ONLINE DATING

FOR

THE NERVOUS

ONE PERSON'S JOURNEY
THROUGH A WHOLE NEW WORLD
OF ONLINE DATING

BY

MARK R MORRELL

CONTENTS

ACKNOWLEDGMENTS

I want to thank my partner, Diane, for planting the idea inside me to create this book, and for her love, encouragement and critique that helped to make it much more memorable.

I also want to thank my daughter, Rose, who is a constant source of support along with having the courage to critique my early draft and tell me it needed a complete re-write – tough but correct.

DAY 1: SATURDAY

I am Chris (not Christopher or Chrissy) Davison. Exactly one year ago today my life as I had known it for nearly 25 years completely imploded. It has taken me 12 months, 12 whole months, to piece back together my life, weave in some new threads, and get to where I am today: day 1 of my new life.

It has been a long journey, exhausting at times, with setbacks along the way to get to where I am today. This will be my launchpad to propel me into the unknown, to seek out new life, to boldly go… Hold on a minute that sounds a bit too familiar to me? Let's just keep it at the unknown for the time being or the vaguely familiar from a very distant past.

I stand at a crossroads. I can look back, look forward and if I need to, glance to my left or right to see where I have gone and where I may be going from now on.

365 days ago (and probably a few hours to be precise) my wife Emily, but known as Em, after 25 years of marriage told me to leave

her, the house, and our children and not to come back.

I have thought a great deal on what I want to do today and probably even more importantly how to do this. Just deciding to try online dating has been tiring enough! Several times I almost talked myself out of it. Why do it and spoil what I have? It isn't perfect although it is okay but is it good enough? For the time being it will be but I want someone who can give extra meaning to my life. If I don't do something now it will keep recurring, nagging away at me, with increasing urgency.

I recalled the conversation I had the previous evening with my two children, Daniel, 21, although he likes to be known as Danny, and Elizabeth, 19, although she likes to be called Liz, and younger, as Danny constantly reminds her, by 30 months from her brother. How to best describe my two children to you? Well, they are a mix of Em and my genes. There can be little doubt that their mum and dad are Em and I.

I will start with Danny, as he was the first to arrive into my world of parenting. He has his mum's brown wavy hair, blue eyes to match and her pointy nose. Combine this with my height and mouth, even the same smile and it will always remind me of Em.

Liz on the other hand has my dimple and chin with green eyes and my darker hair colour minus the grey flecks increasingly showing in mine now. Shorter in height than Danny, like Em is to me, she also has a similar slim build, a fair mix of her mum and dad's features and another reminder of Em.

Danny and Liz both want to know how I am doing with it being one year since I had separated from Em, their mum. They were very pleased when I said I had some good news for them. They had been increasingly concerned by my mood swings recently and had been reluctant to have any contact with me beyond texts and emails for the past few weeks when I am angry and raging about everything.

"I saw my counselor yesterday. We had a good meeting and we discussed the progress we have made over the last nine months. As you know, my divorce from your mum is slowly moving forward. We have finally agreed the finances and who will pay what to balance out everything equally. It means mum will stay in the house and has agreed to buy out my share so I can look for my own place."

"I am looking for places that are by the sea. I want it to be large enough so each of you can stay when you visit me if you want. As long as I can see the sea, I won't feel down for long; I hope it will inspire me to better times. I can't wait to have my own home and stop renting someone else's place but I do know I'm fortunate to be able to do that."

My children nodded their agreement to this decision with Danny adding a grunt. I had been surprised at the time of my traumatic separation how quickly they had adjusted to Em and me splitting up. Maybe they saw cracks in our relationship that I didn't? Maybe, being younger, they accept change more easily than I have?

They had given up trying to find out from Em exactly when it had gone wrong with our relationship. All she had offered Danny and Liz was that she realised one day she no longer loved me and wanted a life away from me. The children were still welcome at our house, well her house now, so that helped minimise the dislocation in their lives.

I carried on. "My business is still successful. Since separating from your mum, I have kept my clients and added a few more that keep me busy as well as pay the bills for the divorce and living here. It's a good balance; working here developing training material and then training people at their place of work."

I stressed to them. "I am alone but I am not lonely so much now as I am busy working. I read a lot to keep up to speed with new ideas and trends that I can use to improve my business."

I continued, "I appreciate that both of you have withheld judgement on who is to blame for this mess. I know it's not been easy for you Danny with your studies at university but you are getting good enough results and you are finding it interesting. And for you Liz, waiting for your A level results, I hope you get the place at university you want. Both of your support has helped me start rebuilding my life so I am now more content, confident and happier than over the last year. Thank you."

I took a deep breath and paused for a moment before I made the most important point.

"However I have gradually realised that there is something or rather someone that is missing from my life. I'm making new friends with the locals here that I want to keep, as I hope to buy a place nearby. I also meet people occasionally who share the same interests as me here. As you know, I'm not someone who is regularly in the pub most evenings and finds it easy to chat to women I've not met before. But I have this huge gap in my life that your mum used to fill deep inside me and I think a "special friend" will help."

I paused again, more I think for my benefit than for theirs. "And so I have decided to do something about it. This weekend I am going to start looking for someone who may meet this need I increasingly feel inside me since your mum and I split. I don't intend to give you a blow-by-blow account of what happens but any advice or information you can share that may help me will help me."

"My friends talk about 'online dating'. It seems to be the best option for me to try finding a "special friend". I've heard of a few sites. Maybe you have heard of them, maybe even tried them? Do the names 'Tinder, Grinder… '"

At the mention of the second one Danny guffawed out loud. "I don't think you should be looking at that one dad! It's a gay one and I don't think you're gay. I'm not sure you want to find someone 'that' special!"

Danny continued, "I don't know much about online dating sites but some of my friends have tried them. They do vary. The worst ones are like 'meat markets'. People aren't so much looking for a special friend as for 'one night shags' - you know like another notch on the bedpost or something to boast about to their friends. You need to try ones that are more mature and likely to have women also interested in a relationship like you want."

"You need to think carefully which site to try. Walk before you can run should be your approach. When did you last date? Must be getting on for 25-30 years ago! It's all changed since then but it's the best way if you want to find this person who will be special to you."

"You should do what you think is best. You've been through a tough time. Everyone is entitled to some happiness. If that means finding a person to share your life with and fill an empty space then go for it. I won't criticise anyone you meet… as long as they are always nice about me, buy me treats, say 'yes' to my every wish and whim!" he laughed.

I was surprised by the maturity, knowledge and extent of Danny's advice. "Thank you," I said. "I wasn't looking forward to telling you in case you didn't take it well. Now I'm glad that I did and I am so, so, grateful for your support."

While Danny was making his speech and it was a surprise for him to say so much in one go, Liz was quiet and still. When I turned my gaze from Danny to her after he finished talking I noticed for the first time her eyes glistening.

"What do you think Liz?" hoping she supported my plans too. That's when my carefully planned evening went off the rails as Liz stood up, burst into tears and ran out the room.

I turned to Danny bewildered. "What did I do?"

"About the worst thing you can possibly do dad."

"Uh?" I was still perplexed by what had happened.

"Liz secretly hoped you and mum would get back together somehow, some way, despite all that's happened. You saying that you're looking for someone other than mum brings those hopes crashing down all in one go."

"Oh shit! I didn't know she thought that was still a possibility. When we split she took it badly but I felt she accepted it more as time went by but obviously not. How comes you know?"

"We do talk sometimes you know! It's not something you ignore about your sister whatever else is going on between us."

"Yes, of course. Sorry, I've just been so wrapped up in my own problems recently. I feel as if I'm starting to see the light of day again after being in a very dark place for ages. Shall I go and talk to her?"

"Nah, let her sort it out in her own way and time and then she'll come back in. Got any more beers dad?"

That brought a smile back to my face. Danny wasn't one to miss out on any free hospitality going no matter how grim a situation looked. I got up and grabbed one from the fridge and gave it to him, which he quickly opened and drank from.

While we waited for Liz to come back I asked how his studies are going. Danny never opened up too much on this subject but I squeezed out from him that his grades are ok, no major panics and planning to do more of the same.

Danny asked how my local football team, Brighton and Hove Albion, were doing knowing it was a good subject I would be happy to talk about. After many years moaning about its plight in the lower leagues, a new owner, new investment and new ground had led to promotion to the Premier League for the first time last season. Life was good for the Seagulls and I waxed lyrical for a while on how good the team is now.

Before it became a specialist subject on Mastermind for me Liz came back into the room and I stopped talking, rose and gave her a big cuddle. We then sat down together on the sofa with my arm round her shoulder as she stayed close to my side.

"Do you want to talk about?" I said gently in her ear.

"Not really." She mumbled back to me.

"OK, but I would like to know why I upset you so feel free to share anything with me when you're ready."

"Yeah, I will do… when I'm ready to."

I knew Liz well enough by now not to push a point. Liz would talk when she wanted to and not before.

The rest of the evening was spent talking about happier times when we were a complete family and our plans for the future with Liz hoping to go to her first choice of university if she got the right A level grades and Danny continuing with his next year. For me it was continuing with my business and building a new life for myself. We didn't touch on me finding a special friend again.

So when I woke up the following morning I decided on the

anniversary of that fateful day when I had left Em after she had confronted me with her momentous news that our marriage was over to turn those thoughts into reality. This story is about what happened next.

Where I'm living now, I feel I am spoilt by what there is on my doorstep to enjoy. It seems a privilege to have such natural riches available for me to indulge in, as many times I want. Without a doubt it has been the right decision to move to the seaside. I find no two days are the same as far as the sea is concerned. It always looks different to me whatever the season, high or low tide, wind direction or strength or if it is sunny, cloudy or raining.

When I have dark, gloomy, days it is consoling to watch the waves crashing on to the beach, hearing the sound of the pebbles restlessly moving with the tide. Sometimes just the exercise of walking along the seafront will lift my mood, realise things are not so bad, even help me think through what is causing the downward mood swing and start correcting it.

For me there is nothing better than a day by the seaside when it is warm and sunny. The bonus for me is I don't have to leave it behind. It is there when I go to sleep and when I wake up the next morning. I can enjoy every single day like that if I choose to. That uplifts my soul and strengthens my spirit to renew my life.

For Day 1 of online dating I prepared by shopping for enough food to sustain me over the whole weekend and yes, a few bottles of red wine, which are on special offer at my local supermarket; honest, and I took it as a sign! I am not expecting anyone to call round and disturb me. The scene is set for me to start this journey. I haven't slept well recently; it was at the back of my mind at the start of the week and at the forefront more and more as Day 1 loomed into view.

To find a 'special person', someone who can potentially be with me for the rest of my life, feels a very daunting prospect. It's more likely that I might find someone who fills some of the emotional gaps in my life. I have thought a great deal about the person that I hope to meet. I will be happy even if it is only for a brief time; as long as it is positive then it will be good while it lasts.

After making my regular cup of tea that I always need to start my day with, I think about my preferences for who I am looking for:

1. Someone local, ideally in the same town or close by.

2. Around my age or maybe a little younger.

3. Similar outlook on life as me, wants some fun and to see new places.

4. Overlapping interests, they didn't have to match mine exactly.

5. Separated, single or divorced (but nothing extra-marital please!)

In parallel there are some things that I don't have any preference for:

1. Background: I am not into the working, middle, and upper class thing.

2. Ethnicity: I didn't mind where someone comes from.

3. Looks: I am very clear that Em will not influence my choice. They did not have to be a replica or the exact opposite of her.

4. Work: It doesn't matter if they did or not.

5. Children: It doesn't matter if they have any or their age(s).

Digesting these thoughts I feel refreshed by my cuppa and ready to tackle some breakfast; my usual mix of cereals to eat with orange juice to drink. After that I shower and dress as I want to feel good before starting this task. I am partly dreading it but also excited about because it is like nothing I have done before.

I find when I'm about to do something important that I need to settle first. The chair is just right, facing the right way and I'm comfortable sitting in it. The desk, table, etc. are clear apart from what I need to use; in this case my laptop, notepad and pen. I often find a pot of coffee helps to focus me on what I need to do. It will certainly be needed for this task, maybe more than one pot!

Do you find that things can distract you? I do! I try to remove them from my mind. I know from experience that it helps me start more easily whatever I need to do. So, I browse the websites for the latest news, check my emails and the weather rather bizarrely as I don't plan to go anywhere this weekend. Finally with my mind settled I start to look for online dating sites.

Now, if you're like me then you will be familiar with using the Internet - Google, Facebook, BBC News (and Weather of course), maybe local news… that sort of thing. If you're not as far advanced as me then online dating will be even more of a shock to your system when you go to these dating sites.

I start searching for 'online dating' to see what I can find. I don't know what I expected to find but it isn't this! At the top of the page with results are sponsored sites that I have learned from my work are not always the best ones to start with. Just because a site has paid to boost its ratings to the top doesn't necessarily mean it is the most relevant. In fact because they have paid to boost their site it may mean it isn't what you're trying to find.

After navigating past these sites I see sites claiming to have the 'best 5 dating sites… ' or 'best 10 dating sites' or most daunting for me 'best 20 dating apps'. What is an app? How does it work? Is it something I use on my phone? How many dating sites are there? There does seem a lot and I wonder if it will take weeks rather than one weekend to find the right one for me!

It gets better because online dating sites are listed next. I recognise some from my conversation with Danny and Liz. I remember to avoid that one site so I don't make a challenging day even more so! Remembering that I am determined to keep an open mind, I start to click on the link to each dating site and explore this new online world that is opening up before me. I also pour the remains of the coffee from the pot in the hope it will help me make more sense of what I see.

I have to admit I am seduced to try the first site, boosted by advertising, despite all I've just said. I am presented with a big picture of a much younger man than me (we're talking decades, not years, if I'm truly honest with you here), and a woman looking romantically into each other's eyes. A picture of a (very young compared with me) woman says she can be my coach. Does this mean I have to be trained to be ready for the challenge ahead? She wants to know everything about me: date of birth, location but when she wants to know my name I call a halt.

While I appreciate the slow, seductive, approach to tease my personal details from me I want to check out the competition first. I am intrigued by the heading 'meet real gents', which seems to say to me that some men are false. I open doors for women, stand up to let women sit on buses and trains some of the time. Does this mean I am a 'real gent' too?

The more I look around, the more it raises questions in my mind. Am I going to fall at the first hurdle? Online dating seems more daunting and different than I feared it would be. I use the Internet most days for my work to find stuff I need such as train times, hotel rooms, traffic routes, but this is different! I make some more coffee and settle down to find out more, intrigued by my first glance at this new world opening up before me.

I move on to the next dating site that catches my eye. It shows emojis (small image used to express an emotion) of a young man and woman. Like the last site it immediately makes me feel I am 'too old' for it. I just don't feel comfortable; I can't explain why just how I feel about looking around. If you don't feel right about a site then I feel there isn't a good chance of finding the right woman for me. I am asked for information about myself before it will try to find me suitable choices. Again, I am reluctant at this early stage to do this and move on.

The next site I again have doubts about before I even click on it this time! It is different from the first two; it's also definitely not for me. Images of couples, young couples (this seems to be a recurring theme) of different sexes, one of two women and I am pleased to see, of different ethnicities and dress. All these people are obviously happy with each other and having fun. I just feel that I am old enough to be their father rather than their partner and I am not interested in dating someone half my age. It is a definite no from me to trying this site!

So three sites almost certainly dismissed so far as I move on to the next dating site. A big image of a young woman smiles back at me and less information is requested about me here, which makes me feel more comfortable. Someone apparently finds love every 14 minutes it claims. This reminds me of Prince Charles' fateful answer "whatever 'in love' means" to the question "was he in love?" when his engagement to Princess Diana was announced. Can it be this simple I wonder? Sign up and 14 minutes later find I'm in love? I muse about this as I read through their blurb about online dating.

As I scroll down I see steps to take to help find a person I am interested in. I need some help so I can learn to walk before I can run with this dating experience. I then see my first picture of a man with grey hair with a woman who looks over 30. It looks like this site actually admits mature people date too! Hooray! Yes, this is the first possible site that interests me.

I realise that most of the morning has gone already. Time is moving fast as I absorb this totally new world I am finding. Maybe time for one more site before a break for lunch and some much needed sustenance?

I am more hopeful with this site as I see pictures showing people of various ages, not just in their 20s. Like the one before it shows me how to join, how they will help, and what gives this site the strongest tick of the box, there are success stories to read *and* they include mature couples. Most of the members of this online dating site have similar views to me on issues like politics, education, values, etc. It may be a better chance of finding someone who I will like and will like me.

This seems a good time to take a break and refuel as Danny tells me when he eats. I put together a cold lunch of ham, salad and half a baguette. I want all my brainpower functioning 100% for what may be one of the more significant weekends in my life. I don't think I am overstating this. It doesn't feel like it will be easy finding the right online dating site, let alone the person who can become the special friend I am looking for in my life.

As I sit down and start eating my lunch, I think again about yesterday evening and my conversation with Danny and Liz. Mentally I compare notes on how dating has changed from my time. I recall saying, "The last time I started dating anyone it was by chance or through a friend. Take my meeting your mum for example. I was in a disco with a couple of mates and see her with Sarah, her best friend at the time, sitting at a table chatting. I overcame my nerves and surprised myself by asking her if she wanted to dance and was stunned when she said 'yes'. I couldn't believe a woman so good looking as Em could be interested in me. Anyway, the point I am making is that it's different, very different now. I work on my own so I won't meet anyone in that way. I meet clients but that has been and will always be purely on a professional level. It will be too complicated if there is a personal relationship developing as well."

Danny and Liz said it is hard to meet anyone if it isn't through some online contact now. To me it feels like their mobiles are the gateway to dating someone, probably meeting or arranging anything with anyone. I use my mobile for work emails, texts, and calls but not for personal stuff like they do. Is this going to be the next challenge for me once I find a suitable online dating site? I groan as it just feels like one thing on top of another. Rather than getting closer to finding my special friend it feels more and more remote with these unforeseen barriers standing in my way.

After some fresh fruit and a fruit tea – yes, I am being *very* healthy this weekend – I take a short walk along the seafront to sharpen my senses and put me in the right mood for what may be a long afternoon. Focusing my thoughts I sit back down, again clearing my mind of any distractions, and open up my laptop. I click on the next site that claims it is a serious dating site using intelligent matchmaking to bring like-minded American singles together. Clearly that excludes me, as I am not American. It does make me wonder if the other sites I have found have more of a US than UK focus but decide not to revisit now but possibly check back later.

Tindr turns out to be exactly what I expected and it's not for me.

Asking me to immediately login using my mobile number, Facebook login or using the Tindr app sends all the wrong messages to me. I'm cautious about giving out any of my personal details online.

The next site claims to be the best for conversations with more than any other online dating site. One billion messages a month! There is even a relationship predictor which I'm sure is a great feature and encourages members but I just find it all too overwhelming. I feel like a very small fish in a huge ocean. It is too big, too much for me when I just want to dip my toe in the water at this stage before taking the plunge.

I carry on skimming through the results and see a few more online dating sites. None of them are what I am looking for. It seems the prime audience for online dating are two-three decades younger than me for most sites. I take stock on what to do next. I am a little flat because I expected something more from the dating sites I've found so far today. There only seems to be a couple of sites that I feel I can try. Which of these possibilities will have the pleasure of becoming my first route to… whatever? I am keeping an open mind on what I am looking for; there is no need to narrow my options over who that will be yet. It is hard enough deciding on the best site to try to date this special friend. Time for a cup of tea and then review the finalists again I think.

As I sip my tea I reflect over what has happened today. I remember the so-called advice given to me by two friends, Gordon and James, who I meet at all the home games and some away games to watch our local football team.

I met up with Gordon and James after the football season had ended a short while ago and they both had been away on holiday with their families to avoid missing any games. They picked up my mood quickly and I unburdened that I had split from Em since I saw them at our last game. They were stunned and didn't know what to say. To be honest touchy feely stuff like this isn't their strong point but they knew Em. We had been season ticket holders for many years sitting together watching our team win, lose, or draw in stoical despair or unbounded joy.

I realised it was time to go when Gordon said, "Every cloud has a silver lining. It means you can go to more away games next season." The look I gave him shut him up immediately and I said a quick goodbye and left them in the pub. With friends like that who needs enemies, I briefly thought. Next season still seems a long way away and how many more games I see will be the last of my worries.

Maybe more away games are an easier option than choosing an online dating site? This is even before I start choosing the special friend I feel I need to fill this widening gap in my life. It gives me the resolve and strength to decide on a site. If the worst came to the worst I can always try other sites… or as a last resort even go to more away games with Gordon!

While I feel the possible sites left have something to offer me, which will I feel more comfortable with entrusting my personal details to? My friends tell me that I will be attractive to women as I am not that bad looking, I have my own place, am reasonably fit and healthy, run my own business and I am financially independent. Surely that will appeal to some women out there looking for their special friend?

I go back through each site carefully, clicking on the headings, reading the guidance and success stories. They reassure me they can help me but when it comes to crunch time I feel one just has that little bit more to give me, appealing to more of my wishes and hopes.

I think of trying more than one at the same time but I am not sure I have the emotional strength to cope with the inevitable rejections or missed opportunities from both; one will be enough for now.

So, one big decision made today! The next is to start my online dating journey. There is still some of the afternoon left and my dinner, like my lunch, will be a simple affair, deliberately so I can focus all my efforts with online dating this weekend. I think about how I will join my no.1 choice for online dating and consider the options. Basically did I want to be a bystander and just look for other women and wait for one to contact me? Or do I want to subscribe and become a member so I can contact anyone I like? It feels like a good place to pause and think.

After dinner I am relaxing with my second glass of red wine, the open bottle beckoning me to not forget it and about to start watching a comedy programme I had recorded. It will relax me and put me in the right mood. Today has been exhausting and I need to go to bed early as I am tired but that plan is interrupted. The doorbell rings; it is two short rings followed by one long ring, the signature call of my neighbour, Meghan, from the flat below.

I have lived at this place for four months. I reluctantly agreed a tenancy for 12 months at the time despite not wanting to be tied down for that length of time, being anxious to buy my own place. However my divorce (more on that another day when I'm stronger!) seems to be taking forever as it moves at a snail's pace and now that extra time looks like a good decision. I have gradually got to know everyone living around me. Having the top flat means I pass neighbours on my way up or down four flights of stairs. No lift helps to keep me fit, some days when I am in and out several times, very fit!

Meghan has lived there in the flat on the ground floor for many years. Originally born in north Wales, she moved away when she got married. She still retains a little of a Welsh lilt when she speaks even after all these years away from her homeland and keeps an eye on everything as she now lives alone with her dog, a corgi called Blodwyn. Privately I think that she just wore her husband down and into an early grave with her relentless curiosity and nosiness. While it is great if you need a parcel taken in while you are away, the downside is Meghan wants to know the ins and outs of everyone's life and, as I found once to my cost, share your confidences with anyone who she happens to bump into… and she doesn't forget any details either!

I momentarily think of not answering the door but decide to do so rather than risk a later long interrogation of why I didn't when we next meet up. Meghan does have a very persuasive method of extricating a few details and then exaggerating and speculating wildly on what it all may mean. It making sense or being close to the truth are factors quickly discarded if it is likely to spoil sharing a tasty bit of gossip with her friends.

I am determined to say the minimum and keep the conversation short but polite. That went out the window so to speak as soon as I open the door though. In rushes Blodwyn yapping and wagging her tail, sniffing at everything her neck can stretch up to. Distracted by the dog I open the door wide and in marches Meghan peering around as she moves. She clutches three envelopes close to the cardigan she always wears. Again I think to myself that it will need to be surgically removed from her one day. I always see her wearing it, rain or shine. For all I know she probably sleeps in it!

"Looks like you're having a quiet evening in by yourself again Christopher," she starts by saying. I bite my lip to stop the immediate retort that my name is Chris not Christopher. She hasn't stopped using it despite me repeatedly telling her whenever we met over the first few weeks.

"Yes," I reply. "It's been a busy day for me." Hoping that she will not stay because I am having a quiet evening by myself. However my hopes are dashed when she continues.

"I don't like being on my own for too long either. It's always nice when there's someone you can pop round to for a chat. Oh, I see you've got some wine. It will be nice to have a drink if you don't mind playing host and pouring me some."

I sigh inwardly and hopefully silently and go to the cupboard that contains my wine glasses. I brought an old one out, remembering Meghan smashing one of a set of six glasses I bought a few months ago. I don't normally entertain for more than two people so it isn't critical but it's the careless way she knocked it over that annoyed me. Thankfully it was nearly empty at the time so the stain is now contained to a small area but I can still see out of the corner of my eye that part of the carpet.

"So what have you been doing today with yourself then Christopher?" she said in a pointed way.

"Nothing in particular, just taking it easy, getting a few chores done." I am determined not to say anything about online dating. If Meghan finds out the Spanish Inquisition will seem like a tea party in comparison.

"Well," Meghan said, "it stopped you from coming down for your post today. You've had three letters that I brought up to you… just in case any of them are urgent and you had forgotten."

She opens them like a fan and looks carefully at each one before passing them to me. "Looks like bills to me, nothing handwritten on the envelopes." I just nod; I have no intention of opening them in front of her.

When Meghan realises this she turns her focus to what my plans might be. Again I am noncommittal and offer little for her to feed upon. I didn't think she had reached the stage yet of making up lies. I ask about her and her plans and get the usual litany of mind numbing moans about Blodwyn and her antics with other dogs and her own aches and pains. She grumbles again about the people in the flat between her and me and the noise they make scraping their chairs on the wooden floor. I said she should talk to them knowing she won't; there is more mileage for her by moaning about it than resolving it.

After a longer pause Blodwyn starts whining and scratching the bottom of the door. I am grateful that she wants to be let out to relieve herself. Picking up on this I said, "Looks like Blodwyn needs a wee to me."

Meghan has many faults but she is very attentive to her corgi's needs. With a groan of frustration at missing an opportunity to interrogate me for more morsels of gossip she reluctantly gets out of the chair and moves towards the door where Blodwyn continues to whine.

"I suppose I'd better take her out. You don't fancy walking with me do you?" I politely decline this last attempt by her to extract more information from me, claiming tiredness forcing me to turn in for an early night soon.

"But it's only nine o'clock!" she exclaims. I shrug my shoulders and start to yawn slowly as I open the door.

Thanking her for the mail and saying goodbye I watch as Blodwyn scampers down the stairs with Meghan following more slowly. I listen to the footsteps until I hear the communal front door open and close as they go outside. I sigh with relief at the narrow escape while accepting there will be more encounters that I will need to parry to avoid giving anything away. At least she didn't open my letters or parcels; she does have some red lines she won't cross.

I rinse the glasses out, turn off the light and walk through to my small bedroom. After getting ready for bed, I pick up a favourite book of mine *History of Britain* by Simon Schama. I am fascinated by history and like reading these types of books. I hold to the adage that what we are can be traced back to what happened in our past. For Britain that is a fascinating past, if sometimes uncomfortable, that I am always interested in researching and reading about.

After a couple of chapters I feel my eyelids getting heavier and it becomes difficult to concentrate and take in what I am reading. I drift off to sleep and dream several times of weird situations meeting women for the first time. Little did I realise that reality will at times be even more surreal than I can dream about tonight!

DAY 2: SUNDAY

After a restless night I follow the same routine as yesterday with tea, then by breakfast, shower, dressing and sitting down with my trusty laptop and freshly brewed coffee available nearby. I am starting to crystallise my thoughts on how I will approach today but as I start my mobile alerts to a message received. Who will text me? Meghan of course! Did I want to have coffee with her this morning? I choose to ignore it. A conversation with her is the last thing I need now.

As I collect my thoughts again my mobile sends another alert. This time it is a message from Rachel who has been a close friend for many years. She just wants to wish me luck knowing what I am about to do today and will try to call later. It is a familiar trail she has trodden several times while trying to find her special friend.

I recall one conversation many months ago when she surprised me by her reaction to my news about Em and I splitting by not being surprised! Rachel couldn't understand why Em had stayed with me so long.

I asked her, "Why?" genuinely puzzled by this.

She replied, "Because you love your business so much. It's your baby; you created it on your own; it means everything to you."

Rachel had seen this coming from a long time ago but didn't feel it was her place to mention it and risk interfering in my marriage. Her advice was to try to reconcile but if Em was unresponsive and determined to move on then I must do the same.

"Why make the pain you're suffering any worse or longer than it has to be?" she summed it up with her pragmatic advice and realistic view.

She has been through one divorce and three separations from long-term relationships. Each was different in the intensity of pain she felt but after the long drawn out process that ended her marriage, Rachel's approach now is to move on as quickly as possible and agree as much as possible on the finances. Advice based on her own hard-bitten experience when one ex-partner 'took her to the cleaners' for far more than he deserved.

Pouring a second cup of coffee I gaze out the window and reflect on her advice that I still feel is profound. It focuses me on what is happening with my life, to start taking more control of things rather than keep drifting expecting someone to sort me out or wave a magic wand to put it all right. No fairies appear to do this, which confirms my view that I don't believe in them. Who actually does?

Finally putting all these distractions to one side I take a deep breath and open the online dating site I chose yesterday after much soul searching. The first decision is choosing how to join. One option is to register for free and have limited use of features. Basically it seems that I can view other members but not contact them and hope that I catch the eye of someone who will contact me.

The other way is to sign up and use all the features. That way I can make the first approach to someone I like and wish to contact and hopefully meet.

Over the course of last evening I decided, confirmed by feeling the same today, what to do. If I am serious about finding a special friend through an online dating site then I will take the plunge; just dipping my toe in the dating water isn't going to move me forward. That means subscribing, in other words paying, so I give myself the best chance to help find that special friend. I can join for one month, three months or six months. I choose the last option; I don't think it is likely to work out that quickly in my favour. I don't get that sort of luck!

I click on the subscribe button and it immediately presents with an unexpected dilemma. The site wants me to have a username, not my real name that I want to be known by. I just didn't anticipate this could be needed at all! Of course, as I think about it more it makes sense with the need for anonymity or a persona especially for women. I will want to know someone much better and feel safe before I share my name and location. If it doesn't work out then I won't feel there is someone I didn't get on with who knows my identity. That will be for a later stage if things start working out.

I struggle to think of possible names. I am trying to market myself to have the widest appeal to women. That means some obvious usernames or nicknames will not be appropriate. I regularly go to support my local football team but I will not use the nickname given to me by my friends to me for this purpose! The more I think about it the harder it becomes. What was a stumbling block is now rapidly becoming a serious barrier.

I get up, put on my jacket and go out for another of my seaside walks. I always find being by the seaside stimulating and helps clarify my thinking. I don't always sort out a problem but I usually return clearer in how to start tackling it. This time it did work as my mind drifts remembering a comedy series I enjoyed many years ago, so much that I bought the box set of 'The Good Guys'. It's a mockumentary, a spoof documentary, of how a police squad operated by the way. I will have 'A Good Guy' as my username.

It is a name I feel I can live up to and aim to be that all my life. Whether it will appeal to women I hadn't a clue. There is only one way to find out and that is to go with it and then find out their reaction. And I can't think of anything else for a username that will remotely be likeable by anyone let alone a female special friend. That settles it in my mind; 'A Good Guy' it will be.

I realise the morning has gone finding out that I need a username and coming up with one. I next look at the packages; do I want to have for one month, three or six months? While six months will be the most expensive it is half the price of the one-month package when spread over that time. I am not that confident to believe that I will contact anyone and they will become my special friend. I reason that whatever I pay it is a small investment to make if I do succeed and find happiness with someone for the rest of my life.

The next step is a long list of questions to answer split into three types; easy questions about my age, colour hair, etc.; harder questions with a list of answers to choose which is most relevant; lastly difficult questions describing myself and who and what I am looking for. Time to pause for a break, have some lunch, and reflect over what I've done and need to still do.

I follow the same routine as yesterday but chose some mackerel as I believe fish feeds the brain, and I will need to concentrate on those questions this afternoon. My mobile alerts me to another text and it is from Meghan again. This time she is asking if I am free for tea. I have to admire her persistence. She never is one to be put off easily or at the first attempt. Again I chose to ignore her, as it will severely diminish my chances of finishing today with my online dating profile launch. She really can be irritating with her timing.

I had to creep down the stairs and quietly close the door behind me when I leave the building. I take the longer route to the seaside to avoid her seeing me pass her window. Knowing my luck it will be just as she is looking out and she can quickly open the window and call me back!

After stretching my legs again with a seaside brisk walk I sit down with my laptop and start answering the questions. I know the more information I give the better my chances of being contacted. I understand that some people lie or are selective with what they say. I am determined not to do this; being 100% accurate and honest is critical. I want someone to want to meet me right from the start, not discover I'm not who they think I am later.

I work through the easiest questions first. I know I am male, my age, colour of my eyes and information like that. Moving on to the next group of multi-choice questions and I select answers from the choices given, I am determined to answer them all and not skip any by leaving them blank. The questions tend to cover lifestyle, my interests, my views, and my activities. Again by adopting an open and honest approach it is reasonably easy to select an answer that reveals some of the things that make me tick.

I feel good now with most of the questions answered. There are just a few left but these are crucial and the most difficult. Time for a cup of tea and a chocolate bar to refuel before I tackle these! While I wait for the kettle to boil, I think about how to describe myself and whom I want to meet. The second part feels almost unreal to me when I consider it after 12 months of independence following living and being married to the same person for 25 mostly happy years.

I start describing what I want from a potential special friend; I really don't have a certain type of woman in my mind. I am not looking for a replica of Em; neither am I trying to find someone who is the complete opposite. I think about people I got on with generally and specifically what attracted me to Em, not physical features, more what made me laugh, kept me loving her, would brighten up the greyest of days.

Slowly the space fills as I sketch out in words the special friend I am looking for. It doesn't feel complete but it is a solid start. Next I describe myself; I don't know about you but I find this difficult. If I start writing about my strengths I wonder if I am being too bigheaded and overbearing. Then again, if I start with my weaknesses then I'm hardly likely to be the new kid on the block when my profile is seen.

I look through my business CV to get some ideas and excerpts to use from it. I struggle to get the right balance between my achievements e.g. my business, marriage for 25 years, my personality and how I behave, and what I want from my life.

After several edits, one of them a major edit radically changing my approach, it feels like I am clearer whom I want to meet and whom they will be meeting. I hope it gives away enough to interest women but not bore them with too much detail. I read that the more you reveal the more likely it is that a woman will be comfortable contacting me. I also know that photos of me are vital with the more recent and varied the better. No pictures of Em and I torn in half and none of me 10-20 years ago to be shown either.

I feel it is time to park my profile for a while and have some dinner. I haven't published anything yet but I want to do so by the end of the weekend just leaving this evening to reach that goal. After something to eat I can check through everything again with a fresh pair of eyes. After a nourishing meal with only one glass of red wine I feel ready with the dishes washed to review everything. I change a few answers to questions realising some have more than one answer e.g. types of films I like, rather than just a single choice. I tinker with the wording about myself and the special friend I am looking for, change a few words here and there to describe my feelings more clearly.

Eventually after a couple of hours I realise I am tinkering for the sake of it. I am putting off the moment when I press the submit button and launch myself on to an unsuspecting world of women searching for their special friend. After one last read through I take a deep breath, press the button, and hey presto my profile is there for anyone to find if they are interested in me.

I stand up and walk round the room a few times before gazing out the window at nothing in particular. I feel huge relief that I have achieved my goal of joining an online dating site. Whatever happens next it is going to be a journey into the unknown for me. I heard anecdotally of people finding their true love within a few days or not having any interest shown in them while they were with a dating site. Time will tell which side of that scale it will be for me.

I treat myself to another glass of wine, after all this is a special occasion. It isn't every day you start looking for a new partner to maybe live the rest of your life with. The days are almost at their longest now and darkness is only now starting to descend. I sit down and let the room slowly darken as I reflect over everything I have done this weekend and the events of one year ago that had led me to where I am now. I am determined to make the most of any opportunities. Anyone I meet I will aim to get as much as I can out of each meeting. I will not rush to judge rashly, assume or decide on the spur of the moment.

Feeling very tired I look forward to lying in bed and hoping I sleep better than last night with my restless dreams. I am more relaxed because of what I have done and curious rather than wary of how events will now unfold. He who dares, wins I drowsily think as I drift off to sleep.

DAY 3: MONDAY

I wake up and my mind immediately flashes back to the events of the last two days. A feeling of relief mixes with one of satisfaction and flows through me as I reflect on what I've achieved after weeks of psyching myself up for this next stage in my life. There is a spring in my step as I get out of bed to make some tea because today my future special friend may contact me! As I put the kettle I think that anything could now happen; the sky is the limit!

Working from home for the next three days means time to focus on developing a training course for one of my business clients on Thursday. Preparing for this course is the perfect antidote to stop me dwelling too much over online dating. The time goes quickly as I set out what I want to cover on Thursday; it is work I really enjoy and get satisfaction from doing.

It means I have time for anyone who views my profile; assuming someone will of course. There are three ways that I can see if anyone shows interest in me. Firstly, my profile can be viewed by anyone whose criteria I fit e.g. location, age, gender, etc. Secondly, my profile can be liked; I get an alert when/if this happens. Lastly and most significantly, someone can send me a message; I will get an email alerting me.

As the day wore on so my spirits start to drop with no alerts to show anyone is interested in me. I try to be logical about this; 'early days', 'just the start of the journey' but emotionally I feel I am missing the spot that I should have reached. Of course, my vulnerabilities and insecurities started coming to the surface as the day drags on that are harder to ignore.

After I finish work I prepare, cook and eat dinner; I still haven't received any alerts from someone (anyone!) showing interest in me. I have a quick call with Liz who asks how my weekend has gone. I summarise what has happened with my online dating and she sounds relieved.

Danny also calls out of curiosity to ask how my 'big dating adventure' is going. I tell him my 'big dating adventure' hasn't got off the ground yet with any interest. He cautions me not to expect too much too soon. I reply that I have signed up for 6 months and accept it will take some time. But it will be nicer if it happens sooner rather than later.

After the call I go to my dating site and see there have been two views of my profile. So at least I exist online even if neither person was interested in me. To be honest with you, the weekend drained me. I know I should search for that special friend but I don't have the energy to start just yet.

That will have to wait for another day. I view my profile and wonder if I can change it and get caught in a maze of contrary thinking that can't decide if I am too detailed or too vague or too...

what! I stop myself going into a well of uncertainty that risks becoming worse. This is only my first full day on this site; there are many more days to come before my six months is up.

DAY 4: TUESDAY

Nothing. No views. No likes. No messages.

I check a couple of times – lunch and evening – but no activity.

I concentrate on preparing my training course and trying to keep busy but eking into my consciousness every few minutes is no contact, no one interested in me, what is the point?

It alarms me how much something I hope will make me happier risks dragging me down to levels I last experienced months after separating from Em.

I try to stay calm, patient and positive. I pick up my book I had been reading about the history of Vietnam since 1945. Maybe not the most uplifting subject I agree! But it is engrossing and helps distract me from my situation until bedtime.

DAY 5: WEDNESDAY

Today is a repeat of yesterday: nothing is happening. I wonder if I am doing the right thing. Yes, probably, is my response. Message to Chris "Keep going it's only three days since you started".

Should I start looking for my special friend rather than wait for her to find me? Yes, but only when I feel strong enough to. Maybe this weekend will be a good time?

Meanwhile I complete my training preparation, print off the handouts, collate everything, and feel confident about tomorrow's event. I am relieved that I can still separate dating from business; I still need to earn a living I remind myself but it isn't easy.

After dinner I feel pretty low and unsure if the gap I am seeking to fill with a special friend is worth the uncertainty and anxiety I am feeling. I call Liz but get no reply. I try Danny next but I also get no response. I next try Rachel but again get no reply. Just when I really want to speak with someone they aren't there for me.

I'm starting to feel sorry for myself; it's not a pretty sight I can assure you, when I get a text from Rachel. She is busy for the next hour or so but will call me later this evening. I am grateful for this response and it restores some of my equilibrium. I text back 'I would love to hear from you later'.

It is a couple of hours actually before Rachel does manage to call me back. By then my mood has sunk lower filling up with insecurities caused by my marriage ending. Why had it happened? What a failure I am! Why bother with another relationship when the pain of the last one is still strong?

All of these don't help my mood and bring together all sorts of random but negative thinks. I am renting a place still, partly because it suits most of my needs now but mainly because finding a place of my own to buy seems frightening. No decision is better than the wrong decision I reason with myself but it isn't right and I know it deep down.

On top of my pending divorce and online dating, just feeling normal with my single status is sometimes too much for me. I yearn for a quite life, at the moment I yearn for Em and the nice relaxing evenings we used to have chatting over this, that or nothing in particular while enjoying a bottle of wine or two. Yes, two, hmm, maybe I had been drinking too much for longer than I care to admit sometimes? It hasn't got any better since I left Em either. It isn't that I can't get through a day without wine or I'm distracted thinking about my next bottle but...I *do* enjoy wine and it seems a shame after opening a bottle to then not finish it rather than leave it for tomorrow even if it is only me drinking it.

Yes, something else to think about. Luckily my mobile rings to break my thoughts up with Rachel calling me back as promised. As soon as I answer she picks up my mood and starts asking why I am like that. I quickly summarise my day and what has happened or rather hasn't happened with the online dating.

She gives me a masterclass in rational thinking, managing my expectations and coping with my mood swings. To sum it up Rachel says, "I think you should do what comes naturally to you. When we do that, we are happier with the decisions and paths we take. Having time to process everything you've experienced and are still experiencing can be a big help. Don't add pressure to yourself, do what works best for you and what you're at peace with within yourself. Sometimes doing that is the best way to manage things, recover and ultimately move forward."

These words act like balm on a running sore as it sooths my emotions and calms me down. Based on her own experiences Rachel knows the ups and downs that I face. After about an hour chatting we are both yawning and take that as a sign to end our call. I put the stopper in the bottle of wine I haven't finished; a minor victory I register with myself.

DAY 6: THURSDAY

My sleep is disrupted by wild dreams and strange scenarios involving dating and bizarrely buying a house. Every place I look at with a view to buying is owned by women I have seen on the site or dated. To make it worse they all take a dim view of me wanting to view and buy their place. I am reminded by each of them in very clear tones how poor their experience has been with me when we have met.

Feeling frail and doubtful about the whole adventure into online dating and if it is a wise decision to start down this route, I go through my morning routine automatically, barely conscious of how I end up getting into my car with my bag containing all the training material and plugging my mobile into the car kit that will keep me in communication with the outside world. To be honest I'd rather have solitude and my own thoughts. What decides the matter is that I have little idea of the best route to get to my client's place for the training. Realities therefore triumph and the satnav-automated voice accompanies me. I arrive with plenty of time to prepare and feel comfortable with my surroundings today.

Thankfully the training day goes very well. The room is set out as I have asked and all the attendees come that I expect with only one a few minutes late.

The group is interested in the training content, most people are engaged and contribute their views, asking a few questions to clarify. It is everything a trainer can dream of setting the scene for an ideal training day.

I feel that my time preparing has been well spent. My fees to carry out the training offer good value. I am confident that when I follow up with people who attended I will find their behaviour has changed since this training and they and their employer benefits too.

The intriguing part of the day is with one of the attendees, Gill. She is very pleasant generally but particularly attentive to anything I say or do or ask. She maintains good eye contact and whenever there is a break, comes close to me if I am queuing for a coffee asking me questions about my background. One might think she could even be flirting with me!

As the training ends people drift away in twos and threes on the way back to their workplaces. As I am packing up getting ready to leave, Gill stays and chats generally about the work she does and how long she has been working there. I don't feel we are crossing a line yet over my professional approach of not getting too friendly with a client but it feels like I am getting close to it. I look more closely at Gill while we chat.

She is a little bit shorter than me – I'm around six feet in old language – with lovely blond hair down to her shoulders that looks natural, an attractive face with blue eyes, an infectious smile, and a cute dimple on her chin. But most appealing is her interest seemingly in what I say and about me. Along with her eye contact is the intensity she shows me. All I remember is her deep blue eyes fixed the whole time on mine, giving off their own message. Her body language indicates I also have her undivided attention.

I sense I can ask her to continue the conversation and she will be willing. However I don't feel comfortable doing that today. Gill seems to sense my hesitation and solves it by asking for my business card because she knows a friend in another company who may be interested in my training. She says,

"Having my details means its easier for my friend to refer you to the right contact."

I always carry a pack of business cards around; it's a cheap and easy way to find new business. There's always a chance that someone wants to find out more and a consultant never says "No" to a possibility of new business. I am not crossing any lines by giving her my business card although I wonder if she really has a friend or just wants it for herself. I thank Gill for her interest, wish her the best and make my excuses about the traffic and avoiding the congestion home, leaving with a handshake.

As I drive home I am intrigued by what has just happened and how I feel. This hasn't happened to me before with a client although strictly Gill is not my client but we did meet through business. Maybe it happened before but my attitude and married status sent a signal that I was off limits to any female? Maybe I am flattering myself too much thinking that! It does make me think more about how to take the first steps finding my special friend.

It is now four days since I had joined the dating site and I am feeling ready this weekend to start looking. Is it another natural step along the online dating journey? Or is it a slightly desperate hurried step reacting to indifference or disinterest in my profile? I don't know but feel I have to make this next step to find out. I prepare my mind for this like I did for the last weekend. My social life (what social life!) will have to stay on hold again.

I spend the evening going over the events of the day from a personal and emotional viewpoint not business. To have someone, especially a female, show any interest in me is a pleasant change. It certainly won't harm my self-esteem even if it is nothing more than a connection leading to new business; something I will never say "No!" to.

DAY 7: FRIDAY

Friday starts off with me waking up from a dream about Gill, not as a potential business connection but as someone lying nude next to me in my bed! It is pretty obvious by how I feel and how she is lying that we've had a passionate night together. I remember feeling very content and happy as the dream faded away only to be replaced by the reality of my life today – alone in bed, work to do, etc.

After breakfast and showering my working day starts with a phone call to the client I had delivered the training for. I always do this to check that I have met their requirements; can anything be improved; did they want more; any other feedback – hopefully positive comments – and if a follow up call or meeting is needed. Thankfully the client is very pleased but wants some time to check within their organisation on the next steps. We schedule a call in one month's time when this should be clearer.

Before I say goodbye I suddenly have this wild thought in my head to ask her about Gill! I didn't of course but it disturbs me that my personal life encroached so easily into my business life; normally I can easily separate them, keeping one detached from the other. I make a pot of coffee while I wonder what is happening inside of me.

I haven't thought about Gill since I woke remembering that dream. Clearly something is going on with my subconscious though. I try to put further thoughts about Gill to one side until after work which is straightforward and I ease down satisfied this has been a good business week. I have two other clients I am working with and one wants me to meet with him and his team on Monday to scope out the next stage of a large project changing managers thinking to be less controlling and more empowering with their teams. It is a subject I am familiar with and so I feel prepared for the meeting.

As I unwind and prepare dinner, I think again about Gill. I don't expect to hear from her and decide to wait for her to make the next move if there is to be one. However while I am eating my meal all that starts to change as I receive not one, not two, but three email alerts from my dating site all within 15 minutes of each other. My profile has received two likes and my first message! I want to be in the right frame of mind and place to read, maybe even savour, this first message and wait until I finish my meal, then pour myself another glass of wine, before finding out.

Excitedly I log in to read my first message; seeing the 1 next to the heading 'Messages' feels great. The message is from a woman called Daisy Chain that says, 'I like your profile. What do you think of mine?' Short and sweet I think, straight to the point, no messing about. So I do what Daisy Chain wants and look up her profile. She says she lives in London so not local to me and she is a university professor but doesn't say where she lectures. Her background is a mix of Asian and American, she is interested in travelling and I seem to tick most of the boxes that she is looking for in a man.

I am not sure if she is who I am looking for but I have nothing to lose by responding and seeing whether it leads to something. How should I respond? I didn't want to appear too forward or desperate but I did want to show her I am keen. I hum and haw for a few minutes over what to say before deciding to hedge my bets and keep my reply short but friendly. I type 'Thanks for liking my profile. I like yours too and want to find out more about you. Would you like to?' It feels like the right tone I want to set as I send the message.

I move on to the two likes my profile received. One is from MaryJane who viewed my profile a few days ago. I guess my reciprocal view triggered her to like mine; this may be a slow burner. I like her profile and return her like with mine – 'like for like' I think and smile to myself.

I will wait to see if she wants to up the game and message me or maybe I will do that if I hear nothing in a few days. It is hard to know what is the right or wrong thing to do in this brave new world of online dating! I suspect I'm going to learn some things the hard way. As long as I *do* learn there isn't much else I can do.

The other like is from JeanGenie. Maybe a David Bowie fan? Again reading through her profile I don't see anything that gives me a strong like or dislike for her. I haven't closed my mind to any type of woman I want to meet. At the same time, I don't have any idea who I do want to meet. I like her profile and again choose to wait and see if she will message me.

My busiest evening this week by far! Like London buses, nothing for ages then three dating contacts, one quickly after the other. The evening got busier when my daughter calls to ask how I am and how the dating is going. When I tell her what has happened in the last half hour Liz goes quiet. She thinks I am brave and hopes I find someone to be happy with but it sounds lukewarm as if her heart isn't in it. Danny texts a few minutes later to ask how my dating is going. After I tell him he feels I should take the initiative and start looking. I say I am about to try over this weekend to find women to contact. Danny wishes me luck.

I start to experiment with the dating site. It is similar to searching with Google. The default setting will look for any woman within a radius of 20 miles of where I live and within 10 years of my age. I can then use filters to narrow or widen the area and the age range. I can choose origin, height, eye colour, and interests or other key words or phrases that may be included in a profile. I can only cope with a standard search to start with, which comes back with over 100 women.

What do I want to do? I check the time – it is coming up to 9pm. The results show each woman's profile picture, name and location. I view these and click on a few profiles to see if I like anyone enough to make contact with.

The results don't seem to be in any particular order and so SassySal who registered over four months ago has the unknown privilege of being my first profile I view on the dating site. I can't tell whether she is still looking for or has found someone. The main thing is she lives in West Sussex and is interested in men up to 60 years of age. Great, I have five years leeway in which to decide and still meet her criteria in age!

Emerald 3 is next and joined today. Maybe I am the first person to view her profile? Unfortunately her profile is incomplete with nothing about her interests and who she is looking for. It makes me appreciate the pain I went through is worth it to launch a complete profile. She may be one to revisit and check when Emerald 3 has written more.

Then there is Dusky Di who registered earlier this week. Again, her profile isn't complete but Dusky Di says more about herself and it is clear that whoever she is looking for it won't be me as her interests and plans don't dovetail with mine.

I am about to click on the next profile when the Alert heading flashes for a new message or rather in this case, a response from Daisy Chain. The message is again short and to the point. 'Would you like to meet up?' Gosh, within one week I may have a potential date! I didn't expect things to move so quickly or for it not to be me asking for a date. Times have changed from my previous dating time; I can get to like this! I see no point delaying a response. She wants to set the pace so I will let her decide where and when. So I just say, 'Yes. Where/when?'

It is now gone 11pm and I am not really in the mood to burn the midnight oil and read through all the profiles. I am seeing a couple of football friends tomorrow evening so it won't be a complete online dating weekend like the last one. Today's dating experience has been surprising, with the promise of something developing over the weekend.

DAY 8: SATURDAY

The flat looks appealing; it's on the ground floor, bedroom is at the back and the living room at the front has a view overlooking the sea. Sadly it is only a figment of my imagination. Since I woke first thing this morning all my plans for the dating site went out the window because my brain can only think about one thing. Where can I move?

I have put off for some time, too long to be honest, finding a place to buy. It will be the very first place of my own. So far, I have lived with my parents, shared rooms and houses with friends or lived with Em until our break up and my move to my current pad although temporary has given me a taste of life on my own after settling into a new routine.

It was a PS from Rachel at the end of our conversation last Wednesday that has been slowly germinating in my mind. She said, "Where exactly will you live with your special friend?" nothing more and I couldn't think of anything to say. Rachel urged me to make my own life and a big factor in that will be having a permanent place that is mine. When all around me is falling in, I can run to my little bolthole, and be safe and happy in my own home.

As I breakfast, shower and dress I am thinking about a place of my own. What do I want? How big a place? How old? How much? Where? That last question is critical because I have a strong desire to live by the sea, literally right by the sea. My place has to have an unrestricted view of the sea from my place, at least for the living area, and that means being right on a coast road.

That makes it simpler in one respect; there won't be many that meet my criteria. But it makes it more difficult if I can't afford any or compromise so I can have most of what else I want. It is the thought of failure that prevents me starting this journey. Why I should be compelled to start now with everything else going on is a good question! A masochist some might say, an avoider others may say, worrier as I won't find a special friend so don't start it or just so mixed up still with the big things that happened 12 months ago.

Either way there is a clear determination in my approach today. I am going to find a place. I know what I am looking for. I am prepared for disappointment. I start a task that becomes a daily grind by going through the property sites, applying my criteria and seeing what the results throw up. Bizarrely it feels like trying out dating sites, me trying to match myself with a place to buy that meets my wish list.

As I work my way through the flats listed – there aren't many in my price range that meet my criteria – I reflect back on the two places I bought with Em. We rented for the first couple of years after we got married. We were so full of love for each other that our surroundings didn't seem to matter as long as we had each other.

Our first place was a small, two up – two down, terraced house that needed updating. It felt like our first real home, something we were investing in, building our lives together. I only remember sunny days there but knowing how our weather is that it wasn't that really. They were happy times, before Danny and Liz, freedom to do what we wanted outside of work, we only left because we needed an extra bedroom and a garden for the children we planned to have.

And so we moved to our family home where our children were born and started their lives, played in the garden, went to school, watched films together, cooked, played games and generally enjoyed a happy time. Looking back now, my business needing more of my time, Danny and Liz leaving for college and university all contributed to Em buying me out and staying in our last home.

Finding a place to live in those days involved countless number of visits and daily phone calls to estate agents checking if anything knew was 'coming on to their books' for sale. At least now more information is available on websites that stop me making wasted journeys to visit places with a huge block of flats next to it or on a very busy and noisy road or overpriced compared to similar properties, etc.

I spend the morning and early afternoon viewing all types of flats that can give me what I want. I realise with a sinking feeling that flats in most towns nearby are outside my price range by a considerable amount; that does feel depressing. I try to be positive focusing on a few towns that have flats meeting my criteria. The one thing I am determined not to compromise on is the sea view; the flat can be bigger or smaller, older or newer, cheaper or pricier, but it has to have that view.

I remember with a bitter memory the last time I had been in my last home with my family. I went to try one last time to reconcile with Em before I instructed my solicitor to start the divorce proceedings she wanted. I felt at the time that I was just putting off the inevitable but I clung to some hope that time and distance from me might change Em's view about our marriage. Don't they say that distance makes the heart grow fonder? Em finally text me back after I left regular voicemails, texts and emails for two days. She gave a date, time and duration (which seemed a strange thing to do and felt a bad omen at the time) to meet at our house.

I spent the time leading up that last meeting trying to think through all the scenarios that could unfold. I kept to myself and avoided talking with my children or friends about it. Either I was going to solve this on my own or I would fail. It was my responsibility and I would go with my instincts. The trouble was the more I thought about it, the more troubled I was, the more wine I drank, the more angry and frustrated I got and the less sleep I had. It meant I wasn't in the best state of mind when the meeting with Em finally happened.

Em was in a similar mood to me and was not willing to give ground or reconsider what she had done. Our meeting quickly moved away from reconciliation and on to blame games and deteriorated as we argued over who should have what and how the children should be supported while they completed their studies.

Very little was being achieved when the doorbell rang. Em immediately stiffened and her face went very pale. She didn't move and stayed quiet. Up until this moment Em had been in full control of her actions and mood but she suddenly changed to indecision and doubt as if she was calculating whether to answer the door or not. It slowly dawned on me that it was her boyfriend at the door and a sudden compulsion to confront him and find out whom he was made me jump up and run to the door. Em shouted, "No!" to me but nothing was going to stop me.

I wrenched open the door as the doorbell was being pressed again. I saw a man who I didn't recognise with a goatee beard, greying hair, muscular with tanned skin and a little taller than me. He was wearing a dark suit with shirt unbuttoned with no tie. He was surprised for it not to be Em opening the door and stepped back. I just said sharply, "Yes, can I help you?" He was confused, then his eyes looked behind me as Em rushed to the door and showed some recognition.

We all just stood still. I glanced over my shoulder and saw the pleading look in Em's eyes towards the man. In that moment I could see that I had lost the woman I had loved for over 25 years. The energy just emptied from me and I felt cold and desolate. I pushed past him without saying a word and walked to my car parked in the road without looking back. The only sound I heard was the door shutting behind me.

It was a long and lonely journey home to my place but must have only been 30 minutes. As soon as I got in, I opened a bottle of wine, poured it up to the brim of a large wine glass and gulped it down. I felt it burn my throat, warm my insides and give me the strength to move to the chair in my small living room. I sat there for the rest of the evening, watching the light slowly fade, only moving to reach for the bottle and top my glass up. A second bottle got the same treatment. I just wanted the wine to obliterate all my bleak thoughts and this sinking feeling in the pit of my stomach. I knew for certain IT – WAS – OVER between Em and I.

That memory now spurred me to contact three agents and arrange viewings of five properties. One of them I find out has gone under offer today but I am able to book dates/times to see the other four early next week. None of them are really what I am looking for; I reason that I need to see what is out there first with my own eyes and get into the swing of looking for my own place.

Glancing up at my clock on the wall, I realise time is marching on. I still haven't done any food shopping, there is no dinner for tonight and I really don't fancy eating out alone. I am meeting up with Gordon and James this evening. We rarely meet during the football close season, May through to August, but James asked and arranged it. A first for James as I can't remember him ever doing it before!

Rushing around the supermarket, picking items almost randomly, I manage to get enough shopping to see me through the next few days and a cheap pizza on special offer for tonight's dinner beckons to me when I get home.

As I am about to put the pizza in the oven, whistling to myself to reflect my good mood at the prospect of seeing two friends for a drink this evening, my mobile alerts me to a text. Putting the pizza to one side I check it. It is from James 'Sorry going to have to cancel this evening.' No reasons why or whether Gordon wants to still meet. Typical James, even when he does try to organise something it doesn't happen. I reply 'OK.' then send a message to Gordon 'Still want to meet up?' and wait for a reply.

Trying to stay positive I heat up the pizza and aim to still meet up unless Gordon says otherwise. I need this change of scenery and conversation. After eating and getting ready I still haven't heard from him and text again after calling Gordon and getting his voicemail. Still confident that we will meet up, I start going down the stairs and walk to the bus stop to take the journey to where we plan to meet. However as I get to the bus stop so my mobile rings; it is Gordon saying he can't make it either.

I am annoyed and show it. "Why?!" Gordon just says something has come up around the same time as James cancelled and he couldn't get back to me before now. Exasperated still I realise there is little point arguing with him without causing a fallout between us that will take time and effort to recover. "OK. Bye Gordon." I say and end the call.

By then I am at the bus stop with nowhere to go and no one to see now. I am angry that my friends so quickly and lightly cut out an evening of potential laughter and entertainment without (at least to me) much if any thought for my wishes. It feels pointless catching the bus to walk around bars and pubs on my own. I don't want to be 'the oldest swinger in town' as that song in the '80s was called. The alternative is back to the flat and a bottle of wine but as I make my way, something makes me carry on walking until I reach the seafront. I use the stiff breeze blowing in my face to calm down and to take stock of everything.

As I get back to the front door of the building where my flat is Meghan turning the corner, calls out to me. She has been walking Blodwyn while 'taking her constitutional'; I still don't understand what this means or can be bothered to ask about it again after her first rambling explanation. With an inward groan I turn and smile, greeting her; I know whatever she asks I will do after ignoring her last weekend.

Meghan invites me into her flat with a wave of her hand as if she is royalty. Her place on the ground floor is a shrine to her family, her husband who died five years ago; her three children who have moved away to other parts of the world (Africa, America and Asia apparently from her last update). The photos are everywhere on the walls of the flat. Although I have never met them personally, it seems as if I know them intimately from their faces, their families, and Meghan's detailed descriptions about each of her three children.

Things get a little better when Meghan goes to her fridge and produces a bottle of white wine, her favourite, and offers me a glass.

She pours the wine into two glasses, brings them over and places them carefully on the table between two armchairs before sitting opposite me. While I am sampling a rather dry but tasty French wine she starts one of her long monologues all about her life over the past few days.

The gist of it I gather is her relationship with her friend Jim. He wants it to be more than a friendship; in fact he wants to marry her (good luck with that mate I think) while she just wants to be friends. I am used to hearing this story or rather it feels like it is becoming a saga after the past few months. Things are now coming to a head it seems as he has invited her to spend a long weekend away with him at a hotel. While Meghan is flattered and agrees to go with Jim, she is not prepared to sleep in the same bed or room with him. It has to be separate rooms or no break. Understandably Jim is reluctant to agree to this as he is paying for the break.

It makes me think of two questions. Firstly will I ever be having this conversation with a special friend in future? I certainly hope to although it seems a million miles away based on the current progress. Secondly are the holidays in the past, I mean distant past before the kids, when Em and I had been at our happiest? Probably, we had all the freedom and none of the responsibilities of parenthood to consider while away.

As my mind came back to the present, Meghan is getting close to the inevitable question she usually asks, "What would you do if you were me Christopher?' Inwardly I sigh to myself; Meghan loves to ask that and I suspect takes great pleasure after hearing the answer to ignore it and follow what she wants to do all along. I take the plunge and give my view on what she can do, why she can do that and any consequences she needs to consider. Partly it feels a waste of time and partly it stops her asking about me and I realise I do need some company, even Meghan's, this evening.

She considers my advice for a moment and I sense she has dismissed it and is about to ask about me. Quickly I ask, "What will you likely do Meghan?" which results in her puffing out her cheeks and giving me a ten minute diatribe on all that is going wrong in her life, how poorly she is treated, how Jim doesn't really understand what she wants. I nod empathetically while sipping my wine. When she finishes I compliment Meghan on her choice of wine and accept a top up in my glass.

I know what is coming next and Meghan doesn't disappoint me. "What have you been up to Christopher? I haven't heard from you for a while." I know she means that I haven't responded to her messages last Sunday. I tell her about my last week leaving out any reference to online dating. As she doesn't really (or wants to) understand what I do it is easy to give the impression I am very busy (I emphasised the very) to explain why I haven't been in touch. I ask her about her family, always a rich source of fresh conflict between either Meghan and her siblings or children, and she quickly got in her stride with the latest events, fallouts and gossip. It confirms my view that I won't say anything about my dating because it will be common knowledge within 24 hours and lead to a relentless set of questions about its progress from Meghan and from anyone else she tells who bumps into me.

Thankfully Blodwyn starts whining and looks anxiously at the door. This is my cue to leave while Meghan takes her outside for a walk and a wee. With a quick goodbye and a promise to keep in touch we make our departures and go our separate ways. By the time I get to my place it is after 9pm and I just want to relax and unwind. I am grateful for some company, any company, this evening and being with Meghan has been better than just sitting on my own moping about being on my own.

Tomorrow will be when I plunge into seeking a special friend to prevent me worrying about having low moments on my own like this evening has almost been.

DAY 9: SUNDAY

It already feels like a very long time ago when I sat down last Saturday and started to look into the world of online dating. I feel that I am finding my feet more now and starting to take the initiative. My goal today is to put out some tentative feelers with any women who I find interesting.

What created this positive state of mind and spurred me on is a message sent very late yesterday from Daisy Chain that I read first thing this morning. It says 'How about London next Saturday?' and is short and to the point like her other messages. I am not doing anything next Saturday so reply 'Yes. Where exactly and when?' hoping we can agree today on more details.

While I wait for her reply, I settle down to look again at the dating site. I notice the weather outside is wet and windy for this time of year and pleased I will be in the warm and dry, reinforced by a pot of coffee to help me this morning. I search through women matching with my profile for wishes, interests, ages, locations, etc. and mentally compare them with my preferences. Using the process of elimination I remove any women that clearly don't interest me first of all. That takes a while but I find it's easier to do when deciding whom to contact.

I pause to take stock of the progress made. It seems impossible to find the needle in the haystack, loads of women's profiles to search through and find *the* one, my future special friend. Now I have reduced the profiles down to a more manageable number I feel able to seriously consider the next step; contacting someone. I imagine how Neil Armstrong feels taking 'one small step for man, one giant leap for mankind'; it is a similar experience for me as I step out into the online dating world.

With more coffee to sustain my thinking and keeping a clear head I select Moody Blue for my first message; but what shall I say that will set the right tone?

I write down some words and start playing around with them: 'Hi, I liked reading your profile. What do you think of mine?' or 'Hello, I like your profile. Do you like mine?' or 'Hi, I like your profile. Are you interested in mine?' I will decide based on how they have written their profile to how casual or forward I feel like being. Playing it cautious feels okay with me as the natural approach, avoiding being presumptuous or too familiar.

I pluck up courage and say to Moody Blue 'Hi I'm A Good Guy and like your profile. How about looking at mine and letting me know if you want to find out more?' Yes, I know this is different to my examples and probably too wordy but it is my first attempt. At least it looks grammatically correct I think pedantically to myself as I send the message.

I slowly work my way through the remaining profiles, discarding some, liking others and for around a dozen send a message expressing interest in their profile and encouraging them to do the same with my profile. With a break for a cold lunch and short walk around the block it is mid-afternoon when I send the last message to Angel Clare (probably an Art Garfunkel fan using his debut album for her username).

Exhausted, I make myself a pot of tea and sink into my armchair by the window and gaze out at nothing in particular. I am pleased, even satisfied, that I crossed over a big mental barrier to start the daunting task of finding and contacting women I have never known before today. However, I expected to have heard back from someone, any one of the women I have contacted, especially Daisy Chain. Logic said she is busy with her life like I can be, emotion and anxiety however shouts "Now, now, now… don't delay replying!" at me.

I message Liz and Danny to ask how they are and briefly update them on my day. Their interest in me is appreciated although their responses vary – Liz cool, Danny warm – to my taking the initiative with my dating sojourn.

It seems like an alien world I am entering. It would be similar if I visit a country and don't speak the language or follow the customs and behaviour of everyone there. Not knowing what is the 'right' thing to say or do is draining. I am learning a side of life that I never knew existed or thought I would join. Yet here I am learning a new language, ways of behaving, as each day of online dating goes by.

Maybe many of the women I have contacted feel the same? How do you get the balance right? Showing that I am interested in someone who doesn't respond will leave me dejected and rejected. I want to leave everyone who contacts me or I contact with our dignity and self esteem intact. Think before you speak was a saying my mum taught me when I was young and it has stuck with me throughout my life. It amazes me how appropriate it is now as I apply it to online dating.

Still no responses come back to me and I try not to fret about it. I distract myself by cooking a chili con carne. I haven't heard from or seen anyone so far today and I am feeling that loneliness. I play some music to fill the silence and drown out my insecurities voicing their concerns inside my head. It is going to be a long evening at this rate!

After dinner, I go out for a walk and some fresh air in the hope that it will help improve my state of mind. The seafront always feels fresher after some rain and with a strong breeze blowing. The exercise and change of scenery helps but what helps even more is a surprise message from Gill following up on her conversation after training. She contacted her friend who is interested in finding out more about my training at Gill's workplace.

To say I am surprised is a big understatement. I am used to people I do business with promising one thing but for all sorts of reasons; forget it, not mean what they say, change their mind, and it doesn't happen. Because of the way Gill engaged with me I hoped rather than expected to hear from her again. Well, she has come back to me and is now suggesting we meet with her friend after work one day next week. I am up for that!

The week ahead looks very empty; some are like that, other weeks can be too hectic to cope with. Apart from some flat viewings with agents I haven't much planned. I suggest a couple of evenings when we can meet up. Gill quickly confirms Tuesday will be the best for her and Linda, her friend, to meet up. After agreeing a time and place for our meeting we wish each other well until we met.

It gives me a massive boost and makes me walk around my place with lighter footsteps. I iron my work shirts, sort out a few other domestic chores; put clothes away, load up my washing machine, etc. Exciting stuff… not! At the end of the day I still feel despondent with nothing back from Daisy Chain or anyone else I messaged. Ah well, one of those days I say philosophically to myself before retiring to bed.

DAY 10: MONDAY

I wake up after another restless night dreaming about women snubbing me, whether I am asking for something, just saying hello or even in one case crossing the road to avoid walking past me on the pavement. It means I am not in the best of moods or as prepared for my meeting with a potential new client as I want to be.

It is raining as I leave my place and I curse the long walk to where my car is parked several streets away. Of course, I have again left without my umbrella – a small collapsible one that I had bought exactly for these occasions – and feel my clothes match my mood as I start the drive to where Dave Donaldson, my client, wants to meet me.

I always aim to leave with plenty of time to spare in case of a problem with my car, traffic congestion or like today, bad weather. I arrive at the place for my meeting with over half an hour in hand to give me time to compose myself. I don't normally check my personal emails, just my work emails, before a meeting in case there is a sudden change of time, place or people. However on this occasion I do and see an alert from the dating site. Deciding to check it rather than have it in the back of my mind during the meeting, I eagerly go to the site.

The message is from Moody Blue, the first woman I contacted yesterday, but it isn't good news. She thanks me for my message and will be in touch if she is still interested later. I am both puzzled and disappointed by her response. 'If still interested later' doesn't make sense to me and I am tempted to ask her to clarify but realise I need to meet my client so stop.

The meeting with Dave goes fairly well. He is interested in my proposal and has checked there is budget. But he needs more details about what I specifically will do. Timescales are still on the vague side; it is hard to get a feel for how urgent it is needed, only that it is. I am used to this with new clients; most are genuine with the need for more details. Others however can receive these and then mysteriously not show any further interest. This is because they use the details to carry out the training themselves. The trick is to get the balance right – cover the 'what' but not the 'why' or the 'how'.

Anyway, after the meeting I walk round to a local café to eat some lunch and collect my thoughts about Moody Blue. As I'm eating a rather tasty quiche with salad I think about all the possible reasons why she said that. I am still puzzled by it and whether to respond or not. Eventually I decide to reply just saying, 'OK'. It shows that I have read her message – I am being polite – and will wait. I hope it may elicit more information on her thinking.

After driving home I receive another alert. When I quickly check who and what it may be I am again disappointed. It is a 'Like' from Angel Clare but no message, just that. That feels like a failure although I tentatively hope it might be a slow burner. I reciprocate and like her profile to show I have received hers. There are five more views, four from women I messaged yesterday and a new woman who I guess didn't feel I warranted any contact with – fair enough I think.

All in all it means my efforts yesterday, which so drained me, have not borne fruit so far. I will persist after I meet Gill and hopefully hear back from Daisy Chain.

DAY 11: TUESDAY

Another restless night dreaming about unsuccessful meetings with women who reject me one way or another. My subconscious is very inventive in the different ways I am snubbed or humiliated again and again. One of the dreams (or should they be called nightmares now?) is a meeting with Em, the first time in many months I have dreamt about her. It brings back how our marriage spectacularly imploded in vivid detail that awful day twelve months ago.

I know I have my moods and can be difficult to communicate with at times. Pressure from work can lead to me drinking one too many glasses of wine some evenings. But they are relatively rare and otherwise I feel I am a funny guy, a loving, supportive, father to two wonderful children. Em also has her bad times and will stay with a friend for a weekend to get a break from everyone.

My first reaction when she told me that she wanted a divorce was to be stunned and unable to respond, even move, as I started to absorb what she was saying in an emotionless, matter of fact way.

After a few moments of sitting there paralysed by shock I stammered out "What? Why? Are you ok, Em?"

Em, the name I had called her with great affection since the first few weeks we started going out, responded "Because I don't love you and I don't want to live with you anymore."

Again, I paused for a few moments as I took stock of this clear statement. I remember hearing birdsong outside and Steve, our neighbour from two doors down, washing his car while playing a radio loudly. The house was still, both the children were away, obviously planned by Em so this conversation could happen.

Em then proceeded to list all the concerns she had about our marriage and what she wanted to happen:

1. She had fallen out of love with me.

2. She was tired of my moods and drinking.

3. She was in a rut and wasn't sure what she wanted.

4. But she was sure it was without me.

5. There might be someone else.

6. She has already contacted a divorce solicitor (really!!!).

7. She wanted me to pack my belongings and leave.

8. She would tell the children I am away for a few days on business.

9. She didn't want me to call her – emails and texts would suffice.

10. She didn't want to discuss it further or try any couples counseling.

"What? Why? Are you ok, Em?" were still the questions I thought even if I wasn't asking them, particularly the last one. I had never seen Em behave like this or picked up even a hint that this was brewing inside of her. I sat down, feeling weak and helpless and paused for a moment to try to collect my thoughts.

The silence grew between us. Normally we communicated well, able to express our feelings – good and bad – with each other honestly and openly. Fair enough, recently there hadn't been so much of that but all couples went through phases like that. Didn't they? Maybe not? Was that why this was happening?

The mood started to become ominous; it was clear Em had nothing else to say. She just wanted me to accept the situation, pack and go. No words of explanation, evidence, just leave before the children or anything happened to interrupt what she wanted to happen next.

I don't consider that I am an awkward man. I believe you should treat people you meet, as you would expect to be treated too. Up until this moment I had total respect for Em and her views even if I didn't always agree with her. I would support her actions such as telling the kids off, making a stand over an issue, meeting her halfway if we didn't agree on the way forward Em want.

But all that changed when this stranger who looked like Em but certainly wasn't acting like Em stood a few feet in front of me. Staring intently at me, waiting for me to act on her suggestions, proposals, well it feels more like a set of instructions to be followed to the letter!

As I sat absorbing what had been said… and not said by Em I tried to find a response but words wouldn't come out of my mouth. Neither could I summon up the strength to move any of my limbs. The silence gradually became more oppressive as time slipped by.

I was still not sure what possessed to me to do what I did next. It might have been the combination of what I felt along with how Em was behaving. I suppose we all do things we later reflect on and wonder if we took the best option.

I just said loudly, "I'm not doing it Em! You can't make me leave and you can't force me. So tell me why or I'm not moving from this chair." Em responded by calmly and softly repeating her list of concerns.

I replied sharply, "You've already said that but you haven't said why and why now."

"I don't have to." She whispered to which I sat back and said, "Fine but I'm not moving until you do."

A long silence enveloped the room. I started looking at my smartphone to show I was not likely to move. Em knew by my actions that I meant what I said and she sat down opposite me and looked intently at me. I can tell she was furiously thinking about what to do or say next. After a few more minutes Em stood up and hunched her shoulders and started speaking.

"I haven't loved you for some time now Chris. We haven't had sex for a while because I don't want to with you. I don't have the same feelings that I had for you. What I want from life and what you want have diverged so far it isn't possible to be compatible any more. Lastly, I've met someone else, I think it can become serious and I will not give you his name. There isn't room in my life for both of you and it's not you that I want to be with any more."

"I've thought about this for a while and I haven't changed my mind. I'm sorry this has come as a surprise to you but when you sit down and think about it you will realise the signs were there. You should think about how you have changed and the impact that's had on me. The children will need to be told but they've both left school and are becoming adults now. It won't be the first marriage split they will have heard about or witnessed. So now, will you go?"

Wow! I've got my answers although I didn't like what Em had said. I sat and thought back over the past few weeks and the distance that had grown between us; her lack of interest in my life; her early nights if I am staying up or her late nights if I am tired or fancied some loving with an early night. I had been very absorbed in my work recently. I hadn't much time for Em and hadn't really noticed until now that she hadn't taken up my thoughts or time.

OK, I got that but… another man… already! Either Em was a quick mover or I was so submersed in my life that I just hadn't noticed the change in mood or time away for no apparent reason. To be fair, I am not the jealous type; neither did I check up on Em who I had trusted 100% up until now. That did tip the balance of my mind into more of an inferno as I dwelled on what she said and what she hadn't said about this other man. My resentment grew rapidly and it exploded.

"No!" I shouted. "I won't go! If anyone should go it's you as you're the one who's destroying our marriage. I've not been running around with other women, sizing up whom your replacement can be, then dropping the bombshell. Give me one good reason why I shouldn't pack your bags and tell you to leave now for your darling boyfriend."

"I'll tell you why you will go Chris. I won't sleep with you ever again. My new boyfriend is a much better lover, more considerate, lasts longer and has a much bigger penis than you. He makes me happy and more satisfied then you ever did. He has shown already that he is very committed to me and to our future. I don't want you and frankly I don't need you any more in my life. You never loved me like he does. Just face it, you're so consumed in your own life that little else matters to you. Being on your own will be the best thing for you and for us... so leave now before this gets messier and nastier. Try to avoid unnecessary pain. There has been plenty these past few months... at least for me

"Why didn't you talk to me Em, instead of running off and finding someone else? I've always tried to understand and to meet your needs, whatever they are, haven't I?"

"No, you haven't; you used to. I've tried talking with you but it was never the right time. You were either too busy to talk, always needed to be somewhere else, too tired, too distracted by work or football or reading or sometimes all of them. You're impossible and have changed too much from the man I first loved to want to try a fresh start with you now."

"That's you making excuses, using my behaviour to cover for your own passions and actions. I still say you should go. Give me one good reason why I should go now."

"To avoid you being humiliated. You won't be sleeping in my bed tonight or any other night. In fact it's going to be full soon, maybe even from tonight, and you will have to sleep in the shed, garage or on the floor of one of the children's bedrooms. I told you why I want you to go. I'm trying to avoid it being any worse than it is. Just accept what is happening and move out now."

The fight suddenly left me. I hadn't slept well for a few nights and it was taking its toll. I felt deflated. Maybe I needed time and space to think this through better? I needed to act with my head, not my heart, now.

I stood up and strode quickly towards Em. I raised my arm up and Em flinched as I moved past her and pushed open the door to the hallway and climbed the stairs to our bedroom.

As I entered I found my head had cleared sufficiently to think logically about what I needed to do. I looked around the bedroom where we had slept together for the 15 years we had lived here. The bed, matching bedside cabinets, dressing table, his and her wardrobes, were still where they had been this morning, nothing had changed physically. The window still looked out onto the garden, the sun shone over the grass and shrubs, leaves gently moved in the breeze.

And yet, it wasn't the same. The atmosphere was cold, stale, and lifeless. Everything intangible had changed, gone. I knew that I would never feel welcome or comfortable in this room with so many happy, intimate, memories.

I took a deep breath, moved towards my wardrobe and reached above it for the suitcases normally used to pack clothes for holidays to be enjoyed. I put two of the largest onto our double bed and opened them. I moved to one of the chest of drawers and started mechanically to lift clothes out from each drawer into each suitcase.

After taking what I thought would be enough for a few days, I opened my wardrobe and removed trousers, shirts, jumpers and a couple of suits that are hung inside. At the back of my mind was the thought that at any moment Em would say it was all a joke – not a very funny one - or a test to see how much I did love her.

I certainly didn't realise these would be my last precious moments here. At best my confused state was thinking it would only be for a few days. We would both quickly see how absence makes the heart grow fonder as the saying goes. We would be back together, stronger from this mini crisis, happier than ever before with each other. Whoever this guy was, was either a fantasy or a chancer, taking advantage of Em who was feeling vulnerable at the moment.

I now know that my hopes will be dashed. This will not be the outcome, quite the opposite in fact, I am never to see this bedroom ever again.

It felt like an out of body experience as I lugged each suitcase down the stairs. Em was nowhere to be seen, presumably still standing in the lounge. I went in there to say "Bye." There was no response, just her looking intently out the window with her back to me, so I turned and left.

Feeling despondent with that dreadful memory still fresh in my mind even after this period of time, I try to raise my mood by thinking about my evening ahead when I will meet Gill and Linda. It doesn't feel like how a normal business meeting should be. It certainly isn't like yesterday before I met Dave. Although it may lead to new business with Linda's employer, it also seems like a vehicle chosen by Gill to see me again.

It isn't a date - like with "Daisy Chain" - although she still hasn't confirmed anything for this Saturday yet which I am getting a little anxious about. It is with difficulty that I focus my mind on the training proposal that Dave wants approval for that we discussed. Slowly, very slowly at times, I work through the details, deciding how much to give and what information to hold back, as Dave is a client I haven't worked with before. He seems sincere with integrity but I am not ready to trust him yet with too much of my intellectual property. Less about my methodology and more about expected outcomes is my approach.

By the time I complete, read through it again, check for any grammar errors and email it to him, it is late in the afternoon. With only 2-3 hours before my meeting with Gill and Linda my mind drifts towards what to wear, eat and say to them this evening. I haven't been to the place we are meeting before so that adds to my anxiety. Where will I meet them? Should I be there early or 'fashionably late'? All this and other thoughts are swirling round in my head at the same time.

Somehow over the next couple of hours I eat, shower and after a few changes of clothing settle on 'smart casual attire', a shirt, jacket and trousers (no jeans) that match reasonably well. More importantly I feel most comfortable and confident wearing these than anything else.

I look in the mirror and see a man with brown hair, thinning and receding a bit at the front, with flecks of grey showing round the sides above the ears. My frightened, pale face has worry lines etched across its forehead. Set inside it are two blue/green eyes – they never seem to stay the same and might reflect my mood. A pointed nose, not too long, is set above a mouth that is very tight with pursed lips but is capable of a big broad smile that people always comment upon liking about me. I'm sporting a (fashionable?) short growth of beard; salt and pepper as far as brown mixes with grey hair. Hmm, not the best I've ever looked in my life!

As I start towards the front door and pick up my car keys blind panic paralyses me. Is there a way to get out of this without embarrassment? An evening watching the TV, any programme on any channel suddenly is very appealing. I stand still for five, maybe ten minutes, trying to think clearly and breathing slowly to calm down. I convince myself that it will be far worse to cancel at this late stage than to meet even if nothing comes of the evening.

This all makes sense of course but my mind isn't being logical; it is full of emotions instead. It is a chance to chat with two women who are strangers to me and try to find out what makes them tick, laugh, test out what might work in situations that I am going to have to get used to now.

The pub we are meeting in has two small car parks separate from each other so I choose the one with the least amount of cars there and park well away from the few already there. I always have a fear of coming back and finding huge scratches all the way down one wing of my car in any car park, especially supermarkets with shopping trolleys being an extra hazard. There are ten minutes before the time we agreed to meet.

The mirror when I glance in it still shows an anxious face, perhaps a little less lined, looking straight back at me. I take a deep breath and open my door to step out. Looking up I see the weather has cleared and it is dry for the moment. Checking I am still smartly casual or casually smart, whatever, I walk towards the entrance. When I get to the door I move aside to let a couple out first. They are laughing and holding each other's hands. It is a nice image and makes me wish that it were me with my special friend. I'm not religious but I feel like offering up a prayer, something along the lines of "For what we are about to receive…" as I enter the pub.

There are two bars inside the pub, one blaring out loud music and crowded, and the other quiet and with a few people sitting round tables. I quickly move into the quiet bar and glance around. Neither Gill nor Linda is there but I can see tables free still as I reach the bar. Ordering a pint of Harvey's best bitter, lovely local brew, that I can nurse and make it last, I take in my surroundings. It is full of brass rubbings and horse paraphernalia; bridles, saddles, horseshoes among other stuff. It gives a false feel to the place, as it isn't in the country, trying to be something that it isn't. The Horse and Groom is its name but I suspect there hasn't been any grooms for many a day frequenting this pub!

After paying I weave my way in between the tables to one that has four seats and is reasonably private. It gives me a clear view of the entrance to this bar so I can spot Gill and/or Linda when they arrive. I try to relax, taking slow deep breaths, sip some of my drink and make myself as comfortable as it is possible; realistically slightly less uncomfortable. Inside I am knotted up and my stomach feels like it wants to be sick. The clock on the wall ticks slowly as 5, 10, then 15 minutes go by while I sit on my own waiting.

As I am thinking this must be what people call 'fashionably late' and not my type of fashion I hear the sound of loud laughter and glancing up see Gill and Linda enter the bar. Gill instantly recognises me and beams a large smile and nudges Linda towards my whereabouts. They are both wearing dresses; deep red for Gill and light blue for Linda. Make up has been applied generously by Gill who looks as if she is aiming to be glamorous in her appearance. I note that she has made a big effort and hope she approves of my efforts.

Then began the strangest business meeting I've ever had. I ask if I can get them both drinks. After a quick look at each other, they ask for the same drink, white wine. I ask if they have a preference and Gill says anything but Chardonnay. That gives me plenty of scope and I leave them to sit down while I weave my way back to the bar. Returning with two large glasses of wine I notice they are sitting opposite each other not side by side. It presents me with a dilemma of who to sit next to but as I pause Gill pats the seat next to her and smiles to indicate where I should sit so I do, as she wants of course.

After further introductions and clinking of glasses together I sit back and look more closely at Linda who appears a little awkward with me. After a short silence Gill starts the conversation.

"Well this is a nice change for me on a Tuesday evening. No Eastenders or other TV to watch. Just some nice company to enjoy."

I nod my agreement and look towards Linda who nervously smiles and drinks some wine.

Gill continues, looking at me "So what have you been doing with yourself since we last met?" I obviously am not going to say I'm messaging women on a dating site so keep it concise by saying I am preparing for some new work. By doing so I am hinting to Linda about the purpose of our meeting. But Linda doesn't seem to pick up my hint and stays silent.

"Sounds interesting," said Gill. "What is it about?" I briefly summarise what the work will be and that it is similar to the training I delivered last Thursday. "Oh, that's good. I like what you did last week. Maybe you can do some again for us?" I think, well that is exactly why we are meeting again with Linda but instead I say that her employer may want more training but it isn't certain at this stage. Again Linda just sips her drink and stays silent while looking at Gill.

I am about to ask Linda directly why we are meeting when Gill seems to read my mind and anticipating my question to her asks about my football team. Surprised by this change of subject I briefly say that I am looking forward to the new season and watching whom my club signs as new players. Gill says she isn't much of a football fan but Linda goes to a few games with her husband; they are both Crystal Palace supporters. It feels like a stake going through my heart at hearing those words. Brighton is a deadly rival of Palace and the banter between both sets of supporters isn't always for family hearing.

"Oh!" is all I can respond with and again look towards Linda.

This time Linda does speak. "Yes, me and Adrian go to games whenever we get a chance. Who do you support?"

I simply say, "Brighton," nothing else.

"Oh," says Linda, a little surprised. "Our clubs are not always the best of friends are they?"

"No," I reply. I don't know what else to say, this meeting isn't going as expected, in fact it doesn't look like it will even start – the business part of it at least.

"Wouldn't it be nice if we did get on better? I suppose being in the same division doesn't help. How did all this bad feeling start?" the longest statement yet from Linda so far this evening. I could have given her chapter and verse over the origin of the rivalry back in the 1970s when Alan Mullery and Terry Venables were the managers and didn't get on, creating the fertile ground to feed fans with the excuse to show their feelings whenever there was a tasty action packed game… and there were many.

"It all started a long time ago and has continued because we seem to stay in the same divisions most seasons. Have you been to any of the games against Brighton?"

"One at Selhurst Park but it wasn't a pleasant atmosphere as we were near the Brighton fans in the away end. I don't want to hear that language again for a while. I just let my hubby go on his own if it's a Brighton game now."

"Yes, I rarely go to the away games with Palace but always go to the home games at the Amex. I find the atmosphere can be nasty and all avoidable so don't enjoy them much… unless we beat you big time of course!"

That brings a smile to Linda's face. There is a thaw in our relationship. I start off by saying "Gill mentioned to me…" but don't get any further because Gill interrupts me "Linda, will you be a darling and get us some more drinks please?" Linda looks questioningly at Gill but stands up and moves towards the bar without saying anything. She comes back a minute later to check what I want to drink and returns to the bar.

What is going on I wonder? I turn to Gill and look closely at her face. There is no denying I do find her attractive. There is something about her expression and how deep and blue her eyes look that I find very appealing.

"Well?' I ask.

She just smiles and says "Well what?"

I don't know what to say and feel completely out of my comfort zone. Something is happening which I don't understand.

"Why are we here?" I ask the direct question to Gill out of frustration with what is and isn't happening so far.

"We're just catching up after last week, aren't we?"

"But what about the training?"

Before Gill can reply, Linda returns with the drinks Gill asked her for. I wait for an answer but again Linda sits down without saying anything and Gill sips from her fresh glass of wine.

Excusing myself I walk off towards the toilets only to find it is where the Ladies toilet is. Embarrassed, I ask at the bar and move slowly in the opposite direction, out of the bar and down a corridor to where the Gents toilet is. Once inside I find a cubicle and just sit down and take a deep breath. What is going on? Am I missing something? It is beginning to feel like Linda is being used by Gill as a vehicle to test me out. Surely not! Can I be that lucky? The only way to find out is to wait and see what happens next. My nerves mean I am tongue-tied and unsure what to do or say.

When I return the atmosphere has changed; Linda is more relaxed and Gill more confident. What have they been discussing while I was away? As well as taking a break to collect my thoughts, I hope they talked about what they will do next. I am in their hands so sit back, sip my beer and wait for whatever is going to happen.

Linda again looks towards Gill and I follow her by also looking at Gill who seems to be preparing to say something. I sit expectantly as Gill clears her throat and sips her wine. Silence and sipping seem to be the in-thing this evening, Linda mirroring Gill's action now. I join the trend by lifting my beer to my lips and keeping it in my hand on the table. Seconds feel like minutes as we both wait patiently for Gill who adjusts her stance next to me.

Gill finally speaks. "Sooo… the situation is like this Chris. Linda has asked around where she works about your training but her bosses are not sure if they need it. Sooo… it means that it isn't possible at this stage to get you any work with them. Ummm… we wanted to tell you face to face rather than call or email you as you be may be disappointed or have questions and feel awkward responding."

My reaction is mixed. Firstly it is presumptuous, I haven't gone searching for this work; Gill approached me. Secondly, I am not disappointed; there is enough work from my existing clients to keep me busy. Lastly, what is wrong with an email or call or text? Why did we need to meet this evening unless there is another reason?

Being in two minds on how to act and unsure what to do next I feel the evening is a big letdown and I am here on false pretenses. However it may all be a ruse so Gill has another chance to talk with me again without feeling awkward.

Quickly processing all these thoughts I look at Gill, then at Linda, and say, "OK, so what else shall we talk about? Seems a bit early to call it a night." It must have been the right response as the atmosphere lifts and we all smile at each other. Over the next hour we chat about our interests, likes and dislikes, holidays planned or taken. I am beginning to feel comfortable for the first time in ages with women I didn't know socially.

It is gone 10pm when we rise from our table and say our goodbyes. Linda and I have an awkward handshake but Gill gives me a tight hug, sparkling smile and a kiss on my cheek. I drive home feeling on a high. I can meet women and be reasonably OK with it, a small step along my dating learning curve.

Back home I pick up a message from Gill wishing me a good night's sleep and hoping we can catch up again. I am not sure how to respond so leave it until tomorrow when I can think better on how to respond and what I want to do.

DAY 12: WEDNESDAY

From the moment I wake up my head is buzzing with dreams from last evening's events. One probably led to another and reflected how life has been limited since my separation from Em. They are rather erotic and vivid dreams that involve me and Gill and one that includes Linda; a threesome no less, something that is only a fantasy or an erotic dream rather than my experience like a lot of men I hasten to add.

The last message from Gill late yesterday is still unanswered. It isn't that I don't want to continue our friendship to see where it may lead to; it is more a fear of the unknown. After being with Em for so many years then no one for 12 months, mainly out of choice rather than necessity I am almost afraid of being intimate with someone different. I am not confident about myself, my body, how I will behave whenever I meet someone new.

From the moment I met Em our relationship had been monogamous until Em's confession about her infidelity over the last few months. I had been happy with everything that she had brought to our marriage. There didn't seem anything I wanted or needed that Em couldn't provide physically, emotionally and sexually. Life was pretty good with Em; she had been my best friend as well as lover. That's why it had been so devastating to part from her and such an enormous challenge to even imagine I can be happy with another woman.

I decide to reply to Gill's message by saying, 'Really enjoyed last evening. Will be good to meet up again. Maybe just the two of us next time?' Within a few minutes my phone alerts me to Gill's response. 'That sounds good to me. What are you doing Saturday?' Oh no, Saturday! I am still waiting to hear back from Daisy Chain and have to think what to say before trying for an alternative day. 'Not sure about Saturday but can meet anytime Sunday if you're free.' I wait and wait but no reply comes back.

It is Wednesday; there are still three days before I hope to meet Daisy Chain. It's the anxiety and uncertainty that is the worst part with this new online dating experience. I don't want to appear desperate and decide I will wait until tomorrow evening or Friday morning before contacting Daisy Chain. Instead I will sort out a few business emails, visit my mum, and then see the first of several properties this week. I am not looking forward to either event.

Even with my mum suffering from dementia and generally frail physically, it was difficult moving her 2 years ago from her home where she had been for 40 years, to a nursing home. Her nursing care is good, the savings from selling her house still pay her bills, but it is a two-hour car journey each way to visit my mum which limits how often I can go. I aim to go fortnightly, sometimes more frequently, but it depends on how often she needs me and how busy work is.

Driving the car along roads I am very familiar with, noticing the changes in the trees and hedgerows as the seasons unfold one into the next, I reflect on how much she has deteriorated recently. The last time she hadn't left her chair to see me to the door out of her room because she was so tired. She is increasingly forgetful and confused by her surroundings and whom she was talking to.

We aren't a particularly close family. My mum and dad only had one sister each. Dad passed away over five years ago from lung cancer; smoking for many years hadn't helped of course. My mum and dad were still very much in love when he died and she missed him dreadfully and has never really got over it. I can't prove it but it seemed to me she deteriorated from the day after his funeral with her low mood. She had stayed often with Em and me; seeing the children helped to lift her spirits while she was with us but it didn't last once she was back home.

I had a distant relationship with my dad. I respected him for loving my mum and looking after her but I didn't love him. His time as a prisoner during World War II affected him deeply; he never opened up about it to me and always seemed afraid to show his true feelings to me. It made me feel starved of love and affection and it was a relief when I got married as it put the same distance between us physically that it always was emotionally.

My mum is always full of love, seeing the positives in everyone even when I couldn't. She and I are very close because she could give me the love and affection my dad couldn't. She was the glue that bonded our family together and meant I look back with fond memories of my time growing up. I do have an elder sister, Mary, by four years and that age gap as well as being different sexes always seemed to limit how close we were from my earliest memory. We didn't argue much – just went in parallel with our lives as we grew up.

I rarely speak with Mary now even with our mum being unwell.

When she got married for the third time a few years ago, she moved up to Scotland which reinforced the distance between us like it was with my dad and me.

I was closer to my Aunt Ruby, my mum's sister, than to my sister. My aunt is happily married with one son who is a few years older than me. Ruby and I speak on the phone every few weeks, mainly about my mum's health. I last saw my aunt a few months ago when we bumped into each other at the nursing home. It made a pleasant change to have company while chatting with my mum as well as catching up on Ruby's news.

I do not belong to the closest family in history but my mum is the most important person to me after my children. With my dad's death and separation from Em, our relationship is closer than ever. My mum's frail health and poor memory means she doesn't remember that Em is no longer in my life.

As I park the car, I can see they are painting the outside of the main building. My mum is in one of the rooms in the Annex with a view of the car park, building that was being re-painted and some of the gardens. I had pushed hard for this room as it gave her something to look at, to stimulate her interest, when she was inside. The home had a library, social room with activities and restaurant where all the residents who are able to will eat their lunch and dinner. My mum thinks it a wonderful treat to have her breakfast brought to her to eat in bed; something she had always done for my dad on Sundays but sadly it was never reciprocated even on special days like her birthday.

Mum smiles at me as I enter her room; that is a good sign to start with. I say hello and give her a big kiss on each cheek and a long and warm hug. Then her smile leaves her face, replaced by a puzzled look.

"Is it Chris?"

"Yes mum."

"Are you my son?"

"Yes mum."

"Oh, you look different. Are you sure?"

"Yes mum. How are you today?" I try to break this loop of conversation.

"I suppose I'm ok. Is Em with you?"

Inwardly I sigh. "No, Em isn't with me. Em and I split up. Don't you remember?"

"No, I didn't know. When did you tell me? What happened? Why aren't you together?"

Annoyed with myself for questioning her memory; an increasingly touchy subject with her these day and frustrated that I am reliving moments of my life I want to forget about I tell her again why Em isn't with me any more. It is probably well into double figures the number of times I have now told her this. After I finish she looks ahead silently. It is hard to tell where her thoughts are.

"Danny and Liz send their love and hope to see you soon when they break from their studies."

"Danny? Liz? Oh, your children… where are they?"

"Danny is at university and Liz is at college and hoping to go to university."

"Oh, I remember when they were small. They always wanted to see nana and give her a hug. I remember when you first met Em and you started courting, going out or whatever they call it these days. You looked the perfect couple together; your hair was as long as

Em's. Lovely seeing you together... but not now; so sad."

I didn't know what to say; this happens every time. My mum without realising it knows my Achilles heel and goes for it like a rapier thrust into an open wound. It adds to my upset at how my mum is slowly but inexorably deteriorating. How long will she remember me when I come to see her?

The rest of my time is spent asking my mum questions about her childhood, her favourite period of her life. To be honest, I like to hear about a time I only read about in history books or archived footage in History programmes on TV. It means when I do leave after a couple of hours she is happy, a smile on her face that only disappears temporarily when she can't remember my name as I leave.

Thinking hard over how my latest visit has gone with mum, I run to the car as a heavy shower of rain starts. While listening to the deafening patter of rain on my car roof I check for any emails or messages I received while I was chatting with mum. Apart from the estate agent sending me an automated text reminder of my appointment there isn't anything. I have the long drive back but there is plenty of time before the viewing.

However 40 minutes into the drive I come to a stop before a long traffic jam. Temporary traffic lights have been set up because of some problem with the road. Inching forward a few feet at a time, I finally after half an hour (30 minutes!) of crawling along, move past the offending road works where surprise, surprise, there is no one. One digger stands forlornly on its own, whoever worked it has gone home/away/never turned up, you guess... and I am now likely to be late for my viewing.

Chuntering away to myself I try to catch up for lost time but fail as the traffic for the evening work commute delays me further. While

I am still 10 minutes away and already 15 minutes late I see the agent's number come up on my mobile but I can't take the call. I regret not investing in a hands-free facility for my car. It seemed a lot of money at the time but at this moment it is worth any price. When I get there the agent is just about to drive away. He is rather curt about how long he waited, that he has another appointment now and asks why I haven't let him know I would be late.

We leave it that I will call tomorrow to make another appointment and if it is still available, he or someone else will show me round the flat. By the time I get home I feel drained. I quickly shove something from my small freezer into the microwave, uncork a bottle of wine and sit down to watch TV while I unwind and settle in for the evening.

After my second glass of wine and lasagna that is piping hot and nearly burns the top of my mouth off I open up my computer to check if anything has happened while I was out. The news is both good and bad. The bad news is nothing from Daisy Chain leaves the ball rolling into my court to act upon tomorrow, something I want to avoid. The good news is I have two Likes for my profile from women I haven't contacted. I view each profile and Like one and Like and send a message to the other (I feel bold or desperate or probably both) saying I like her profile and did she want to follow up?

I realise it is a few days since I sent all those messages which have elicited a mute response and no replies. Before I start this I get a text from Rachel asking if I want a call later. I reply 'Yes!' Any comforting words from her will help lift my spirits. My search finds six women who joined since this week but only one that interests me. I send a message similar to ones I have sent before. I reason it isn't the message but the receiver that is the problem.

Just after that Rachel calls me. The call starts off fine with us both updating each other on what is happening. It is when I talk about Gill and Daisy Chain that our call takes a downward turn. While I suppose I bragged a little bit about Gill and how we met it didn't seem too bad but Rachel sees it in a very different light. After she questions me about Linda's at times strange behaviour her advice is clear.

"Don't see her again."

Surprised by her reaction I ask why she thinks that.

"She's only playing with you Chris. You will be just another notch on her bedpost. She isn't interested in the type of relationship you want or need at the moment. If you're still unsure why not ask her for Linda's contact details and then ask her directly what Gill's real motives are?"

I am not expecting this from Rachel and we argue for five-ten minutes about what is right for me and why Gill is wrong for me. We agree to disagree and move on to Daisy Chain and why I haven't heard from her. Rachel thinks it is probably because she is busy and there is still plenty of time before Saturday. It should only take a few minutes to agree where and when to meet. Why am I getting so hot and bothered about it? I can always suggest somewhere can't I?

Put like that it is hard to justify why I am getting into such a state about it. It is my first online date. Am I am being unrealistic about what to expect? Probably and the chances of my first date being the special friend I am looking for are astronomical. More likely I will win the jackpot in this week's National Lottery!

Reluctantly I accept that I can wait until Friday evening and only if I still haven't heard from her, contact Daisy Chain and check if our date is still on. Rachel urges me to stick with it, keep checking for new women every few days and not be downhearted if I don't hear back. People are busy and may take some time before getting back to me. All good advice that I accept, Rachel finishes by saying again,

"Be wary of Gill and women like her. They're not worth the effort. Don't be fooled by the attention they give you. They're not after the same thing as you."

I spend the rest of the evening troubled by the events of the day; messages with Gill; the visit to my mum; the property viewing; Rachel's call and what hasn't happened with Daisy Chain. I feel my life is in a state of flux, something that makes me feel uncomfortable, but what I need to get used to and realise will continue for the foreseeable future.

DAY 13: THURSDAY

The sun is shining through the curtains when I wake up. It may be bright and sunny outside but my mood doesn't feel like that. I struggled to get to sleep last night going over and over my conversation with Rachel. Rarely do we disagree about anything so it unsettles me that our views about Gill are so far apart. It reminds me that Gill asked me about meeting this Saturday and she hasn't responded to my offer of Sunday instead.

I don't like uncertainty as you've probably gathered already about me and yet that is exactly what my online dating experience so far is like. I am going to have to get used to it and learn to be patient and accept I cannot control events like I can with my business. That makes me check my emails and see there are a few that I need to respond to this morning.

My day is a mix of viewing properties – hopefully I can get to them on time – and catching up on work stuff. There are three viewings today, the first being in an hour's time so I quickly shower and dress so I'm ready to go. As I am looking for my car keys my mobile rings, it is the estate agent.

"Good morning, is that Mr. Davison that I'm speaking to?" I confirm that it is.

"I'm sorry to be the bearer of bad news but the owner of the property we are due to view has just accepted an offer for it. It means I'm going to have to cancel our viewing. I hope that isn't going to inconvenience you too much." I say that it won't, thank him and end the call. This property viewing isn't going as well as I hoped either and I need to check for new flats as often as online dates.

Sitting down with a coffee I open my computer to start on my emails, trying to clear my mind of online dates and flat viewings, but with little success. There is a lull in my workload for the next week or so that should enable me to focus on these matters. I can't motivate myself and get my jacket and go for a walk along the seafront to clear my head, which feels like it is buzzing with bees inside, and I struggle to think at all.

As I leave Meghan is coming back from taking Blodwyn for one of her many 'constitutionals' and stops as I pass her. She can't resist asking how I am and what I am doing. I brush her off by saying I am just taking a short walk for a change of air (I am tempted to say I am taking my constitutional but resist the temptation). She accepts that and I quickly walk round the corner and out of her sight.

I sit on a bench and gaze out to sea; the waves mesmerise me and make me drowsy. Closing my eyes I drift off to sleep for a few minutes. I certainly come to with a jolt and I'm not sure where I am or what is happening. My head is much clearer now though and a glance at my watch shows it is a good time to leave for my second flat viewing.

When I get back to my car parked outside the building that contains my flat Meghan is on the porch watering the plants.

"You look like you're in a hurry Chris."

"Yes, just a bit."

"I hope it's nothing untoward."

"No, it's fine, just need to be somewhere soon. Bye."

With that I get into my car and quickly drive off. Arriving with plenty of time I check my mobile and see an alert from the dating site. Piqued by this I quickly log in and see the woman I messaged yesterday has replied. Again though it is a holding response like I had earlier from Moody Blue, she will get back in touch later if she is still interested. Hmm, well at least I heard back this time even if it isn't what I want to hear.

The agent arrives and is very business like, a quick "Hello" and he hands me the property details, which as I glance through them are the same as on the website. As soon as we walk though the front door to the flat I know instantly that it isn't for me. The décor is shabby and the layout of the rooms isn't great either. I want a small space – hallway or corridor – between the front door and the living space but there's none. The bedroom is very small and not ideal for a double bed with furniture that will suit two people (yes, I am optimistically thinking ahead again). Still I listen to the whole sales pitch to compare this with other places I will view.

The agent points out the council tax band, ground rent, maintenance, service charge and length of lease; things I haven't even thought about. All in all it is a good benchmark to compare with other places and a wake up call to check all these features and charges. After a quick chat, the agent says farewell and moves on to his next appointment. I stare at the place from the outside. It is on the first floor of a three storey converted property and needs painting and a new roof sometime soon; all expensive costs I want to avoid.

Parking the car in the same space, Meghan is coming out the front door without Blodwyn. I sense trouble; without the dog there is no pressure for her to move on. I say hello and try to walk past without engaging her in conversation.

"You're busy today. That's twice we've met already and it's still the morning. Sometimes I don't see you all week. Anything interesting going on?"

She is right; sometimes I don't see her for days. Maybe subconsciously I time my entrances and exits when I know she will be occupied or away.

"No, just getting a few errands done today. Keeping myself busy."

"What is it that's keeping you busy Christopher?"

Why does she not call me Chris like I asked her to countless times?

"Nothing of importance. Bit of shopping and stuff."

"Oh, well you seem to have left it behind because you've just got some papers in your hand."

Damn, she is right! Trust her eyes to spot that.

"I need to pick it up later when it's ready. Must dash as I've got an urgent work call in a few minutes and need to be ready for it. Bye."

Meghan looks very suspiciously at me all the time until I close the front door.

Back home I eat a cold lunch and scan the property sites for anything new. There are a couple of flats but nothing better than those I am already seeing. I call the agent about the flat I was late to view yesterday and we agree I will view it tomorrow morning. After that it feels natural to look on my dating site for any new women. There are only two but neither interests me. My profile has been viewed a few more times but there is no more interest than that.

At a bit of a loose end now I message Liz and Danny to check how they are. Both come back within an hour to report they are ok. Liz asks how I am so I gave a quick summary of my dating experiences and my visit to her nan. She promises to go when she finishes her studies and pass her love on when I next speak to her nan. But there is no comment about my dating women from Liz.

I go to view the second property I'm booked to view today. It is slightly better than the first in that it is located on the top floor and the building looks in better condition. I ask more of the right questions however the agent has forgotten to bring the details and the layout is very cramped even for one person to live comfortably there, let alone two. The agent can see I am not that interested and compounds my gloomy mood by trying to persuade me to see other flats he has that I have already dismissed when viewing online. I point this out but he is programmed to transmit messages not receive them so it is 15 minutes of wasted effort and we leave each other with just a nod.

As I walk up the steps to the front door so Meghan opens it, this time with Blodwyn. It is almost as if she waits for my arrival to time her departures today! This time she is a little more pointed with her remarks.

"I see you still haven't collected your shopping yet." My reply is "No."

"Hmm, well I hope you don't forget. Anything else going on today?" She really can be nosy and push her luck sometimes.

"Nothing worth mentioning but thanks for asking. How about

you?" A good tactic because Meghan can't resist talking about herself even if she is itching to find out what someone else is doing.

"Well as you asked Christopher, I am visiting a friend nearby. She's invited me round for tea and it gives Blodwyn some exercise there and back. Her son and mine used to go to the same school. We've been good friends ever since. Of course her son hasn't been able to progress with his career as much as my son has but she doesn't seem to mind."

There is her motive; another chance to score a point and find out what her friend's son is doing. I don't know who her friend is but immediately I feel sorry for her but also grateful that I am not the target for her curiosity for a while.

The rest of the afternoon and evening is spent eating, drinking, watching TV or reading a book. Nothing really lifts my mood and it is a relief for bedtime to come and I slowly sink into another restless sleep.

DAY 14: FRiDAY

It is Friday at last and my day gets off to a better start with a call from a potential new client. David who I met earlier in the week calls and says he is interested in my proposal. Can I give him more details? After a good chat we agree to meet next week and I will prepare some options for us to discuss then.

Next up is my re-arranged viewing of the flat I was late for. It is better than the previous two although still not what I really am looking for. The service charge and other costs are the highest and clearly not sustainable for the long time I plan to be there. It is a different agent today and she is more helpful and hints there are likely to be more flats coming up for sale soon that may interest me.

I then have an urgent call from my mum's nursing home. My mum is very concerned how I am and will not be pacified unless she can speak to me directly to confirm that I am fine. This hasn't happened before and I worry that she is entering a new phase of her illness. I speak to her, reassure her I am well, send Liz's love to her and say I will see her again soon and not to worry about me meanwhile. My mum is calmer, less agitated, when we finish our call.

I spend the rest of the day working out my business accounts. Spreadsheets and me have a love/hate relationship. I love it when it is complete and the right figures are in the right columns and all the formulae work correctly but I hate what I have to do to get to that state. I exchange a few choice words between my spreadsheet and me at one stage!

Finally after much frustration I complete it to my satisfaction and most importantly hopefully that of my accountant. Paul takes great pleasure in pointing out in excruciating detail any errors he finds. He is a friendly, helpful, reasonably priced accountant and has looked after my business accounts and tax affairs for some years. However, he can be very annoying when pointing out any errors as if I am a child. Several times I have been poised to tell him where to go but stopped realising how difficult and time consuming finding another accountant will be. Better the devil you know… as the saying goes?

With dinner cooked, eaten and washed up, I sit down with my second glass of wine and start composing a message to Daisy Chain when two things happen within five minutes of each other. First Gill texts me to say she can meet on Sunday. What about the same place at the same time?

Next an alert from my dating site to a new message. Quickly logging on I see it is from Daisy Chain at last! She wants to meet me at 6pm in a pub near Warren St station.

Rachel was right and my patience has paid off and I am grateful for her advice. However I am frustrated we won't meet until the evening. I haven't made any plans for the day; I wasn't sure what might happen.

The same now applies to Sunday with Gill. While it will be great to meet her again I was hoping it would be during the day, maybe Sunday lunch in a pub, but it isn't to be. I sigh, life is never simple and straightforward when you want it to be is it? At least I have something certain to work on now.

Replying to Daisy Chain first I say that I'm looking forward to meeting her. I follow that with a text to Gill saying that same place, same time on Sunday is good for me too. It leaves me with another gap to fill during that day.

Pouring myself the remaining red wine in the bottle into my glass I sit back and contemplate how to prepare for my two dates this weekend. I don't know where to start! What to wear? What to say? How to act? With Daisy Chain I won't have met her unlike Gill and it is definitely not a business meeting either. It will have to be something different to wear and to say. I text Rachel and Danny with a variety of questions to get some help; I don't think Liz will want to help sadly.

Rachel comes back first warning me again about the perils of meeting women like Gill. I respond saying fair enough, I am warned but I am a grown man over 18 now and make my own decisions. When I ask for advice about meeting Daisy Chain she doesn't respond again. Danny's advice is basically to just be myself and to stay as relaxed as I can and to wish me good luck.

DAY 15: SATURDAY

I woke early around seven and immediately wonder how many hours before I am due to meet Daisy Chain. How will I fill the hours until then? While drinking my first cup of tea I work backwards from our meeting time. I decide to catch a train to Victoria and walk through London to the pub near Warren St station. It will use up time, keep me active and help my nerves that are jangling already.

After breakfast, showering and dressing, I go for a walk. I realise as I come back with all that is going on in my life that I haven't checked my post for the past few days. There is only one letter but it looks official and I sit down to open it while making coffee.

That is when the bombshell broke! It is a letter from my solicitor handling my divorce from Em. I read it twice and very carefully to understand its implications. After making the coffee I slump down in a chair and put the pot and cup on the table by my side.

The letter states that Em has changed her mind about giving me my share of the equity that we previously agreed. She now wants to sell the house first and then give me my share from the sale price. That may take ages and will cause me unnecessary stress from the uncertainty. I am fuming and stomp around my flat ranting away at her and all that she has done.

We managed to get to the first stage of our divorce with the decree nisi being issued to confirm legally our marriage was over. I instructed my solicitor to petition for divorce on the grounds that my wife's unreasonable behaviour because of the affair she admitted having. She accepted this and matters had been progressing at as good a pace as is possible with these things. The court's actions and the process of law grind along very slowly.

Then we got to the sticky bit of splitting up all our assets including my business, which I particularly resented. I had built it up single handedly and now I had to share some of the profits when I am not the one who had an affair. I start finally to find a flat to buy because Em agreed to re-mortgage the house so I have the funds to buy one.

The letter ended with my solicitor asking me to contact her at my earliest convenience me to arrange a meeting. My 'earliest convenience' adds to my stress because her office now isn't open until Monday, two whole days away. I want to know what to do *now*, not next week! I curse myself for forgetting to check my post. I don't get much but when I do it is normally important like this letter is. Damn!

I sit in despair and frustration for a long time until my mobile rings. It is Danny calling to check how I am. I decide not to mention the letter until I am more in control of my emotions. With typically bad timing Danny then asks (the real reason for his call I suspect) if I can lend him (by that he means give) some money to tide him over the revising and exam period for next few weeks. With a sigh I ask him how much and agree to transfer that amount to him. Danny thanks me and appreciates that I can do this quickly and without arguing.

His call breaks the cycle of thoughts I was having. I decide even though it is just after lunchtime (I am not feeling hungry) to catch the train to London. A change of scenery, change of mind, etc. is what I need. But first I need to change into my dating gear for meeting Daisy later.

I will never, ever, ever criticise a woman who takes a long time getting dressed to go somewhere after my experience. All I need is a shirt, trousers, jacket and shoes but trying to work out the right combination of these leads to many changes, I lose count how many, until I give up and leave wearing close to my first choice of outfit over an hour ago. At least it uses up some of that spare time I console myself with.

I can't remember much of the journey apart from being appalled by my solicitor's letter and frustration that I can do nothing. Em changed her mind over several major things in her life, some which affected me, since we split. Maybe this is her reacting to the stress of our divorce? Whatever it is, it isn't good news for me.

I want to keep on looking for flats; it has taken me so long to finally get round to this after putting it off so many times. But how can I buy it without my money and I suspect trying to force the issue will take more time and money, create even worse feelings and may not even succeed.

This on top of my mum, business and online dating is shredding my nerves. I will either have to 'man up' or stop dating and concentrate on my business and my mum. Why does life have to be like this I think again and again? I don't want much, a place to live, some happiness with someone, be able to support and advise my kids. Is that too much to ask? Obviously yes it is at the moment I conclude.

I do love London, despite six years of commuting up to it from Brighton each working day. Two hours each way, door to door, had an attritional effect on me. Danny and Liz were young, pre-school age when I started, but Em and I agreed it was a great career opportunity, nice pay rise, and I could always rethink things if it wasn't working out.

And that is how I started my business. After all that time the travelling wore me down. The train service wasn't getting any better, each year the fare rise didn't always match my pay increase. But the experience I gained gave me the confidence to start out on my own and I never looked back or regretted doing that for a moment.

However while I love visiting London to see the sights, meet with friends or business clients, I never want to live there. The noise, so many people, pollution, and heat in summer always put me off living there. The best I can do is stay in an air-conditioned hotel room. Ha ha if only I can afford that!

As I get off the train at Victoria I wander through the concourse and make my out towards Buckingham Palace. Wherever possible I want to walk through the parks and avoid the pavement and traffic. I find a place on a bench in Green Park and watch the ducks pestering people to feed them bread by the side of the lake. Some geese are honking away loudly and a few are flying around having been disturbed by someone probably getting too close to them.

I watch people passing by me, couples arm in arm walking slowly, gazing into each other's faces not caring where they are going. An elderly couple, both on motability scooters slowly move around the lake, chatting to each other and pointing out birds, statues and trees.

Children run noisily around through the shrubbery and trees playing their own games or trying to eat their ice creams before they melt down the side of their cones.

It is a lovely scene and it helps take me away from my solicitor's letter and my meeting with Daisy Chain. I could have stayed there for hours but unfortunately a smoker sat next to me, lit up her cigarette and started puffing away as if her life depends on it - quite the opposite to what will probably happen to her I muse. I am downwind of her and the smoke is blowing into my face. She makes no effort to hold it away from me so I gather myself together and move on towards Trafalgar Square.

The skies are clouding over and it is very humid now. I can hear the distant rumble of thunder as I make my way to The National Gallery, always a great favourite of mine. I go inside as I have plenty of time to kill before meeting Daisy Chain. I don't want to arrive ridiculously early and lose control of my nerves while waiting for her. I feel the most relaxed that I have been all day as I walk around admiring my favourite paintings and painters including Turner, Constable, Van Gogh and many others.

I sit in the café and nurse a pot of tea for over half an hour silently practicing conversations, especially openings that I can use with Daisy Chain later. I reckon the time to Warren Street means I only have to find places to visit for about an hour before reaching my destination. A wander through Chinatown and around Shaftesbury Avenue reminds me that I haven't seen a show in the West End for years; something I need to put right after seeing what is showing now.

I arrive at the Duke of Wellington with ten minutes to spare (is that fashionably early?) and order myself a pint of London Pride. I find a seat at one of the few tables still available that has a spare seat next to it. Placing my rucksack strategically across it I keep my eye on the entrance to spot Daisy Chain when she arrives.

The pub is busy with people chatting and drinking but no music playing loudly to drown out any conversation not conducted by shouting. It feels like a local pub judging by the atmosphere and the bar staff are friendly with many of the customers. Six o'clock comes and goes but no sign of Daisy Chain; I try not to be anxious while I wait.

At ten minutes past six she arrives or rather I think she arrives. I get up to approach her smiling when I realise it isn't her as I get close up. Thankfully I haven't spoken to her so she just gives me a funny look and walks past me to greet a friend seated at the back of the pub. I sit back down but thankfully it is only a couple of minutes longer before a lady comes through the door that is clearly Daisy Chain. Again I stand up and walk towards her and she smiles as she recognises me. We awkwardly shake hands and I point to where I am seated and offer to buy her a drink. She asks for a Peroni and carries on in the direction I pointed while I order her drink and bring it over to her.

We clink glass against bottle and toast each other then sit back and gaze at each other for a few minutes. I notice that Daisy Chain has a few more lines round her eyes and grey hairs. Her hair is cut in a 'bob' style compared with longer hair in the pictures. Her face is attractive but not beautiful to me. She is taller and slimmer than I expected based on the photo she uploaded to her profile. My mind has gone blank about the details on her profile, what questions I want to ask her and the interests we share.

Daisy Chain is probably doing a similar thing. Whatever it is we both sit in silence and gaze at each other. She finally breaks it by asking me if I have travelled far. I explain briefly my journey from Worborne to Victoria and my walk to here. I ask how she had got here and she just says that she lives nearby and walked.

"You are what I expect you to look like." I am relieved to hear this as I had made sure I followed the advice over photos; recent, not cut in half to not show your last partner and one showing your full length.

"Thank you. It is easy to recognise you from your photo," I replied.

"What is your name 'A Good Guy'?"

"Chris, and yours?"

"Emily." That hits me like a bag of cement going into my stomach. She notices and gives me a puzzled look. I quietly say, "That is the name of my ex."

"Oh, aah, that's not a good sign is it?"

"Why?" I say, puzzled.

"Because whenever you call my name you will probably think of her."

"I've no idea. Maybe, maybe not."

"What do you do exactly?" I briefly explain my business and what I do. I ask her the same question.

"I'm a Vice Chancellor at the University of Richmond, Virginia. I'm here on a three month secondment to research how human relationships are impacted by different environments."

"Wow. That sounds amazing and an enormous area to research."

Emily smiled briefly. "Yes, it does sound like that but I've narrowed down the area to fit with the subjects I teach. I've taught for many years since I moved to the U.S. I was born in Cambodia and emigrated to study at college in Philadelphia before moving to where I am now. Do you know any of these places?"

"I confess that I don't know any more about Cambodia than what I see on the news or read in books – travel and history – and websites. I stayed twice in Philadelphia for business conferences and explored and enjoyed the sights there; the Liberty Bell, signing of the Statute of Independence and where Rocky Balboa runs up the steps in the movie and of course, sampled a fantastic Philly cheesesteak. Delicious!"

"Do you drive?" she asks.

"Yes, I've got a car."

"Are you a UK resident?"

"Yes, I've always lived here."

"What are your plans for the future?" Crikey! What are they, I think?

"To continue with my business, find my own place and hopefully a special friend to enjoy my life with."

"Do you want to travel?" Hmm, well yes but I am not sure where to, when or how often. "Yes but nothing specific."

Emily then opens up, "I was married once many years ago and divorced after three years; no children. I've not been able to meet anyone since because I can't drive. Without a car to get around it's pretty difficult to meet anyone."

I feverishly try to digest all this information, work out how it changes how I feel about Emily and how to respond. Before I can reply, Emily continues.

"I feel isolated in my community because I've not been able to travel to meet anyone. I quite like England and I've visited London, Birmingham and Manchester before. It is nice being driven around to see places; I love that. You can see so much and meet so many great people with a car. How old are you Chris?"

"I'm 55."

"And how long do you plan to work before you retire?"

"I don't know really. Five or ten years?"

"Hmm, interesting." Is it? I feel like this is becoming an interview, not a conversation.

"Are you divorced or just separated?" I think briefly back to the letter I have in my rucksack from my solicitor. "I've got my decree nisi but not my decree absolute yet."

"Oh, so you're still married then?"

"Well not quite. My marriage is over but I still need to agree the final details to be divorced."

"How long will that take?" Great question! One I have been asking myself all day without a clear answer.

"I'm not sure to be honest. Maybe a few weeks or months?"

"You don't seem sure."

"It's a little complicated."

"Are you still with her?"

"Good God no! We haven't seen or spoken to each other in nearly a year."

"Oh, ok, I just wondered. And it is your car? You own it?"

"Yes that's right." Why this interest in my car?

"Well, thanks for the drink. It's been great to meet you Chris. I need to go now but I'll be in touch if I want to meet up again. Bye."

And with that farewell and a brief smile, Emily rises and walks out of the pub without looking back. She doesn't give me time to stand or respond. In fact I don't know what to do or think about what just happened. One thing is for sure, I need to get out of The Duke of Wellington pronto as I now find its atmosphere claustrophobic and I want to breathe some fresh air.

Outside the noise of the traffic, rush of people walking past, even the smell of the car fumes is liberating. I look around but can't see Emily and wonder if I will ever see her again. Do I want to even if she does after this? What to do? I check where I am. This isn't a place I am familiar with. I can see the Underground sign just up the road; it seems to beckon me towards it. I don't resist; I've had enough of London and of today. The journey home and a bottle of wine are enticing and I trudge to the entrance and start my journey home.

It takes nearly three hours before I am sitting down in my comfy chair, wine bottle open, lights off apart from the low light from one corner lamp. I have worn myself out going over and over my meeting with Emily as I travelled back from London. I try to summarise what happened:

1. I now know Daisy Chain is called Emily.

2. She lives near The Duke of Wellington.

3. She is here on a three months secondment.

4. She has been divorced for many years.

5. She likes being driven in a car.

6. She likes me being a UK citizen.

She was keen to find out a few things about me in great detail but showed little interest in me generally. I can't see what the attraction will be for me in someone only living here for a maximum of three months. I have no plans to visit let alone emigrate to America. Maybe Daisy just wants a bit of fun with a man while she is here? Unless something exceptional happens this is a date to put down to experience and learn from before I meet Gill tomorrow evening. With that thought I make my way to bed.

DAY 16: SUNDAY

I wake up feeling refreshed and decide it is a day to take a good long walk along the coastline, get some exercise, take in the beauty of the natural scenery that I love and generally chill out ahead of meeting Gill later. After getting myself ready and feeling in good spirits I pack a rucksack with a picnic, book, water and sunscreen; yes, it is going to be a lovely, lovely day, lovely day as Bill Withers sang.

Texts from Rachel and Liz ask how yesterday has gone but I don't want to be distracted from making an early start so I am back in plenty of time to relax, change and get to the pub for Gill. I will reply when I stop for a rest on my walk.

I have been fortunate to visit for business and pleasure many places around the UK but for me nothing can beat the breathtaking beauty of the Seven Sisters, a set of cliffs on the Sussex coastline, including Beachy Head with its dubious reputation sadly. Just seeing the white cliffs jutting out from the land with waves crashing against them make me feel privileged to enjoy looking at them as well as walk over them like today.

It is a short drive in my car before I start my walk. Usually I wear my walking boots; they feel like walking on cushioned air, but it is hot so sandals will be better for my poor old feet I think. I set off at a steady pace moving towards the first of the seven cliffs, well actually I understand it is seven valleys in between the tops of each roll of the chalk that make up the Seven Sisters.

Anyway I digress, the fresh sea air is filling my lungs. With very few people out at this time of the morning the silence is therapeutic and I can think clearly and positively while walking. Making good progress I get to Birling Gap and the café there around coffee time and sit down outside under a parasol with my coffee and Danish pastry. I hear the waves crashing on to the pebbles on the beach below and gaze out at the English Channel. The French coastline is too far away and over the horizon but I imagine someone sitting at a café like mine gazing towards where they think England is also enjoying the sea view between us.

Feeling like all is well with my world, I reply to my messages giving a brief update on what happened with Emily. With the passing of time I look back more philosophically on my meeting. I am certain that I will not hear from her again; neither will I contact her. If she is trying to find someone to live with here within three months then she must be under a lot of pressure. It makes me appreciate that my position is much easier; no time limit, no real pressures except to find someone to love and to be loved. Easy peasy I reflect finishing my coffee and make a move.

It is getting hot as I apply more sunscreen to my face and exposed limbs. It won't be good to turn up this evening as a good imitation of a lobster I think and smile to myself. I feel peckish as I arrive at

Beachy Head. Apart from toilets, the ubiquitous ice cream van, and the lighthouse there is a restaurant/pub where you can eat and drink if you want. I can't imagine walking back with a heavy head befuddled by alcohol consumed here with a hot sun to add to that effect but some people I notice are taking that path.

Finding a nice bench to share with a couple who look like the ideal advert for retirement as they sat together eating their sandwiches, chatting quietly to each other, looking healthy and reasonably fit. If I can be like that at their age I won't have too much to complain about health-wise. After we exchange pleasantries – they drove here from Tunbridge Wells – I eat my sandwiches, slice of pork pie and fruit while drinking the cool water I poured into a flask to keep it cool but isn't too heavy to carry.

After letting my stomach settle – a habit my mum taught me to do from an early age to avoid indigestion – I start my journey back, nodding to the couple sitting side by side who are still enjoying the views and each other's company. The sun is shining more into my face as I make my way back westwards across the Seven Sisters towards where my car is parked. Even though I am retracing my steps the view going back is different with the distant coastline and ups and downs of each cliff to negotiate. I don't stop at the café but rest for a few minutes on top of the next cliff head.

Again I have a few messages including from Rachel and Liz but choose to leave them until I get to my car. With this heat it will take a few minutes with the car windows down before I venture inside to sit down. I bump into two sets of friends walking in the opposite direction to me and we express the same views; the coastline, weather and how many people are now here. The peace and quiet I enjoyed earlier is replaced by the buzz of conversation, insects and birds flying around.

Finally getting back to my car, I read my messages as the car interior cools a little with the windows down. Liz is non-committal and asks what is next or rather who is next so I tell her I am meeting Gill again this evening. I don't mention the contents of the letter from my solicitor yesterday. James from football asks if I fancy watching Brighton's pre-season friendly match in a few weeks time. Having no idea what is happening then I say yes in principle but will confirm nearer the time.

Lastly Rachel's message is supportive about Emily but still warns me about Gill advising me not to see her. What does she see in Gill that I can't? Why is she so negative? Can't she trust me to use my own judgment? After all it is me who has met her twice, not Rachel; the next installment will be after this evening. I am not going to let this spoil my mood. It has been a lovely day so far and I feel on top form, invigorated by the activity and scenery.

Arriving back at my flat, I make a light tea and relax in front of the TV to catch up on a couple of programmes I recorded a while ago. There is about an hour or so until I meet Gill, enough time to shower, change and drive there to be at the pub with 20 minutes to spare; the traffic flows smoothly despite the good weather bringing out all the Sunday drivers as my dad used to moan about forgetting he was one of them!

This time Gill parks in the same car park but I am disappointed to see Linda get out of the driver's side and Gill from the front passenger's door. She hasn't said anything about Linda being there again and I wonder what her plan is. I decide to stay in my car as they haven't spotted me and leave it a minute before entering the pub. The last meeting wasn't straightforward and this one has the signs of being the same. Oh well, here goes, nothing to lose I say under my breath as I open the door to the bar.

Standing at the bar are Gill and Linda waiting to be served and looking around for somewhere to sit and wait. When Gill sees me approaching she beams a big smile while Linda smiles nervously. I give each of them a quick hug and kisses on their cheeks, both cheeks for Gill. I ask what they want to drink but Gill waves me away saying it is her shout first and what do I want. I choose a long drink first, a lemon and orange mix, to keep a clear head and rehydrate after my long walk earlier.

Gill says to Linda that she thinks I am looking very well this evening and I explain where I have been today. It impresses Gill that I can walk that distance and she seems to see me in a different light after that. She makes a joke that it will be difficult for her to walk that with the heels she wears pointing down at her shoes. Indeed I agree with four-inch stiletto heels it will be a challenge for her and for me too! Linda just smiles and seems to relax slightly as if the first hurdle of the evening has been jumped. What is going on in her mind I wonder?

We sit at a table in a corner. The place is half full or half empty depending on your outlook. The main thing is no music playing and no one within easy listening distance so we can chat comfortably in our normal voices. Gill is keen to start doing that straight away.

"Well this is lovely. Meeting you twice in a week is lovely. Did you have a lovely weekend?" Lovely seems her favourite word this evening.

"Yes, took it easy yesterday and enjoyed the exercise today. How about you?" I look at both of them separately. I want Linda to engage more in this evening's conversation.

Gill answers first. "I went out yesterday to London with a couple of girlfriends to see 'The Sound of Motown' and have a few laughs and drinks. Like you yesterday, I took it easy today. A girl has to have time to prepare for evenings like this."

Linda squirms a little at that last comment while I am recovering from the shock of Gill being in London like me yesterday and an irrational fear that she was in The Duke of Wellington at the same time I met Emily.

They both look at me questioningly so my shock must have shown on my face.

"Something we should know about Chris? Got something to share?"

"No, no, just brought back an unexpected memory. Nothing worth sharing."

"So what can you share then Chris?" Gill is very good at applying pressure I realise.

"What do you want to know?"

"When did you split from your wife?" Wow, straight to the point!

"Just over 12 months ago."

"Why? Was it you or her or was it mutual?" I am going to be honest here.

"It was her."

"Why?" I take a big gulp before I speak next. "She found someone else." I am being honest but very economical with the details at this early stage.

"Have you seen her since your split?"

"Twice, to collect my things and to try to sort out stuff but that was months ago and it's been through solicitors since." I am not going to mention yesterday's letter though.

"That is interesting." Is it? I guess so but I am not prepared to divulge more.

"What was your weekend like Linda?" I ask changing the subject.

"Oh!" said Linda slightly taken back. "We went to a barbeque on Saturday at my in-laws and then lunch with some friends today. Both were nice."

"How long have you known your husband?"

"Um, well, we've known each other 20 years on and off but we've only been married for the last five years." Interesting; there's a story here for another day I'm sure.

"When did your last relationship end Gill?"

She is silent for a few moments then says, "Recently."

"Oh." I am surprised by her one word answer. "How recent and how long had you been together?"

"Two weeks ago. We'd been together for 18 months."

Wow, that is recent! I don't know why I ask the next question, some instinct makes me, because it is direct to the point of being rude even.

"And before that?" Now it is Gill not Linda who is quiet and withdrawn.

"Um, I'm not sure I want to go there if you don't mind. Is that ok?"

For the first time since I had met her Linda took the initiative.

"Gill's having a tough time, her ex didn't treat her very well." Linda said to me then turning to Gill. "Steve was a right bastard to you." I am surprised by Linda describing him in that way but even more by Gill's response.

"Steve's not that bad when compared with Pete. He was a

complete bastard to me at the end!" Gill replies to Linda, then turns to me and says, "Pete is my ex ex."

Crikey it is becoming an interesting evening of surprises now. Will all evenings with potential girlfriends be like this? I wonder what will happen next.

"As I said I don't really want to talk about it. Will you excuse me?" Gill gets up abruptly and swiftly moves towards the ladies toilet and disappears holding a tissue to her eyes.

I look at Linda and she glances at me then looks down at her drink, picks it up and takes a long gulp, places it down on the table before composing herself.

"I said this isn't a good idea to her. It's too soon. She's not ready. But she is very headstrong and won't listen. Always thinks the next man will be the right one for her, 'Mr. Right'."

I sit in silence, not knowing what to say or do. This is difficult and unexpected. The look on my face must have shown this.

"Chris, I'm not saying you're like the others. Even if you are the right man for her I don't think it is the right time or place."

I nod my agreement.

"I only went along with this to help her get over Steve splitting from her. You made a big impact on her when you did that training. She badgered me to go with her when she met you. There's no training I'm afraid, sorry."

Again I just nod, smile and reach my hand out to gently pat Linda's hand on the table. She doesn't withdraw it and I remove it quickly but it has been the first natural exchange between us in two evenings. We both smile at each other.

"I've probably said too much already. I'll go to the loo and see how she is. I should have gone with her. You won't say anything will you - please?"

"No, I won't. This is just between the two of us," and smile which reassures Linda so she can focus on Gill. She quickly leaves to find Gill.

I sit back and puff out my cheeks. Phew, this dating business is throwing up a new side of life I haven't experienced before! While Em and I had our ups and downs they were only verbal, never physical, and normally over in minutes with the making up afterwards normally very enjoyable.

Drinking my orange and lemon mix I feel the need for something stronger to relax me when or if we have another round of drinks. Five minutes become ten, eventually after half an hour Linda emerges with Gill following after her. She looks like she has been crying a lot with her eyes puffy, small mascara marks down her cheeks and something about her hair that I can't quite put my finger on.

While they come and sit down with me at the table the evening is clearly over as far as everyone is concerned. I offer to buy them a drink but I know the answer before I ask which they confirm as they shake their heads. I am at a loss what to say, Gill looks miserable and spent, so it is left to Linda to wrap matters up and suggest we all leave and see how we all feel tomorrow.

Walking with Gill and Linda to their car I say goodbye to each of them; a quick hug and kiss on the cheek for each of them as I silently see them off before getting into my car. Driving home my mind is full of thoughts. They continue after I get back to my place, open a bottle of red wine, pour a large glass and take a large gulp from it.

A weekend that started full of promise and hope ends on a rather flat note. There is no chance of Emily and I developing a relationship; we are clearly incompatible. With Gill there may be a chance in the distant future but not now and who knows what will happen with online dating for me in the meantime.

Two steps forward then one step back; I try to assess it optimistically and learn. Certainly I need to find out more about any woman before I meet up with them. While I have an open mind and will not pre-judge anyone I have to apply a stricter criteria to avoid the last two meetings. How to do that is the question? I have no idea how. Rachel can help but has been restrained in her advice because of my insistence about Gill. I will call her tomorrow and see how she feels. Yet another evening is finishing with me sitting alone with an empty or half empty bottle of wine to console me. That isn't good either as I get ready for bed.

DAY 17: MONDAY

As I wake up I become aware that I need to do three things today:

1. Talk to my solicitor about her letter.

2. Talk to Rachel about this weekend.

3. Talk with a business client.

I don't expect to talk with these people in my priority order but I start by texting Rachel asking if we can have a call this evening. My client's meeting is from 11am until 2pm, a business lunch, to agree a communications and training strategy and how to implement it. It means I have time to see my solicitor before or after this meeting. Thankfully neither is a great distance away from me or from each other so it is feasible to do both.

As soon as 9 o'clock comes I call my solicitor but just get her answering machine. I leave a message but I will call again as it is urgent. I try again 15 minutes later but this time it is engaged. At least she is there I hope and leave it for another 15 minutes to try again. I am a minute away from calling her when my mobile rings; it is my solicitor.

"Hi Chris, it's Debra. I got your message and called you back as soon as I can."

"Hi Debra, thanks for doing that. I've done nothing but think about your letter since I opened it on Saturday." Not strictly true I know but only a slight exaggeration.

"Yes, I'm sorry to be the bearer of such news. I've got some room in my diary for later this afternoon. I'm guessing you want to meet me as soon as possible. I think it's better in person than over the phone if you don't mind." I don't mind it is exactly what I want.

"Yes I can do that. What time are you free?"

"How about 4pm? I've got an hour spare which should be enough time to cover all the points we need to discuss."

"Yes, that will be great. See you later Debra."

"Bye Chris."

That's what I like about Debra; available, accessible and professional at all times. It removes a load off my mind ahead of my business meeting and I can now make last minute preparations for it.

I like being a consultant; it is an overused phrase and sometimes said or received in a negative way. I define a consultant as 'a person who provides expert advice professionally'. That's what I aim to do. Someone is willing to pay me for my expertise on work they need help with. If they have the necessary skills and experience then they won't need me. I make the difference – fill that gap.

Work can vary from creating a policy, developing a strategy, implementing a plan or training. Sometimes I get to do the whole thing from start to finish. That is where I get the most satisfaction.

Unlike being employed where you get to see a project from start to finish and beyond, I often just get to do my piece and then leave it for others to implement or take it to the next stage of the work. This contract is for the entire project, one of those rare occurrences for me, and I am really enjoying it so far.

We meet or catch up on conference calls regularly but haven't met often. I know my strategy aligns clearly with their business requirements. It is now about agreeing priorities, timescales, budgets and who will work with me. This meeting with Brian Deverill, Communications Director, is the first after a board meeting to approve the strategy and implementation plan. The other good thing about being a consultant is you can keep the inevitable politics at arms length. Brian will handle that while I get on with what I am best at, using my expertise to help his organisation.

It is a welcome distraction from online dating too! As I drive to Brian's office Rachel texts back to say she can make a call with me this evening. Everything is moving forward and my ducks for today are starting to line up nicely. I tune my radio into some old hits from the '70s and '80s and hum along to some of my favourites from that era. Not even a shower of rain can dampen my mood.

Traffic hold ups mean I arrive five minutes late. Brian is on a call and waves me in pointing to a chair opposite his desk and smiles. When the call ends he welcomes me and we move to a bigger table. He pops his head out the door to ask his secretary to call two other managers in who are involved with the project.

After exchanging pleasantries with each other, the two managers Alan and Roger, join us. Brian sets the context for our meeting today and what happened at the board meeting. The good news is it has been approved but the budget is more limited than we want. It is a typical story these days as organisations tighten their purse strings. The cut isn't draconian and it will be possible to deliver most of the key priorities; there is maybe more money when the board sees the benefits.

Brian hands over to me as the project leader; I know everyone from working with them on the proposal that has been approved. They are impressed I created the proposal on time, with minimum fuss and most importantly, got it approved. We are as they say 'all singing from the same hymn sheet' and I quickly go through how the strategy will develop and be implemented.

The main discussion is over what comes first and if we can do things quicker so the work is completed earlier. I am relaxed about this and had built some slack into the plan; we reach agreement in time for a buffet lunch to be served. The conversation moves on to wider areas of interest; football, holidays and weirdly dating.

Roger divorced sometime ago recently tried speed dating. When he explains what happened one evening last week it makes me want to laugh and cry from his experience. Spending five minutes with a stranger and then scoring them while they do the same with you feels very stressful. To have your scores read out and then know if anyone you score highly has also scored you feels false. But for Roger it means a second date later this week with a woman who scored him highly too. Well, there is an alternative to online dating if that fails.

As lunch finishes and we each go our separate ways, we agree follow up calls and meetings that Brian's secretary will send invites out to everyone. I am very pleased with the progress made; the meeting hasn't overrun and I have plenty of time to get to Debra's. One big meeting for my working life followed by a bigger meeting for my personal life!

Debra is part of a small firm of three solicitors that focus on personal rather than corporate clients. I like the personal touch and plan to use Debra for my will after my split from Em is confirmed and my share of the assets can be disposed how I wish rather than as agreed when we were together. The receptionist welcomes me with a smile and nods to a chair in the waiting area. I am familiar to her after meeting Debra a few times about my divorce. Debra doesn't charge more for personal meetings than phone calls and it is good to meet and hear from her in person.

As Debra beckons me into her office I am impressed by how good she is, good at her job, good looking, good personality and happily married to a surveyor with a young child. The pictures and certificates on the walls and desk testify to this. Always professional she greets me and shows me to a seat opposite to her across the desk. The only things on her desk relate to my case apart from a phone, pictures and laptop.

"Thanks for coming in Chris." From the start she puts me at ease and I feel that she appreciates me making the effort.

"No problem Debra. I'm glad you can see me today."

She then summarises the situation so far with my divorce; the decree nisi confirming my marriage has ended, assets agreed on 50/50 basis to be shared with no custody issues for our children. The problem is the timing for this will change because of Em's decision to sell our marital home rather than re-mortgage it. The amount can change and may increase if she sells it for more than it has been valued at.

"When will this happen? I'm finally starting to look for a place to buy. It's taken me ages to be in this frame of mind. Can't I insist on my money now and she sell it later?"

"It is possible but the time, effort and resources you will need make it counterproductive. Do you know why your wife changed her mind?" Wife I note, not ex-wife until everything is settled, which may be way in the future.

"No idea why, I can ask the children. I can see this going on for ages. It may even be a game, a tactic, to change what she pays. Who knows?"

Debra responded, "It may be in your interests to find out. I can ask her solicitors but they're not obliged to find out or inform me. We need to be patient for a little while longer than we hoped before we settle on the basis already agreed."

I know deep inside that she is right but I find it hard again to know that my life is still being directed by Em even though we parted over 12 months ago. I am depressed that I can't live my life as I choose to yet.

"Technically there is nothing to stop you looking for a place but… and it is a big but, you can't exchange contracts unless you can show you have the money. It might all fit together time-wise but it is a risk that only you can decide if it is worth making."

"Okay, I will try to find out why via my kids. Let's keep in touch if anything new happens."

We part on that note and I drive back home seething with anger and frustrated by what Em is doing. I will have to involve Liz and Danny to find out more. I prefer them to be bystanders rather than participants but I have no choice.

Once home I call them, get voicemail for both, leave messages and text them to make sure they respond quickly. I sit back and (yes,

I know I shouldn't) open a bottle of wine and order a pizza for delivery. I am not in the mood for cooking! I text Rachel to ask what time we can speak as I am desperate for some sound advice from her.

Instead my phone rings and it is Gordon wondering how I am and will I be going to the same pre-season friendly as James already asked me about. I give him the same answer that I am interested but can't confirm yet. Clearly Gordon and James don't communicate directly but through me; I am the link between them. I ask how Gordon is and get general, non-committal answers and leave it that I will be in touch nearer the time.

My second glass of wine is almost empty when Rachel calls. At last someone I can pour my heart out to and feel safe! And I did, telling her all about my weekend from the moment I opened the letter from my solicitor through my meeting with Emily, walk over the Seven Sisters, meeting with Gill, and finally today's discussion with my solicitor.

Rachel shows why we have been good friends for so many years. She doesn't respond like many people will have done after hearing my news with "I told you so." over the outcome with Gill. Instead she is analytical and supportive about my situation and the way forward. This includes:

- Suggesting I can get a bridging loan to help me to buy a place without waiting for Em to sell and share the proceeds.

- Applying the lessons I learned from my dates with Emily and Gill.

- Keeping positive and continue online dating.

Feeling more upbeat after our call, I start searching for new women who joined the dating site recently. Three have but none of them really interest me so I leave that. Instead out of curiosity I search for Daisy Chain's profile to remind myself of what she wants but I can't find it. Intrigued I search further and find she has blocked me; not only did I fail the interview, I needn't bother re-applying to be her partner! It makes my life simpler even if it feels a bit over the top for her to react that way.

Next I search for new properties listed but there is only one and it doesn't interest me. More importantly, I am determined not to be blown-off track by Em's decision to sell our house before sharing the equity. I will continue seeking my first place to buy just for me and worry about the consequences when or if they arise later.

Danny calls back concerned by my message that something must be wrong. I am a little irritated because he thinks it will be affecting him after I explain what happened. He needs a little more encouragement than I think should be needed to contact his mum and find out what is happening. Even more when I stress the urgency to find out; I don't want to find out in a week or so's time. Tomorrow at the latest is vital for my state of mind as well as my plans. It won't mean the difference between a pass and fail with his degree because of a 10-15 minute call with his mum either.

Half and hour later Liz rings in response to my message and, having been with her mum today can shed a little light on my news. Em had a huge bust-up with her latest boyfriend resulting in her deciding to move and sell our house. Where she will move to Liz has no idea but it all happened in the last week or so and Em is still livid about the split when Liz spoke with her. She says she will try to find out more at the end of this week when she normally calls her mum and allow Em to calm down. I thank her and she promises to keep me up to speed. No mention from either of us about my dating.

There is plenty of food for thought after these conversations for me to digest tomorrow and contemplate. With it getting late I make my way to bed. It takes a while to settle, hard as I try to, the events this evening churn over and over in my mind. It isn't that it is bad news, more the amount of news that means I lie awake for a long time before finally dropping off to sleep.

DAY 18: TUESDAY

I'm woken late after a disturbed night's sleep by my mobile ringing; I normally set it to silent but forgot with everything else on my mind last night. It is the estate agent seeking feedback on my last viewing. Trying to recall what I felt I gradually explain why it isn't the place for me. To be fair he listens, takes the feedback on-board and checks what I am looking for. In fact he thinks there are two flats that may interest me that are likely to come on to the market soon when he will contact me to arrange a viewing. I thank him and confirm I am interested.

Feeling that is a vaguely positive move I make a cup of tea and come back to bed with my laptop. The main objective this morning is to start the work agreed at my meeting with Brian, Alan and Roger. While I look forward to doing this I am lethargic as if it is the weekend and I can do what I want. Maybe it is about what happened over the weekend that is causing this? I slowly make breakfast also bringing it back to bed as I read through my emails, both work and personal.

It is a personal email that catches my attention most; it is from my mum's care home. I rarely hear from them by email or letter so this is unusual. As I read it my concern grows; the care home are troubled by my mum's dementia. They are so anxious they want to discuss whether other homes that specialise in dementia care could be more suitable for her needs. Wow, this is an unexpected turn of events! Considering I visited my mum last week it is very sudden. Maybe they didn't want to tell me in person but more formally like this?

As if I don't have enough on my plate already I add contacting the care home to my list. My lethargy increases after this and I don't shower until late morning. With coffee by my side, I sit on the bed and slowly start setting out the next steps in a project plan to share with Brian & Co. I break for a call with the care home and speak to Veronica Wallis, Chief Nursing Office and author of the email. However she is in meetings and can't get back to me until this afternoon. Fair enough, at least I can get some work done before then.

Gradually I settle back into a work mode and apart from a break for lunch and a quick walk down to the seafront I complete enough of the work to send it to Brian & Co., more for information than for approval. I continue with the tasks I am responsible for without delay. With perfect timing Veronica then calls me back. However she is reluctant to discuss the email further over the phone and wants me to visit instead.

I say that might not be possible this week, testing how urgent this is to her. Obviously it is as she explains that she feels it is better for my mum's dementia that I find a different care home now. I ask what made her decide this now but all she can offer are observations by the nursing staff that she is getting worse. I feel uncomfortable about something she says or her tone, I can't quite put my finger on it, and say I will think about it. Veronica ends our call saying she will need to formally give me notice to terminate her contract. I don't respond or say goodbye as she hangs up.

I make a cup of tea and sit by the window staring out while I run over the conversation I just had with Veronica. The more I think about it, the more it unsettles me. I can't recall any formal dementia assessment or her doctor contacting me about this; I will research more before I do anything. Looking for a new care home will be daunting; it was hard enough finding this one. I don't want my mum disturbed by moving unless absolutely necessary. It took time to settle her in this one and she was happy to move there; she won't be happy this time.

Before my dinnertime I top up my shopping and clear and clean my flat. It helps shape my mood and after dinner I settle down to check through my dating site after it alerts me to a message from someone. It is Moody Blue who liked my profile a week ago. 'I like your profile. Can you tell me more about yourself?' I thought my profile covered enough but on reflection it does feel a bit stuffy and business-like, reading more like a job application than a life story and interests that appeals to women.

I re-write some parts and edit others until I am confident it shows me more as the person I am now; my life story, interests and what I am looking for in a "special friend". Once I upload the changes and a couple of new photos of me I ask Moody Blue to read it again and let me know what else she wants to know and share about herself (her profile says less than mine).

I go through every profile again; some that I viewed before but didn't follow up for one reason or another. It takes a couple of hours but it is good use of my time as I contact two women I overlooked previously but have updated their profiles so they interest me now.

Next I like two others just to see if I get a response, then follow up on three women who viewed my profile but didn't contact me who I feel are worth my while trying to engage with.

As I am about to log off from the site, one of the women, Primrose 4, confirms she is interested in me, possibly to meet, after asking me where I live. I reply that it is Worborne; I know she lives in London and that is enough for me at the moment. She likes being by the seaside and wonders if we can meet. That will be great I reply, when will suit her? She says next Friday afternoon is a good time for her. Will the balcony at the Royal Festival Hall be ok to meet? Yes (I went to a reception there a long time ago and I'm fairly familiar with the layout). After closing my laptop I'm pretty content with my day.

DAY 19: WEDNESDAY

Wednesday starts out much better than yesterday. I slept well and wake feeling refreshed and at an earlier time but at a loss what to do today. There is some work remaining from yesterday for Brian & Co. but nothing more in the offing workwise. I don't panic about the lack of work as I find it normally sorts itself out – famine or feast – and I shall make the most of this free time.

Researching dementia is top of my list after completing the work. Sitting down in my favourite chair with a pot of coffee I read more about the condition. A few things come into prominence as I carry this out:

1. Dementia isn't just one condition. There are variants and I suppose the better known is Alzheimer's.

2. There are procedures to assess what type of dementia someone has. You can't just feel it is that; it needs proper assessment.

3. Treatment varies and my mum, being diagnosed fairly early, can take drugs to reverse some early signs and reduce the rate of decline.

4. There is no cure; it is how to manage it the best way.

The more I research, the more premature the care home's decision feels to me. A proper assessment is needed to a) know how bad and what type of dementia my mum suffers from and b) help me to decide the best type of home if she does have to move. Dementia UK and other charities I contact are very helpful and reinforce my view that a proper assessment is the best way to help my mum have the right care she needs.

I am unsure whether to contact the care home to share this or wait until I receive the formal letter Veronica mentioned. Not really feeling up to that type of conversation at the moment I leave it to see how I feel tomorrow or whenever the letter arrives. My mobile alerts me to a message on my dating site.

It is from one of the women I contacted yesterday; one that I overlooked initially because of little content on her profile then. She is called Angie Baby. 'Hi, would like to find out more but not sure about meeting yet. Where do you work?' It is an interesting if slightly surprising question. I make my profile look less like a CV and I'm asked where I work. How ironic! I say that I work for myself and from home most of the time. I ask where she works and what she does.

There have been five new views of my profile. I wonder if updating my profile brings it to people's attention or just coincidence. Whatever the reason it is a boost to my self esteem and after viewing their profiles I decide to like one and message two others to see if they want to take their interest any further.

I call my mum to say 'hello' and ask how she is. I normally ring every few days; it isn't because of the letter but it is especially good to hear her so chirpy and recalling that I am her son, where she is and how her grandchildren are. She doesn't mention their names so I prompt by giving their names then saying what is the latest news for each of them. It is a good half hour before mum feels tired and will stop talking and have a rest, which I am happy for her to do saying I will see her soon.

The evening passes uneventfully apart from when I go for a seaside stroll and bump into 'yours truly' yes, you guessed it, Meghan and Blodwyn walking in the same direction. Slowing my pace (reluctantly) I come alongside and ask how they both are. For the next 10 minutes I get a monologue on every little thing that has gone wrong or she has a bad view of. It is being so miserable that makes her so happy it seems. Blodwyn decides she wants to relieve herself and I move ahead without causing (too much?) offence.

Back at my place I relax reading my book and wind down before going to bed.

DAY 20: THURSDAY

My day starts out well with a new message on my dating site. Angie Baby (a Helen Reddy fan after the song?) replied to my question; she works in the Civil Service at Croydon. That ties in with her profile showing she lives in south London. The problem for me is it just answers my question, nothing more than that. Do I ask more questions or leave it for her? I decide to leave it for the time being and see if she follows up later today with another message.

I notice that my profile receives more views but no more contact. I leave it for the time being before I consider if anyone is worth a like or message. I laugh as I think this because these words are something I have never used or had a need to before.

Two things happen to change my focus for the day. The first is a call from Harry Stokes, Internal Comms Manager, who wants to know if I am interested in helping train their managers on how to communicate better. Of course I say "yes" and ask for more details but he wants to check my CV with his boss before sending me anything.

Fair enough, that's what I would probably do if I was in his shoes.

The second thing is a call from Liz who spoke with her mum this morning. Her assumption on the reasons why Em is selling the house is correct. Em has been living with her latest boyfriend for three months before it fell apart dramatically when she asked him to contribute towards the cost of food and other essential costs. Apparently he thinks it is a privilege for Em to pay for the pleasure of his company when he is with her. This didn't go down well with Em and he found himself out on the street with all his clothes late one evening. The next day she contacted estate agents and our house is on the market within a week.

Liz then threw me by asking me when I am going to Scotland. I am puzzled by her question, as I can't think of any business clients I know there. She then reminds me that I am going on a coach holiday.

"What! When?" I say.

"You are going to Scotland. You told me ages ago."

"Oh no! Argh, I remember now. That *was* ages ago! I'll have to check and get back to you."

We end our call and I start going through my emails to find out when I am going. With everything else going on I completely forgot about the holiday I had booked back at the start of the year. My plan then was to have a stress-free holiday with some company.

I had gone away last year for a break on my own soon after I separated from Em but I had missed having some company with me. Apart from chatting to the staff at the hotel, cafes and pubs it had been just my lonesome and me. I don't mind my own company but there are times when I want to chat about things and for a few days while I relaxed, that joy wasn't available to me and I missed it, I really did miss it.

I had booked a coach holiday to the highlands of Scotland; I have always wanted to visit there but Em didn't fancy it so we haven't gone. Now is my chance to do that and a coach picking me up and dropping me back in Worborne seemed ideal. The hotel had entertainment in the evening; breakfast and dinner included, as are trips to Aviemore, Inverness and Isle of Skye. All I need to do is find my lunch and some company for it to be a great break I thought at the time.

I read through my email and find to my horror that my holiday starts on Saturday morning, *this* Saturday morning that's two days from now! As the implication of this sinks in I realise I risk making a mess with my date on Friday and my work with Brian & Co for next week. The first thing I do is call Liz back to confirm the dates and outline my problems with them. After I explain this Liz's response is,

"What problems?"

"I've got my online dating to check, my work with clients, properties to view and nan's care home problems for starters..."

Liz replies, "Will you have your mobile with you?"

"Yes."

"Will you have your laptop with you?"

"Yes."

"Will you have Wi-Fi?"

"Yes, I think so."

"So, what's the problem? What's stopping you from enjoying yourself, seeing somewhere you've wanted to all your life, while still being in touch?"

"But I might need to see a client or a date or a property." Even I know this sounds a bit weak as an argument.

"You might but the likelihood is you probably won't and if you do you can arrange to meet after you get back. It's only one week you're away for."

"Yes, that's right." I reluctantly accept Liz's rational and logical approach. It is a case of managing this rather than it forcing everything else to stop or go wrong. It is only one week away and I had been looking forward to it when I booked it.

I am very grateful to her for mentioning the holiday. Saturday may have passed me by without me realizing I was missing my holiday. What a state of affairs I have got into!

It changes my plans for the day as I realise it is free time to prepare before I pick up the coach on Saturday morning. With my meeting on Friday with Primrose there will not be much time spare for packing.

Washing and drying clothes, sorting out what to pack, finding where I put away the suitcase, etc. takes up most of the day. I nip downstairs to see Meghan, one of the few times when I do want to, and let her know I will be away next week. I also politely answer all her questions about where, how, who, what, and why I am on holiday. When she feels satisfied she has extricated enough information to share she asks me if I want to leave my spare keys with her "just in case" but I decline. One thing I swore never to do is to give her free rein of my place and its belongings for her to dwell over at her leisure while I am away.

By the time I eat dinner and pack as much as I can, I relax and catch up on my email, calls or messages. Nothing urgent has come up work-wise, all is okay with Brian & Co. and Harry hasn't followed up on our earlier call yet. A text from one of the estate agents says one of the properties they talked about is now likely to come on the market early next week. Am I interested in viewing it? Hmm, good question but it can wait until I see the details and reply but it does sound promising.

Next I go to my dating site where two new women have joined and both attract me. I send them messages saying (again) that I like their profiles and what do they think of mine. Apart from a couple more views there hasn't been any more interest in me after the initial flurry earlier this week. Maybe a week away will be what I need before returning to the online dating scene?

Lastly I text Danny and Rachel; Danny just to say I will be on holiday in Scotland, Rachel to update her on my dating and holiday.

DAY 21: FRIDAY

This is date no. 2 day with Primrose. I sleep in until around 10am this morning, late night packing and unwinding combining with a bottle of rather fine red wine. An easy morning lies ahead of me with a few items of clothing to iron ready for packing last thing tomorrow morning. Making sure my laptop, electrical leads and charger are by or on top of my large suitcase so I won't forget them and save me time tomorrow.

After a leisurely breakfast, following it with a shower and dressing it is coming up to noon and time to check train times for London. I want to be there with a few minutes to spare and not be late. Working back from that goal means I need to leave within the hour. I choose to catch the first available train partly so I am not late but also to occupy myself and limit my anxiety. It is just as well as the connection to London Bridge is cancelled and the half hour wait means I will be on time if nothing else goes wrong. I buy a BLT (bacon, lettuce and tomato) sandwich, one of my favourites, from the railway café, water and a latte coffee to kill some of the waiting time and make sure my tummy isn't going to rumble while we meet.

Munching on my sandwich at the station I look around at the other passengers waiting for the same train. How did they meet their partners? How long have they been together? How happy are they really with each other? What secrets do they keep from each other? I muse at each couple and speculate what the answers are. I wonder if anyone is curious why I am catching the train and can come close to guessing why. Very unlikely they will but my face shows the strain as my stomach tightens as we leave each station stop as the train nears London.

Leaving the station I walk towards the Thames riverbank walk. I love seeing the strong current of the Thames tidal flow, outwards to the sea now, as I walk slowly through masses of tourists enjoying the sights of Tower Bridge, the Golden Hind, HMS Belfast, The Globe theatre and of course the London Eye. As I near the Royal Festival Hall on the Southbank my nerves tighten and I feel I need to rush to the nearest loo every few minutes.

Finally I enter the Southbank entrance, I'm early, as I wanted to be. That is the good part but inside I feel a complete mess and quickly dive into the nearest toilet, open a cubicle and sit down to try to compose myself. Taking deep breaths I tell myself to be calm, it is one person I am meeting; she is probably as nervous as me. Checking my watch I see it is 3pm and I leave the toilet and make my way up to the balcony where we agreed to meet.

There are several people so I walk around, glancing at each woman as discreetly as I can, trying to see if Primrose is there. I don't see anyone looking remotely like her picture so stop in a place where I can be seen. With two entrances at opposite ends of the balcony it is difficult to check if she arrives. Five minutes become ten minutes, then fifteen and at twenty I doubt she will turn up.

I regret not having her full name, just first name and no means of contacting her. I am determined that with any future dates I will achieve that level of disclosure or I won't meet up. If this is a test of my commitment then I am not impressed. Should this be a sign of how she lives her life then I am not attracted to it. I decide that 30 minutes is my limit and it is close to that when Primrose suddenly appears as if by magic by my side.

"Are you the Good Guy?" she asks with a smile. I am caught by surprise, convinced she had stood me up.

After a slight pause I say, "Are you Primrose?" to which she nods and smiles which I return hesitantly.

"Shall we go somewhere cheaper for a drink and chat?"

"Err yes, where did you have in mind?"

"There are plenty of places nearby. I'm sure we can find one where we can talk."

"Okay, lead the way Primrose."

With that she leads me back to the Southbank and starts walking in the direction I came from before turning right onto a path, then round a corner to a place that is empty, obviously closed.

"Oh!" said Primrose "I thought it would be open." For someone who claims to know lots of places I didn't think this was a good start.

"So where to next?"

"I'm not sure. Let's go on and see what there is round the next corner." I am not filled with confidence hearing this but leave my doubts unsaid.

We continue round the next corner and a few others after that before turning round one more and Primrose gives a surprised, "Oh!" as we take in the view of an outside bar and café situated between two blocks of flats. There are people sitting at seats and tables in the middle enjoying the bright sunshine. Some reggae music is playing in the background from the bar. My mood lifts as I take in the scene and we move towards a free table that is slightly apart from others to give our conversation some chance of privacy. I ask Primrose what she wants to drink but she insists on buying and I choose a pint of lager.

Primrose comes back with a cocktail for herself and my pint, sits down and clinks glasses with me.

"Well this is nice," she says.

"Yes, it is."

"Well where do we start?"

"What about first names – or do we want to call each other Good Guy and Primrose all afternoon?"

There is a pause, as if she hasn't expected this question, followed by a sigh.

"Call me Clare." I am unsure if this is her real name or a persona for first dates. It is progress anyway.

"I'm Chris."

We then tentatively talk for the next hour about our lives so far. I find out Clare lives nearby, works for one of the local authorities as a Social Worker and has a daughter, 30, who needs help from time to time while living independently on her own. She doesn't talk much about previous partners and I sense the father is not in touch and there hasn't been anyone recently in her life.

Clare is interested in my relationship with Em and why it fell apart, a little about my children, but mainly where I live in Worborne. She wants to know what it is like, how long it takes to get there, the sea, the coast, the town, how long I have been there and the place I live in. I am careful not to give precise details of where I live or how to get there at this stage.

After buying the next round of drinks (Clare's is a cocktail of her own concoction it seems) I sense a change in her mood. Clare is petite, mixed-race (Caribbean father and English mother), about five years younger than me, and five inches shorter. She is wearing a loose dress with a colourful flower pattern. Her smile is appealing and the freckles on her face add to my attraction for her with her plaited hair and brown eyes.

These eyes stare intently at me as I think mine are at her. I suspect she is sizing me up. Am I worth a second date? Is there a spark igniting or one just fizzling out? We are both comfortable with sharing a silence for some time, soaking in the sunshine, enjoying the conversations and music playing around us. Clare then interrupts the silence.

"I've got a course nearby I need to get to in an hour. I'm not sure about it but I think I'll go."

"What is the course about?"

"Oh, just something I'm interested in finding out about."

Sensing this as a brush-off I don't ask any more about it. I want to finish my drink and go soon. I can't think of anything more to say now. Clare then says.

"I do like you but I'm not sure about where you live. Maybe I need to come and see it? How long does it take again?"

"It varies depending which London station you leave from but normally about 90 minutes or so with a good connection."

"Hmm, I'll have to think about it." She looks at the clock on her mobile and gets up smiling at me.

"It's been good to meet you. I've enjoyed our chat. Maybe I'll see you next in Worborne soon?

"Maybe." I get up and we move together and give each other a hug and quick kiss on the cheek before we part and Clare walks back the way we have come in.

I sit down for a moment. It has gone past five by now. This is peak commuter time and one to avoid if possible. I have a sense of déjà vu as if this is a repeat of last Saturday's date in London. I decide to have another pint here and reflect on what's happened; it is better than being alone at home reflecting and there is little packing left to do.

Sipping my pint I think:

1. I like Clare; I am not sure how much, but I want a second date.

2. She is also like Daisy Chain, meeting in familiar surroundings.

3. Our first date lasted longer and I feel better for it.

4. She doesn't seem to appreciate the effort that I made travelling here.

5. Her background is very different and that appeals to me.

6. Worborne is a big deal for her and I am not sure of the outcome.

I realised that I don't know what will happen next and I will have to be a little more assertive after each date. Knowing the name of my date and having contact details are vital should anything last minute change.

The sun goes down behind the flats and I take this as my cue to drink up and make my way back to the station. Picking up a hot

Cornish pasty (I haven't had one for ages and fancy something different) to eat on the train journey home my mood is better than last Saturday. I still don't understand how online dating plays out when you start meeting up. Perhaps I never will but I can try to learn from each experience so it gets better in future.

Reaching home late evening I check for any emails or texts (I don't like doing that on a train in case anyone is looking over my shoulder) and had received a message from Gill that just says 'Hi". I call Rachel on the off chance and find her free. We chat about my date; she thinks that Clare will make up her mind if I am too far away rather than if she likes me or not. Rachel reasons that if she didn't like me, Clare wouldn't even be thinking about where I live. That makes sense to me and I feel good that I may have found someone who likes me as a date.

Rachel cautions me again about getting emotionally involved too early, first dates are all they are at this stage, and to expect more rejections. I only need one to be right and all this churning up of my feelings will be worth it. The chances of finding my special friend recede in my mind with each passing day it seems to me. Thanking her and yawning at the same time, I trudge along to my bedroom, strip off and fall asleep as soon as my head hits the pillow.

DAY 22: SATURDAY

I am grateful that when I drink a few pints or glasses of wine I sleep deeply but not so much that I oversleep. It is with a start that I wake up wide-awake, panicking that I have missed the coach only to find it is half past seven. Quickly jumping into the shower, dressing and grabbing a bit of breakfast I pack my bag, check everything is switched off and walk briskly to the meeting point for my coach.

The meeting time comes and goes so I call the helpline to find out the coach has a fault, which delayed its start, but it will be here within the next quarter of an hour. It isn't an auspicious start but when it does finally turn up it isn't my coach but something called a 'feeder' coach. Apparently there is a big interchange for coaches somewhere on the M1 where I change to another coach for the rest of my journey; more new things that I never knew about before.

Driving a little faster than I prefer we make up some of the time and I arrive at this interchange, more like a service station except only coaches park outside, while people mill around getting hot and cold drinks, food, etc. I finally board my coach into the front seat I picked before we set off for Scotland. I am now excited that I am going to somewhere I always wanted to go to. If I hadn't split from Em I may never have gone so I try to think of this as a good thing.

Quickly I become aware that I am the youngest person on the coach, not just by years but probably a couple of decades compared to the average age. My companion next to me for the journey is Audrey who is 88, a pretty lively 88 years young not old and very proud of this person. The only problem is having a conversation with her is interrupted by her suddenly going quiet as she drops off for a nap then waking up to continue talking about a subject I've forgotten about.

We reach our overnight stop at Preston, which solves one mystery for me. I haven't read through the itinerary and imagine we will travel through the night! The sun is shining when we arrive at the hotel for our overnight stay and the meal gives me a chance to hear from a few characters keen to proudly say how old they are and share installments of their life with I feel the promise of far more to come during the week, whether I want to hear them or not!

It is early to bed as it will be early to rise for a full day journeying up to the Highlands of Scotland tomorrow. I am not in the mood for checking properties or online dating. It can wait until I arrive at my temporary base for this week.

DAY 23: SUNDAY

Up early and down for breakfast after showering and most importantly leaving my suitcase outside my room to be collected at some early god forsaken hour. Once on the coach we settle back into the same familiar rhythm of chat, rest, chat, rest break, chat, gazing out at views, chat, break, etc. as we drive up to and through Scotland diagonally from the south west to the north east until in pouring rain we arrive at our hotel, north of Inverness.

The weather isn't inviting but the welcome is and at first sight the hotel is warm and inviting. The hotel has seen better days but still retains its old majestic splendor if a little tired at the edges. The good thing about my room is the marvelous view across the valley full of trees, hills and rooftops of the village beneath us. The bad thing is no broadband or Wi-Fi connection, even worse no mobile signal either. Damn! I hadn't checked the small print or reviews and to be honest, didn't think it would be important when I booked. Now I will have to hunt around for scraps of time when Wi-Fi is available wherever we stop.

Certainly the scenery is breathtaking, the air bracing and clear and it is good that our first day includes a visit to Inverness. There must be some Wi-Fi there I hope to use. Sure enough with a few hours to visit the sights I am able to separate from the other groups and find a café that serves a hot lunch with free Wi-Fi thrown in without any pressure to eat up and get out. It is just as well because there are a few messages I need to respond to.

Alerts from my dating site get my attention first; a message from Clare saying she is thinking of visiting Worborne but wants to see me again this week before deciding. I can read Clare's message both ways. Does she mean to meet me first before deciding whether she wants to "see" me? I spend most of my lunch debating inwardly what she means. I reply:

'Hi Clare, I can't make this week as I'm away in Scotland until Sunday. Can we meet the week after?"

I do like her but it is out of my hands now. All I can do is hope she wants to see me so much that she will be willing to wait.

Next message is from "Angie Baby" who finally wants to meet up. I answer,

"Yes! Where and when is best for you?"

One woman calling herself "Great Dane" replies saying she likes my profile and asks if I am divorced or not. A strange one but easily answered as I say I am separated, have had my decree nisi and am waiting for my decree absolute. I end by asking what her situation is.

Finally I search for any new women who joined in the last few days and read their profiles. One gets my attention with her interests and lives near me so I send a variation on what is becoming my standard enquiry.

Next on my list are texts starting with one from Danny wishing me a good break and asking me whether I can lend him another £50, the real reason for the message I suspect. I choose to ignore this for the time being. He asks too often and never repays a loan. Liz also wishes me a nice holiday but doesn't ask for money, which I reply to saying where I am and that it is okay so far.

Lastly, I reply to Gill's text saying, 'Hi. How are you?' I am not sure if it is good to have any contact. If I knew Linda better and had her details I would speak with her to find out if I should reply or not. Time will tell and it doesn't feel so critical when I'm this far away. A quick text to Rachel updates her on progress with online dating and the holiday so far.

I have some time left to look round Inverness before boarding the coach and moving on to Loch Ness. While there are plenty of beautiful views to impress sadly there are no sightings of Nessie, the Loch Ness monster, despite many claims on posters and encouragement. As hard to find as my special friend I muse as we make our way back to the hotel.

The first evening without mobile or Wi-Fi is weird but also strangely liberating. Communication is by person, what feels vital at home doesn't feel so this far away. Then it dawns on me that I have been so engrossed in my dating exchanges that I forgot to check my work emails. No one has called so that is a good sign but I know clients can quickly turn from easy into difficult ones if they perceive they aren't getting your full attention. I make a note to check first chance I have tomorrow and settle back with a beer to some traditional Scottish entertainment for the evening before retiring to bed. The air feels very healthy but tiring too and I am pleased to be tucked into my bed by 11.

DAY 24: MONDAY

A trip to Aviemore is on the cards for today. The weather forecast is good for today but not later in the week so the visit has been brought forward. When we stop in the town of Aviemore for a break I dive into the first café offering free Wi-Fi, buy a coffee and grab a table to use my laptop on. Two people on my holiday want to join me but I politely apologise and give my excuses about work I need to catch up on.

It is just as well as Brian & Co. has made a few points about my plans, nothing major, but it means making adjustments to when some work is planned and adjusting who does what and by when. I manage to complete these and send them back for further approval. The other email is from Harry Stokes - he is becoming my star client. Not only does he want me to do the work but also has his boss' approval and, even better, the budget to pay me for this work. Result! He wants a call this week, which is a challenge not knowing when I may have a good signal for long enough to have the call. I am reluctant to say I am on holiday instead I say I am committed much of this week but will try to. When is best for him?

Grabbing my stuff I run back to the coach and carry on to Aviemore taking the Funicular up to the restaurant and platform to view the mountain scenery from all points of the compass. It is truly breathtaking and therapeutic for my mind putting everything into a better perspective. The rest of my day is taken up with the drive back to the hotel, changing and then eating dinner followed by some Scottish dancing. Bagpipes are not my favourite musical instrument but the enthusiasm shown by the player, volume of noise and range of notes makes it endurable for me.

Tomorrow I must check for properties available and updates on my dating site.

DAY 25: TUESDAY

Today is a trip around the Highlands with no particular destination in mind called 'The Loop'. My problem is whether there will be some free Wi-Fi, just a small morsel that's all, anywhere en route for what I need.

And so the day becomes a battle between me trying to enjoy the beautiful mountain scenery and appreciate the driver's knowledgeable commentary and my increasingly urgent need to stop and find some Wi-Fi to check properties and my dating site. Each time we stop the view is amazing, the welcome friendly, the food and/or drink tasty but the Wi-Fi is non-existent.

Finally, late in the afternoon as the coach winds its way back to the hotel I make my way down to the front and ask the driver if he knows anywhere that has Wi-Fi that I can use. He doesn't but he offers to drop me in the village so I can try the café there before walking back to the hotel.

"Yes please!" and I thank him profusely; soon afterwards he stops to let me off.

Hoping against hope that it is a) still open and b) has Wi-Fi I walk up to the café and find it open and has Wi-Fi. Not believing my luck I open the door and enter. Ordering a cup of tea and a scone with butter, jam and cream I find a table in a corner and take my laptop out. My joy becomes more confined when I realise how slow the broadband connection is, almost glacial in its progress.

I click on a link, drink my tea, click again, butter my scone, click again, add cream, click, and add jam; you get the idea of just how slow it is. But it is still better than nothing although the owner wants to close in 15 minutes. I check my online dating site first and find no reply from Clare but Angie Baby and Great Dane have!

Angie suggests we meet in Eastbourne as it is near to where I live next Sunday as she is visiting her parents there and can meet me at lunchtime. Argh! Will I be back in time? I suspect not but… I reply, 'Yes but need to confirm as I'm away this week. Will let you know ASAP. Really looking forward to meeting you.' I hope that won't deter her.

Great Dane replied saying 'Good! I want a man to be straight with me. I am not interested in any charlatans.' That is all. I don't know how to take her reply. Is it approval or dismissal? I will wait and see.

I then check my emails before moving on to properties. Two work emails are quickly answered and with four minutes left I go to the first property site. As the owner politely says she has to close and can I eat up and leave I find it, a flat with a direct view of the sea. I missed checking this site earlier in the week when it was first advertised for sale just within my price range. I didn't hear her second call being so absorbed in reading the details and checking the photos again. Her sharp tap on my shoulder and look remind me not to outstay my welcome here.

I scramble to pack away my laptop, grab my coat and finish my scone mumbling my apologies and sprinkling crumbs in my wake as I hurriedly leave the café. Thinking frantically about what I can do being so far away until Monday I can't remember the route back only that I find myself in my bedroom sitting on the bed staring into the mirror opposite. I can make and receive calls and texts and decide to try calling the agent who is… damn, I can't remember which estate agent is advertising the flat!

My evening consists of partly listening to conversations with people I am eating with, part of my attention on the evening entertainment – another local singer doing the hotel circuit – while another part is working out when I will find the next Wi-Fi, who the estate agent is (I narrowed it down to two) and whether any of my dates will respond to my enquiries. It feels like a very long evening.

DAY 26: WEDNESDAY

I didn't sleep as well last night; either the effect of the Highland air is wearing off or my mind is still going over what it has been on since last evening – properties, dating, work, divorce, and mum – in no particular order of play. At least Wi-Fi should be on the agenda as we are going to the Isle of Skye after visiting Kyle of Lochalsh, somewhere I remember from a TV programme when Michael Palin took a train journey that I will retrace today.

We board the train and I enjoy the most wonderful views as the train transcends the valleys, lakes and surrounding hills towards our destination. I bound off the train down the platform partly because I want to see the Kyle and Skye but also because there will be broadband… somewhere hopefully that is warm (it is blowing a strong cold wind in June!) and a hot drink. Winding my way past the chip and confectionery shops busy with customers from my train eager to top up after their hotel breakfasts I find a café down a side street with a 'Free Wi-Fi' sign on the window.

Ordering a latte and a small bun I find a table and take my laptop out of my rucksack, log on and navigate to the property site. Quickly finding the details I see the estate agent selling the property is the one who gave me advance warning of its sale. As my coffee and toasted bun arrive at my table I speak with the agent about the flat. It is still available although people have already shown interest and some have viewed it. The main thing is no offers have been made yet. I briefly explain I am away for a few days but want to see it next Monday. We agree I can view it at 10am... if it is still available.

Tucking into my bun while slurping my coffee I check my dating site and find that Angie followed up on my message,

'Will you meet me on Sunday?'

I haven't checked when we will be back that day, probably not until that evening I think. I am annoyed with myself that I forgot to find out. I need to do that and get back to Angie quickly.

Great Dane also followed up on her last message asking me if I drive a car. I say that I do, a little nonplussed by her request. This might get interesting!

With two more likes from women I contacted a couple of weeks ago I am slowly learning the rules of this "game" of online dating; basically there are no rules! I sigh, so much to learn; it is like wading through mud as you try to make headway. The sad thing is Clare still hasn't been in touch.

Checking other emails takes up the time to finish my coffee and toasted bun. Feeling better from my online dating and food and drink I venture back out into the town and make my way back to the coach. The rest of the tour is very enjoyable - all the more for me after my coffee break's achievements.

As I enjoy the evening entertainment - Scottish dancers

performing to traditional Scottish songs – I recall memories performing in a school concert the same songs. I remember being in the descant so I must have been young - before my voice broke. Ah, another budding singing career brought to a shuddering end by adolescence; I smile to myself.

I think about the week so far. Yes, it is frustrating not having the internet on demand but it is also liberating to have that freedom to spend time doing things in the real world knowing there isn't the constant digital distractions of emails, websites and other apps and communications to monitor. If only I can enjoy it with a special friend wouldn't life be wonderful?

DAY 27: THURSDAY

Checking with the coach driver I find we leave a day earlier than I thought. My thinking is really out of kilter for this holiday! It means I'm ok to meet Angie Baby.

According to the holiday itinerary it is a 'free day for everyone to explore the local surroundings, enjoy the scenery, amenities and take advantage of last minute gifts and mementoes from the local retail shops in the village.' The first part sounds better; I'm not a great one for holiday gifts for others or myself. If I come back and give away fridge magnets, Highland toffee and, Scottish jumpers they will be viewed suspiciously and with concern for my wellbeing.

Without any Wi-Fi (the café is closed every Thursday) I will use it to my advantage. One day without access to the outside world won't hurt me; surely I can cope, I am made of sturdier stock.

After breakfast the weather encourages me to walk up into the hills to enjoy some spectacular views. Although only a couple of miles or so from the hotel the silence is deafening and wonderful to enjoy, no traffic or chatter from people, certainly no mobile phones pinging all the time like when you're on a train to London during the week.

I find when I am down in the village afterwards for a light lunch that it is therapeutic and I am in a very relaxed mood. After lunch I stroll through the village and on to the valley below. Sitting by a babbling brook while reading my book helps me appreciate how good this week has been. I vow to try retaining this mood for as long as possible when I get back to my turbulent world back home.

After one last evening meal and first part of the hotel entertainment I head back to my room to pack my bags ready to leave early tomorrow morning.

DAY 28: FRIDAY

We start to make our way back on the long journey home this morning. After forgetting the dates for the holiday I also mess up on when I get back home; late Saturday, not Sunday. First chance I get I need to let Angie Baby know that I can meet on Sunday when she wants.

The journey back is tiring and boring for me. My destination was a wonderful base to explore some of the Scottish Highlands; the scenery breathtaking at times. But it is a distraction from the main event of finding a special friend and a place to buy.

Having limited use of my mobile I will aim to avoid checking it every few minutes, just in case there is a new email or message or news bulletin. Maybe even leave it in one central place in my flat instead of carrying it around everywhere with me? A special friend will change my focus anyway.

As we pull into yet another garden centre outside Edinburgh I resent the number of them we stop at for a toilet break and drinks with snacks or meals depending on the time of day. Does the coach company have shares in garden centres? A little more variety wouldn't go amiss.

But the one bit of good news at this garden centre is free Wi-Fi for 30 minutes each visit. Making the most of this chance I check my dating site. Firstly, I let Angie know I can make Sunday. When and where does she want to meet? Secondly Great Dane replied,

'Good! So do I.'

I don't know what to make of it and leave it while I think of a suitable reply.

Taking the eastern route down south to the interchange we stop for the night in Middlesbrough. While the hotel is warm, welcoming and the food appetising, the location is in a business park devoid of any views, nearby entertainment or venues and leaves a lot to be desired. At least the Wi-Fi is free and the signal consistently strong as I catch-up on everything.

Angie Baby confirms she wants to meet me at Eastbourne railway station at noon. That is OK for me and I give her my mobile number. I say my name is Chris. Is she happy to give me her name or mobile in case there are any last minute hitches before we meet?

There is nothing more from Great Dane or from Clare but there are a couple more views, both from women I messaged but nothing further. I realise that means no further interest. I systematically start blocking women who haven't responded to my tentative romantic overtures or I am not interested in meeting. De-cluttering the profiles helps me to see a couple I overlooked. I quickly rectify that by contacting them.

I then check my emails and respond to a couple from my accountant about my tax affairs. A message from Rachel asks how my holiday is going. I reply that it is good so far and is she free for a call. She declines as she is spending time with her new boyfriend at his place this evening. Good for her! I hope this will be her Mr. Right. Apart from that there is nothing else I can do before I am back home on Sunday.

DAY 29: SATURDAY

This is the dreariest day I have spent in a very long time. Up at the crack of dawn to leave my suitcase outside for the driver to pack in the coach's hold, I am tired and my tummy is a little bloated by the full English breakfasts, cereals and coffee (here it was rather good to be fair to them) this past week. My body is pleading with me to detox with fruit and a small breakfast; I reassure it I will do just as soon as I can. Meantime I paid for this food so my approach is to take advantage of it and fill my boots with one last large breakfast like most of the other passengers on my coach as I glance around are also doing.

Then begins the journey that seems to take forever as we stop at one garden centre after another on our way south to the coach interchange near London. None of the garden centres have Wi-Fi so it is a case of strolling around looking at the ranges of plants and garden equipment. By the time we leave the last one I almost feel like I can say and spell the Latin names for all the plants displayed.

Finally we arrive at the interchange and again we disembark from the coach and mill around waiting for our feeder coaches to have the luggage loaded and passengers called. It amuses me how I am now seemingly invisible to people who I chatted to most days over a drink or meal on the holiday once they are seated and halfway back to their normal lives. It isn't that I desperately want to keep in touch or see them again, it's just unnecessarily rude. Am I extra sensitive because of my situation?

Finally after waiting the longest 67 minutes of my year so far I embark on my feeder coach, which then proceeds slowly round the M25 (Europe's biggest car park?) and then to various drop off stops before arriving at Worborne for me to disembark. Thanking the driver and with a quick "bye" and wave of my hand to the remaining passengers I trundle my suitcase to my home. I don't pass anyone I know on the way, which is good as I am not in the most talkative of moods.

After dumping my bags in the flat I pop out to the corner shop and stock up on bread, milk and a few other essentials before making my way back to my place and settle in for the rest of the day. There is a pile of post to go through; the usual circulars, spam mail but a few nuggets of interest including a letter with details of the place that is for sale I hope to see on Monday if still available.

I let Danny, Liz and Rachel know that I am back home now. I also call my mum at her care home a) because I want to see how she is and b) because I received the formal letter giving me four weeks notice of her stay being terminated. My mum sounds frail and a little under the weather. She can't remember I have been away in Scotland but can remember the names of her grandchildren. After saying goodbye, I put a pizza in the oven and open a bottle of wine. It is nice to go away but I love that I can do this or anything else I want within the confines of my own place.

It made me realise with the holiday ending how much I have changed. Some of it was done consciously but other ways not. My daily routine, choice of food and drink, even clothes are different from when I was married. The main thing is I feel so much better for the changes. It is another moment to take stock of how far I have moved along the journey to independence. I know I can give up some or all of this if I do find a new partner.

And that got me checking my dating site to see what was happening. Angie Baby thanked me for my mobile number and she will call if there are any problems and her name *is* Angie! Very cautious I think but with one flaw. What if *I* have a problem and can't make it or I'm delayed? At least we are on first name terms but there is nothing from Great Dane.

At that moment I get a text from Gill

'Hi, how are you? Hope you're ok.'

Again, I hear Rachel's words of caution in my ears and decide to wait until tomorrow before replying, if I do even reply. Coincidentally Rachel rings to ask how my holiday has been. I briefly describe the itinerary and she laughs at my comments about the hotel, garden centres and age difference.

When I say that I am seeing Angie tomorrow she is pleased and hopes it will go well but her tone changes when I say Gill has texted me. Again, she warns me to steer clear and not complicate my life more than it is already. Still unsure of why she holds such strong negative views but respectful of her advice I promise to think very carefully before I do anything with Gill.

I reflect on life again and on tomorrow and finally meeting Angie. Eastbourne isn't that far from me but it feels like it has been a long journey already to get to this first date.

DAY 30: SUNDAY

What a let down today has been! How crushing can disappointment be after you raise your expectations too high? Very crushing I can confirm.

The day starts out well. Before I leave home Angie texts me saying how much she is looking forward to seeing me at last with kisses at the end. Hmm, this does sound serious! I reciprocate with kisses back. I am nervous but it is becoming a familiar feeling now. I can control my anxiety a little better this time.

I get ready to meet Angie, don't cut myself shaving even, drive to Eastbourne and park the car with plenty of time. More texts from her with endearments and kisses are exchanged between us. It really is becoming very lovey dovey between us and we haven't even met yet!

I wait at Eastbourne station for ten minutes before Angie appears trundling a suitcase behind her. We exchange hugs and hold each other's arms for a few moments. Seeing her in person for the first time I am not sure if I am attracted to her as much or at all. Angie's face is plumper than her profile picture, she is bigger in size also not that it affects me much. She is also shorter than I expect and I realise she is probably insecure and bolstered her details to paint a more flattering picture. Her lovely smile shows her warm personality that shines through and warms me instantly.

I sense that life hasn't been too good since the photo was taken. We are a little awkward standing there until I suggest we find a coffee shop where we can sit and chat more. That seems to relax Angie however Eastbourne on a Sunday around the station is not the best place to find a coffee shop. I expected to find one just around the corner but it takes an awful lot of corners to walk round before we finally find one and sit outside.

That is the trigger for Angie to start divulging her life and current situation. She is here because her parents are staying at a hotel for the week. She spent a boozy evening with her sister until late into the night. The coffee is helping to clear her head.

All of this doesn't impress me very much. I hoped she would have given our meeting more of a priority. For Angie to meet me while suffering with a hangover doesn't help my self-esteem. Maybe I should have gone in a pub and drunk something before meeting her? Maybe I should before I meet any date in future? Dutch courage they call it, don't they?

Angie then told me about her last relationship. She is still sharing the house with him. It's complicated but the gist of it is he owes her money, she won't move out until he pays her and his new girlfriend has already moved in with him.

Wow, that's a lot to digest! While I try to do that, Angie asks about my situation. I briefly explain I am now on my own and my divorce is almost complete. I notice as I tell her that she is looking very intently at my face, so much that I feel awkward by the attention. When it continues I stop and ask her if there is something wrong about me. She responds:

"Yes, I want to see how closely you look like my ex."

"What! You mean the one you're still living with?"

"That's right. You're a little thinner in the face but very similar."

"And that's why you want to meet me?"

"Of course. You do look so like him."

"But you've just ended the relationship?"

"But you don't seem to have the same personality."

"Oh…"

I am thrown by her comments and just sit back and drink my coffee. This is certainly *not* going the way I hoped! Angie fills the silence by speaking very fast about yesterday evening. She hasn't seen her sister since the break-up and they bonded over alcohol and failed relationships until late in to the night.

She finished that by saying she is hungry and can we find somewhere to eat. Almost like on automatic pilot I get up and we start to find a place, not any easier than with the coffee. A fish and chip restaurant has some space and we can sit in reasonable privacy to continue our date over some food.

Angie finds it fascinating that Em had an affair and asked me to leave and wants to draw parallels with what her ex has done. I am not happy about that close comparison and change the subject by asking what her plans are.

"I'm going to move in with my sister for a few months after the bastard has paid me my share of the money for the property. I'm not leaving until I get every penny first and he knows that. Then I'm hoping to buy somewhere around Milton Keynes and a new job too, fingers crossed."

Fingers crossed indeed! Angie doesn't seem ready for a new relationship with all her other plans. I can see how far I have managed to move away from my split with Em when I can see how raw Angie's experience is (and she had several relationships before). It isn't like this is the biggie unlike mine has been for 20 odd years.

She needs to catch a train to London after this and I look up the train times on my phone. The choices are one in 15 minutes or an hour after that. We agree it is best if she gets on the next one. As we walk to the station I realise I do like Angie as a friend but she is never going to become my special friend.

I feel a bit of a fool as I have got carried away with my emotions, exchanging love notes with Angie earlier today. I am not embarrassed but feel awkward that I behaved like that. I guess deep down it is feeling hope for someone again after so many years that is at the root of my thoughts. The drought of so many years turned into a flood of emotion, which has prematurely ended.

We kiss each other briefly on the cheek, smile and briefly hold each other's arms before Angie boards her train, glancing back and waving as she does so. I wave and smile back before turning and making my way back to my car.

The journey home is without incident and I don't play music, sing or do anything but just concentrate on the drive. When I get back, I reflect on what happened feeling let down, flat and used. Was I a curiosity rather than a date to Angie? She is certainly in a mess emotionally and I can't be too harsh. I hope she will get her money and move quickly; it must be unbearable for her there.

I open a bottle of wine and my laptop; one to console me, the other to give me hope and it works! There are two messages for me on my dating site. Neither message is from Great Dane or Clare but from two women I haven't communicated with since my first standard (as it has now become) introductory message. In Melanie's case it is 2-3 weeks ago and in Magic Triangle's case earlier this week.

Melanie says she likes my profile and would I like to meet up soon. That is pretty straightforward and acceptable by me. I respond that I will and ask her where and when can me meet.

Magic asks me if I would like to meet up tomorrow! She suggests meeting at Worborne station and if the weather is good, walking with her and her dog along the seafront. Apart from viewing the flat everything else workwise can be moved around to fit with this. So I reply that I can and ask Magic what time will be good for her.

While sending that reply a message appears from Angie. She is back home and thanks me for seeing her and is sorry it didn't work out as well as she hoped. I quickly reply that it doesn't matter and wish her well for the future.

Feeling on a bit of a roll while pouring a second glass of wine, I search for new women who joined the dating site. Reading through their profiles I am interested in three and send messages to each of them with my standard introduction.

Pulling together a cold supper I message Rachel, Danny and Liz with a brief update of my day and then settle back to watch some TV. Not appreciating the full emotional impact of today's events on me I am surprised when I wake a couple of hours later on my sofa with the room dark and the programme finished long ago. Rubbing my eyes I curse my bad timing; too late to do anything and too awake to go to bed.

Determined to make the best use of this time I start drafting the content needed for Brian & Co. How to guides, processes for work, communications standards to be implemented flow easily until around midnight I feel tired and relaxed enough to settle for sleep again. As I go to bed I think none of today has gone as I hoped and the more I learn about dating the less I seem to know about it. Yet I feel as if that invisible force of momentum is slowly starting to move in the right direction for me.

DAY 31: MONDAY

The flat viewing and my meeting with Magic Triangle are the top items on my agenda for today. I sleep in late after my disrupted evening and wake with an hour to go before I see the flat. The agent hasn't said it isn't available so full of hope I quickly wash, dress, eat so I am ready to leave with just enough time to arrive on time. As I am rushing to leave, Meghan comes out of her flat.

"Oh hello Christopher, I haven't seen you for a while. Can you possibly help me with a little chore now?"

"Sorry Meghan, I've got to rush now and see a flat."

And there it is, out in the open, in a moment of weakness and distraction I have told her the one thing I promised myself not to do. I quickly glance back as I go out the door to see an expression I never thought I would see. Meghan with her mouth opening and closing, like a goldfish does as it breathes, but no sound coming out as she looked at me in shock.

I ran to my car aware of the impending fallout when I next see

Meghan. The longer I put that meeting off the worse it will be when I meet her. Shit, shit, *shit!* I don't need this on top of everything else. I put it out of my mind as best I can when I arrive and see the agent outside waiting and smiling at me. The building that contains the flat is right on the seafront road.

Quickly exchanging greetings while handing me the details we make our way up the stairs to the top floor. The flat I am viewing is to the front of the building; there is another flat to the back at the same level. We enter into a small hallway with stairs leading up to the top floor; technically this is called a maisonette, as it isn't all on one level.

Then the grand reveal as he opens the door to the lounge and all I can see out of the windows is sea, right in front of me and to the side. A wonderful, absolutely delightful, view; I am spellbound and just stop and stare for a few moments at its beauty. This is what I have been dreaming of finding and it can now be mine. With a slight cough, the agent brings me back to where I am in the room and shows me what is inside the rest of the maisonette (not flat).

The place is empty and newly decorated but even so I can appreciate the size of the lounge and small separate kitchen area with fitted appliances. The stairs lead round to the landing, a back bedroom with views out to the town centre and countryside in the distance, a bathroom and front bedroom with a view to die for; absolutely stunning views of the sea that I can wake up to every day for the rest of my life and not tire of. I am in love with the place, deeply in love, already!

"What is the situation with this place?"

"There haven't been any offers yet but there has been one second viewing."

"What is the position with the owner?"

"He has moved out to live with his partner in Brighton while he sells this place before finding his own."

"Oh, okay, umm, let me think about it. I am interested but will probably want to see it again with a friend, maybe tomorrow if that's possible?"

"That can be possible. Give me a call after you've thought about it. I don't think it will hang around for long so don't delay."

"Thanks, I won't."

My mind is trying to process all that I am feeling about this place into some cogent thoughts. Yes, I really like the flat, sorry maisonette. Yes, I can just about afford it but that isn't the real dilemma. Will I have the money to buy it? That is in Em's hands and makes me frustrated and angry even more because there isn't any easy way round it. I breathe a very deep sigh as I open the door to my place avoiding Meghan on my return.

While I make my coffee I call Rachel. She is the only one I want to view this place with. Her views are different about what to look for and she knows what I am looking for. She doesn't answer so I leave a voicemail asking her to call me urgently. I message her with the same request. Next I sit down and work through my options while drinking coffee. I do find that after coffee I think more clearly and quickly.

Sure enough a rough plan starts to emerge that, depending on how events work out, there may be a way forward. Rachel calls back anxiously asking what is wrong. I explain my need and she says that within reason she should be able to make a viewing in the afternoon with me. That is just what I hoped for and I call the agent to ask for a second viewing. Will tomorrow afternoon be possible? It is and we agree to meet again at 4pm.

I finish my second cup of coffee and take stock of things. I am still meeting Magic Triangle later. I answer a few work emails and then check my dating site where an alert tells me I have a message from Melanie who wonders if we can meet up in Brighton. That is no problem for me and I suggest Friday after work for a drink. I did that as part of my new approach to try to get things onto a more equal footing over location. There is nothing from Great Dane or Primrose who I write off now as not interested in where I live or me or both.

I decide that I am not going to make such a big effort dressing up for Magic Triangle and try to dress more like my normal self. It is a lovely day, warm and sunny, so a t-shirt and jeans make me feel more comfortable and relaxed than smart trousers, shirt and shoes. I make my way up to Worborne station and wait for her train to arrive. I recognise her from her profile picture, which is a relief and we exchange a brief hug and greeting.

Magic has a thin face with angular features, which I like immediately. Her hair is fair, shoulder length and straight. She is slight, small, very nimble and fit from walking her dog I surmise. Magic knows Worborne and suggests we walk through the town to the seafront where her dog, Dusty, can be let off the lead and we can have time together to get to know each other.

Following my new approach, I make the first move and introduce myself as Chris and ask for her name. Magic is Sue who lives in Brighton alone with her 11 year-old dog that is half blind. That is good news because I am not the greatest dog fan. I am relieved that I won't face years of doggy walks picking up Dusty's poo and disposing of it in all types of weather to please Sue and show my love for her.

We discuss what each of us does for a living. Sue writes plays for the theatre, has her own website and is a sign writer and working at big conferences for enlightened organisations with an inclusive culture helping people with hearing difficulties. I am impressed; she is impressed that I've run my own business successfully for so many years.

Sue has had many failed relationships and isn't sure why. Certainly she has dated many different men but whatever is missing the spark hasn't stayed burning for long with anyone so far. We contrasted that with my marriage over such a long period of time. We also find that we share the same politics and discuss climate change, food banks and social issues. In fact over two hours we find we have more things in common than not.

It is going so well that I ask Sue if we can meet again. She seems keen and suggests we meet somewhere in between us in a few days time. I walk back with her to the station but we don't exchange kisses this time, just nods and a brief hug, before she boards her train to Brighton. I walk back feeling good about meeting Sue. For once I am home before my date!

Sue feels like a good match intellectually and our conversation was entertaining and interesting. Her career is amazing and different to mine although we are both self-employed. Do I see Sue as my special friend rather than a friend with similar interests? I could but it is only our first date and that feeling needs to grow. I still have no type that I am looking for on my dating site. I am not sure if that is good or bad. I have potentially every woman to contact but maybe I will miss the 'right' one with so wide a remit?

Once I am home, successfully avoiding Meghan again, I log on to my dating site. Having just left Sue I do feel a little "unfaithful" that I am searching for other women. Then again I have only met her once and she may do exactly the same thing, even seeing other men as well as me. The rules for online dating seem to be whatever you make them to be or change them so they suit your situation.

Melanie replied agreeing to meet me at Brighton train station around 7:30pm. That is perfect for me and I confirm that I'm looking forward to seeing her, giving my first name and mobile number.

There are no women who joined who take my fancy and make me want to contact them. Two women have liked my profile but I don't reciprocate. Am I getting fussy? Lastly three women viewed my profile but again, I don't contact them beyond viewing their profiles. It feels a confusing picture to me with potential dates, real dates and follow up dates all happening at the same time.

My feelings are in turmoil. Yes, it is great to have such love interest with so many new women in my life but how do I separate one from another when I contact them? Is it different online to meeting them face to face? I don't have a clue to be honest with you! I am trying to keep up with the online dating game I joined that is being played. Am I the only one who feels like this or do women who contact me feel the same? It isn't a question to ask on a first date for certain!

I message Danny about my maisonette (not flat) viewing and call Liz who thankfully answers my call. I explain my day and how the maisonette I viewed may be *the* one I am looking for. The big question is 'will I be able to buy it?' as my money is tied up in the home that Em decided to sell; no sale – no purchase it seems. Unfortunately Liz hasn't been in touch with her mum since our last call because Em is on holiday for two weeks. Our house may have been sold for all I knew but I will be the last to know! I try to keep my anger out of my voice but Liz does pick it up and says she can't cope being the go between over this and ends the call abruptly. Oh dear, where do I go with this?

DAY 32: TUESDAY

I wake up with my stomach knotted and exhausted from dreaming about the flat I viewed and will see again today, dates I met or hope to with their bodiless profile pictures drifting in and out of the rooms of the flat and of course it isn't a flat; it is a maisonette. What a way to start the day!

As I slowly emerge from this sleepy maelstrom of feelings I check for any emails or messages left since last evening. A short text from Danny thanks me for my update but he has nothing else to say and hasn't heard from his mum. Well, at least I know anyway. It is the two messages on my dating site that grab my attention next.

The first is from Melanie who is looking forward to seeing me and shares her mobile number which sounds like a positive step to me. The second is from Sue saying she enjoyed yesterday but doesn't want to meet me again as there was no spark for her about me. I feel crushed; yet again I had got carried away with my impressions, fast-forwarded to a future that won't happen now. Why did I do that? Am

I ever going to get beyond a first date?

Although I have Melanie to look forward to meeting I still feel disappointed about Sue's message but she has been open about how she feels and I can hardly expect her to meet me just because I like her more! It isn't any different to how Emily and Angie probably feel after meeting me but they haven't expressed it like Sue has.

The morning passes slowly with calls to Brian & Co. emails and work to do resulting from those calls. It keeps me busy and distracts me from the impact on me from Sue's message for a while. I don't go for a walk after lunch as usual, partly because I just want to be at my place and partly to avoid bumping into Meghan.

Finally, I leave around three and arrive by the flat, sorry, maisonette with plenty of time. I took the train to test the transport links and walk to get more of a feel for where I may be moving. I know the area a little but want to see what goes on around there as well. Nothing unusual happens, people walk by along the seafront, traffic passes but isn't too busy and no lorries and buses, just cars and motorbikes. None of the residents in the building come or go while I watch.

The agent arrives a few minutes early but he doesn't see me and I wait for Rachel who gets there a few minutes late, apologises and has clearly rushed to get here. We introduce each other and then enter through the main door and walk up the four flights of stairs to the maisonette (I am getting to like that term). Even though I have seen it before, the view from the lounge stops me in my tracks to take in again. Rachel does the same thing, the agent just moves to one side and stays silent. He doesn't need to say anything as the view is doing all the talking and selling itself to me.

After a few moments Rachel remembers her role and starts asking the agent questions about the place, its history, neighbours, condition, etc. Meanwhile I wander around and take in the place, its décor, atmosphere and most importantly to me its views. I realise whichever window I look out from has a stunning view; even through the bathroom window in the roof that slants down I see the countryside in the distance.

Eventually I make my way back down to the lounge where the agent and Rachel turn and look at me. Trying not to show a great big grin at being here again, I smile and ask how they are. The agent says he and Rachel have discussed the maisonette and building in general. Is there anything I want to ask? Apart from the asking price and if anyone else is interested, I reply "No". He repeats the asking price and that no one is due to see it for a couple of days as things stand.

I know estate agents can be stereotypical, don't trust them, they don't tell you the truth, never stop talking, etc. However, I do like Robert, who has a sense of humour and appears to be open and honest. We leave the building together and with a handshake we part.

Rachel said, "I caught the train here as my car is in for some repairs until tomorrow. How about we drive back to your place to discuss everything?"

"I've left my car at home too so I can take the train. How about we stop at a pub on the way to the station?"

"Sounds good to me. I'm in the mood for a drink and a chat."

We find a nice pub and beer garden where we settle with a bottle of red wine between us. We both sip from our first glass of wine before Rachel starts with the obvious question first.

"What do you think of the place Chris?"

"I love it, I really do. It has everything I hoped to find for my own place. But what do you think?"

"I agree it does tick a lot of the boxes you have. But I wonder about how much it will cost to maintain? It's great on a day like this but what about a cold, wet, windy day though?"

"Yes, that's true. I see the roof was repaired this year and Robert said they plan to replace all the outside brickwork next year."

"True and the maintenance costs look high but that's to your advantage if it is for this work. What about the stairs?"

"What about them?"

"Well you're fit and healthy now but what if you are ill or in years to come unable to climb up the stairs? You're not getting any younger!"

"Are you being cheeky?"

"A little but I wonder if you are thinking that far ahead."

"I haven't but I look at it this way. Whatever time I do have there I will enjoy every minute of it. This is the place of my dreams, somewhere I've always wanted, and a paradise place on holiday except it's my home every day. It just feels so right, almost perfect, for me now."

"And what if it isn't just you? What if you find your special friend?"

"She will have to like being there to."

"And if she doesn't…?"

"She won't be my special friend then. Whoever is in my life will need to enjoy being by the sea too."

"Is that a deal breaker for you."

After a little hesitation I said, "Yes."

"Hmm, ok. Actually I don't think it will be a problem. I love the views and its situation too. To be honest I think it will be a chick magnet and you will be fighting them off!"

We laugh, clink glasses, smile and look around at the flowers in the garden among the few other people drinking in the warm sunshine.

"This can be my local."

"You can do a lot worse. In fact, you have done a lot worse!"

We laughed again.

"What do you plan to do next?"

"I'm going to make an offer and see how it goes from there. If need be I can pay the full asking price but anything spare will help furnish it. I'm fine with the décor so that will save me a lot."

Then Rachel asked *the* key question.

"How will you afford it?"

We both knew that she meant Em's decision to delay the final part of the divorce by putting our marital home up for sale.

"I need to sort that out. I'm going to see my solicitor for advice."

"That's good but you'll also need to convince the agent that you have the funds. They may want hard evidence."

We drink again but this time not laughing or smiling. The atmosphere isn't so warm, as if a cloud passes over the sun for a moment. I move the subject on.

"How are things with you? How's your new boyfriend?"

"Oh, don't ask about *him*! He's been a complete bastard the last two times we met. Thoughtless, late, forgetful... where do I start?"

For the next 20-30 minutes Rachel offloads about the past few weeks. Apart from yet another relationship fragmenting and falling apart, work is very stressful with a threat of redundancies on the horizon. Her family are being difficult over sharing the care of her mum and dad so they can stay independent at their home with help and support from their children... except only Rachel seems to turn warm words of support into action that actually helps. I think of my mum and her care home as she pauses because the bottle of wine is empty.

I go for a comfort break, take a break from Rachel's outpourings and replenish our drinks with another bottle of wine. Will I be like Rachel in five or ten year's time? One failed relationship after another, bitter about women, distrustful of anyone new. I certainly hope not although I admire her resilience and optimism that her Mr. Right is still out there waiting for her to find.

Rachel looks more composed when I arrive with wine bottle and fresh glasses but asks to be excused and spends a long time in the loo before we resume our conversation. This time she wants to talk about my dating. Apart from some texts and a couple of calls we haven't sat down to discuss in detail what has happened, is happening and may happen next.

Slowly we dissect my approach, progress so far, my anxieties and hopes. It isn't easy and my head is feeling heavy from the sun and wine or the subject discussed or maybe all of them. Gradually it feels my inadequacies and low esteem is winning out to such an extent that Rachel calls a halt and said another bottle of wine is called for, gets up and is off to the bar before I can object.

When she returns Rachel has thought while at the bar about everything I have said.

"Chris, you've got to be more positive about this. You're drawing on all the negatives, some are real but you perceive others. You're not seeing a balanced picture like I can."

"I'm not sure what you mean. I've not even managed to get beyond a first date so far. It hardly seems that positive to me."

"But that's a typical example of you being in your own little bubble. You are so exasperating at times! Women *are* interested in you; they have contacted you; they have met you; they trust you with details about their personal lives, even contact details. I know people who have been on a dating site for months and got diddly squat attention for all their efforts and troubles. Don't underestimate your efforts, fortunes, and luck, whatever… it's working for you. And you will get a second date; you're still testing out what attracts you to someone who feels similarly about you. It takes time and patience… believe me, it does!"

"Thanks Rachel. That makes me feel a little better. I just keep going over what I do or don't do to make them not want to see me again. I'm not confident that a second date will ever happen or with a woman who isn't right for me but is happy to meet again for whatever reasons."

"I recently saw Malory Blackman interviewed about her latest book in London. She is a real inspiration to people. She wrote many books but her first book was rejected 82 times, yes 82, before a publisher offered to publish it. Her words of encouragement to the audience were 'Don't give up!' and that's all you need to remember with each encounter, don't give up."

I nod with agreement. If an author can keep going through 82 rejections by publishers of your book then I am sure I can cope with a few rejections from women on first dates. Of course if I get past that 82 benchmark then I may need extra help I muse but not seriously.

By now the sun is leaving the garden and it is much cooler. We peruse the food menu, choose two dishes and move inside where it is warmer and we can continue our conversation. The issue that still niggles away at me is why. Why don't women want to meet me again? Why don't they respond to my messages on the dating site? Why don't they return my likes? Why, why, *why*? It eats away at my heart and makes me anxious all the time.

Rachel offers no more succour beyond what she iterated already to me repeatedly. She starts to get frustrated with me as I keep mumbling away about it, probably the effect of four (now) bottles of wine and the food not soaking it up yet. Maybe that is causing me to maunder so much about it too?

After polishing off the fourth bottle and eaten our meals we check train times and decide to make a move. It has been helpful discussing all these things with Rachel that churn away in my head and it is always good to see her anyway. But the anxiety remains after we say goodbye dwarfing my thoughts about the offer on the property I will make tomorrow. It doesn't help that it I am dependent on Em accepting an offer to sell our house and give me my share of the money.

DAY 33: WEDNESDAY

I wake up far too early with a head far too heavy. When I do drink a lot it I sleep heavily and Em said I am very hard to wake from it. However the wine induced heavy sleep can't compete with the thoughts of my offer to buy the maisonette. Part of my thinking is how much or maybe more precisely how much less than the asking price. But mainly it is how to answer questions about my ability to buy it. I hope my solicitor will help there.

I have a letter from my mum's care home demanding an update from me when she will be leaving. That really annoys me and is another thing to act on today. What with dating, flats and care homes to deal with I'm relieved that work isn't full on at the moment.

After getting ready for the day I do the most important task first; I call the estate agent who is, naturally, pleased to hear from me. I give him my offer that Robert says will probably not be acceptable as it is too low and the property is still relatively new to the market. All the usual estate agent speak that I expect to hear; I will await his response.

The next task isn't so quick with my mum and her care. I haven't done anything yet except research dementia and the best ways to care for someone with it. Now I have been reminded about their termination notice the ball is firmly in my court now. I call Dementia UK and again explain my situation to the nurse who answers my call. He suggests that I call or write to the care home setting out my concerns about how or if the dementia had been assessed and to contact my mum's GP to arrange a formal assessment. That way I will have the evidence to help with my next move.

I thank the nurse and write the letter without delay. I know what I want to say and it flows so quickly on to my laptop that I print, date and sign it within half an hour of starting. With that out of the way for the time being I call my solicitor to find she is in meetings for the rest of the day. Annoyed with myself for not calling her first I ask her to call me about my divorce.

The afternoon is clear and I decide on the spur of the moment to visit mum at the care home. I take the letter with me and leave quickly, again managing to avoid Meghan, and drive that familiar journey to where my mum now lives. After signing in at reception I make my way to my mum's room without seeing anyone on the way, which suits me fine. Entering her room I can see instantly that she isn't her normal self and quickly reach her standing by the window looking out at nothing in particular.

Still staring into space I turn her gently round until my mum can see it is me except that she doesn't see me. Whatever she does see it is definitely not I because she screams out loud and tries to beat me away. Shocked by this unexpected turn of events I let go and back away quickly falling over her chair behind me. With me shouting from pain and my mum screaming in panic we make a right pair but the most worrying thing is no one comes to find out what is happening! It seems like it is the Marie Celeste care home; deserted except for the two of us. My mum then snaps out from wherever she is, looks down at me grimacing in pain as I roll over from my back and try to sit up.

"Who are you? Are you hurt?"

"Mum, I'm your son Christopher, you know Chris. I've hurt my back but I don't think it's serious."

"Chris? My son?"

"Yes, you're my mum and I'm your son Chris."

"If you say so. Your face is a little familiar now I think about it."

"That's good. I'm here to see you. I visit you regularly to see how you are."

"Oh, well I'm fine as you can see."

That is my first problem as mum clearly is not fine. Next is my concern at the lack of attention when we both shouted out. Hardly a place that gives me confidence that she will get the care she needs now or in the future. Lastly, how to get her the right care; I call her GP and leave a message for him to call me urgently, briefly explaining why.

We sit down and look at each other; mum with curiosity, me with concern. What to do next goes round and round in my head. I will leave the letter at reception; clearly I am not in the mood for a general discussion about my mum's situation. The sooner I can move her to the right place the better but what and where is that place? I need to find places nearer to my home or maybe my new home. Oh God, this is getting horribly complicated and I can't cope with the permutations. What has been a spur of the moment decision to see my mum now becomes a very different proposition.

"Would you like a cup of tea mum? I'm gasping for one!"

"Yes that will be nice son."

Son, she had said "son". I can't tell you how much that touches my heart to hear that word from my mum again. I put the kettle on and busy myself getting the tray ready, putting cups and saucers on it, then warming the pot as my mum loves to do and pouring hot water into the pot with two teabags, the only concession to today's convenience instead of tea leaves and a strainer. Bringing it to the table between our chairs I sit and smile at mum who smiles back at me.

Over the next hour mum returns to normal or rather how I see her now when I visit. She is calm, relaxed and able to converse with me about my children and me. She doesn't seem to realise that Em and I are divorcing but that doesn't seem important. I feel more comfortable when I leave that she is safe within her room. As I leave the home I give the envelope with the letter to the receptionist who accepts it with a nod and "goodbye".

As I get to the car my mobile rings, it is my mum's GP. I briefly explain why I called, what happened and my wish for an urgent assessment so I can find the right place for my mum. He promises to see her later this week, update me, and start the ball rolling by contacting Living With Dementia to assess my mum's condition.

I thank him and have a more relaxing journey home after that call. I park the car and walk back to my place but as I open the door a tight-lipped Meghan looks straight at me confronting me.

"Hello Christopher."

"Hello Meghan."

"Is that all you have to say?"

"At this moment in time, yes that is all."

"When are you going to tell me about your plans?"

"Why do I need to tell you anything?"

"There is no need to take that tone with me Christopher!"

"I'm not, just asking why you think you have to know what my plans are."

"As a friend and close neighbour I naturally think you will want to tell me."

"Well firstly you're not a friend and secondly you're a neighbour while I live here."

"How rude! Who do you think you are after all I have done?"

"Just remind me Meghan what exactly you have done?"

"I've… I've taken parcels in for you. I've offered to mind your place when you're not there. I make you welcome and invite you into my own home. It's not everyone I do that to."

"Thank you for taking in the parcels but I can easily pick them up from the Post Office if you don't. I bet you check who they are from and what they may contain."

"How dare you!"

"I haven't given you my keys because I don't want you nosing through all my stuff trying to find out things about me that I want to keep private."

Meghan gasped, "Really!"

"I know you need a ready supply of information to gossip to your friends about and I don't intend to give you that."

"Christopher!"

"No one who knows me calls me Christopher. I told you when we first met that my name is Chris but you ignored me and carry on calling me Christopher, something only my mum calls me."

"Well really Christopher, I mean Chris."

"I'm very happy for you to not invite me any more into your place and for you not to invite yourself into mine again. Are we clear?"

Meghan again gave her impression of a goldfish as her mouth opens and closes with no sound coming out. I take advantage of this to walk past her and briskly climb the stairs before entering my place and closing the door on her and the world outside.

I open a bottle of wine and drink the first glass down in two large gulps. Topping it up I move into the kitchen and start cooking dinner, decide I am not in the mood and order a pizza takeaway instead. While I wait for it to be delivered I relax in my easy chair and just close my eyes to absorb all that is happening.

I awake with a start as my door buzzer sounds loudly; I must have dozed off. I quickly descend the stairs, thank the delivery guy as I take the pizza and mount my stairs quickly to avoid a repeat encounter with Meghan. I sink into my chair; sink another glass of wine into my mouth along with slice after slice of pizza.

While eating my mobile rings, it is the estate agent. Eagerly awaiting his news I am disappointed to hear that Robert has not heard back from the seller about my offer. He promises to update me as soon as he does; there has been no other interest so far in the property. I thank him and end the call. It is the "so far" phrase that makes me anxious. Why hasn't the seller been in touch? It is one more worry to add to my growing list; I haven't heard from my solicitor either.

I reflect on what happened today. I don't regret a word of what I said to Meghan; I just wish it hadn't happened or maybe not happened today. I am sure she will exact her revenge; what and when I will wait to find out. The incident with my mum is more worrying.

To be shouting out like that and no one investigating is awful. It means the emphasis is on me to get mum's dementia assessed and to find a new nursing home with the right level of care she needs.

Tired and worn out by all that is happening needing me to act on this, that and the other I am in bed early but struggle for ages to sleep with everything whirling around in my head.

DAY 34: THURSDAY

After several attempts at having a lie in after a night of broken sleep I surface for breakfast just before 9am. Before I can take my first sip of tea my solicitor calls.

"Hi Chris, it's Debra. Sorry I couldn't get back to you yesterday. How can I help?"

"Thanks for calling back. I've got an update on Em and the sale of the house and a new problem because I've found a place I want to buy."

"Ah, ok. Yes I think I can guess what you're going to say. Do you want to discuss it later today on a call or in person?"

"In person will suit me. What time do you have in mind?"

"I agree, better in person. I'm free at 2pm for 45 minutes. Shall we meet then?"

"Yes, that's fine with me. Thanks."

"See you at two, bye." That fits one piece into today's jigsaw puzzle.

Next is a call to my mum's GP who will call me back after 11 when he completes seeing his patients. I ask if it can be as soon after as possible but the receptionist can give no guarantee. I thank her; at least I try to get an urgent response back.

I'm working through my emails when my mobile rings again, this time from my estate agent. I jump up and stand still as I answer the call. As soon as I hear his voice I know my offer hasn't been accepted.

"I've heard back from the seller and your offer isn't high enough for him to accept at this stage." So, not completely dismissed and with a caveat.

"What offer will he accept at this stage?"

"The full asking price is ideally what he is looking for."

"I am a cash buyer with no mortgage." I am stretching the truth a bit here.

"Yes, that's why he hasn't completely dismissed your interest. If you want to make a higher offer I will be happy to refer that back to my client."

"I'll think about it and get back to you. If anything changes meanwhile will you let me know?"

"Of course I will Mr. Davison. Bye."

I decide to wait until I see Debra before going back with another offer. Everything is still in play and I am at the front of the queue, in fact the only one in the queue at the moment.

As I get back to my emails there is a loud insistent banging on my door. I know who it is because my intercom hasn't buzzed; it has to be Meghan. I am definitely not in the mood for her and ignore it but she isn't one to be put off easily.

"I know you're in there Christopher… Chris. You were very rude to me yesterday and you're being rude again. I demand an apology for the way you spoke to me and upset caused. I can only think you're not feeling well."

I don't move or say anything in response.

"I know you're there you know. I've not seen or heard you leave this morning."

Proof if any is needed how much she keeps tabs on the comings and goings of everyone in the building. I continue to stay still and silent.

"Really, this is intolerable! I've never been treated like this before. So rude! This won't be the last you hear of this from me!"

With that I hear her slowly and deliberately stomp down each stair to her flat.

Breathing a sigh of relief I quietly move to the kitchen and prepare an early lunch to eat. Meghan has drained me of energy. Clearly things are not going to get better unless I make an abject apology and whatever else is needed on her terms. That isn't going to happen - ever!

Next up is my mum's GP calling back as promised. He listens, asks a few questions and notes my concerns about yesterday's events at the home. He has contacted Living With Dementia who carries out the assessment but it may take a few weeks but it will confirm her health. Meantime there is nothing to stop me now asking care homes certified by the Care Quality Commission as qualified for dementia care. I thank him and mentally add this to my ever-expanding list of tasks to do.

After lunch I walk to my car thinking the flat I want to buy has to happen somehow. The idea of renting my flat for months or years is unthinkable, especially with Meghan as a neighbour as well as the monthly rent that can be saved. Somehow I have to make it happen but how escapes me for now.

Debra as usual is ready for me when her secretary escorts me into her office. The desk is clear apart from my papers that are open at the relevant sections. She radiates competence and gives me confidence that she can help me find the best route through my divorce and flat purchase.

"Hello Chris, would you like any tea or coffee?"

"Coffee please." Her secretary nods and leaves to make my coffee.

"How are you? I understand you have some news and some questions for me."

"Yes I'm fine, well to be honest, I'm stressed and even more anxious now than at any time since I started divorcing Em."

"OK, I'm sorry to hear that. Shall we start with your news?" I pause while Debra's secretary comes back with my coffee.

"I've found out why Em changed her mind about my share of the equity. She had a big bust-up with her latest boyfriend, told him to move out immediately, next day she phoned an estate agent for a valuation and put it up for sale without telling me. Now she is away on holiday and not contactable until next week when she returns."

"Well the fact she has not informed you is a serious concern. Your wife or her solicitors should have informed us before your marital home was put up for sale. The court may take a dim view should this come to light in any dispute over the settlement. What action do you want me to take?"

"First let me ask you a question over what happened yesterday and today." Debra looks intently at me as if trying to read my mind. "Go on."

"As you know I started looking for a place of my own to buy. On Monday I found it and I made an offer that has been rejected. I want to make another but with the uncertainty over the house sale I don't know how to fund it or whether it can work itself out later. I need advice, legal advice Debra."

Debra sits back and pauses, presumably thinking over what she can say for a few minutes then looks at me.

"You will need to convince the estate agent that you have the means to complete the purchase. They may accept your word when you make the offer but at some stage you will be asked for evidence either by the agent or the seller's conveyancer handling the sale. It's not something that I'm qualified to handle but I can recommend a good friend who may be flexible once she understands the full picture."

That last sentence Debra says gives me the first chink of light that a way through this property minefield is possible. Eagerly I accept her recommendation and Debra calls her friend, Maureen, and makes the introductions, before passing the phone over to me. Maureen asks if we can meet tomorrow at 9am to discuss how she can help me. I confirm I am happy to do that and get her details on where to meet. Turning back to Debra I say,

"I'm not sure if contacting her solicitor will delay or help me. Can't it slow down the sale if Em wants to be difficult and drags her feet?"

"Yes it can but any delay completing the decree absolute will be frowned on by the magistrate when approving any settlement or if forced to, deciding on how assets are apportioned."

"Hmm, well I'm guided by you Debra as always."

"My advice is I do write to your wife's solicitor and inform them of what has happened. I suspect they will be surprised and want to find out why their client is not informing them also. It can embarrass them and no solicitor relishes being in that position. I certainly wouldn't."

"OK, whatever you believe is best gets my vote. Thanks again Debra."

With that I leave her office and walk to my car. I feel my steps are lighter and the weight shifts a little off my shoulders. I sit in my car and call the estate agent but he is taking people round other viewings until later in the afternoon when he can call back.

I drive home and of course time my entry just as Meghan is coming out to walk Blodwyn. We pass each other with a frosty silence and avoid looking at each other. I prefer the silent treatment to the relentless poking of her nose into my life. The Tremeloes song 'Silence is Golden' sums up my mood as far as Meghan is concerned.

While waiting for Robert to call back, I stare out the window and gaze while sipping my tea; it is too early to open a bottle even for me today. After nearly an hour he calls back to ask if I have reconsidered my offer. This was £10,000 less than the asking price. I offer to split the difference if the seller is ready to start the sale. It is an obvious suggestion and doesn't surprise Robert; he will relay my offer and let me know what the seller says.

Knowing how long it took for an answer to my first offer, I am not expecting any news today. With nothing better to do I start searching online for nursing homes that care for people with dementia. There are a lot so I narrow the search down to within a five-miles of where I live. That makes it a more manageable number to look through. Of course, they all sound good on their sites but there are no fees shown, just the services and facilities offered.

I reduce the list down to a top 10 and make a note of the numbers to start calling tomorrow and arrange visits depending on how my enquiries go. After I eat dinner and clear everything away I check my dating site. There is nothing from Great Dane, Angie or Melanie who I see on Friday. There is nothing else from anyone I contacted and no one joined since my last check. All in all there is nothing - full stop!

I sit down and watch TV, catching up on a few programmes I have missed, then take my book up to bed to slowly bring to an end a very quiet evening, very quiet indeed.

DAY 35: FRIDAY

My alarm wakes me early so I can be ready to hit the road and be with Maureen for 9am. I sort out key documents like my birth certificate to help prove I am whom I am and where I live to help move things along should my offer be accepted to avoid unnecessary delays.

Maureen is very welcoming and puts me at ease. She listens intently to my situation and only asks a few questions to clarify points that help her understanding. After I finish she smiles and says she believes she can help me. The main thing is to reassure the estate agent and flat owner that I can pay for the flat when we complete. The bonus is she knows Robert and believes their relationship is good and they will reach an understanding.

However, if there are changes to my financial situation I must let her know immediately. She specialises on conveyance with multi-occupancy buildings; in other words she knows a lot about flats, even maisonettes as well! The leasing agreements will need careful scrutiny she warns me. Relieved that I found someone who will help me I make my exit after thanking her again.

While I am with Maureen I hoped for a positive call from Robert to say my offer has been accepted so I can start the ball rolling. Sadly when it finally comes around noon it is neither one thing nor another. He has heard from the seller's partner that they are away and will give an answer when they are back on Monday.

"Why the delay Robert?" I ask.

"I don't know, I really don't. It's not unusual for people to take their time considering offers."

"So, I've got a weekend to have this on my mind!"

"I'm afraid so unless you want to offer the full asking price."

"That doesn't really help me does it?"

"I'm just saying what the other options are."

"Are there any viewings planned?"

"Only one, tomorrow." One is one too many for me of course but what is the alternative? I will just have to wait it out and hope my nerves stand up to the strain.

"OK, thanks for letting me know Robert. I know you're doing your best."

"If I hear any more I will update you as soon as possible."

"Thanks, bye."

So I have a weekend with this in the back of my mind. At least I have Melanie to look forward to this evening; it is some consolation. My other distraction is rectifying a problem of my own causing but I want to respond first to an alert from my dating site. It isn't from any of the usual suspects but a new woman, Blossom, expressing an interest in my book writing career that she shares and wanting to meet up this weekend.

My writing career consists of one book that a friend helped me to publish. It covers my area of work and is a practical guide to help solve some of the common problems organisations face. It did sell a few hundred copies in a niche market that I am very proud of. In fact if I sold just one I would have been pleased! It was more as a marketing tool to raise awareness of me, as most people will still want you to help them rather than do the cheaper but harder and time-consuming way of acting on the books' recommendations.

After checking her profile I am not sure if she offers the attractive qualities that I want but I decide there is little to lose and maybe a lot to gain. I naively think that we can meet as writing friends if not as lovers depending how the date goes. I say that it sounds good; where and when does she suggest. Within minutes she responds saying Lewes can be a good place for her. How about lunch on Saturday and see where it leads to from there? She is rather bold I think for a first date and assume that we will click. I confirm Lewes and lunch; does she know anywhere good to meet? Again a quick response suggests a café near Lewes station for coffee and lunch around noon. That sounds ok so I let Blossom know that I will meet her there.

The rest of the afternoon is spent planning the training for Harry Stokes. Luckily Harry is that rare phenomenon for me, a patient client. With everything else going on I forgot to get back to him as promised while I was away in Scotland. After explaining to him that I am putting the finishing touches to how to rollout the training, I find a similar plan for another client. This helps me to save time as I adapt it so it is relevant to Harry and give him what he needs.

By the time I email him the information I realise I am cutting it

ONLINE DATING FOR THE NERVOUS

fine to meet Melanie. Not wanting to be late I quickly change into some smarter clothes than the t-shirt and shorts I am wearing. It isn't my preferred option but I decide on the spur of the moment to eat at the first or only place I will go to with Melanie and bring my best table manners with me. The main thing is I get into Brighton at just the right time; crossing my fingers the train will be on time.

One good thing is I haven't time to feel anxious about meeting Melanie like other dates. As the train journey starts I think about how to play it differently to other dates. No instant judgment, be open-minded, try to control nerves and not have unrealistic expectations. Yes, that sounds like a good approach; the difficulty will be remembering it as the evening unfolds.

The train arrives at the time I am due to meet Melanie; walking quickly I exit the platform and look for her. I don't see her as I glance around so walk about looking for anyone resembling her profile picture but I can't see anyone who does. Five minutes become ten and I pause before carrying out another survey; the station is busy at this time and she may be sitting out of sight although why will be puzzling.

As I am about to walk a lady I only vaguely recognise is walking towards me. When she gets close to me she looks into my face quizzically.

"Are you Chris?"

To which I nod, "Yes."

"Good, I'm Melanie." My disappointment is palpable but I hope hidden as I look deeply into her face. The woman standing in front of me looks a good five years older and her face more lined than her one profile picture on the site. Her blond hair in the photo is now lined with grey although she has a lovely smile, beautiful blue eyes and is clearly even more nervous than me.

Now I'm not expecting an absolute stunner who is years younger than me hankering after a more mature male partner so don't get me wrong here. But there is a clear difference that she must be aware of when she uploaded the photo or she is fooling herself or hasn't looked in a mirror for the last five years or so. Whatever the reasons I still have an evening ahead with Melanie and I remember my vow to how to approach this date.

"Well it's good to meet you Melanie. Where do you want to go?"

"I've no idea Chris. I don't normally go to pubs."

"Oh, well let me think, there is a nice pub just over the road that I went to sometime ago. We can peep through the window from outside before we go in."

"That's ok with me."

We cross the road, look in through the window, see there are some seats and tables available and decide to give it a try. The bonus for me is it serves hot food.

Inside we find a table with three chairs and sit down. I explain my need for some food, which Melanie doesn't object to and ask what she wants to drink. Then I order our drinks with a pie and chips for myself, Melanie isn't hungry. After taking our drinks back, I sit down and we gaze at each other before I break the ice again.

"So Melanie, how many dates have you been on so far?"

"Umm, this is my first." Wow! A newbie and it makes me feel like an old hand at this dating game.

"How about you?"

Gosh! I had to stop and count for a moment, "Three so far." I don't include Gill, as that was different.

"You are a mover then!"

"Not really, none of them have worked out; no second dates so far."

"Oh, it's all new to me."

My (obviously microwaved) pie and chips arrive very quickly. I ask Melanie if she wants to tell me more about herself. I feel she wants to talk, I need to eat and that way we can do both at the same time. As I tuck into my hot pie and chips she starts unburdening to me. By the time I finish I am aware that she was married and has one son who graduates next month that she is very proud of. She lives locally and has done since she split from her husband when her son was young. Melanie trained and worked as a nurse before getting married and returned to it after her divorce. Her nursing career in the last couple of years has moved on; she visits patients needing care after an operation and back at home.

Melanie really enjoys her work and finds it very satisfying. She confides that she hasn't dated anyone seriously since her divorce focusing on her work and her son. However he said recently that he will be living where he had graduates away from home so she should consider dating to fill the gap he will leave and find some happiness and company in her own life again if possible.

I realise that I am her first date in many years and don't feel comfortable with that responsibility, typical of me! It seems like I have to make it a good experience whether we meet again or not because she is like Angie very brittle after bad experiences with men. Again, I feel in uncharted waters with dating. I think of myself as the newbie to the dating scene however Melanie sees me as someone experienced with dating and an expert compared with her.

Seeing that I have finished my meal Melanie asks me for my story about why I am here this evening. I reveal more about why I am there to support what I said on my profile. She is interested and asks questions to clarify anything unclear to her. Once she knows how my split had happened, she is surprised that my wife had cheated not me, and my close contact with my children relaxes her. Our evening becomes more about general views and interests; they aren't the same but there is enough of an overlap to keep the conversation going. I buy her another drink and we chat for most of the evening in the same pub.

The atmosphere is relaxed and we open up more as we get to trust each other. Part of me is trying to work out if I could love as well as like Melanie. She brings the evening to an abrupt end when she looks at her watch and says she needs to catch a train in five minutes. Leaving the remains of our drinks we hurry to the station thankfully only a couple of minutes away. A quick goodbye and she rushes to her train saying she will text me as we exchanged mobile numbers during the evening.

A quick check of the timetable shows my train will leave in ten minutes and is waiting at the station already. I board it and sink into a seat in my own bubble processing all that happened while the usual noisy, boozy crowd of revelers at that time of night are all around me. I am torn between two lines of thought based on my feelings.

As a friend, Melanie will be good company. We have similar views and seem genuinely interested in each other's work and respect what we have achieved. On the other hand as a special friend I am not so sure. Counseling myself against rushing to judge prematurely, I really don't know if the Melanie I met this evening rather than in her profile attracts me or not. A second date will of course help but I want to sleep on it and wait for Melanie's text.

I am exhausted from the day, concentration during the evening, and churning over my conflicting views on Melanie. A text from Liz said she had more news about her mum and to call her but I am too bushed to have a proper conversation about Em now. I reply that I have been out and will catch-up tomorrow. It may or may not be significant but it will have to wait until I have more energy.

DAY 36: SATURDAY

Today is one of looking back at yesterday evening with Melanie and looking forward to lunch with Blossom. Add into the mix the text from Liz and it could become an interesting day. While I contemplate this over breakfast my mobile pings again with a message from Gill! It says, 'Still think about you Chris. Would like to call.' I had no answer to that and stall with my response until I can think clearer. That messes my day up further!

My first priority is to speak with Liz but I know she will be sleeping in and not appreciate being woken by her dad. Best to just let her know she can call me when she is ready and be patient. I slept better so I am in a relatively relaxed mood for my date. All the time I compare her with my other dates, even when I first dated Em.

When we first went out texting and mobile phones were not part of normal living. Neither of us had mobiles because they were so expensive. Even if we could make calls and texts they weren't cheap and not essential to our daily life or dating like they are now. An arrangement was made in advance on a home or office phone and you trusted the person to remember. I wrote Em's home number on my wrist and almost forgot when I washed my hands afterwards and nearly removed it! I'm sure I am not the first man in history to risk accidentally destroying their chances of a potential date that way.

It's hard to appreciate how much dating has changed since then as dates are messaging each other seemingly every minute before they meet. I find it amazing they have anything left to say when they actually meet in person but they do of course - or do they just text each other across a table? I'm not saying one is better than the other but I feel that if I committed to meet Em than it was more likely to happen than now when it seems too easy to put someone off, postpone at short notice or just be too distracted by other messages and potential dates.

Em and I normally met on Friday evenings and all day Saturday. It feels boring now but we kept those nights free to see each other. Sunday was usually catching up on chores, preparing for another week at work and maybe chatting over the phone if our parents weren't around. A call during the week was unusual and only from an office phone, a meeting during the week very unusual. Yet we accepted it, saw mates or girlfriends during the week, and romance flourished as it has done for decades.

Talking nostalgically about the past my instinct with Blossom is not to share my name or mobile until we meet. Taking the train (because parking in Lewes is a nightmare) I walk the short distance to the café she wants to meet me at. They are very friendly and I ask for a latte while taking a seat at a table with a view of the road. As I sip my latte I think back to meeting Melanie and wonder if I will recognise Blossom by her photo or not.

The clock ticks on past our meeting time though I am now getting used to this happening now. Then I recognise her, hesitating as she walks towards the café, taking her compact out of her handbag to check her makeup and I know she is very nervous. What follows over the next hour or so is my most embarrassing meeting with a date so far.

After initial introductions and getting her a coffee we sit at the table and look at each other. It is clear she is attracted to me and sadly it doesn't look like I feel like reciprocating. I realise now that meeting Blossom when it will only be for friendship is a mistake. Blossom thinks I can be her special friend and tries to be throughout the lunch. It takes me three attempts to get her to look at the lunch menu and choose what she wants.

She talks about her writing and I am interested in the subjects she writes about from parts of the world that I have never been to. Slowly it dawns on me that she wants a fellow author and my published work book qualifies me in her eyes, to travel these parts of the world with her. I try to be neutral, avoid saying yes or no to her implied requests. We are interrupted by a call from Liz which I answer saying I am with someone and will call her back. She guesses what is happening and ends the call abruptly.

The most excruciating moment is watching Blossom gather up a forkful of food and with her hand shaking from nerves drop half of it on its journey from the plate to her mouth. I feel great affection for her and how our date means so much to her but there is no spark. My only wish is for her next date to be the one who can help her fulfill her dreams about travel and writing.

After we leave the café it dawns on her that lunch with me has not been the success she wanted it to be. I am polite and attentive to everything she says or does but can't offer her the affection, a hug or kiss, as I am not who she yearns for. We part at the station and I go to one platform while she goes to the opposite one and slowly moves along it while looking across at me. I often want the train to hurry up – don't we all – but on this occasion as each excruciating moment passes with Blossom looking at me pleadingly, almost shouting at me to change my mind, I have never wanted it more. I feel very bad as I board my train for leaving her like that and vow there and then to only meet women who I fancy rather than just like. I catch a last glimpse of Blossom standing forlornly looking at me as the train slowly gathers pace leaving her behind.

To distract me while traveling back home I call Liz back. The information about Em isn't earth shattering; she is back from holiday and has a new boyfriend she met while there. I am impressed by the rate and ease that she can pick up men. While she is very good looking to me, it is obvious that others share my views. It is still hard to take, like a punch to my stomach, even though I am looking for someone and we haven't been together for over a year.

However it is the postscript from Liz that interests and upsets me most. Em said she'd received a letter from her solicitors asking her about the sale of our home. She is annoyed with Liz for sharing that information with me and causing her this headache. She is going to see them next week to find out more; so, Debra had made contact with the expected outcome. I hope it won't delay me being able to buy my place jumping several hoops ahead.

However Liz doesn't care about that, only the pain that her mum and I are causing her. For the rest of the journey she shouts at me, blaming me for her unhappiness, berating me for splitting from Em, accusing me of being selfish by dating until she just cries and ends the call. I didn't have my mobile on loudspeaker but the passengers around me could clearly make out some of our conversation and looked at me disdainfully.

I am shocked and stunned into silence as I leave the station and walk to my place. I didn't know what to do after that call; maybe call Danny? Maybe Rachel? I wasn't going to call Liz back today for sure! I couldn't cope with all the raw emotion again so soon.

Instead when I get home, I sit down reflecting on my two dates in two days. I don't think I am any closer to finding my special friend or even a second date. I make a cup of tea and review my dating site; no messages from new or existing women who either I contacted or have contacted me – it's depressing.

And then there is Gill! What do I do about her? It is tempting to ask Rachel's advice but I already know she won't be pleased that I am still in contact. I feel like a moth to the flame – I know it's bad but I can't resist the urge for contact.

Part of my problem is that no one else seems interested in me after one date and wants to meet again yet Gill stays in touch. I decide to reply with, 'Hi Gill, yes I would like a call.' And then I sit back and wait to see what happens next.

Within ten minutes my mobile rings, I tense up and prepare myself for a possibly difficult call but to no avail, as it isn't Gill but my football friend Gordon. The football fixtures were released earlier this week but I missed the excitement; Gordon and James haven't of course and want to know if I will go with them to the first game away at Liverpool. Even though it is two months away they want to know if I will be going now.

Not having a clue what my life will be like then I give a hesitant "yes" and ask what will happen. Gordon goes into detail, too much detail, about the ticket booking and who will do what. The bottom line is he wants my money by next Thursday to make the booking; travel arrangements can be sorted out nearer the time. I promise to do that. We then continue a general chat about how we each are and what we have done since the last time we met. He is amazed when he hears my dating exploits; having married young to his wife for over 30 years I feel like I am talking a foreign language to Gordon.

When I finish my call I noticed my mobile shows I missed a call while chatting with Gordon. I don't recognise the number but guess it was Gill and groan. Was it her though? What to do? Call her back? Leave it with her to call again? I hate these emotional dilemmas and finally decide to wait as she wants to call and hasn't left a message...if it is Gill of course. One should never assume of course. Nevertheless I feel awkward that I missed that call when it was just general chitchat with Gordon about nothing really important. I give a deep groan and slump further into my chair and just stare out the window.

Eventually I decide to start preparing something to eat. After a few minutes my intercom buzzing interrupts me. I am not expecting a visit or delivery today so answer quizzically, "Yes?"

A breathless voice answers, "Hi this is Colin you don't know me. We're moving into the flat below you but have mislaid our front door key. Can you let us in please?"

"Um, let me come down and let you in. Won't be a moment." He may be genuine and is my new neighbour but I am cautious about who I let in without checking first. I make my way down to the front door and open it to find a sweating young man puffing and trying to catch his breath.

"Thanks for letting me in, I'm so grateful. It's been a nightmare and neither Emma nor I can find the blasted key! We've looked everywhere in the car but it hasn't turned up."

He seems genuine but I want to be sure and find out a bit more before letting him in.

"So, do you have keys to your flat?"

"Yes!" Colin dangles a set of keys from his extended hand. That is reassuring.

"When did you take over the flat?"

"Yesterday but we both work so haven't had a chance to start moving stuff in until now."

"Have you bought it or are you renting?"

"Renting for six months to start with and then we'll see how it goes." By now I am convinced he is genuine.

"Sorry for the interrogation but I just want to be sure you are who you say you are before giving you free rein." I open the door and extend my hand to shake his, which he accepts with a firm grip.

"Phew! It's nice to finally be inside. I dreaded no one being in and having to cancel with everyone helping us move in today." Moving in today? It is nearly 6pm already!

"Have you got much to move?"

"Not really and it shouldn't take too many trips."

"Well, I'll walk up with you and leave you to get on with your move. It's great to meet you; if you want to pop up one evening for a glass of wine and chat I will be happy to see you."

"Thanks, that will be nice."

I leave Colin outside his flat and carry on up the next flight and let myself in. You never know who your neighbours are going to be, noisy or quiet, private or nosy? It is better to have someone there than the whole building to be empty even I suppose with Meghan living here.

I carry on preparing my dinner only to be interrupted half an hour later by Colin asking again if I can let him in. I press the buzzer but for whatever reason the door won't open so I walk down to let him in with a friend and some boxes. With a quick "hi" and "thanks" from Colin I go back to my place. I cook a lovely Bolognese and just finish the spaghetti and open a bottle of red wine when the buzzer goes again. This time it is a different male voice but asking the same thing. I go down the stairs, open the door, check who they are and lead them up to Colin and Emma's flat before carrying on up to my place.

After two mouthfuls of my meal the buzzer goes yet again and I answer it to hear a female voice giggling and asking if I can let her in to Colin's flat. I walk quickly down the stairs to meet a smiling face that introduces herself as Emma. It is nice to meet Colin's girlfriend and I welcome her and lead her up to Colin's flat. I wait with her and after he answers and gives Emma a hug and a kiss, I ask if anyone else coming can buzz his flat number and spare me the extra exercise. He promises to do that.

However half an hour later after I am starting to wash up the buzzer goes yet again. I answer and go down to Colin and Emma's flat where no one answers the knock on the door although I can hear music and people talking. Trying not to get irritated by this I continue down to the front door explaining what has happened and let them in and leave them outside Colin and Emma's flat. With a deep sigh I carry up to mine only to hear my buzzer going again as soon as I get there. Answering it tersely I tell whomever it is to press the buzzer for Colin and Emma and replace my intercom phone. I am tempted to leave it off the hook but don't want to make any of their friends feel unwelcome.

I repeat this process another three times during the evening as people forget the buzzer number or it seems just press the first one they can reach. Either way it isn't a normal evening; it would have been nice if Colin or Emma popped up to say thanks or sorry but never mind. I have done my best to show I can be friendly and accommodating. In the back of my mind is how their first meeting with Meghan will go and what she will say about everyone especially me.

Luckily I haven't anything planned apart from catching up on some TV so it doesn't cause a problem but I don't want too many repeats and hope they find their front door key quickly. I don't hear back from Gill and wonder whether to text or call but undecided by what to do I choose to do nothing. Neither do I hear from Blossom or Melanie, one with relief the other with hope I still will.

DAY 37: SUNDAY

For days I've been moaning about going on a first date with someone new but it never leads to a second meeting. Well today that changed and I am asked for a second date not once, not twice but three times today. But I'm not sure I will go on any of them! I know, I know but let me first tell you what happened!

The morning passes quietly with me catching up on a shedload of chores that I left and now need doing around the place. By lunchtime they are out of the way and I look forward to a nice stroll along the seaside to reflect on how things are.

As I leave I bump into Colin and Emma who give me a brief nod and "hello" as we pass on the stairs. I am underwhelmed by their lack of warmth after all that happened yesterday evening. The air outside is fresh, just right for me to think as I absorb the scenery with the sea crashing onto the beaches.

After walking until where the promenade ends and the beaches turn into cliffs I sit on a bench and check my mobile. I received an alert from my dating site. Quickly going to it I see a message from Melanie as she promised to do.

'Thank you for a lovely evening Chris, you are so nice to me. It is strange to be dating men again after so many years. My son prompted me to, as he didn't want me to be lonely when he left. His graduation is soon and I want to concentrate on that first before meeting up with you again. Hope that's okay with you. I like you and what you said. Melanie x"

My reaction is mixed, great that someone at last likes me enough to want to see me again. However, I am unsure Melanie is for me and to have to wait for sometime before meeting again doesn't send the right vibe to me about the relationship I am looking for. I decide not to stall but reply straight away to Melanie.

"Hi Melanie, it's lovely to hear from you again. I enjoyed our evening too. It's a pity we can't meet until after your son's graduation. If we can meet earlier please let me know. Take care and I hope all goes well. Chris."

I look at it for a few moments, make one or two small changes, decide after Angie that I am not going to show my feelings online with kisses and message back. I wonder what Melanie's reaction will be. Will it be what she expects? I think she is taking a chance that I won't meet anyone else. Maybe she doesn't know how online dating works? Then again, I am not so sure either.

I walk back home but I find my pattern of thoughts broken by Melanie's message. Gazing out at the sea I know I need to hear from Great Dane. Maybe I will take the initiative to increase the momentum? However, by the time I get back my dating site alerts me and I see that Blossom has left a message.

"Hello Chris, it was lovely to meet you for lunch. I love how you talk and the interest you showed me. I want to meet up again and discuss how we can use our mutual love of writing and travel together. I really do love your smile and face and want to see it again. I think we have so much in common and I hope you are the man and travel partner I have been looking for, for so long now. I hope and wish that you want to see me again. Blossom."

I read through the message several times to make sure I understood everything and then lay back on my sofa and stare up at the ceiling. What a wonderful, thoughtful, loving and caring message from her! I feel terrible because I just don't feel the same about Blossom. And I obviously hid that while we met even if at the end when we walked to the station I showed how I felt... or did I? Oh dear... I really don't know what to think or do as I go over the sequence of events that unfolded during our date.

By the time I run and re-run through what we said and did yesterday I am more confident that my feelings are true and it will be pointless meeting Blossom again. I console myself with the knowledge that it will be harder and more painful to say later that I don't have the same feelings for her that she has for me rather than now. But I am determined to communicate this, unlike my first dates who hadn't even bothered to say anything to me. I have my standards and I'm determined to treat my dates or rather ex-dates with the same decency as I expect to be treated.

Now came the really hard part, expressing my feelings in words that will have the right effect. I realise there is no way she will be happy with my reply but maybe she will see why in the future if not now. I struggle to start it and then go through several edits and re-drafts until I feel ready to reply.

"Hello Blossom, it was lovely to see you too. I enjoyed meeting and talking about your writing and travel plans. While I like you as a friend, I don't have deep feelings of love for you that you want or have for me. I feel it is better to end things now rather than continue to see each other. You are a lovely lady and will make the right man very happy but I'm afraid that isn't me. Take care, Chris."

I make myself a pot of tea after sending the message and don't feel very good about what I have done. But I know in my heart of hearts that it is the right thing to do now – it would have been worst to continue seeing her and let her feelings grow when it wasn't going to lead to anything. And to be honest it wouldn't be easy for me to continue seeing her knowing this.

It feels like my dating options are narrowing swiftly. I search through the latest recruits to the site and message four women who I have not seen before. Always the need to find fresh blood; it seems my life resembles that of a vampire. At least I can operate in daytime as well as at night!

The rest of the afternoon passes without incident apart from an exchange of messages with Rachel about our last meeting. We apologise to each other for drinking too much wine and for anything we may have said that wasn't right. It was a good if drunken evening and I aired thoughts and anxieties that I had bottled up for too long.

After dinner I still haven't heard from Gill. Remembering it was a Sunday evening three weeks ago that didn't go to plan for either of us, I sit down and call her. She picks up on the fifth ring.

"Hello Chris, it's nice of you to call back."

"Hi Gill, I thought I would call you as you haven't been able to call me," I said generously and encouragingly as she had promised to call me.

"Yes, thanks for doing that. How are you doing?"

"I'm fine. How about you?" I don't want to be distracted and keep it short.

"Well, that's a good question. I don't really know to be honest with you."

She stops but I keep silent because I need the call to go deeper to be worthwhile. No more superficial chitchat and dancing around the problem. Still I get nothing from Gill so I go straight to the point.

"So what was it you wanted to talk to me about?"

Again, silence but this time I am not going to say anything. Eventually with a deep sigh Gill speaks.

"I miss you. I want to see you."

There it is out in the open. What I can also hear is Rachel saying, "No, No, NO!" to me.

"OK, but what about how you were when we last met? How do you feel about your ex?"

And your ex-ex it is tempting to say too.

"I'm different now. I've been on my own since then. I've talked with Linda who's helped me. I feel like I'm moving on."

"That's good to hear but I'm not sure if you're ready for anyone new in your life."

I am not going to say 'me', trying to keep some distance between us.

"I feel I'm ready and am calmer about life and everything. All I want to do is meet with you Chris - I'm not asking you to marry me! Can't we just do that, meet again, maybe just once more?"

It is difficult to avoid saying "No" to a plea put like that.

"OK, let's meet up, just the two of us this time – no Linda. When did you want to- I'm busy so not sure how quickly I can?"

That isn't strictly true but I don't want to rush into this without thinking everything through first.

"Maybe one evening this week? You can come to my place if you want."

That sets alarm bells ringing. I haven't had sex with anyone since my split from Em, I am not into one-night stands or taking advantage of a vulnerable woman like Gill seems to be.

"Thanks Gill but I prefer to meet somewhere neutral but not the same pub. How about having dinner after you finish work at a place you are familiar with?"

"I suppose so. Are you sure you don't want to come here? I can cook you a nice meal with a bottle of wine."

"That's tempting but I don't want to put you to any trouble."

"It'll be no trouble, quite the opposite, a pleasure."

"OK, let me think about it and get back to you."

"Oh, if that's what you want to do."

"It is. Have a good evening and I'll be in touch."

"OK, you too and hope to hear from you soon. I do like you and miss you. You do know that don't you Chris?"

"Yes, I do Gill."

"Good, well see you soon Chris. Bye."

"Bye Gill."

After I end the call I feel exhausted. I am unclear if I said the right things or am doing the right thing. I just don't know what to do or what else I can have done apart from following Rachel's advice to the letter and saying a blunt "No!" and "Bye." Whatever I choose to do it is not going to be decided by me tonight.

Absent-mindedly checking my mobile for emails I see I received an alert ten minutes ago. Great Dane has followed up finally on our last contact and again our journey takes a great swerve in its direction.

'Will you meet me next Sunday?' she is direct and to the point again.

I quickly reply,

'Yes. Where?'

The one thing about Great Dane I like more and more is that I know where I stand with her. She gets straight to the point unlike other women I met such as Gill just now. I feel I will be clear on how we feel about each other and what is happening. It is something I am beginning to yearn for with online dating.

DAY 38: MONDAY

Today starts with the best possible news! My offer for the maisonette (not flat remember) has finally been accepted and I have the green or maybe just amber light to buy it. Robert calls me just after 9am as I am finishing a leisurely breakfast combined with a pot of coffee. He asks who will handle the purchase and is pleased when I give Maureen's details, acknowledging that he knows her and has completed sales and purchases involving her. Robert ends by saying he will write to all parties involved with the sale and purchase of the maisonette.

Maureen congratulates me on hearing my news when I call immediately after I finish my call with Robert. She will put our plan into action and is confident there won't be any problems as long as my marital home is sold before I exchange contracts on my place. That of course is the weakest link in the chain and out of my hands; all I can do is hope.

I make more coffee and prepare for my first of two visits to nursing homes today. I started calling care homes last week and worked through a list of questions so I can try to compare them. The key question of –"how much are the fees?" providing a surprising variety of answers with some giving the full costs while others give a rough amount, one refusing to give figures over the phone insisting I see them first.

Both nursing homes are near enough for me to walk to each of them having left plenty of time to travel between each appointment. Each home goes to great lengths to show me all the facilities and a typical room my mum will have. However on fees it becomes a greyer area and depends on their assessment of the level of care. When I ask why the dementia team's assessment isn't enough they become vague over why it is needed and, of course, there will be a charge for it too. To say I am not entirely satisfied or convinced by either home would be an understatement.

Back home I call my mum and have a reasonably normal chat. She isn't sure who I am to start with but remembers Danny and Liz and, of course, Em, who she is still convinced is married to me. Thankfully she doesn't recall our last visit and what happened. I hope she will be happy with what I am doing to give her the right care even if she is not fully aware.

I update Danny, Liz and Rachel with my news about my offer being accepted and ask my children not to share this with their mum for the time being. I want Em to be aware when and if it suits me. We still need to sort out who is having a few remaining furnishings. I am not like one divorced husband who gave his ex-wife half of everything, literally by cutting every piece of furniture in half, but there are a few items we both have sentimental attachment to rather than of high value and I won't give them all to her.

After a busy morning I go through my emails while I munch on a sandwich with more coffee for lunch. Great Dane replied,

'Will you be driving your car?' to which I said

'Yes.'

While I am not sure why she said that at least they are easy questions to respond to.

The rest of the afternoon I spend preparing for another meeting tomorrow with Brian & Co. at their workplace. It isn't difficult to do just time consuming. I am interrupted by two calls: the first is from Maureen with a quick update on the conveyance. Robert has been in touch and seems fine with the information she gave on funding. I breathe a sigh of relief with the first hurdle behind me now.

The other call is from Gill asking me if I have decided when to meet. I admit that I haven't because of some urgent work today but promise to let her know later today. Her call put me in a place where I don't want to be. I feel I have little choice about meeting but where is open for debate. Maybe a meal at her place will be good after all?

After completing my work for Brian & Co. I eat a convenience meal and drink deeply from a bottle of wine I open. Is it Dutch courage I need before calling Gill? Yes, if I am being truly honest with myself. After pouring the remains of the bottle into my glass I call Gill who answers after one ring. I guess she was waiting for me to call her.

"Hi Gill, it's Chris."

"Hi Chris, I'm glad you called."

"I've now had time to think about what you said."

"Oh, and what have you decided?"

"If your offer of a meal at your place still holds then I'd like that."

"Great! Wonderful! What about this Wednesday?"

"Yeah, that sounds good to me."

"OK, I'll text you my address and expect to see you around six o'clock. Is there anything you don't like or are allergic to?"

"Not that I can think of. As long as it's hot and tasty and there's plenty of it then I'll be happy."

"Ooh, well I'll make sure that's the case with everything!" Gill said flirtatiously.

Not aware until then of my double entendre I laugh a little nervously.

"I'll see you on Wednesday then Chris."

"Yes, look forward to it. Bye."

After the call I vow never to tell Rachel about this whatever happens afterwards. Speaking of the devil as they say moments later Rachel texts to ask how I am. I know it isn't a spooky coincidence more her normal routine of regular checking in with me. I reply with details about Great Dane, Melanie and Blossom but nothing about Gill.

Next up is another alert to my site where I find a message from Great Dane

'I will be outside Battle Abbey at 3pm.'

It is a statement, not a suggestion, rather short and abrupt even but all I need to do is say 'OK'. Something to look forward to this weekend!

Nothing else happens that evening apart from the sound of loud music for an hour from Colin and Emma's flat below. They really aren't making themselves good neighbours but it isn't the right time to see them. I don't want anything to disturb my mood; my offer has been accepted on the place of my dreams and I have two dates. Life can be better but it can also (and has been) a lot worse.

DAY 39: TUESDAY

The day starts early with a 'wakey, wakey, rise and shine!' type of alarm that startles me out of a deep sleep and rushing for the shower. Once I have breakfast and dress for my business meeting I check I have everything before departing.

The journey is difficult and the traffic is busy but my mood remains positive because I am confident about the meeting ahead and about my flat (sorry maisonette) purchase and date with Gill. I arrive with only minutes to spare but pleased I set the alarm so early to allow for congestion. After a warm welcome from Brian I sit down with his team.

The meeting goes as planned; Brian is pleased with progress so far and encourages us to keep to the plan. There are some changes planned within the organisation but he knows no more about them or how or if they will affect our project. I heard rumours like these before and sense they will have some impact but can do nothing more than note them and focus on what I am being paid to do.

After a long day by the time I get back after driving at commuter time the last thing I need is to see Meghan on the doorstep. Even more of a surprise, she is smiling at me!

"Christop… Chris, I wonder if you can either pop in now or after your dinner for a quick chat please? There's something important and maybe in both our interests I want you to know about."

Intrigued by this sudden change in Meghan's mood I just say, "Err, yes. Later?"

Meghan smiles and lets me in whilst she returns to her place. Wondering what it can be about I let myself into my place and relax in a chair after opening a bottle of white wine. I normally drink red but today I fancy a change. Remembering there is lasagna in the freezer I pop it in the oven and settle back to finish my glass. A good business meeting, no flat hunting, two dates ahead, yes life is good.

After dinner I respond to Liz's message congratulating me on my offer being accepted and call her. We chat about the maisonette, her nan (more nursing home visits tomorrow) and how life is now she's left college for the summer. I asked her if she knows what Danny is doing but all she can say is that he isn't back home yet, only mum and her are there. We do not cover my recent dates. I know I will have to broach this touchy subject with her but this isn't the right time.

Having washed up and changed I see Meghan, unable to contain my curiosity any longer. Blodwyn greets me very warmly as I bend down and stroke her while Meghan beckons me in to sit and offers me a glass of wine. Life is really looking up I think as I accept her offer.

"Thank you for coming down to see me Christopher, I mean Chris." I smile inwardly as she corrects herself. "I hope the wine is to your taste." It is a bit sweet for me but I am never one to turn down a free drink especially on the rare occasions it is from Meghan. "It's fine Meghan."

"I'll get straight to the point. Have you been introduced to our new neighbours yet?" I reply, "Yes."

"Oh! When was that?" asked Meghan thinking I have stolen her thunder from her.

"On Saturday night when they moved in."

"Oh, I was away for the weekend so didn't have that pleasure."

"Have you been introduced to them?" I am not expressing any opinions yet until I am clear where Meghan stands on this.

"Well yes I have actually. I have to confess it hasn't been as good as I might have hoped it will be."

"Why's that?" Now I sense we are getting to the nitty gritty of why I am here.

"All day my buzzer has been going. Whenever I answer it is either one of them or the other wanting to be let in. I asked them if they have their front door key but both said they must have mislaid it and can't find it with all their clutter to unpack. Frankly Christo... Chris I'm at my wit's end worrying what's going to happen next."

"Have you explained how it is affecting you?"

"Well yes I have but it doesn't seem to make any difference."

"Have they asked for a replacement key?"

"They didn't say and I'm not sure I asked them. I assumed they will have but there's been so many times I'm confused about what's happened. Oh dear..."

"What would you like me to do Meghan?"

"I don't know. Can you talk to them?"

"I did when they did the same to me the evening they moved in. I'll try again but maybe I can call the property agents who are responsible for the key? Maybe Colin and Emma have called already?"

"Colin and Emma?"

"Yes, the couple who moved in."

"Oh, I never got their names with all the toing and froing going on."

"OK, leave it with me. I'll try them and/or the agent about the keys tomorrow."

"Thank you Chris." I finish my glass of wine, get up and make my exit before she becomes her normal self and starts interrogating me.

I do hesitate outside Colin and Emma's door but hearing nothing I decide not to spoil a good day with a bad argument. I am not in the mood for any more excuses from them and have time tomorrow morning to try to sort things out.

DAY 40: WEDNESDAY

I wake up thinking, 'I'm going to spend the evening at Gill's. Am I doing the right thing?' and that one thought stays with me throughout the day either at the front or back of my mind. Now the day arrives I am uncertain if this is the right thing to do. Rachel's advice is always there about avoiding Gill yet it seems like I'm still like that moth drawn to the flame. It's something I have to go through and hope it is the right choice.

The evening ahead is still a long way off. I have care homes to visit along with the front door key to take care of first. As soon as it is open I call the property agents for the building and explain the problem but they are reluctant to help me. Apparently it is each flat owner's responsibility to equip their tenants with the front door and flat keys. When I ask if they can contact him they say it isn't their responsibility. Eventually after much discussion they give me a contact number for me to ask him to ask them. Madness!

For most of the day I visit three nursing homes to check if any are suitable for my mum and if they have any vacancies. They are better than those I visited last week but none have space for my mum but two could have something available soon. I don't like to ask why in case I don't want to hear the reasons. At least there is a little light at the end of the tunnel but more visits are needed.

When I get back I phone a few more homes to visit. Once I complete the calls I start to get ready to see Gill, to be honest with you I don't know how to get ready for seeing her. On my way back I pick up a bottle of white wine, as she is cooking chicken. Dressing for dinner isn't difficult either. It is trying to get my head into the right frame of mind; it is at her place, our second or maybe third date, the first on our own and unsure quite how the evening will go.

I get out after parking my car on the opposite side to her home, a nice terraced house in a tree-lined street with a small front garden. I am a nervous wreck. I even forget to lock the car until I press her doorbell and turn round to check my car is parked safely. As I turn back Gill opens the door wearing a very nice black dress, very nice indeed, that is strapless with a plunging neckline. It is the happiest I have seen her; she looks positively radiant.

"Hi Chris! Welcome to my humble abode. I hope you like it." Stepping aside to let me in but not quite enough to avoid me having to brush past Gill and feel the outline of her body beneath the dress.

"Thank you. It's very nice from what I've seen so far." Handing over my bottle of wine to Gill as I spoke.

"Ooh, wine! It will go with my bottle I've chilled in the fridge. Yes, I hope you get to see it all!" she said with a twinkle in her eye.

Not knowing how to respond I just smile back. I follow Gill who is now leading me into the kitchen with a dining area that looks out on to her garden at the back.

"Now the dinner is cooking in the oven, there's nothing I need to do for a while so why don't I open my wine that's chilled in the fridge and replace it with yours for later?" I just nod.

Holding two large glasses of white wine, she moves towards me and hands me one. "Would you like me to show you round my place or shall we just sit and chat?"

I respond, "I'd like to sit and chat please." Why did I say "please"? My nerves are shredding me of normal thoughts.

"How has your day been?" Gill asks smiling brightly at me.

"It's been a boring day visiting nursing homes for my mum to move to, asking the same questions and so on."

"Oh, I don't remember you saying anything about your mum. Then again, not sure if I asked."

"It's all happened recently so there won't have been much to say. It's such a grind seeing one after the other and trying to check which you feel she will like."

"My mum and dad are still around but not together any more. They've each got new partners now. They separated when I was young; I hadn't left school. I see my mum quite often but not so much with my dad."

"My dad died some time ago, my mum and dad were still in love when he passed away. She still misses him and doesn't want anyone else in her life apart from me. Neither of us sees much of my sister so it feels like being the only child. My mum and I are close so my mum being happy is important to me."

"You may remember I told you I have an older sister and younger brother but we're not close. There are a few years between each of them and me. We never really had that much in common and so on.

I can't remember the last time I spoke with either of them."

We both pause and sip our wine. I look around at the kitchen with its units and worktop with various containers.

"It looks like you're keen on cooking looking at all you have here." Gesturing towards the worktop.

"It looks like that, mainly collected from each time I've been with someone. I'm terribly lazy when I'm on my own and just warm up something from the freezer. I like to cook for someone rather than just me."

"I find it a new experience as my ex really liked cooking and was very good at it. I tended to do other chores around the house that she didn't like so much. I dreaded cooking the first few times, found it stressful, but now I enjoy it. I haven't had too many disasters and have cooked the odd meal when a friend's come round and no one's died of food poisoning yet." Gill giggles a little.

"Well I hope you don't judge my cooking too harshly. It's a chicken casserole; everything is in one container. It should be ready in about 20 minutes."

"I must do more dishes like that. It's easy to scale up or down with recipes. What's your favourite dish?

"What, apart from you?" Gill laughs and smiles; I just blush. "That's a difficult one but I do like a piece of red meat, cooked to perfection, that just slides into my mouth and down my throat." There is a twinkle in her eye that makes me wonder if she maybe thinking of something else.

"Why don't I show you round?" said Gill getting up and going to the fridge to top up both our glasses, handing mine back to me and walking into the hallway in one seamless movement - I just follow meekly.

Gill gives me a tour of her house, the stairway, landing, bathroom and both bedrooms finishing with her own. It is nicely decorated, maybe not entirely to my own taste, and the bed looks very comfy with plenty of pillows arranged at the top with vivid colours.

"What do you think?"

Again I am unsure of the exact meaning of her question so I remove any doubt, at least in my mind, with my answer.

"Your house is lovely, I like the way you have decorated each room."

"Thanks, that means a lot to me. I want it to be a home as well as a house."

With that we move out of the bedroom and down into the kitchen where I sit at the table while Gill serves dinner. She also uncorks my bottle of wine and tops up our glasses, we clink them and toast each other before eating our chicken, which is very tasty.

We discuss over dinner our different work situations. Gill is pleased; partly I feel out of guilt, that my business is going well with other clients. I am interested in some of the office gossip about the attendees and what to expect with my next check-in call for further work soon. After another top-up of our wine glasses by Gill she brings a large bowl of strawberries, raspberries, mango, melon and blueberries with a jug of cream from her fridge.

It's one of my favourite deserts and I smile widely in anticipation; Gill sees this and smiles back appreciatively. I take several spoonfuls of fruit that fill up my bowl almost not leaving any space for cream to complete the perfect mix for me. After waiting for Gill to serve herself a smaller amount I tuck into mine enthusiastically. Little is said beyond my praise for her choice of fruits, their taste and how she cut them up.

Gill says, "I never knew you were such a fruity man." Again I just smile at the hint of double meaning with her comments.

Clearing the table Gill asks if I want coffee, real ground filter coffee, not instant from a jar to which I say, "Yes please!" sit back and watch her make it. As I relax a few random thoughts come into my mind; firstly I can't remember when I last enjoyed a meal like this; secondly Gill is a great host; thirdly and bizarrely I must call my sister about mum; lastly I have drank a lot of wine and can't drive home. The last just hovers in the back of my mind without an obvious solution.

As if Gill is reading my mind she asks, "When is the last time you had a meal like this?"

"I really can't remember it must be when I was with Em but we both seemed so busy and our lives so distant from each other. That will be quite a few years ago! How about you Gill?"

"My ex wasn't into cooking like this. He was more dinners that you warm up from the freezer to sit and eat in front of the TV. My ex ex was probably the last time I cooked a meal like this and that was a while ago."

Our conversation moves to past relationships. While I talk about a marriage that lasted around 25 years before fragmenting, Gill talks about a dozen relationships that had foundered for one reason or another - some her fault, some her boyfriend at the time. It really does seem Gill had a very messy love life up to this point. She was also unhappy, insecure and anxious still to find the right man for her. Who that will be she didn't seem sure.

"I want to find someone whose arms I can fall into and feel safe and warm; someone who is capable of loving me as much as I love them; someone who is always there for me. Is that asking for too much Chris?" she looks directly into my eyes.

"I don't think so. Have you come close to finding that yet?"

"I think I have with each relationship I enter into. But then things go wrong or I realise they're not the right one after all."

"What's the longest relationship you've had?"

"Ooh, that's a hard question. I don't know off the top of my head. I bought this house with Chris yes, same name as you, over 10 years ago and we were together for at least 6 years before he took a job in Dubai, not for a short contract, it was permanent. He said it completely out of the blue just before he left for work one morning. So casual with it he was as if it was something that happens every day. I felt so bad I stayed at home and cried for most of the day."

I didn't really want to pry into her previous relationships but try to see if there was a pattern that emerged about why they ended.

"What's the longest time you've been on your own?"

"This period. I told my ex to leave three months ago."

That didn't seem long especially to me. I have been separated from Em for over a year and only recently dipped my toe back into the dating pool.

It also opens the floodgates for Gill to offload what happened with her ex. Basically he was cheating on her with one of her friends. That was doubly devastating, to lose a friend as well as her boyfriend. Gill met him within one month of splitting from her ex ex as she refers to him and he moved in soon after. They were together for six months, hardly any time at all to really find out who each other are in my opinion.

It seems this followed a similar pattern for Gill. She can attract men easily but not necessarily the right man for her and finds it difficult to make it last for any length of time. They either lose interest in her or she in them after a few months of bliss.

Gill also doesn't stay on her own for long either before a man attracts her or a man is attracted to her or just because she doesn't want to be on her own for long. Maybe she doesn't like her own company for long or is more prepared to put up with the lows in any relationship because the highs make it worthwhile?

Whatever other reasons there may have been, they are interrupted by Gill suddenly moving from her chair to sitting on my lap, putting her hands either side of my head and giving me a full-on kiss; lips, tongues, the whole lot. After what seems like a lifetime we part, both our faces flushed, eyes sparkling and dive back in for another locking of tongues as we kiss passionately.

When we part this time Gill settles in my lap, her legs across the arm of my chair and her body close to my chest. I put my arms around her shoulders as if it is natural and what we have done forever.

"I think you are the one for me Chris."

I can't think of anything to say. I don't know what to think. I seem to be moving automatically without consciously thinking about it. We just sit together wrapped up in the moment, maybe fearing its magic will go if we think more.

It is getting dark but we just stay in each other's arms holding on, enjoying the warmth of each other. I can't recall when Em and I last had a moment like this. It feels so romantic and makes me yearn for more times like this. While my life is independent and satisfactory, I realise a chasm exists where no love, romance and care for or by someone special. Is Gill my special friend after all?

Eventually we move and Gill pulls the curtains but instead of putting a light on she beckons me to follow her through the door into the hallway. I move towards her and instinctively hold her hand, so warm and tender. As we climb the stairs all thoughts of how I am going to get home, when I am going home or how much I have drunk disappear into the recesses of my mind. For now my world consists of just Gill and me.

DAY 41: THURSDAY

I would love to tell you that last night was the most romantic night of my life. I'd love to say we made mad passionate love the whole nightlong. I wish I could say we moved together as if we had known each other all our lives. I also wish we had sworn undying love to each other, never to be parted. I want to say all these things but I will be lying if I do.

It started off well. In the soft light of her bedside lamps we embrace and slowly untangle each other from our clothing. I don't recall any awkward moments as parts of bodies not normally shown publicly come into view for the first time to each other. I can't speak for Gill of course but she never recoils at any time as she disrobes me. In fact our clothes seem to come off at an increasing pace along with frantic holding and feeling of each other for the first time.

I haven't been this aroused or excited in my life. Holding, touching, looking and loving a different woman to Em is a revelation! I burst with love and energy and excitement for Gill. She is like Em except she isn't. Everything is where it should be yet it is different in shape, texture, amount and it is all so lovingly given to me for my enjoyment.

As I say it starts off well, very well, but then we hit a snag when Gill asks if I brought any 'protection' meaning condoms. I haven't and said so. How can I be that presumptuous that we will end up making love by the end of the evening?

"Oh, it's just that I came off the pill after my ex left. It gives me side effects. I've got some condoms somewhere. I keep some spare ones here… just in case."

"Ok, ok," I said, feeling my erection shrink with each word we exchange. 'Spare ones' and 'just in case' somehow takes the edge off what is a special moment.

After a few moments fumbling around in a drawer in her bedside table she brings out a box. "Do you know what size you are? You know, small, medium or large? What about ribbed or smooth? I'm up for anything!"

I felt I was making love; sweet beautiful love but the way Gill describes it, it sounded like she is just having sex and making do with any condom sheathed penis that find its way into her vagina. The magic goes for me along with my erection. I just don't know what to say… or do.

"What's the matter Chris? Do you need a helping hand? Are you a shy one?" Gill says in a seductive voice but in an insensitive way that doesn't help. Still I don't say anything, just try to shrivel up like my penis has. What was a magnificent high comes crashing down to an ignominious low.

After wrestling with the wrapper I ask Gill if she can stimulate me so I am ready for action again. To be fair she does succeed and it is enjoyable again but it is more fumbling around with frustration than steady progress with an explosive climax. Needless to say after half an hour of this we call it off and lie down side by side in silence, both looking up at the ceiling lost in our own thoughts. Then Gill deals the hammer blow to my feelings.

"This has never happened to me before." There it laid, her damning indictment on my manhood, to grow and engulf our evening, our hopes and our expectations. What can I say? It's all too soon for me? I need wooing first? I am not a 'wham bam, thank you ma'am' man before I started seeing Em. Notches on bedposts are never my idea of fun.

"It's never happened to me either. Maybe it's all a bit too much, too soon?"

"Well that's never been said to me before either! It's always been the other way round."

"Well I'm sorry this has happened. What do you want me to do now?"

"I don't know. It's all such an anti climax isn't it? Do you want to stay? We can try again in the morning? Seems a bit pointless if you go now."

I don't fancy calling a cab and then getting one back tomorrow morning when I'm sober and can drive my car again. Staying the night and seeing how we both are tomorrow sounds more tempting.

"I'd like to stay. Let's see what tomorrow brings."

"OK and I would like someone to cuddle up to tonight. It gets cold and lonely in this big bed."

But the following morning, this morning, neither of us really wants to pick up on the night before and see where it leads to today.

The cold light of day gives a different appearance to my situation and I want to withdraw with grace and review rather than plough on whatever the consequences. Gill doesn't deter me from being like this I notice. Maybe this has all been a horrible mistake? I am sure that will be Rachel's view if she ever gets to hear about it of that I am 100% certain.

I don't bother with breakfast; Gill is going to work although she hinted last night she could take the day off or work from home. I want to be out before her and drive back home as soon as possible. We do make an effort and promise to call each other but apart from a hug and some kissing there isn't a fraction of the warmth we showed to each other last night.

Getting back home I take stock over a pot of coffee of what did and did not happen, trying to rationalise it to make sense of it all… and fail miserably. My mood is interrupted by a call from the estate agent, Robert, who wants to know who will be surveying the property. I don't because I haven't thought about it! I say I will get back later today with their details and start searching online for any surveyor who is local. After wasting 45 fruitless minutes trying to find one I suddenly try Maureen who may be able to help. One short call to her later and I am able to give Robert the name and contact details of a reputable, local, independent surveyor who Maureen recommends as ideal with flat purchases.

The interruption causes my mood to lift and as I collect my thoughts I realise there are two nursing homes I am due to visit this afternoon. Changing my focus from Gill to my mum helps keep my spirits going and it is a fairly good afternoon as both homes are the best I have seen so far. In fact either will be suitable for my mum; the problem is neither has vacancies in the 'foreseeable future' with the caveat that one could become 'unexpectedly available at short notice should a resident depart'. I knew what they mean by 'depart' and partly want someone to die and partly dread that being how a room becomes available.

By the time I am back home after doing some food shopping and wine too of course, I check my emails and find some awaiting me from my clients including a cryptic one from Brian of Brian & Co. asking me to call him urgently. It is too late now but I will call him first thing tomorrow. The rest are follow-ups on work I bid for or how things are with some business colleagues I network with. Dinner beckons me.

After eating I sit down with a glass of wine and check my dating site. There are some likes but no messages from women I contacted. I check for any new women and message two with my standard enquiry. Maybe I need to change it? It doesn't seem to be working too well recently. Maybe it is my profile, not the message and I? Maybe I just need to be patient and keep plugging away?

Which makes me come back to what is in the back of my mind – Gill. How do you solve a problem like Gill (not Maria as the song title goes)? I have no idea whether to text, call her or do nothing and see what happens. I go over and over the pros and cons for a long time without coming to any conclusion. It seems Gill may be doing the same thing as neither of us contacts the other.

DAY 42: FRIDAY

I am up early so I can take my car to a garage I have used for years to service and MOT my car. It is a few years old now but I am attached to my car. It has been a loyal servant and I am happy with it; my car is nippy, ok for motorways, economic around the town and can carry four passengers (six on one mad journey) and my bags when I am food shopping. A 'good runaround' if not a 'real belter' will best describe my car although I haven't gone so far as to give it a name.

Dropping it off early means there is a good chance I can pick it up before the rush hour congestion slows down my journey. I catch the train back to my home and settle down to a relaxing day sorting my work and personal emails. However all these plans change as soon as I turn the corner and see Danny waiting on the doorstep with a big rucksack and suitcase that looks very full of clothes and other stuff. This doesn't look good; it doesn't look good at all.

"Hi Danny, I wasn't expecting to see you today. In fact I haven't heard let alone seen you for a while." I stay standing on the pavement indicating to Danny that he needs to speak before he can enter.

"Mum's chucked me out. Can I stay with you?" Danny mumbles sheepishly, looking down at the steps. Straight and to the point with the minimum of words and effort, that is Danny all over!

Not wanting to draw attention to us in front of Meghan's front room window even if she is still in a good mood I quickly say, "OK, but I want to know why."

Inside we go, I help Danny with his suitcase, we climb the stairs to my place. I realise it had been some time since Danny or Liz have been to see me, what with uni and all that, and I should ask Liz round - for a meal, not to stay too – I'm not sure my nerves can stand both staying here or the discussion with Liz I keep putting off having!

While I put the kettle on to make coffee, strong coffee - I need it – I quickly scan my emails and see a new message from my dating site. Leaving that until later I focus on making coffee while Danny merges into the sofa trying to make himself as small as possible. We don't say anything until I put the coffee pot on the table with two cups, milk and cream (Danny hates cream with coffee, I love it).

"Well son, it's always good to see you but this is a bit unexpected and to be honest you haven't been in touch much recently. So, what's going on?"

"Mum chucked me out first thing this morning." Danny repeated and looks at the coffee pot waiting for me to pour him some. "Can I have some coffee?"

"It needs to percolate for a few minutes. I want to know what's happened since we last spoke a few weeks ago. You're hardly Mr. Communicator!"

"I don't really want to talk about it."

"Well if you want to stay I will need to know why and for how long. I hope to move from here soon if my flat purchase goes through ok."

"It'll just be for a while, nothing permanent."

"Too right it won't be permanent... and I haven't said yes yet! You need to talk or this is going to be a very short stay."

Danny stays silent, weighing up his options, working out his story no doubt; while I plunge the filter down the percolator then pour coffee into each cup. I pass Danny's to him to put the milk in while I pour cream into mine. As I sit back my mobile rings and I see it is Brian of Brian & Co. calling. Thinking it must be urgent I excuse myself and walk into the kitchen area.

"Brian? How can I help?"

"Hi Chris, just following up on my email. Is there any chance you can come to see me today? Something urgent has cropped up." Brian doesn't sound like his normal self.

"My car is in the garage being serviced today and I've got a bit of a domestic crisis with my son turning up on my doorstep just now. Can it wait until Monday?"

"Oh..." clearly deflated at my response "If that's the first chance then it will have to be Monday. Can you make it first thing please?"

"Yes, sure. Is there anything I can help you with now over the phone?"

"No, no, best wait until Monday and talk in person."

"OK Brian, have a good weekend meanwhile."

"Yes, bye." And that was it, not the usual Brian at all. What has happened? I am drifting off into possible reasons for this change when I hear Danny cough which brings me back into the room.

Turning round and sitting back in my chair I say, "So Danny, it's time to spill the beans now…"

"I've screwed up a bit dad. Things haven't gone to plan."

"Oh? Do go on…"

"I met a girl, Cass, in my last semester and we got on really well; she's studying Economics. Anyway one thing led to another and we've pretty much been together 24/7 for the last few weeks at uni what with studying for our finals and so on." I silently drink my coffee not wanting to interrupt Danny.

"Well after we finish our exams she asks if I want to stay at her parents' place. They live in Lancashire and she says it will be OK. They're really nice, just a bit strict on what Cass can and cannot do with boys at their home. Anyway one thing leads to another and while we are in separate rooms we spend a lot of time in hers…" I think I am starting to guess where this may be going but keep quiet.

"Anyway one night while we are together there is a knock on the door and her mum interrupts us if you know what I mean. It is embarrassing and there is a big scene with lots of shouting and from her mum and crying from Cass. Then her dad comes in and starts shouting at me. The end result is I go back to my room, pack my bags first thing in the morning and leave without even saying goodbye to Cass."

It is tempting to stop it there but I want the full version. "Go on Danny."

"Well I call mum and ask her if she can send me some money to pay for my train ticket. I then buy my ticket and get home. When I get there Liz is staying at a friend's and it is just mum's new boyfriend and I; he's creepy. When I tell mum what happened she just says, "Go and stay with your father. I'm not having you stay here if you behave like that. I mean! What right has mum to say that? She's gone through a string of boyfriends since you left. Every time I call it's a different voice answering the phone if she's not there! I did plead but she won't have it and just says I can stay one night, that's last night and now I'm here. Please let me stay dad." The last sentence is said in such a plaintive way. Danny is desperate.

"OK Danny you can dump your stuff in the spare bedroom and stay until you can go back or find somewhere else."

The relief on Danny's face will be something I will cherish for a very long time. Part of me is pleased to have him here; part of me dreads the end of my independence and freedom to do whatever I want in my own home. I would never have done what Em did if, and it is if, Danny's version is complete and accurate. He does have a habit of editing out any bad stuff and must have thought about what to say while travelling to me.

Danny scampers to the spare bedroom quickly in case I might change my mind. I start to think through the consequences of my decision; food, bathroom sharing, spare bedding, who watches what on the TV, the list is endless. I decide I have enough on my plate without adding any more to that list.

Opening up my laptop I go to my dating site to read a message from Great Dane. As usual it is direct if surprisingly revealing about her.

'Hi Good Guy, you are the first man I will be seeing since my husband died of cancer 8 years AGO. My two children still miss him.'

That is all she says, nothing else. I don't know what to say to it, there isn't really anything that feels appropriate. It makes me think the stakes become higher and I feel pressure that she chose me as the first man to see. Why? What is so different about me? Maybe I will find out on Sunday?

I make more coffee; I need more fuel for my brain to think more about Danny. The only people who can confirm or challenge his version of events are not people I can contact. Em obviously not and Cass I had no idea existed until half an hour ago. It seems some father-son bonding is needed and see where that leads. I walk up to the door of the spare bedroom, knock and enter to find Danny spread out on the bed with his eyes closed, suitcase open and contents strewn across the floor. I cough and Danny quickly opens his eyes.

"Looks like you've made yourself at home already. If you're going to stay here until things are sorted we need some ground rules so we live together happily. OK?"

Danny grunts and nods his head as he sits up on the bed. "Put your clothes away in the drawer unit and hang everything in the wardrobe; there are plenty of spare hangers. If you leave it like that I might be tempted to think you want to leave now." Danny shakes his head quickly then; I feel I have struck a nerve. "When you've done that we can have some lunch."

My mobile rings as I leave Danny's room; it is my garage. Thinking this is a record time for a service and MOT for my car I answer in a cheerful tone.

"Hello!"

"Mr. Davison?"

"Yes."

"It's about your car."

"Yes."

"I'm afraid we've run into a bit of a problem."

"Oh?"

"When we checked the brakes we found they need replacing. They're very worn down and will become dangerous soon."

"Oh! Well thank goodness you did. I've said I'll pay for any parts and labour on top of the service and MOT."

"Yes, thank you, we know but that's not the problem. The problem is we can't get hold of the parts until Monday at the earliest."

Silently cursing for choosing a Friday rather than another weekday for the service I grit my teeth.

"Isn't there anything you can do before then?"

"Not really. It's not like we can cannibalise another model for the brake parts these days. Breaker yards aren't what they used to be and with brakes you really want brand new parts with a warranty. I'm sure you can understand our position."

I do but it is a blow. Not having my car feels like not having my mobile or right arm. It just doesn't feel normal.

"OK, thanks for letting me know. Can you let me know if something happens to change things today?"

"Sure Mr. Davison and I'm sorry for the bad news. Have a good weekend."

"Thanks, likewise."

Weekend… oh no, how will I get to see Great Dane at Battle? Bugger! I don't know if any alternatives will work; a bus or train on a Sunday isn't a prospect I look forward to. What should have been a straightforward day is rapidly going pear-shaped. Just then Danny appears.

"What's for lunch dad?"

"I don't know. I think it will be cold, you know bread, and salad and whatever goes with it that's in the fridge. Can you put it on the worktop and help yourself? I've just found out my car won't be ready today. I've got no transport for the weekend now."

"Can't you hire a car?"

"Yes I can but it will cost a fortune at such short notice."

"Guess you'll have to train and bus it like me then."

"Looks like it."

Between us we get lunch together and sit down for our first meal in ages. We munch our meals contentedly and chat about lighter stuff like the Albion's chances next season. We also moan about Sussex having another bad cricket season, not that either of us ever goes. Danny used to go to football when I got him a ticket if either James or Gordon couldn't make it but hasn't since he's been at university. With lunch finished I want to find out more about Danny.

"What are your plans Danny?"

"Dunno, nothing at the moment."

"Are you in touch with Cass?"

"Nothing since I left her. She's not answering her mobile."

"Do you want to continue seeing her from long distance?"

"Not sure, just want to talk and then see how we feel."

"I'm not doing much today or tomorrow but I'm off to Battle Sunday afternoon."

"You're going to fight?"

I laugh. "No Battle not battle, the place. I'm meeting someone."

"Is this one of your dates?"

"Yes."

"Didn't think you'd still be doing it after this long."

"It's only been a few weeks. These things can take a long time. I'd like to find the right person."

"Bet you thought that when you met mum." That hits home and hurts.

"Yes I did and it was for many years. Sometimes people change, drift apart and have different interests."

"Mum's certainly changed!"

"Oh! Do you want to say more?"

"She gets more and more bitter about things. She's no fun any more. Now it's all about what she gave up for us, how her career stalled because of us, how unhappy her life has been, how ungrateful we are for all the sacrifices she made. She's re-written our family history to fit with this. I've never done a thing right and always been trouble from the moment I was born. It's been hard staying at home with this in your face all the time. I leave uni late and go back early to cut down how much time I spend with her. Liz has done the same to a lesser degree but I know she's sick and tired of it too."

Wow! This is revelatory news and also explains the change from re-mortgaging our house to selling it without any prior warning. It doesn't auger well for completing our divorce and worries me about the place my heart is set on buying.

"That's very helpful Danny and explains a few things that mum has done that affect me. I'm really sorry she has become like this and how our divorce is affecting you. It's cramped here with just that small room as your bedroom but you won't be hassled unless the few ground rules I have are broken by you... like leaving the top off the milk."

I smile and Danny smiles back at an old bad habit he had of not screwing the top back on the milk. One disastrous moment had brought it all to a head when I lifted a nearly full carton of milk out of the fridge; the top slipped off spilling milk in a wide arc all round the kitchen as I had moved. It took a while to clean up and Danny spent the rest of the day in his room not playing outside with his mates. The top on the milk has never been loose since that incident.

"This place is really only meant for one person so we will need to tolerate each other; noise, space, washing, etc. All the basics we will need to work together so we're not in each other's way and arguing the whole time. Agreed?"

"Sure dad. Just being here without being moaned at for hours is a million times better than being at mum's already."

"Let's hope that lasts." My mobile rings and I look at the screen to see it is Gill calling. Another surprise to add to others today I think. "Hi Gill! It's good to hear from you."

"Hi Chris! I hope you're OK. I'm at work so I need to make this call short but I didn't want to wait."

"OK, go ahead. I'm listening."

"Would you like to come to a party with me tomorrow night? You'll need to get a train or cab to where it is."

"Sounds interesting. Yes I'd love to go with you. What are the arrangements?"

"I'll text them to you later. Must go. Love you!" and Gill ends the call. It isn't how I thought our next conversation would go but I have another date with her and it is ages since I last went to a party. I admit my dance moves are rusty and probably way out of date. I tell Danny, who is all ears while I take the call.

"Good for you dad! I hope she's better than most of mum's boyfriends." I don't want a comparison; it isn't a competition between Em and I but Danny's support heartens me.

"Better avoid any of your 'dad dancing' though!"

"What do you mean?"

"I've seen you in the kitchen moving to a song and it's a bit awkward watching you. Just stick with being close to her. The more you flail your arms and legs about the worse it gets!"

"Cheek! I'll do my best to curtail those moves. I won't want to poke someone in the eye."

"Especially not your girlfriend! Ha ha ha!" It is good to hear laughter in my place and Danny can be great fun. Maybe this might work out between us?

"Where's the gig dad?"

"Sorry… ?"

"Where is the party?"

"I don't know. She's going to let me know later."

"You party animal. Go dad! Go dad!"

We laugh, smile and pat each other on the back. I am enjoying these moments more than I expected. I am not nervous and tense after the call but feel relaxed and happy.

The rest of the afternoon we spend going over a few ground rules; squeeze the right end of the toothpaste; use up containers open in the fridge first, remote control left on the table not stuck down the side of the sofa, that sort of thing. We both seem relieved to be together for the first time in a long time; there is no stress, no tension, it is lovely and different in a very positive way.

Danny goes back to the spare room to unpack the rest of his stuff and try to clear some more space with all that I have dumped in there that I don't use frequently or still need to sort through for rubbish or recycling. I act on a few work emails from Harry Stokes and Brian & Co.'s team but not Brian. I then ask Danny if he fancies a walk but he wants to "chill" instead.

After I am back, refreshed from the sea air and sunshine, I put the kettle on. I ask Danny if he wants anything but he shakes his head. He knows he can help himself within reason to whatever he wants. I make my tea and go back into his room. He is acting more like his old self, only doing what is necessary, no wasted effort, unless he absolutely has to.

"I will be making a spaghetti Bolognese for dinner. I don't mind doing that but it will be good if you wash up afterwards." Danny looks at me quizzically.

"Is that a joke? Haven't you got a dishwasher?"

"No Danny, no such luxuries here. It's what you find when you rent a place that's not your own."

"Humph, OK then. I'll wash up."

I prepare the meal, play some music to set the scene and within an hour or so call to Danny that dinner is ready.

"Did you want a glass of wine with me? I normally have one with my meal."

Danny's raises his eyebrows, "One? Nah, I'll have a bottle of something. What have you got?"

"I haven't anything else, just wine. It's just me that lives here normally. Have you got any money for shopping or beer?"

"No I haven't. My grant's used up and I'm close to maxing out on my loan. I expected mum to help out."

"She still can. Have you two been in touch?"

"No I am leaving it for a bit."

"Well don't leave it too long. The Bank of dad will only stretch so far."

"OK, point taken."

"Have you been in touch with Cass?"

"Yeah, we finally spoke while you were out."

"And…"

"No dice. It's over. She says she doesn't want to see me now she's left uni. She's too embarrassed to stay with her parents and is staying with a friend. My first real relationship and it's gone in a moment."

"I'm sorry Danny. It must hurt. Maybe you will see the risks with relationships that are long distance in time? Don't be too hard on yourself."

"Yeah… maybe."

"What have you got planned?"

"Nothing really. Most of my friends I have at uni are back with their parents. Most of the friends I have before uni I've lost touch with. Not sure what to do really…"

"Well I've got nothing planned during the day tomorrow. How about we pop into Brighton for the day? Go to a few of the old haunts we did when you were younger."

"Sounds alright," Danny says in a subdued voice. There is nothing worse than a sulky teenager.

"I've got fresh fruit and there might be a tin of peaches but that's all if you want dessert. We'll need to do a food shop if you're staying for a while. Might be a good idea if you can speak to mum for a contribution towards it so you can choose stuff you want?"

"Not now, tomorrow."

"OK, just saying. If you've finished the washing up awaits you. There's gloves and stuff if you want to use them."

"Cheers." Danny shuffles over to the sink and plods his way through the detritus of the meal making lots of noise as he clanks and clinks my crockery and cutlery.

I relax, pour another glass of wine (yes Danny is right about more than one glass) and reflect on what a day it has been. I message Liz to ask how she is and to let her know where her brother is. She quickly replies saying she isn't surprised. Things haven't been good between Em and Danny for a while and she is pleased to be out of their firing line. It is one reason why she is staying with a friend but she might go home earlier now. Again the subject of my dating or how she was on our last call are ignored for now.

Then I send an update to Rachel minus any details about Gill. Her reply is quick too. 'Wow! There's a lot going on! Good luck!' After checking everything is ok with her which she confirms I wait for Danny to finish the washing up that he is oh so slowly doing. When he finishes he flops down on the sofa with a loud sigh; obviously I am working him too hard!

"Fancy watching a film we both like Danny?"

"Yeah, what have you got?"

"I've got all my DVDs up there on the shelf."

"No, I meant what service have you got. Netflix? Prime?"

"None, just terrestrial and Freeview channels."

"You mean to say you've got no satellite channels!"

"Yes."

"Jeez, that's like going back to the dark ages dad."

"Well, it works for me since I left your mum. I don't see the need to change it now... unless you're paying the extra for any of these services."

"Da-a-ad!"

"Sorry son, it's iPlayer and so on for recorded stuff or DVDs for films here."

"This is going to be so boring."

"Well you can always go to mum's." Playing my trump card.

"OK, you win." And he gets up to scan the DVDs several times before reluctantly choosing one, a TV comedy series we used to watch together as a family. I like his choice and put it on.

The rest of the evening is spent laughing and chatting about memories when we first watched it and just enjoying each other's company. I have spent far worse evenings with Danny than this one for sure. I go to bed earlier than him who promises to keep the noise down and switch the lights and TV off when he is tired.

DAY 43: SATURDAY

Two objectives are all I have in mind for today, to have a good time with Danny during the day and with Gill during the evening.

The first objective is difficult when I realise how late teenagers go to bed at night and therefore when they want to reluctantly wake up to face the next day. Trying to wake Danny is like trying to wake the dead. Boy, does he sleep soundly! Finally when he deigns to open his eyes by my persistent calling he passes on the chance to spend the day with his dad in Brighton after all.

Deciding not to waste the day I tell him I am going for a long walk and to make his breakfast, brunch or whatever is the appropriate time for when he finally surfaces and eats some food. The food shopping he will have to do or live out of the fridge and freezer, which I'm sure he will prefer as it involves less effort. Packing a lunch and water into my rucksack I leave for a shorter version of the walk I took when I first met Gill. Maybe it is karma? Maybe it is a good sign for later? Whether it is or not it is good to be out and breathe fresh air drifting in from the sea as I walk above the cliffs and admire the spectacular views.

When I get back later in the afternoon I still haven't heard from Gill with the details for tonight but Danny is awake.

"Sorry for that dad. I feel like I caught up on sleep for many nights last night, a real big catch-up sleep. How are you doing?"

"I'm fine, feel good after my walk. Not as good as being with you in Brighton nevertheless it was energising. My one consolation from the mess my life has been in is to be by the sea. The comfort I gain from it helps me through some of my bleaker moments over my divorce."

"Yeah, I know how much you love the sea. I remember you always talking about it when I was young. I have this weird memory of being rocked to sleep as you talked about how wonderful the sea was. Was it a dream or memory?"

"Gosh! I need to go back in time to picture those moments but I think it maybe memory and not a dream. I never realised how important the sea has been to me until you said that."

"Any time dad." Danny shrugs as he relaxes on my sofa.

Just then the first of a series of texts come through from Gill about this evening. By the time the final message arrives I know where to meet her at 8pm. It is a sort of work party/birthday celebration for two work colleagues mix. Never having been to the venue I check out train times and last train back home. I am not sure I want a repeat of events a few evenings ago so soon again.

With an hour to get ready and have something to eat I ask Danny if he fancies fish and chips, he nods strongly so I give him the cash and directions to the local chippy while I start to get ready with a shower and shave. After Danny returns we tuck into our large portions of fish and chips as we both have healthy appetites. Danny is intrigued with me going on a date never having experienced his dad doing this before. He thinks it is comical about me dating – full stop!

However, I reverse roles by saying goodbye to him and hoping he has a good evening at home while he wishes me a good time out and confirms it is an evening in front of the box for him. Oh the irony comparing it with our past lives! I make my way to the station to catch the train.

Arriving at the venue with a few minutes to spare I call Gill to hear she has already arrived judging by the background noise from music blaring out inside the venue. She meets me at the entrance, pecks me gently on the cheek and guides me into the place where there are at least 100 people either stationary drinking at a bar or in groups around tables or moving to the groove on the dance floor. It seems the party has been going for a while which puzzles me why I haven't been asked to come earlier by Gill. Anyway, things are good and after getting drinks we manage to converse either by shouting during a song or whispering between them.

As the evening unfolds Gill gestures to the dance floor and, avoiding my worst dad dancing moves, we gyrate to a mix of fast and slow music. It is great feeling Gill's body close to mine for the slow numbers while watching it move to the faster ones in a tight fitting outfit that didn't leave much to the imagination. We are enjoying ourselves until Gill excuses herself for the toilets. I weave my way through the throng to the bar and buy drinks while waiting for her to return.

Five minutes pass, then ten and I start to look round more anxiously for her. There is no one I know apart from Gill to ask if anyone has seen her. She didn't introduce me to any colleagues from work. I carry the drinks from the bar and start moving through the spectators without success until I finally get to the other side of the hall without seeing Gill. Pausing to take stock I gaze absent-mindedly at the dancers and see in a corner Gill dancing with a man. Not only is she dancing but also it is very intensive with her arms around his neck, face close to his with a big grin gazing into his eyes, and bodies close almost grinding into each other.

My face flushes partly with anger but also with embarrassment even though no one apart from me knows that Gill is my girlfriend. Girlfriend? If she were my girlfriend then surely she wouldn't behave like that? What is my relationship to her? More importantly what do I mean to her? After all, it is her who invited me here not the other way round. I take a deep gulp from my glass as I watch and wait. I almost drop my glass when at the end of the dance she embraces and locks lips with her dance partner and they walk off arm in arm without seeing me.

What shall I do? Confront her or act as if nothing happened? After a few minutes think I decide what to do and move my way in the direction she took with her dance partner. Eventually I see them both at the bar laughing together as she is buying drinks for both of them. I move up to both of them until Gill turns round and notices me by their side.

"Oh, hello Chris."

"Hi Gill. Who is your dance partner?"

"Oh, this is Jamie." Then looking at him says, "Jamie this is Chris, Chris this is Jamie. Say hello to each other." Gill then giggles which annoys me more. I turn to Jamie and say.

"I like your dance moves. Where did you learn them from?"

Clearly neither realised that I have seen them and I feel the mood change immediately.

"Just stuff I've picked up over the years. You know how it is."

"No, I don't know how it is. Tell me how it is." There is a sharp edge to my voice.

"Hey, don't get heavy. I was just dancing with Gill, that's all."

"It looked more than that from what I saw. What do you think Gill?"

"Don't be silly Chris. We are just having some fun. It's a party after all!"

"You invited me to this party. You didn't have to. I buy you a drink and wait and wait for you to return from the loo only to find after some time you're dancing and from what everyone saw a bit more than dancing with this guy here. Is that how you usually behave?"

Jamie trying to be helpful has the opposite effect "Hey, steady on! Gill is just being her normal party self. Enjoying herself, share and share alike, eh?"

"Is that right Gill?" I turn and look her straight in her eyes.

"Chris! Don't make a scene. Let's go and dance?"

"No thanks. I don't want to follow the same path that Jamie has already taken with you."

"Hey, you can't talk to her like that!" said Jamie.

"Oh, can't I? What do you call what you did then?"

"I didn't know Gill had anyone with her."

Turning to Gill, "Is that right?"

Gill just looks up to the ceiling and doesn't say a word. I make my decision in an instant and turn to Jamie.

"Well she hasn't now. Good luck!" then turning to Gill I say, "Bye Gill. Have a good time with Jamie," and stride to the exit and exhale deeply in the cooler air outside while carrying on to the station. Thankfully neither Gill nor Jamie tries to stop me or call or text me after I leave. I reflect as I wait at the station, I have plenty of time to do this as I just missed my train to compound the misery, on what happened. Clearly Gill can't resist any man's attention it seems to me. Even if we could make our relationship work I will always feel this pressure that it may be only a matter time before it ends. Do I want that with someone rather than be on my own? The answer is clearly a loud 'No!' and I block her number and delete her contact details from my mobile there and then.

When I enter my flat it is empty, no Danny. Nonplussed I walk around my flat ending with the spare room where the door is closed. I knock gently then hearing no response louder and enter. The room is as it was before Danny arrived; all his stuff, suitcase and rucksack are gone along with him. I check my mobile but see I haven't missed a message or call from him this evening. Mystified I walk back into my living area and spot a note beside the coffee jar. It is a hastily written note from Danny.

'Hi dad, hope you had a great time. Cass called me and asked me to join her at one of her friends in London. She says she misses me. Sorry to leave you like this but I can't say no. Wish me luck! Danny x'

Chucked by my son as well as my girlfriend in the same evening!

DAY 44: SUNDAY

Today is the day I will finally get to meet Great Dane, something to lift my hangover after what happened with Gill. Whichever way I look at yesterday evening's events it is hard to see what Gill did in a good light. Most importantly even if behaving like that is her normal behaviour it certainly isn't anything I will be comfortable with. Em never behaved or even wanted to behave like that while with me.

It is another hard, very hard, lesson that I learn. Don't they say beauty is just skin deep? Gill is good looking, maybe beautiful, on the outside but her personality inside has a fatal flaw as far as I am concerned that will mean we can never have a meaningful relationship. I wonder if that is why her relationships keep ending. Anyway, it is no longer my problem and I wish her luck but will never talk to her again; life is too short.

Instead I look forward to Great Dane this afternoon. As I have breakfast, shower and dress it is good to know this follows after Gill. The only wrinkle is my car being out of action and relying on trains.

However it looks like a normal Sunday service and the forecast is for sunshine so that is good. It crosses my mind there may be last minute cancellation or delay; I don't have Great Dane's contact details apart from the dating site.

I go to the online dating site and message her with my mobile number and ask for hers in case either of us are delayed. Something about her site catches my eye and I click on her profile but it takes me to nothing. Her profile isn't there. Perhaps there is a technical glitch with the site? I leave it for a short while.

After pottering around my place sorting stuff as I want it to be now Danny has gone, I try the dating site again but still can't find her profile. Everyone else I am interested in still have their profiles so it increasingly looks like Great Dane has removed it. Why? That is a very big question and either way I look at it I don't like what it may mean.

There are two scenarios I can paint in my mind. Firstly Great Dane is so certain I am the right man for her after eight years of waiting that she decided to take her profile down. Secondly Great Dane has imploded and decided she isn't ready to meet me yet or ever. Either way it doesn't make me feel confident of a good outcome but I will still go through with this and see what does or doesn't happen.

After eating a light lunch (I haven't much of an appetite now) I make my way to the station where for once the connections are easy to make and the trains are on time. Maybe a good sign for seeing Great Dane I hope? I get to Battle with time to walk to where we agreed to meet, outside Battle Abbey. I have been here before, toured the battle site, read that it may not be the correct place where the battle took place and enjoyed the High Street and a few of the cafes.

As I am early I don't expect to see Great Dane when I arrive. I sit on a bench so I am in full view and can look around for anyone looking like Great Dane to appear. The time we agreed comes and passes and as the minutes tick away I start to have that sinking feeling. Checking train times after waiting for 45 minutes I decide she is not going to show and make my way to the station in time for my train so I don't make a bad afternoon even worse.

Whatever the reasons why Great Dane can't meet me it is the lack of contact, thought and natural politeness that hurts the most. One simple message would have saved me the inconvenience and waste of time going to Battle. I have never been stood up before but as is usual with these things it is the way it was done rather what was done that hurts me the most. While I am on the train I reflect on a very bad weekend, probably my worst time dating so far.

Do I really want to continue? Is it worth the pain, frustration and uncertainty that seem to stress a lot of my days and spoil them? I seriously consider cutting my losses and settling for being on my own. Life won't be so rich in emotion and love but it will be less pain and more under my control on what does and doesn't happen each day.

The alternative is to continue but it clearly needs to change from how I have approached it so far. All the way home I swing from continuing with dating through the full spectrum to ending it. While at home alone I realise how much I do miss company, in this case Danny's, and sit down to a cold tea. I'm afraid I drink a bottle of wine far too quickly for my liking; I open a second one to meet my continuing demand.

I slowly move away from deciding to quit online dating. It still hovers close by but more and more I think of how different my approach can be. I want to meet someone local who I can settle down with. When I think back on all the women I dated none are local; in fact not one has appeared on the dating site in all the time I have been searching! Maybe I should spread my net wider? Maybe subconsciously I am too limited in who I am looking for? I am open-minded to who I meet but possibly I haven't fully explored all the possibilities. Maybe a phoenix can rise from the ashes of my dating experiences so far? It can be a phoenix in the form of my special friend whoever and wherever she may be.

I spend the rest of the evening musing over these possibilities. I will sleep on it and see how I feel tomorrow. Needless to say there isn't a message from Great Dane, not that I am expecting one. Sadly I am getting used to dates or potential dates doing strange things without explanation.

DAY 45: MONDAY

My priority is to pick up my car but before I can I need to get an early train to meet Brian and find out what is so important that I have to see him in person this morning. I put my suit on and take any papers I feel may be relevant along with my trusty laptop. The trains again cooperate and I arrive at Brian's office before he does, always a plus point with a client I find.

I sit outside with a coffee, courtesy of his impressively efficient secretary who is already there when I arrive. Wondering what it can be about I sip my coffee and idly scroll through the latest news on my mobile. What catches my eye is Brighton splashing out a club record fee for a player from Germany. My football club is moving into the big time with transfer fees as well as the level of football it will play at – Premier League in every way now!

Brian arrives flustered, acknowledges me then briefly talks with his secretary before beckoning me into his office. After the usual niceties about how our weekends were – my version is severely limited to remove any mention of Gill or Great Dane – we get down to business.

"The situation with the project has changed somewhat since our meeting last week." Brian opens up with, "It means I will no longer be in charge of it, I will not be the project owner. I want you to take over that role. Your fees will increase to reflect the extra responsibility." I let the news sink in and slowly digest it. Questions and thoughts flood into my brain as I do this.

"Why Brian?"

"Because I'm moving on or more specifically I'm moving out."

"Moving out?"

"To pastures new as they say. The company no longer needs my post, my role, and have made a generous offer to encourage me to leave early."

"How early?"

"By the end of this week."

"Wow!' and I whistle, "That is quick!"

"To be honest it feels like it is better to jump now than be pushed later."

"I see. What about a handover?"

"This is it."

"How long have I got to decide?"

"My next meeting is in an hour. The more time you take to decide, the less time for the handover I'm afraid."

"What if I say no?"

"Well of course you're entitled to do that but it will mean that your contract is likely to be terminated and offered to someone else to be the project owner."

"OK, let me have a short break and I'll let you know."

Leaving Brian's office I go to the loo as an excuse to sit in a cubicle and process what he has said. I am not going to say "No" but I want to check there isn't anything I am missing. After considering everything we discussed I go back to Brian's office. Brian looks up from his laptop where he has been typing away.

"OK, I'll take the role of project owner subject to agreeing a satisfactory rate which I'm hope won't be difficult. What do I need to know when I take over Brian?"

Over the next three quarters of an hour Brian covers the project from the owner's perspective, reporting lines and update schedules. The project team will remain the same but they are not aware of his news until his next meeting with them, which follows directly after this one finishes. None of them have been identified as suitable successors as project owner; I take that as a compliment.

By the end my meeting with Brian I feel better briefed with fewer gaps in my knowledge. The time was inadequate so I will have to make the best of this sudden turn of events and show my fees are justified. I wish Brian all the best for the future, ask what he will do next (he is non-committal) and say it has been a pleasure working with him. He thanks me; we shake hands with the promise that my contract and project related documents would be emailed to me later this week. As I leave two project team members wait outside and look at me quizzically; I just smile, nod but don't say a word as I walk past them and out of the building.

The first thing I do is call my garage who have good news for me. The parts they need arrived first thing and are being fitted as we speak. It will take approximately another hour before everything including the MOT is completed. I thank him for the good news. It doesn't make sense to go home to come back out again so I find a café, order the largest latte they serve and sit back to check for emails and think about Brian.

He is a genuinely nice guy who I enjoy working with. He shields me from the politics and leaves me to utilise my time and use my expertise to best effect. I will miss working with him and hope he bounces back quickly from this news. Turning my mind to the future yes, there will be more responsibility and work to do but I hope the increased fee for my time will reflect that. I will wait until I hear from Brian or his team on next steps.

Looking at the time I finish my coffee, walk to the station and catch the next train. When I arrive at the garage there is a smiling mechanic looking at me. Thankfully there have been no snags and my car is fully serviced, passed its MOT and is ready for me to drive away. After paying the bill (prices have gone up a lot since last year!) I drive back home where I face an anxious Meghan on the doorstep.

"Do you have a minute Chris… to come in?"

"Sure Meghan. How can I help?"

"Colin is still disturbing me wanting me to let him in because he hasn't got his front door key yet. I thought you had sorted it out."

"I contacted the property agents but they said I had to talk to their landlord for a key. So far, I haven't been able to get hold of him." I don't want to tell Meghan I forgot and hope she won't press me.

"Oh dear. These things do seem to take so much time! Why are people so difficult to get hold of?"

"I'll keep trying Meghan and let you know what he says when I contact him."

"Thank you Chris. You are kind."

"My pleasure Meghan." I get up to go pleased that I haven't lied and retained good relations with her.

As soon as I enter my flat I call the landlord but only get his voicemail. After leaving a message asking him to call me urgently because of a problem with his tenants I make and eat a cold lunch before starting my next task, deciding on a care home for my mum. Reviewing my notes and the brochures for each home with their fees it becomes a simple choice between two of the nursing homes. It is neck and neck as far as fees and facilities but one has a room available in one week but the other home has a long waiting list.

Before I call the nursing home I must do something I have been putting off – well one of several things I have been putting off as you know – and call my sister Mary. We are not close and she won't be that bothered by my call. It is the indifference, the lack of concern or interest in her mum or brother that hurts me. I know people are different and show their feelings in various ways but I can't remember the last time Mary contacted me. It is as if she never had a family and she keeps herself completely separate from us.

It is more out of a sense of duty than of love that I am calling her now. She doesn't work so this should be a good time to contact her. I am proved correct as she picks up on the third ring.

"Hello."

"Hello Mary, it's Chris."

"Oh… hello Chris."

"How are you?"

"OK, much the same as last time." And when was that – months or years ago?

"That's good. How is the family?"

"They're OK too." This is going to be harder work than I expected!

There is a pause but no further details are forthcoming. I decide to cut to the chase to avoid dragging this out further.

"I'm calling about mum. When did you last speak with her?"

"I'm not sure."

"Well she has deteriorated recently. Her memory has got worse and the nursing home can't cope any longer. I've been looking at other nursing homes who provide dementia care."

"Oh."

"I wanted to tell you before I decide in case you are interested or want to ask anything first."

"I'm sure you've researched it well as you usually do." Was there a hint of sarcasm there? Am I being too sensitive?

"I have looked at several and checked others online before finding the home most suitable and affordable."

The fees for the nursing home come from the sale of mum's house when she first moved into it. We have an equal share in mum's will to her assets so that's not a bone of contention. We also have Power of Attorney to act on mum's behalf although in practice it is I that decide. Mary just acts like a silent partner in a business – she is silent.

"I'm sure you chose the best. I'm fine with whoever you decide to go with."

"Thanks. Is there anything, anything at all, you want to check or ask about?"

"No, I can't think of anything."

"OK, well is there anything else you want to say?"

"No, not really."

"OK, well bye."

"Bye."

"Oh, by the way as you forgot to ask and before you go I just want to say that I and my family are fine too." There is silence from Mary.

"Bye then Mary." I pause for a few seconds then put the phone down, as there is no response again.

After a few moments to collect my thoughts, I really don't want to dwell on the awful call I have just ended; I pick up the phone again to call the nursing home.

It is with a big sigh of relief that I finish the call with the nursing home knowing I have secured the vacant bed for my mum subject to her visiting and being happy with it. Next up I call mum to tell her I will take her out on Thursday afternoon, the day I arranged with her new home.

Now I allow myself time to review my call with Mary. It is hard to believe we are related. As she gets older so she seems to be colder, aloof, remote, I could go on but you get my drift. Why? Was it something I did or said or not do or not say? If not me, who or what turned her into the difficult person she has become?

I am annoyed that I let my emotions show with my barbed ending. To not even ask how I or mum or my children are, even just out of politeness, is really difficult for me to understand. That is not me, never has been, never (I hope) will be. I stop myself from sliding into too much self-analysis. I can't solve it alone and I'm not sure it is solvable by anyone after so many years of it gradually worsening.

I move on quickly and start clearing up my emails, personal and business, before settling to my next important task of the day – online dating. At the back of my mind all day has been developing a different approach. From now on my focus will be not on finding a special friend who is local with the exception being with anyone elsewhere who contacts me. From now on I will widen the radius area and accept that I may meet someone who lives some distance away. That doesn't seem as important now as finding someone who is right for me. The dating well locally has been drunk dry and I need to move on.

I look for anyone within 50 miles so it includes London. The search throws up an awful lot of results to look through. I am determined to review everyone and I can be more choosy in who I contact. Any women I don't like I remove so there is less to check through in future and hopefully more that I want to meet and maybe they will meet me. I can have a bit of fun and contact women who I think are different to anyone I met before. This is *my* opportunity; I want to take it and explore now!

I spend most of the evening searching through page after page of women's pictures to remove those I don't like the look of first; then reading through the profiles of women that I possibly am interested in; lastly to those who do really hit the spot with me I send an updated introductory message to. It will be fascinating to see if women who I have only dreamt of meeting before could be just one response away and then who knows; I find it intoxicating and love it!

I wind my way to my bedroom with a smile, convinced I have made the right move.

DAY 46: TUESDAY

An easier day lies ahead for me today. Apart from popping out for a walk and some food shopping, I can do as I like with a few work emails to keep clients' work ticking over. I can focus on my new online dating criteria and find more treasures hidden before by previous limits. And I am really looking forward to it and can't wait to get my chores done so I can concentrate on the main event.

I speed through my tasks and complete them in record time. Walking to clear my head and let the atmosphere of waves crashing on to pebbles reinforce my good spirits I set a fast pace so I can get back to the dating site. As soon as I get back I make coffee while opening my laptop. Sipping my coffee I quickly open the site and scan the responses. Six women, five of whom I contacted yesterday, have viewed my profile and three also said they like my profile; progress! But no one has sent me a message yet.

Responding to each woman who liked my profile I thank them and ask if they want to ask anything about me or even to meet up. I try to create the impression of being keen without appearing pushy or pressurise. Finally it seems as if weeks of experience with online dating is helping me find the right balance. Of course only time will tell if I am right but I feel the most comfortable since I started using this site.

Now hitting my stride I continue searching for my special friend using my new criteria. I realise I hardly scratched the surface yesterday as there are still many women to I find that I may want to meet. Finding a rhythm and approach that works I start finding women who I really want to meet and I send messages like yesterday. After about an hour I refuel with some lunch and more coffee. From previous times I realise I need to keep an open mind and fresh perspective to make the best decisions over which women I want to meet.

After lunch and buoyed by more coffee I can't wait to carry on with my special friend searching. She is out there somewhere, maybe my next profile, and I want to find her! It is tantalising to think the next profile might be 'the one', the 'right one' that I am desperately trying to find. And she will be so pleased I reached out because I am the 'special one' that she also wants to find. That magical thought spurs me on to continue trying to find her.

Apart for a break to wash-up, make some tea and check for emails I continue for most of the afternoon with the dating site. Time seems to stand still as if I am in my own bubble, so focused on each profile and weighing up whether I should contact each woman or not, that it is a surprise to look up and see it is close to dinner time. My empty stomach now confirms that to be the case with a loud groan! Thankfully only I hear it!

With food, wine and a short stroll along the seafront to revive my energy levels… and satisfy my tummy of course, I start my last stint of the day. I can see there are now fewer profiles left to check than I have checked so far which encourages me. With some gusto I look through one profile after another, carefully assessing each one against my criteria, sometimes after mulling things over, before deciding which ones to contact and which to reject. It still left a few I can't decide upon which depending on my mood I can reject or contact later.

By the end of the evening I feel a great sense of achievement and impending excitement as I wait for any responses. There are still over 100 profiles left to review and I vow to do these straight after breakfast. I go to bed tired but not stressed, convinced I am doing the right thing now after false starts and hiccups.

I'm sure I sleep with a contented smile full of anticipation upon my face!

DAY 47: WEDNESDAY

Waking up refreshed from a sound sleep I quickly get ready to face the day and my first and most important task, completing my online dating search. I see there have been some views and likes but once again no messages. The last set of profiles I want to review again throw up a few women I really want to contact but most do not interest me. When I finish I sit back and reflect on the last few days. It feels liberating, changing my previous approach. Whether it works or not is now up to the women I contacted but I am quietly confident that it will.

While making and drinking my coffee I respond to the women who liked my profile and then log out of the dating site. What now happens is out of my hands and I try but don't completely succeed to put it out of my mind. I need to distract myself with something and I am given two chances to do that. A text from Rachel asks me how my new approach is going. It starts several exchanges as I say how I excited I am with my progress. She wisely cautions me not to get too carried away. I promise I won't but she knows me too well and can see I am very optimistic. Maybe I am being too optimistic? Only time will tell we both know but don't say it.

A call from Liz is my second distraction with news that she wants to stay with me for a few days before going to her mum's for the rest of the summer holidays. Can she come tomorrow? Of course! Liz can come here whenever she wants and for as long as she wants. It will be the perfect opportunity to sort out her issues with my dating and reestablish our previously strong relationship. I will also get an update on her mum's state of mind on our divorce and the sale of our house. She is normally great company with plenty of laughs.

After we chat for about half an hour we agree she will come round early tomorrow so we can drive to see my mum and visit the new care home I chose for her. After lunch I work on some training and communications material that Harry Stokes – at least he is still around unlike Brian – needs ahead of a meeting on Friday. I like this type of work and feel it a privilege to be paid for doing something I really enjoy doing.

By the time I complete the work it is dinnertime. I know I have received a couple of alerts from my dating site but wait until after I ate and cleared everything away before finding out more. Sitting down trying to contain my excitement I see three messages in fact, all from women I contacted this week. Maybe my new approach is showing results after all?

Eagerly reading them I am excited by all three. The first is from a woman calling herself Caribbean Queen. She lives in London and is interested in finding out more about me. Goody I think! I quickly reply giving her the information she wants that I am separated but at the final stage of my divorce and now live on my own. I ask a similar question about her situation as it isn't clear on her profile and if she wants to meet. I don't want to appear impatient but wish to avoid meandering around like happened before to me.

The second woman called London Lady is even keener, suggesting that we meet face to face as that is the best way to find if we are right for each other. I couldn't agree more and ask where and when we can meet up.

The third woman is called Lady Haha. I guess it could be a 'play on words' with the pop singer Lade Gaga although she doesn't look the same. She is more circumspect and asks me to say more about my background and interests. I am unsure how much to say but start off with extra details that build on my profile. I ask is there anything else she wants to know or share with me or if she is keen to meet up.

Determined to keep the momentum going I search the same area for anyone new who registered this week. It throws up only a few results but I find nearly every woman shown to be very attractive to me. Amazing! I eagerly contact each of them including one titled 'A Jewel'; I certainly think she is a gem and cross my fingers digitally she will respond quickly.

Contentedly I laze back on the sofa and put the TV on. Although I am not really watching the programme I am aware of it in the background. My mind is too full of possible dates with beauties I contacted – very sexist I know – but it is lovely to think of the endless options that are potentially available by taking a new approach after Sunday's disaster with Great Dane. Teas, dinners, drinks, walks, cinema and theatre visits - all of these come into my mind as I drift through the cornucopia of women I contacted and who can make my wish come true by becoming my special friend.

DAY 48: THURSDAY

Liz turns up a little later than planned with her case; at least she does turn up unlike Danny who hasn't been in touch since he left abruptly last weekend. Probably too loved up with his girlfriend to consider contacting mere mortals like his dad I guess. Liz hasn't heard from him either so I know it isn't just me, more likely Danny being his typical selfish uncommunicative self.

My mood is good from the moment I wake and remember yesterday's dating activities. When Liz arrives it stays positive as I am determined to sort out matters with her after we have seen my mum. After she drops her suitcase and rucksack at my place we drive off to see my mum and as usually happens the journey is straightforward with no holdups, even the weather is great with wall-to-wall sunshine along the route. Liz finds a radio station playing classic pop music and we sing along loudly together; Liz in tune and me out of tune as usual. Moments like these make all the hard times as a parent worthwhile.

When we arrive we find to our dismay that mum is still in bed. After asking the staff we discover she had a bad night, the latest of several over the past week. It is annoying that no one forewarned me or kept me up to speed on developments. Clearly my mum is very tired and not really aware where she is or even who we are; to visit the new care home today will be pointless.

Reluctantly I call her new nursing home and explain the situation. We agree to try again tomorrow and see how things are in the morning. We stay with my mum for a couple of hours but most of the time she is drifting in and out of sleep. She isn't aware who is with her just that there is someone who she feels comfortable with. Eventually we both leave after saying our goodbyes and I leave strict instructions about my mum needing to be ready to visit her new home tomorrow by the time we arrive.

After stopping off for a quick sandwich and drink at the petrol station the mood back is more sombre especially for Liz. She hasn't seen her nan like this before and I can see it shook her. Sadly for me it is something I am getting increasingly familiar with. Little is said between us during the journey back; the silence enveloping both of us and setting a melancholic mood until we get out of the car.

Seeing Meghan looking serious as we turn the corner to the entrance for my flat makes the mood persist. No more of the recent niceness today she has shown me; it is straight for the jugular, my jugular!

"I thought you were going to contact the landlord for me!"

"I have."

"But they are still knocking on my door or buzzing me to be let in!"

"I'm sorry but I have done what you asked. I called the landlord, I left a message explaining the problem, and I asked him to find a replacement key urgently."

"So you didn't *actually* speak to the landlord?"

"No, she is notorious for not taking calls."

"So, asking you has been a waste of my time then!"

"I have done what you asked Meghan. I can't make people do what they don't or won't do. Can I?"

"That's not the point. You said you would sort it."

"It is *exactly* the point. I have done the best I can. Just stop answering the door and leave them to sort it out themselves."

"Well really, there's no need to take that tone with me Christopher."

"And there's no need to be like that Meghan and it is Chris not Christopher as I have told you a thousand times. Bye."

With that I stomp past her and climb the stairs to Colin and Emma's flat and knock very loudly on the door. Of course there is no reply because they are out. Tired of pussyfooting around this issue I carry on up to my flat, find a notepad and write a note in big letters 'Please get a new front door key now and STOP annoying your neighbours by asking them to let you in.' I then pop the note under their door so they can see it when they next enter.

When I get back Liz said, "Do you feel better for that?"

Seeing the smile on her face I laugh, "Yes, much better, thanks."

"Good!"

"Shall I cook us a nice dinner while you take care of any work and stuff?"

"That will be wonderful Liz. Thanks."

The conversation with Meghan and Liz's offer to cook dinner helps to partially restore my good spirits from earlier today. I received some alerts from my dating site and an update from Harry presumably about his meeting tomorrow that I want to see so I relax into a chair and find out what is happening. I start with Harry's email as my hors d'oeuvre before moving on to my main course of dating alerts.

Once Harry's points have been answered by me I carry on to the dating site where I have five (yes, five!) messages and a couple of likes from women I contacted earlier this week. Wow! I am spoiled for choice on which to read first. That mood did shift down a few levels though after I read the first three responses that are basically along the lines of 'thanks but no thanks'. Still at least they make the effort and not just ignore me. I also know exactly where I stand with them and remove them from my list as no longer of interest to me. That still leaves two that are interested in me, one a follow up message from London Lady.

My London Lady is very clear, a bit like some other dates; she wants to meet in London at a café just outside London Bridge station. That feels just right for me and very convenient. She suggests 2pm, which also gives us flexibility to continue somewhere else or call a halt if we choose to – again just right and convenient for me. I happily agree to meet her this Saturday.

My last message is from a woman in south London who I contacted. She is interested but unsure what to do next. She asks me for some suggestions on what I feel is appropriate. Not really expecting this uncertainty I think for sometime before offering a trip to a museum if it is wet and a walk in a park if the weather is dry. Either should give us a chance to talk and get to know each other. She is attractive to me and I desperately want to meet her.

Lastly I check the women who liked my profile to follow up with a message saying, as they like it do they want to ask anything or keep in touch with me. Satisfied with what I have done I sit back and sniff a lovely aroma coming from the kitchen area where Liz is creating one of her lovely dishes. Seeing me sit back she smiles and says dinner will be in about 10 minutes and would I like to set the table for it. Working smoothly and in sync with her, everything is ready by the time she serves the food, a lovely tasty Spanish omelette.

After dinner and fortified by one bottle of wine shared between us, although I think Liz only has one glass, I grab another bottle and open it, take a deep breath and start the conversation I don't want to have but know I must do.

"Liz, I wanted to chat about that phone call and my situation with dating."

Liz sighs, "Do we have to dad? I'm having a lovely time with you today."

"Sorry Liz but I have to clarify how things are with us over dating."

Further sighs. "If you must but I'm having another glass first." A chip off the old block I ponder as I top my glass up too.

"It's been over a year since your mum and I separated, well over a year in fact, and mum started the divorce and it will be finalised once the house sale is completed. Do you accept that?"

"I guess so."

"Sorry Liz, there is no guessing. That's the reality of our situation even if neither of us likes it."

Silence from Liz as she stares intently into her wine glass.

"I wish I could turn the clock back to when we were a happy family, the four of us together, having great times but that was ended when mum told me to leave and found herself a boyfriend. Yes?"

There is a nod of the head from Liz. I pause and take a big gulp of wine, surprised that I have drained my glass already.

"All I am doing now is getting on with my life a year after mum started doing that with hers in a very hurtful and upsetting way for me. I want someone else who can have a special place in my life, in my heart, and love me in a way you or anyone else can't."

"Don't get gross dad. I get the message. OK!"

"I'm not just talking about sex! It's all the other emotions that two people can show and be affectionate and caring and loving to each other."

"What about me? Or Danny? Aren't we loving to you?"

"Yesssss, you are but there was something that your mum gave that no one else could. I hope there is someone else out there who might fill that gap."

There was a long pause after that. I emptied the bottle into our glasses and we took the opportunity to drink as we thought about each other. I restarted the conversation.

"All I am asking is for you to have an open mind with anyone I am with in future. They are *not* your mum. No one ever will be but one may become the special friend that I need and I would like you to accept her because she will make your dad happier."

Again there was a long pause. I could almost hear the wheels whirring round inside Liz's head as she processed everything before she responded.

"OK." Was all she said but that meant closure to me at least for the time being. The atmosphere lifted with that too.

"Thank you Liz."

I lighten the mood by chatting with Liz about happier times in the past that made us feel nostalgic for when we were younger and part of a family of four people. The memories shared were vivid and brought many laughs and a few tears. Another bottle of wine followed as we move on to Danny and where on earth he is going with his life. Neither of us really 'got it' about his new girlfriend or as Liz thinks his first serious girlfriend. Maybe that is what he needs to go through to find his way forward that he is comfortable with - a rite of passage perhaps?

Whatever it is I can now see more clearly how difficult it is for Liz to keep in contact with her brother. I know he is difficult to communicate with but assumed, wrongly so it seems, that it is I rather than all his direct family.

We move on to her mum lastly and I tell her about Danny's last update to me that had led to him moving out. Liz is more dismissive saying it isn't the first time Em had an outburst like that with Danny. On earlier occasions Danny has just gone back to uni early but now he has broken up for the summer that isn't really possible this time. However whether the outbursts by Em are justified or not are questionable. Liz thinks that her mum has these to disguise her frustrations with her life such as splitting with her latest boyfriend, not having the right career, moving to another place. Sometimes although this it is rare she regrets her marriage ending particularly the way it came to an end.

After we finish and Liz has gone to the spare room, as she feels bushed from that amount of wine, I send Danny a text saying that Liz is with me and ask how he is doing. Surprisingly he replies almost immediately saying that he is OK but wants to meet up again soon.

How about tomorrow? I call him rather than text back and over the next half hour it slowly appears that Danny acted in too much haste leaving me for his girlfriend. Whatever the attraction has been to start with, it seems lust was the motive, it is wearing off quickly and more time is spent in moody silence apart than together in harmony. I say he can come back here after I have taken my mum to visit her new care home with Liz.

DAY 49: FRIDAY

The day doesn't quite start as I planned it to with a flurry of emails from Brian and his team saying farewell, formal handovers of project details and introductions from the team to me as the new project owner. On the face of it they are welcoming and anxious for the continuity I will bring. There doesn't appear to be any resentment that I was appointed. I take the comments at face value but hope there are no bad feelings or anxiety any of the team are keeping inside or shared internally without my knowledge.

I carefully word an email to every team member thanking them for their thoughts, expressing my sadness at Brian's departure while wishing him all the best for the future. I propose we all meet on Monday at 2pm to discuss how we will move forward together and ask for them to confirm this is OK. I am pretty sure it will be and know my proposal is in fact an order they can't nor want to ignore or challenge. Hey ho, back to some good old-fashioned office politics!

One of the emails was from Brian's HR people about my variation

in contract. Worryingly all it shows is a change in the r
are the same. While I haven't agreed a new daily rate, B
clear there will be an increase to reflect the extra respons
little alarm bell rings in the background. I write back along th
of 'surely there is some mistake, the rate hasn't been increased in
with the extra responsibilities?' and wait to see what happens.

There are a couple of messages from my dating site but I will read them later when I can give them the proper time and attention. Liz is never the fastest person in the mornings and I focus on alternatively encouraging or demanding that she is ready when I want to leave. It feels like going back in time to when I drove her to school on my way to work. I always left later than I planned and complained when I got caught in traffic after dropping her off at school that delayed a meeting, call or just catching up on work when I finally arrived.

When we leave 15 minutes later than I planned (some things can't be changed it seems no matter what I try to do!) it feels like a semi-victory for me; sometimes I could be up to an hour late for Liz and her delays, not with school, but to see friends after school or to go to clubs. Why she is late is a mystery to me even after all this time. The desire to find out left me a long time ago. It is always best to stay in the present and avoid the past I find as far as my children are concerned. They have elephantine memories of when I said or did something bad or forgotten to do something that was desperately important to them at the time. All the good things I did are ignored as just part and parcel of being a dad of course. Either way I can't win.

Our journey is good again although the atmosphere isn't as bright as yesterday. Thankfully when we arrive mum is almost ready for us and is looking forward to going out. She slept better and is more alert but sadly isn't sure where we are taking her. I find that appropriate in view of how the nursing in her new home is aimed exactly at

ew home I explain why we are there again
...e since we got in the car. My mum sort of
...and we are warmly welcomed by the staff at
...Taking her gently into the home and giving
...leaves Liz and I to wander around as we
...wing my mum the communal areas and meeting
...the of the residents. The manager nips out of her office and beckons us in for a quick chat. There is a room available in one week and taking the key with her, takes me down to see it. The view from the window is wonderful and it is roomy enough for all of mum's personal effects to be stored or displayed on dressers or hung on walls. It needs a spring clean before it will be ready, that's why they don't want to show it to my mum.

By the time we leave the home everything is settled for the moving in date, monthly fees and visiting arrangements. Mum has enjoyed the visit, being out for a change and seeing new people. I feel she knows she will be going back soon and am looking forward to it. Liz and her chat most of the way back, each sharing their news with each other. I am relieved that Liz can share the burden – sometimes my mum isn't very talkative and the time drags – and pleased by the memories they can still share and enjoy together.

By the time I drop mum back, confirmed when she will be leaving and what I need to pack I manage to just keep ahead of the commuting traffic and be home at a reasonable time for when Danny plans to return. Liz is quiet about the prospect of seeing Danny again and staying in the same place as him. There needs to be some bridge building by him.

When we turn the corner there is Danny sitting on the doorstep surrounded by his stuff waiting already for us. That isn't like Danny and clearly he can't wait to leave his girlfriend I suspect. After greeting each other we march up the stairs carrying his stuff between us and settle down in my place on the sofa and chair.

The conversation drifts from the initial welcomes and "how are yous?" to "what have you been doing?". Danny doesn't want to go into specifics but as I suspect the novelty of being back with his girlfriend and staying with her friend at her friend's place quickly wore off as the week went by. I realise as he finishes his story that the last time we were all together was when I announced that I planned to try online dating. An awful lot of water has passed under that bridge since then.

When Liz leaves the room for a few moments I quietly tell Danny that he needs to urgently rebuild his relationship with his sister. If he wanted to stay then he has to do that first. He questions me with a look but can see I am very serious and he nods his agreement.

When Liz returns, thoughts turn to what we will eat as we feel hungry. I suggest a takeaway but Liz says no and insists that Danny and her will cook while I catch up on my dating correspondence (her phrase, not mine). And that's what happened for the next hour or so.

I am pleased that Liz accepts my situation now and makes a point of showing it with that statement. At times watching Liz and Danny prepare the meal is like a throwback to the 1970's cookery show when Fanny Cradock barked out orders to her partner Johnnie who belatedly and haphazardly carried out each one. Danny is also making a real effort with Liz as he rebuilds his bridge with her so to speak, enquiring about her studies and college friends. There is the odd laughter between them now and again – a good sign.

I smile as I read through my responses from women I contacted.

Firstly my London Lady wants to postpone our meeting by 24 hours so we meet at the same time and place on Sunday instead. That suits me well because it means I am free to spend time with Liz and Danny here. That doesn't happen often and I want to make the most of it, as it may be a while before we repeat it. I reply to London Lady agreeing to her change.

I hit the right spot with my south London lady, known as Desiree, who offers some information about herself and suggests we might have a call one evening next week. That feels like good progress to me and I agree and give her my mobile number. I ask which evening she prefers.

Lady Haha also replied, she is interested in meeting me next weekend somewhere in London. I reply that Saturday is my preference, when and where does she suggest. So far so good with new dates slowly happening thanks to my new approach.

My last message is also positive from a woman in Brighton finally responding to my message I sent at least a couple of weeks ago. Brighton Lolly apologised for the delay due to work and children taking up a lot of her time recently. If I am still interested then she will meet me. It sounds like she left the ball in my court, as if she isn't sure about meeting me. I read through her profile and still like her enough to want to meet at least once. I suggest we meet either one evening next week in Brighton for a drink or meal or at the weekend knowing I may need to juggle dates, times and locations with my Lady Haha.

I am about to finish when a message finally comes back from Caribbean Queen who I had been in touch with a while ago. She likes my information and asks if we can continue by emailing each other for now. I send her my email address for her to contact me. This looks like being another slow burner and for me to be patient.

As I finish, Johnnie (sorry Danny) interrupts my thoughts to say dinner is on the table. I quickly uncork a bottle of red wine I save for special occasions and we sit down to celebrate a three quarters reunion of the family. Obviously Em is unable to join us of course, as they would say at an awards ceremony. Thankfully there is no video link up either! Proposing a toast to my children we drink and eat a lovely meal that Liz prepared with Danny's assistance. Liz and Danny then want to toast me - without my support and love they wouldn't be where they are today. The remainder of the evening is a family lovefest as we recall great times individually and collectively.

It all comes to an end when we realise we haven't sorted out the sleeping arrangements. Despite Danny hoping for something better he is offered the sofa with a promise that neither Liz nor I will disturb him too early in the morning. Knowing that Danny, once he drops off, sleeps like the dead, I can bang a big bass drum next to him and he won't stir - I think it is a safe promise to make that I will keep.

DAY 50: SATURDAY

A very rare family day today! When we all finally surface, Danny being the last, we sit down to breakfast/brunch/lunch depending on when each of us first stirred. As we discuss what we can do today it gradually becomes clear that no one actually wants to do anything 'big' with his or her day. A walk along the beach together is the consensus followed by a pub meal or dinner made by me. I like that as it means we will be together and that is paramount over any other ideas for all of us.

The whole day is one for me to store away in my family album of memories. No arguments, no strops, no negative words exchanged by anyone. After our walk we enjoy one of our favourite family meals as I cook chili con carne and we talk about our hopes for the future. I am surprised how candid Danny and Liz are with me and I am sad how their mum and dad separating affect them.

Interestingly they see me as their continuity figure to rely on now rather than their mum. The constant steam of new boyfriends, the sudden mood changes, the uncertainty of not knowing how their mum will be or what her future plans are badly affect them. I gladly accept the extra responsibility this thrusts upon me. It makes me more determined to try to make the right decision about a special friend and not mess them about.

As the evening comes to a close I realise I haven't thought about or checked my dating site. I decide it can wait until tomorrow. I don't want anything spoiling this special day with my children.

DAY 51: SUNDAY

Today I hope to meet my lady, London Lady, but realise I haven't told Danny or Liz. By the time Danny and Liz stir from their places of sleep I am washed, dressed and ready to catch the train. The Sunday train service for me is notorious for engineering works and shortage of drivers meaning delays or cancellations. I leave on an earlier train than needed as a contingency against this happening.

Danny and Liz are disappointed that I am not going to be with them, Liz especially so. I am not sure if that is because they will miss me or don't want each other's company or don't want me dating. I will have some idea by the atmosphere when I get back whenever that may be, trains and London Lady permitting.

The first train is delayed and I miss my connection to London and I arrive at London Bridge with about five minutes to spare. The new layout after the massive improvements made to the station confuse me and I finally arrive about 15 minutes late at the café where London Lady is sitting patiently waiting for me. After apologising and explaining why I am late I buy each of us a coffee and sit next to her on a sofa. The delay removes some of the tension and we are soon chatting and smiling to each other.

London Lady is very petite with blond hair, a narrow face and must be just over five feet tall. With her blue eyes and broad smile she appeals to me. I like her floral dress; the pattern blends well with her looks and personality. After discussing our backgrounds, she is from south London, lives with her parents, has been married and divorced twice and is a manager in local government, we get down to the nitty gritty.

"What do you want from a relationship now Chris?"

"I'm hoping to find a special friend, someone who is more than a person on the end of the line, meet for a meal or visit somewhere and then not see for a while."

"Uh huh, and what do you mean by a special friend?"

Suddenly an easy atmosphere as we gradually are getting to know each other becomes tense. I feel awkward trying to explain what I mean.

"Well, someone who is more than just a friend. A woman who gives more than just friendship."

"Do you mean a friend with benefits?"

"I'm not sure I know what you mean."

"A friend who you also have sex with."

"Well… I want someone who I love that much and make love to rather than just have sex with."

"Making love, having sex, isn't it just semantics and actually the same thing?"

"Err, I'm not sure it is. There is a difference to me. It's the other feelings that I have before, during and after having sex that matter... how deeply I feel for that person."

"That's one way of looking at it I suppose. I'm not really interested in a deep relationship. I'm up for some sex with men I meet and like but I've had enough of long term relationships after two broken marriages."

So there it is out in the open. A huge chasm between what I want from a special friend and what London Lady does. It exposes that we both want different things from a relationship, something you can't easily say in a profile or in messages, only when face-to-face.

"I like you. You've got spirit, I like your looks and I fancy we'd have a good time in bed... but only as friends with benefits – nothing more than that."

It is bizarre. Here is this lovely petite lady offering me sex with no strings attached. Yet I want more than that. What a dilemma? I can probably leave with her now and find somewhere to have sex with her this afternoon. London Lady interrupts my thinking.

"What's the problem Chris? Isn't this what online dating at our age is all about? We can meet who we want, if we want sex we can, there are no strings, we both move on to meet again or meet someone else, maybe both even."

London Lady encapsulates my thinking in a few simple sentences that I was struggling to say. Is it what I want? London Lady does attract me. I don't think I have been put off sex by my time with Gill. But it feels very cold and calculated, no passion or lingering time to enjoy the moment and repeat it daily. Am I going to turn down sex with someone because it isn't the right type – that's even if I can define it that way?

"Chris! Are you going to talk to me? Should I leave now and on my own?"

I didn't know what to say, never being in a situation where a woman is literally offering me sex for nothing – no money, commitment, or feelings - and it is that last thing, feelings, which means it will be a "no" from me. But I don't know how to express it.

"Last chance Chris. Speak now or we will part now and pick this up if you want to later online."

I am horribly tongue-tied and unable to say anything. I look into her eyes pleadingly but her look is one of bafflement. We met with very different agendas that are incompatible. While London Lady is fully in control of the situation I am all over the place and just want to end it.

"Well Chris, it has been a pleasure to meet you. Maybe we will see more of each other in future?" There is a twinkle in her eye to show me her comments mean to have a double meaning.

I realise we are from different worlds and just nod and smile as she turns and leaves swiftly. It takes me 10, maybe 15 minutes before I stir and get ready to leave. The more I know about online dating the less I know. There is so much ambiguity and nuances that I can't fathom out that it makes what seems like a simple thing – a new partner – complex and maybe impossible for me to achieve.

As I leave the table I look straight at two men sitting at the table opposite me. They overheard my conversation with London Lady. One turns to the other and says, "I would have. Wouldn't you?" who responds "Sure, when it's served up on a plate like that." I walk away without a second glance at them.

All the way home I turn over in my mind what happened in that last 15 minutes with London Lady. What is my problem with what she offered? A commitment free relationship with sex readily available with someone I am attracted to. As I churn this over and over in my mind one word comes back to me – feelings. I want a 'full relationship' – sex with feelings of love, devotion, care, and tenderness. I am not a 'wham bam thank you ma'am' man. I never have been and see no benefit in changing now.

It is best to chalk this up as another hard learning experience. Two Sundays in a row for different reasons have challenged my approach to online dating forcing me to assess why I am doing this. I guessed I won't know if online dating is worth all this heartache and emotional dilemmas until I reach its conclusion – a special friend or being on my own - whenever that will be.

When I get back Danny and Liz (they are still in the same room and talking to each other) ask how my date has gone. Liz wasn't her normal inquisitive self for once, maybe a hangover over her earlier stance over me dating. Danny asking as much for his own curiosity than any concern for how I feel.

I feel too awkward to explain the real reason why it didn't go that well. The embarrassment of saying to my children that I just don't want sex with this London Lady is way too much for me to cope with. I give an edited version with the conclusion that we realise we are not compatible and then ask about dinner as I am hungry and it is getting late.

Danny and Liz can see I am not happy but have the good sense not to delve into my dating experience and heat up what they left for me after eating earlier. I change the subject.

"What have you both done today?"

"We've been discussing mum," says Liz.

"Yeah," Danny confirms. "How we will cope when we go back

home."

"And what did you agree to?" I ask.

"Weeell… we agreed to keep a lower profile when there and if she starts again we will say that we'll stay with you."

"That may be exactly what she wants though," I challenge, not sure if I want them for weeks here over the summer break.

"True," reflects Liz. "But she won't expect us to put on a united front. She can't pick on one of us and not realise it will affect how we both behave. Isn't that right bruv?"

"Sure is sis."

I smile as they put their arms round each other in a mock show of solidarity. I worried how the split with Em could affect them and knew it was difficult. But it has matured them to try to find their own way through the mess their mum and dad are causing. It heartens me to see them trying to help each other. I wonder how strong it will be if Em starts picking on one of them.

I decide to have an early night. The afternoon with London Lady exhausted me. As I turn off the light I groan, realising I haven't checked the messages on my dating site. I resolve to act on them first thing tomorrow before I meet Brian & Co.'s team, now without Brian. Hmm… probably should rename them Chris & Co. I think as I drift off to sleep.

DAY 52: MONDAY

Feeling refreshed after a long and peaceful sleep I nip quietly into the kitchen area and make myself a cup of tea without disturbing Danny who is snoring away on the sofa. Making myself comfy in my bed I open my laptop and go to my dating site where three messages are waiting for me.

The first message is from Lady Haha who is sorry for not getting back to me but she hasn't been well. Can we meet for a drink in London one evening this week or at the weekend? The weekend is much easier for me with no plans to be in London this week. I suggest Saturday near Victoria or London Bridge stations.

The next is from Brighton Lolly who is keen to meet on Wednesday evening for a drink and maybe a meal after she finishes work. That is good for me and I agree to that plan and ask where and when she wants to meet.

Lastly a new message from one of the first women I contacted at the start of last week but it is just to say she likes me but doesn't see me as a future partner for her. I feel a little hurt and think she is presumptuous but accept I am not going to be her cup of tea.

When I open my emails there is a surprise with one from Caribbean Queen now known as Letitia. In a formal way she gives me some information about her business interests that are in Ely and Portugal. This doesn't make much sense to me but I figure out they are like isolated pieces of a jigsaw puzzle. As I find out more things slowly the bigger picture becomes clearer to me, I hope I can keep my interest going that long. I answer her questions but will not be too open at this stage until I feel we are making solid progress. My aim is still to meet as soon as possible.

Hearing movement I stop there and make my way back to the kitchen where a tousled haired Danny is yawning while waiting for the kettle to boil. A grunt from him indicates a welcome to me to which I respond with a nod and a smile.

"Any plans for the day?" A shake of the head from Danny.

"What about Liz?" A shrug of the shoulders this time.

"I'm off in a couple of hours to a business meeting for the rest of the day."

"OK."

"Anything you want or I can do?"

"Nope," and that is my complete conversation with my son. It is probably one of the better ones too!

After getting something to eat then showering and dressing – a suit for today's meeting to set the right tone – I have a quick word with Liz before I leave. Both my children are chilling still and taking it very, *very,* easy again. They are so laid back I can almost see them moving horizontally!

As I drive to where my meeting will take place I go over all the points I need to make. While it is important to keep the momentum going, I feel there is fresh impetus I can give that may have been missing. I am paid to be their consultant not their friend and to get the project completed on time, to budget and meet its goals. If I get a chance I will try to see HR about the variation in my contract too.

That actually happens straight away as I enter the building just after the HR person who is responsible for my contract. A quick hello led to a brief chat and a reassurance that my rate is being reviewed and she will get back to me tomorrow. I am not 100% convinced but can wait another day before escalating.

The meeting goes very smoothly. Everyone is willing to move on and focus on what each of us needs to do. They know me by now so becoming the project leader doesn't faze them. I sense there is anxiety over whether further changes within their organisation can happen which affects their jobs. My continuing presence seems to settle them and put aside any worries they have for now.

By the time we end the meeting three hours later I am confident we will move forward faster while making sure everything will be done as required. The drive home is uneventful and I look forward to having a hot meal ready for me for the third day running. Something to relish, I joke with myself!

However when I got home there is no hot dinner and only Danny forlornly watching the TV from the sofa.

"Hi dad. How are things?"

"Things were fine until I came home. Where is Liz? Where's dinner?"

"We had a bit of a disagreement. She said she is going to see a friend. Not sure who or where."

"Have you eaten?"

"Nah thought I'd wait until you got back."

"Why? So I can cook you something!" I say sharply.

"Nah just not sure what you want," he replies sheepishly.

"Anything hot would have done. I've had a long afternoon working while you've argued with Liz."

"She started it," Danny said defensively. "I don't know what got into her."

"Well this won't get dinner done and to be honest I'm too bushed to cook now. We'll order in pizzas."

"Magic dad!"

"Which you will pay for and make a salad to go with it after you order the pizzas while I shower and change. OK?"

"Fair dos dad." Danny always knows which side his bread is buttered and when he can't win an argument with me.

"Any pizza with pepperoni and mushrooms for me," I say departing from the room, pleased that Danny isn't arguing with me. Obviously it was his fault for the disagreement with Liz and the guilt from it makes him keen to please me.

After the pizzas arrive and I open a bottle of wine for me, Danny says he prefers a beer, I ask him what happened. It is a bit like pulling teeth as I slowly pry out from him the details. Gradually it becomes clear the argument is over their mum and it is over a classic issue – favouritism – shown by Em to Liz over Danny. I find as a parent the need to be balanced and fair to my children the hardest thing to do all the time, not most of it, *all* the time.

Danny feels Em picks on him more and that Liz is either slow or weak with her support for him. I am a little too long in the tooth to just accept what Danny says at face value. There are always two sides to a story, probably three with Em's view, and I want to hear what Liz says before offering any opinion or advice. I am partly relieved they haven't argued about me.

"Let's wait until Liz gets back and we can all have a chat and try to resolve it."

"OK dad, I don't want any more hassle now."

"Want to talk about last week?"

The floodgates open and Danny shares his frustrations and puzzlement with how his girlfriend behaves since he left me to rejoin her. He doesn't understand why she isn't warmer towards him; why she is 'hot' to him then 'chilled'; why he can't seem to do anything right, why, why, why, the questions keep coming from Danny. I feel so sorry for him as it is clear this is his first serious relationship and it has set him back. His self-esteem and confidence are shattered and they need restoring.

I can relate to some of his frustrations and experience them with online dating. Everyone is different in how they see things and people and their previous experiences, unknown to us, can affect greatly how they behave. The main thing is to learn from it and remember the good parts and that isn't just her looks and the sex but sharing her company, conversations, and personality. I feel I am very clichéd but I can only say what I feel and Danny realises I am opening up about my problems since his mum and I split and had to live in a very different world to the previous 20-30 years.

More wine and beer leads to a rare male bonding session between us and by the time Liz is back the mood has lifted considerably. It is clear that Liz wants conciliation not confrontation and soon we are talking amicably about their mum and how they can manage her outbursts. They agree to move back to Em's on Friday and see how the weekend goes. The backstop is my place although Danny cheekily wrings a concession out of Liz that she will sleep on the sofa.

It is the best outcome I can expect after I came home to a dejected Danny and no Liz. But I am exhausted and make my excuses as I go to bed. The thought of checking for any dating activity never remotely enters my tired brain.

DAY 53: TUESDAY

Today is going to be a busy day but I am going nowhere. I have the luxury of working from my bedroom maybe even my bed! I have a load of emails to send and act upon for both my clients as well as checking up on what is happening with my online dating.

After working hard for a couple of hours making good progress with only a break to make some coffee there is a tentative knock on my door. Danny and Liz both poke their heads tentatively round the door and seeing me smile enter together, standing side by side. It feels like two school children presenting themselves before the head teacher!

Liz speaks first. "We are wondering what you are doing today."

"I've got a full day of work ahead of me to do."

"Will you mind if we both met mum for lunch?"

"Not at all. Hope it goes well."

"Thanks dad. We wanted to check with you before we confirm it with mum," chips in Danny.

"I appreciate that. See you both later."

Ten minutes later I hear the front door close as they both leave. I wonder if it is just lunch they are meeting for. Whatever, I am glad they are going together. Maybe their argument was needed to clear the air and establish their priorities? Better to be united than divided as they say.

I continue with my work apart from a break when the HR person I saw yesterday calls me back as promised but not with the news I want. With budgetary constraints they are unable to increase my rate and would have reduced it if my role hadn't changed. I say firmly that I will not continue with the project at all after this week if they don't increase the rate and I will take advice over possible breach of contract. She is a little taken aback by my strong tone; she will seek further advice but doesn't promise anything. I feel they are breaking the terms of the contract and I will take advice and end my role on Friday unless I hear differently.

I complete the work for both of my clients by mid-afternoon and enjoy a long seafront walk to get some fresh air into my lungs and look forward to my dating updates. I look forward to what may happen with anticipation rather than with trepidation since my Great Dane non-show at Battle.

My first message is another email from Letitia thanking me for my reply that she finds interesting. Interesting? Again I think what a formal response. Is Letitia really my type? Anyway she proposes that we meet the weekend after next when she is available.

Apparently there is a lot going on but she does want to meet me and to continue emailing each other. Unsure quite where this is going but knowing we will meet I reply that it sounds good to me and give a brief update that my children are staying with me temporarily. I realise children are important to Letitia but I am not sure why as it doesn't seem she has her own.

Next up is Brighton Lolly who wants to meet me on Thursday at 6pm outside Brighton Town Hall; we can then decide what to do when we meet. Again this sounds fine to me and I agree to it.

After that Lady Haha suggests we meet on Saturday at London Bridge station at 1 and go for some lunch and chat. This fits well with my other plans although there is a sense of déjà vu about it after my London Lady meeting. I don't think lightning will strike in the same place again though.

A Jewel finally responds to my message; I was unsure after all this time if any more women I contacted after my Great Dane debacle would still reply. It is just a tentative hello as she asks me more about myself but there is no offer to meet or anything. I answer her questions and ask her a couple of questions to show I am still interested in her. Do I have the patience for these slow burners who are so slow and cautious?

At least I feel I am moving forward and making progress. Deciding I will cook a Spanish omelette for Danny and Liz I bring out all the ingredients and am about to start when they come into the room. Seeing that I am about to start cooking they quickly stop me and say they are treating me to a meal at the local pub tonight. Immediately suspicious for what the catch is they read my expression and reassure there isn't anything bad behind their motives. It is more a 'thank you' for putting up with them and being understanding. Wow, these are moments I will treasure for a long time to come!

Two hours later and we are sitting in my local relaxing after a lovely meal and enjoying our second drink. Danny and Liz confirm that mum is happy for them to return home together on Friday. Then

Danny drops the first bombshell; Em is engaged! Even though we aren't divorced yet, Em is on the road to marriage no.2 already. Apparently it is a whirlwind romance with a teacher at her school who joined last term. Well, well, well!

Then Liz drops the next bombshell; Em has taken the house off the market. It will now be the love nest for the happy couple. The last bombshell they share between them (they can be a good double act when they want to). Em will be contacting her solicitor tomorrow to start the transfer of funds to me for my share of our marital home. All the uncertainty and go-slow by Maureen can speed up once I have the funds to buy my flat, sorry maisonette.

The waves of relief cause me to break down and sob quietly. The stress of the past few weeks has taken more of a toll than I realise. I sit quietly with tears rolling down my cheeks with a smile on my face. Neither of my children knows what to do having never seen me like this before. In fact I can't remember when I last felt like this.

Slowly I surface and seeing this both my children come over and put their arms around me. It is too much and causes me to break down again and cry with tears of joy. I manage to reassure them I am actually happy; it is just too much for me in one go. I give Danny my credit card and ask him to buy another round of drinks. Liz stays next to me holding my hand and watching me carefully.

When Danny returns with drinks we toast each other and the news they gave to me. My complicated and uncertain life suddenly becomes simpler and brighter. I am more optimistic about my own place, my very own, the first time I can say that. I start thinking about all the calls or emails I need to make tomorrow morning and draw up a list in my mind.

I remind them that I am going on a first date tomorrow evening and they will need to take care of themselves. I also remind them that their nan is moving home on Thursday and will want to see both of them especially Danny who she hasn't seen for a long time. I emphasise to Danny that her short-term memory is deteriorating and she may not remember him. I can see he doesn't fully appreciate she has changed since he saw her some months ago and hope he won't be too shocked.

By the time we leave my local there have been more drinks and we all feel merry and happy with everything and everyone. I vaguely recall getting home and feeling immensely happy and proud of my children.

DAY 54: WEDNESDAY

The first two hours of my day are taken up making everyone aware about my expected change in circumstances. The key call with Maureen also reminds me that my survey had thrown up concerns over the leasehold and some problems with the state of the maisonette that still need resolving first. I am fine now with what is happening and the pace of the conveyance. It doesn't help having to work through a fog of alcohol from last night's celebrations that lifts only slowly – too slowly for my liking.

Danny and Liz slowly come out of their sleepy places they hunkered down into the night before as the morning wears on. They are each seeing different friends and leave by the time I make a cold lunch and another pot of coffee. Slightly concerned that I need to be on top form in a short time with Brighton Lolly I quickly cover off my work emails and check other emails and dating site.

Letitia compliments me on being a good father for spending so much time with my children. Maybe she will be a character referee if ever I need one! She understands my divorce impacting on their lives and sometimes a struggle adjusting for them. The surprise is her divulging that she has two grown up children from a marriage when she was very young. I am looking forward to meeting her! We have a lot in common and to chat about.

I send Brighton Lolly my mobile number in case I am delayed or her plans change at the last minute. Apart from that there isn't anything else happening.

I rest for an hour, walk along the seafront for some fresh air to help clear my head completely then shower and change before going to meet Brighton Lolly (and try to find out why she calls herself that name). Walking to the station I realise how different I am now about meeting women for a first date compared with when I started. Now I am more confident and eager to meet not nervous and awkward.

The train arrives on time on time and I casually walk towards Brighton Town Hall moving against the flow of commuters going in the opposite direction. It helps me appreciate again how fortunate I am choosing where to work and avoid commuting every day. That brings me back to Brighton Lolly who works at the local authority. Can she work where she wants? What exactly does she do? Her profile says Organisational Development that can cover a very broad area of work.

I wait outside the Town Hall for her to show; I am early so don't expect her to be there and try not to get anxious. Six o'clock comes and goes with no sign of Brighton Lolly, I am getting more used to this now and don't mind waiting so much after what happened with Great Dane who is my only 'no show date' so far. At twenty past six a lady who looks familiar walks quickly towards me.

"Are you Chris?"

"I am."

"Well I'm Obi also known as Brighton Lolly. She smiles broadly and I return it with a big grin.

"I am curious about your name."

"Brighton Lolly or Obi?" I feel awkward and a bit embarrassed.

"The first one actually but I am interested in the second name too."

"I laugh a lot so it's a play on words for LOL. I'll talk about Obi later maybe."

"That's as good as any reason I've heard from dates about their names they use for dating."

"Hmm, sounds like you've had a lot of experience. Why did you choose your name?"

Obi is clearly assertive; it isn't going to be a boring evening whatever happens or how it ends.

"Erm, I think I am trying to show who I am. I'm trying to remember exactly. It was a couple of months ago. I hope I am a good guy."

"I'll let you know," Obi said raising an eyebrow and smiling. This could be fun I think.

"What did you want to do?" There are plenty of restaurants, pubs and cafes nearby in the centre of Brighton.

"If you've got nothing in mind I know a nice pub where we can sit and chat."

"Sounds good to me. Where is it?"

"Just a few minutes from here. Follow me."

And I do as we quickly walk through the narrow alleyways in The Lanes; I can't walk beside her and settle down to following her. Obi pauses outside a pub called the Guildford Arms, glances back to see where I am and enters. Inside it is busy but there are some tables and chairs at the back still available. What surprises me is Obi walking straight up to the bar and saying hello to a young woman who recognises her instantly, smiles and comes round the bar to hug her and show her to a table.

I follow - I am getting used to following - as Obi turns round to me and says, "This is my daughter."

Her daughter smiles, "Hello, nice to meet you."

"Hello, nice to meet you too. In fact it's nice to meet both of you."

I turn to look at Obi who smiles at me and then at her daughter. I feel I said something good, maybe significant. We sit down and decide on drinks and food, her daughter taking my order at the bar.

Sitting back down I sigh and smile at Obi. "Well this is different!"

"She has been the Assistant Manager here for the last year so it is an obvious place for me to go to."

"It isn't often I find someone who knows the person behind the bar like that."

The evening moves on with the usual conversation about each other's background. We cover families, a lot of time on our careers, places we have lived and previous relationships. Other than both being married once our lives have taken very different paths to arrive at us now sitting with each other.

The time passes quickly and I am surprised when Obi says she needs to get home as she has an early start the next day. I offer to walk her to the bus stop or train station but there is no need as her car is parked nearby. I then realise she hasn't drunk any alcohol, unlike me with three large glasses of wine.

Outside I say goodbye, make clear I have enjoyed our evening and hope we will see each other again. Obi also hopes we will meet again but isn't sure when with her busy schedule. We agree to continue messaging on the dating site. For some reason Obi isn't willing to share her mobile number or give an email address; she *is* cautious as well as assertive. We part with quick air kisses.

As I make my way home I am not sure how well the evening has gone. While I really like Obi I am not sure if there is that spark between us and she may have similar thoughts. My approach has always been to not judge purely on one date; I am willing to meet Obi again if she wants to and can find time for me.

At least there will be company when I get home and someone to chat to about my evening for a change. Except there isn't and I find both my children are having such good days they continue into the night. I remind both of them that we are moving their nan tomorrow and I will be leaving by 11.

I slump on the sofa and ponder what to do but can't decide so make my way to bed for an early night. It will be a big day for my mum tomorrow and I want to be prepared for all eventualities.

DAY 55: THURSDAY

I wake early feeling refreshed from a sound sleep ready for whatever today will bring. First of all I check my dating site and see a message from Lady Haha asking if I am still OK to meet. I confirm that I will be there as we agreed and that I'm looking forward to meeting her.

Next is a reply from A Jewel to my questions a few days ago and that she has a couple of what might seem to me strange questions but are important to her. Did I mind if she asks me? I am an open book as they say with nothing to hide so I reply that I am happy to answer her questions and hope we can meet soon to find out more about each other. I am a little perplexed if I'm honest with you.

There are no emails from Letitia so our call this evening still looks on. I search for women who joined recently and find one who interests me. My standard introduction is sent; that has worked well recently.

There are a couple of emails from Brian & Co. but I delay acting on them until I hear back from HR. I meant what I said and if nothing is resolved by the end of tomorrow I will not continue with my client and seek advice on breach of contract. I never make threats I am not prepared to carry out. The money is important but being respected matters more to me. I don't want any risk to my reputation; I worked hard developing my skills and experience. They don't come cheap but I always show great value to a client for the money they pay me.

Time is marching on and neither Liz nor Danny have turned up or been in contact. I am annoyed that I have to call both of them and remind them what they promised to do. They are apologetic but neither can get to me on time. I ask both of them to come back and while I am helping their nan to pack their bags and go to their mum's place 24 hours early. They think I am joking but quickly realise I am not by the stern tone of my voice. It isn't how I expect their time to end with me but they need to learn to be more responsible.

So I set off on my own to pick up my mum from her old home and take her to the new home she had visited last week. The difficult conversations with Danny and Liz annoy me and set the mood for a difficult journey. It takes me back to some of the bad times with my dad who could be very strict and lack any understanding when it suited him. My teenage years were fraught with the constant battles I felt he picked with me. It was stressful whenever I came home because I couldn't be sure what mood he would be in or what could be the trigger for our next confrontation.

Yes, my teenage years really did seem to last forever and it was a relief to go to university. It wasn't my first choice but it wasn't the local uni so I would have to stay away in halls and have a break from my dad. Now I reflect back on it my dad was calmer and friendlier especially for the first couple of weeks. I'm sure he appreciated the peace and quiet while I was away and my sister out of the picture at home by then. After that time his patience was flakey and arguments would start without warning. It meant for the long summer holidays I would try to spend as much time as possible staying with friends at their parents' home.

Danny is going through a similar time with his mum. Some of it I am sure is of his causing. He can be annoying at times, like being absent today. Maybe I provoked some of the stand offs with my dad unconsciously. We were of different generations obviously but standards of behaviour had completely changed and he was stuck in his time warp of what to expect from a son and how a father should treat and be treated by them.

I stop maundering more over my dad by playing one of my favourite CDs to lift my mood but I am still annoyed when I arrive to meet my mum. Things get worse when I try to find my mum who is nowhere to be seen. Not having my normal amount of patience, I shout at staff to search for my mum thinking she can be anywhere. I cause that much commotion that one of the nurses knocks on the manager's door only to find her with mum chatting over a cup of tea.

Infuriated by the whole situation I abruptly end the meeting, curtly say goodbye to the manager who caused all this extra wok for me and disruption to my mum, and escort her to my car where I make sure her seatbelt is on before collecting her belongings that are moving with her to the new home. After everything is packed into the boot I sit in the driver's seat to find mum crying; she is upset about leaving, frightened by my shouting and not knowing where I am taking her.

Silently cursing Danny and Liz's absence, I hug her and gently explain that she will be familiar with her new home as she enjoyed visiting it last week. About half an hour later she is settled enough for me to start driving away from the only home she can remember. It isn't surprising she is scared; at least she knows I am her son and that comforts my mum. I love my mum more at this moment than any other time in my life.

The journey is smooth thankfully and uneventful so we arrive at mum's new home in a more relaxed mood. Both Danny and Liz leave voicemails and texts apologising for what happened but I am not in the mood to respond; mum is my only focus right now. Someone spots us as I park my car and a few staff at the home welcome us and help me with mum's belongings. The contrast between how we left her old home and our arrival at her new home is stark. Mum smiles and chats with nurses as if she has been there all her life. I stop and wipe away a tear from my eye as the relief that she will have the best possible care hits me.

Once I drop her remaining bags off a nurse takes me gently by the arm and leads me into a quiet room where there is a pot of tea and some biscuits on the table with two chairs. "How are you?" is all she needs to ask before the frustrations with her last home, my children not showing, my relief that I found this home and my fears for mum's future all come flooding out of me. It takes me a while to recover my composure but the nurse is patient, quiet and supportive and no one disturbs us.

"I hope you feel better now."

"I am. Where is my mum?"

"She is being shown around her new home and room and meeting new friends. We can go find her if you're ready."

I nod my agreement.

"Follow me."

And she leads me through a long corridor and round to where the residents' rooms are showing me into one where my mum is sitting, smiling and chatting with two nurses. She looks up and recognises me straightaway, the best reaction I can hope for. At that moment it confirms to me that I made the right decision and my mum will be able to enjoy her last years here. A huge weight lifts off my shoulders with this realisation.

I don't stay much longer; I don't need to and mum is happy to say goodbye. She is a shorter distance from me now and I can pop in whenever I want to rather than planning when I went to her previous home. The short journey home is uneventful and I have a bounce in my step as I arrive back home… to be greeted by Meghan.

"I just want you to know Christoph… I mean Chris that I haven't been troubled by Colin or Emma or their friends for the past few days. Whatever you did has worked. Thank you."

You could have knocked me down with a feather hearing that from Meghan. Where is my tape recorder when I need it?

"Thank you Meghan."

"I know we've had our differences but we do help each other when we can. You have two lovely children that I was talking with when they came back earlier."

Hmm, you don't know the half of it or seen the other side to their characters!

"Thank you again."

"They say they are planning something special for you!"

"Did they? Interesting, I'd better go and find out."

"Yes and send them my best wishes."

"Err, yes, I will." Intrigued by what she said as I make my way up the stairs to my place.

Hearing music playing loudly I enter quietly to find out what is going on. Instead of coming back to a silent home to relax and find some solitude I enter a hive of music and activity. It takes a while for Danny and Liz to see me standing by the door to my living room watching them, in fact they both jump from shock.

"Surprise!" they say a little hesitantly.

"Yes it is a surprise after what's happened."

"We're really sorry about that," Danny says.

"We want to try to make it up to you rather than just leave before you came back dad," adds Liz.

"OK so what is the surprise?"

"It's our company for the evening and some food and drink courtesy of our fair hands," Danny says.

"Well not so fair in Danny's case probably," adds Liz.

I smile and come over to give each of them a forgiving hug then sit down in my favourite chair by the window.

"A glass of wine will be a good start…"

Danny opens a bottle and pours me a large glass of red wine.

"Dinner will be served soon sir," he says while bending his head in a mock bow.

I nod my head in return taking a large mouthful of wine. They have bought one of my favourites and I savour the flavour as I swill it around in my mouth before swallowing.

It is with a start that Danny touches my arm to wake me and say that dinner is being served. The effect of today and all its emotion has worn me out and I dropped off for a nap in the chair. Quickly recovering I sit at the table to admire a large shepherd's pie in a dish set in the middle of the table, another of my favourite dishes.

Little is said as we attack the pie and enjoy the taste of the meat, potato and gravy made by Liz with some assistance from Danny. They ask how their nan is and what happened today. In between mouthfuls I gradually describe events as they unfolded. Without prompting they both say they will visit next week also pleased that she is now within easier reach for them to see her.

We are still catching up on each other's news when my mobile rings and I realise I have forgotten about Letitia calling this evening. Making my excuses I take the call in my bedroom, closing the door behind me. The call meanders around what we already know about each other, particularly our business interests. It becomes clearer that Letitia doesn't just own the place where she lives but other places too although she doesn't name them. She also likes Portugal a lot. I have been to the Algarve with my family and very early on as part of a golfing holiday that proved to be very boring and I gave up the game afterwards.

The main benefit is I can now put a voice to the profile and we agree to meet in London a week on Sunday. We will have another call next Thursday to confirm the final details. Letitia sounds different to anyone else I have met so far and intrigues me enough to want to meet her and see if there is a spark that seemed to be missing when I met Obi.

When I re-enter the living area the washing up is done, another bottle of wine opened and my children are sitting on the sofa waiting for my call to end. They really do feel bad about what they did I surmise judging by their different behaviour. I tell them about my call briefly and muse out loud where and maybe with who will this all end. Neither of my children offer much of a response, Danny because he isn't that interested, Liz because she is still coming to terms with her mum and dad having or looking for different partners.

The rest of the evening passes quietly but I am not as relaxed as with previous evenings together because of the drama of the morning and pleased when we call an end to the chat and each go to our designated place to sleep.

DAY 56: FRiDAY

Today is a mash up of lots of different things that happen in no particular order but combine to make it a decisive day for me. The first significant thing is a call from Brian & Co.'s HR person.

"After reconsidering the matter we will not increase the rate of pay for the role you now have."

"In that case I will not continue after today. Who do you want me to hand over my work to?"

"You need to give us the proper notice in your contract of 28 days before you can terminate your role."

"I think you will find there is a clause about variations in the original terms negating that and I will leave with immediate effect. You will either increase the rate by the end of today or I will stop the work. Unless you also say whom I will hand over the work to that's not going to happen either. I will not be held responsible for any consequences that result from this as you have caused it. I will also take legal advice over possible breach of contract."

"Oh," is all she says.

"Oh indeed. Are you clear with what I say or do you want me to confirm it by email too?"

"No, no, I'm clear on what you say. I'll get back to you."

"Make sure you hurry because the clock is ticking."

I really don't like this type of negotiation and it is tempting to end the contract but first I want to see if they do increase it and if so, by how much.

Next up is an email from Debra saying Em's solicitors have been in touch with a suggested figure that is around 50% of the property's market value. She recommends I accept it and it will probably be with me within the week, which I do. Wonderful! That is a huge relief and clears the biggest hurdle to me buying my own place. I am still annoyed how Em complicated this final piece in our divorce and can't forgive her.

Checking my dating site next I see a message from A Jewel with her two questions. Have I had a criminal record and when will I be divorced? Her timing is perfect with the second question.

I reply 'Apart from one speeding fine over 20 years ago I haven't broken any law or have a criminal record. I expect my divorce to be finalised within the next month; everything is now agreed for the decree absolute to be pronounced.' I am tempted to ask the same questions but these answers should have a stronger meaning to A Jewel than to me. Let's see how she reacts to my answers.

Next up is yet another call with HR. They have after all reconsidered (yet again?) the matter and decided they can make a small increase as a sign of goodwill and implement this from next month. I quickly refuse the offer unless it is significantly higher and backdated to when I took up the role or I won't continue. I give a figure I think is reasonable based on past experience and say it is non-negotiable; a yes or no are the only replies. She will get back to me.

By then Danny is stirring on the sofa so I make some coffee without disturbing him. Liz joins us and I update them on the news about my divorce from their mum. There is no emotion shown by either of them just acceptance of the inevitable ending of their mum and dad's marriage. There is sadness on my part but it is limited after so many bad things happened; I now feel relief and some optimism for my future.

We chat about their plans for leaving today and lunch together before I walk with them to the train station, hug them both before waving goodbye as they leave for their mum's house. With mixed feelings I return to my place. I could have driven them both to Em's but psychologically I can't go within a million miles of my old marital home after my last few experiences there.

Checking my dating site again, I can't see any new activity so send a follow up message to Obi. I enjoyed our first evening and wonder whether she wants to meet again. If so, when?

Maureen calls and asks me if I can pop in sometime on Monday to sign the draft contract and go through where we are to be ready to exchange of contracts possibly next week. That is great news and perks me up from my mood since Danny and Liz left. While it is nice to have my place back as I like it, their company and personalities fill it wonderfully. I am so pleased my new place has a spare bedroom and at a push the sofa bed is available too.

Just before five o'clock my adversary from HR finally calls back. It isn't possible to meet my demands and if I stop work they will sue me for breach of contract. I know that is posturing and just laugh saying I will stop immediately. They can pick up the pieces next week; if they want me to do anything it will be after agreeing and paying my fees first. I wish her a good weekend and end the call. I am not going to be bullied and I know I am well within my rights.

Dinner is a simple affair; I can't cope with anything complicated after today's events. However there are a few dating activities that complete my day later in the evening. Firstly Letitia wishes me a good weekend and is looking forward to seeing me next weekend. I sense there is something else happening that I am not aware of yet. Secondly A Jewel responds more quickly than before thanking me for answering her questions; she will explain further if and when we meet. She asks me what I plan to do this weekend. I reply cheekily that as I am not meeting her, my first choice, I will be taking it quietly with friends. I follow up by asking her the same question.

The rest of the evening is spent relaxing after another hectic day that is part of a hectic but significant week. Today has been a special day for different reasons. My relationship with my children feels very strong; my first property purchase looks within reach; my divorce that felt like it would continue forever is close to ending and there are grounds for hope that my new dating approach may still prove right.

DAY 57: SATURDAY

Basically a nothing day for me really as I catch up on all those boring domestic chores like washing, hoovering, shopping and cooking that haven't happened during the week. Having a relaxing, low-key day is my ideal preparation before seeing Lady Haha (and I hope we will laugh) tomorrow in London. There is a sense of déjà vu as it will be the same day and vicinity as last weekend's strange meeting with my London Lady. Neither of us has been in touch since we met and I won't be the first one either.

The highlight is an email from Letitia and messages from A Jewel and a new woman who just started on the dating site.

The email from Letitia is intriguing as it raises a number of questions I am unsure about asking now. She asks me how I am - Letitia is very polite I notice - and how my children are. Are they still with me or did they leave as planned? I relish the interest she shows in my wellbeing and me and really warming to her because of this.

But that isn't the problem, these questions are the easy part of her email that I am happy to respond to. The problem is Portugal or rather her plans to travel or move there. No matter how much I am attracted to someone I am dating, emigrating or spending a considerable amount of time in another country is really off my agenda. While it isn't certain, Letitia is seriously thinking about it judging by her email. I sense she is softening me up, testing the waters, to see how I feel before we meet. Is she really expecting me to consider emigrating with her? I know you should "never say never" but surely it can only be after a long period of time and changes in my circumstances. If I love someone that much would I go? That is a very difficult if not impossible question to answer now.

So my response is to play for time by answering her questions, asking how she is, then show interest and ask for more about her thinking with Portugal. It is a lovely country and climate but apart from that I only know the major cities because of the football teams that play in European competitions! Letitia certainly gives me lots to think about that I wasn't expecting to do. Dating!

The message from A Jewel is much easier. While we still haven't agreed if we will meet yet I feel a connection might just be forming between us. A Jewel appreciates the compliment and my humour. That is a step up from other conversations I start with other women I date. She wishes we can meet but it is too early for her to commit without getting to know me better. I am too impatient she jokingly chides me with and needs to take things cautiously; I laugh as I read that. Her weekend is a mix of recovering from an exhausting week at work, seeing her family and catching up on chores. I hope her family balances out the chores and tiredness.

But it is the last message that causes the most intrigue! A woman who I have not been in touch with sent me an invite. The conundrum for me is what to do because she looks like someone close to half my age. While my ego thinks 'hey big man, you can still pull whatever your age' the reality is there must be a catch somewhere, somehow, that I can't work out. Is this some sort of scam? Trying to lead by my brains rather than my loins I respond saying I am interested and what does she suggest. It seems engaging without committing or giving away any more personal information.

My day ends with me thinking about tomorrow with Lady Haha and maybe meeting A Jewel or wondering if Brighton Lolly will reply. I go to sleep knowing I've had worse thoughts going through my mind.

DAY 58: SUNDAY

A sense of déjà vu hangs over my day as I follow the same routine as for last Sunday as I get ready and travel up to meet Lady Haha. I am hoping for a better outcome than with London Lady; that was a weird outcome. I haven't told anyone the full details, not even Rachel, but it will remain one of a few secrets I keep from her. While I am not adverse to 'making love to a beautiful woman' as a character in 'The Fast Show' always says there needs to be an emotional attachment rather than just lust. I never ever thought I would be having this conversation with myself, never!

Before I leave I see A Jewel's reply and it could be significant. She agrees to continue our conversations that are becoming more regular now by email rather than the limited format in the dating site. I'm not sure if it will be worth the effort to be honest. I'm tired of pushing and pushing when the other person isn't so keen. Great Dane really affected me but I hesitate to end it as A Jewel does sort of offer a date for us to meet.

'So humour me and tell me why you want to meet sooner rather than later? Are you naturally quite an impatient person? I'm thinking of us meeting on the weekend in two weeks time, preferably Sunday, as I feel far more relaxed. I can meet you at Victoria, Kings Cross or somewhere in between on the Victoria Line and I'm going to be ultra girly and leave it to you to research the options of where we are going!'

I like her style, how she writes and her thinking and relate to her way and what we may have in common. There is a timeline now that keeps my interest going for now.

'I want to meet you because from reading your profile and our online conversation so far I do like you and think we may have enough interests, attraction, etc., to meet up, have a good chat, find out if we do get on with each other and hopefully be able to move forward.

The more I get to know you, the more I like you. Do you feel the same?

I do like your style of communication; it's very engaging and your sense of humour. Something I love in a person and have myself. Laughing is a wonderful quality.

I didn't realise I am being impatient. It is a compliment for you that I want to see you sooner than later. I also feel meeting in person is the best way to engage in getting to know someone no matter how good we message and email each other.

That Sunday is good for me. So, 'ultra girly' I will research some options based on good or bad weather for you to choose from. Is there anything you definitely DON'T want to do?

I'm thinking of places that enable us to get to know each other, are not too noisy or crowded. Can we meet late morning/midday and see how things go or do you want a set time for how long we meet? I prefer to go with the flow and see how things go.'

This is my longest written message to any woman I have been dating or trying to date by a long way. I haven't had this type of conversation before with any woman I had contacted so far either. I enjoy writing it and sign off with my real name Chris, rather than my username 'A good guy' and hope she will reciprocate.

Leaving for the station with a spring in my step I wonder how today will go. What can the outcome be? Surely not the same as last Sunday! The journey up is uneventful apart from some texts with Rachel who has been out of circulation for a while; a holiday and a new boyfriend explain it. I spend most of the journey updating her on the ins and outs of my love life while she shares her highlights. By the sound of it her latest boyfriend is a good guy (no pun intended) and at least is treating her with a lot of respect so far.

Knowing that Rachel is happier and in 'lurve' with her new beau is wonderful news and uplifting for my mood. That spring in my step gains a bit more bounce as I get off the train at London Bridge. I realise I don't know exactly where Lady Haha will meet me. Maybe the joke is on me for her to laugh 'haa haa' about? I am early so I just walk around the main exits and hope she see or me or I her. It is 30 minutes later when I feel a tap from behind on my left shoulder. As I turn round there is no one there until I realise she *really is* a joker and moved to my right side. She laughs and introduces herself as Lois.

I say, "Hello, my name's Chris."

The rest of my time with Lois aka Lady Haha is exhausting and at times funny but when I want to become more serious I find it very difficult for Lois to be. It seems like I am a new audience to try out her routine on not a dating experience. What makes it worse for me is the place she chooses for our coffee and chat; the same café I was in last Sunday with London Lady. It is a big mistake leaving Lois to choose and for me to offer to buy the first drinks at the bar while she finds a table, virtually the same table and the same people are nearby.

My agony painfully unfolds with one humorous remark after another with my response being either an increasingly forced smile or laugh or repeated attempts that fail to turn the conversation towards more serious and relevant areas that interest me. Matters are brought to a head when the same person who commented on last Sunday's meeting interrupts our conversation. Rather I should say cuts short another attempt at levity by Lois that is already only likely to be slightly funny at best.

"Aren't you the same guy who was here last Sunday?" I try to ignore him and focus on Lois but she is distracted and looks at him quizzically.

"Are you? You are, aren't you?"

Lois asks, "What is he talking about Chris?"

"I don't know. Can we move on to somewhere else?" I reply.

"Why is he asking you that question?" Lois smelt blood.

"He's mistaking me for someone else I expect."

"No I'm not. You were here around the same time but not with this bird." My neighbour at the next table unhelpfully adds.

"Well, were you?" asks Lois.

With a long deep sigh I say, "Yes."

"It was a bit fruity what they were talking about as well I can tell you!"

I groan, trust me to find someone with perfect recall as well as no sense of discretion. I want to shrink into the ground and burrow all the way to the station or in fact to anywhere but where I am now.

"Tell me more please," Lois says to the man at the table next to me.

"They were talking about having no-strings sex whenever they want. I wasn't sure where to put my face they were so open and brazen about it. To be fair to him she was more of a looker than you are." He then turns to me. "Your standards have dropped a bit in a week mate if you don't mind me saying."

I did mind him saying that! However that wasn't the worst thing he said to cause damage. If I had been clearer in my thinking instead of panicking I would grab my jacket and walk straight out of the café. Instead I start to explain what happened last Sunday only realising after a few minutes that it isn't my version of events that Lois wants to hear. Worst of all she turns to me and laughs at me, not a nice one but derisively and sneers at me.

"Looks like the joke is on me after all Chrissy babe!"

"I didn't ask to come here or to sit here; you did."

"And I can see why! Is it normally a different café each Sunday or a different woman or both?"

What is the point? I gradually appreciate that it is best to shut up, close the conversation down and get out as quickly as possible with whatever little dignity I still retain. When you are in a hole, stop digging as they say.

"You are a dark horse aren't you? When were you going to get round to propositioning me I wonder? Well, well, well…"

Trying to remain polite even though it is having no effect I said, "Goodbye, I am sorry it hasn't worked out Lois." Glaring at the man at the next table I gather my jacket and make my way out of the café, tripping over a chair and stumbling into another customer as I hurriedly make my exit. As I leave I can hear the distinctive sound of laughter coming from Lois' direction. Am I glad she finds this hilarious? Will I feel better if she showed more understanding and concern for me?

For the journey home I am yet again feeling fed up with dating, fed up with the vagaries of meeting especially in London now, fed up with... with what exactly? I give up trying to sum up how I feel. It is what happened yet again that gets to me most. I just seem to always be a sucker for a punch when meeting women.

When I get off the train I go to my local for something to eat and drink. I want to be with company rather than be on my own to dwell too much over what happened. I try to be more positive; at least I am in contact with A Jewel; possibly meeting Brighton Lolly again; maybe meeting Letitia but that will be in London and I am already concerned about her plans to move. Well it is better than nothing and I shall take it one day at a time, one contact at a time, and see in which direction my life goes.

The atmosphere is lively for a Sunday evening with plenty of chatter, laughter and music playing in the background. But it doesn't help my mood as I feel remote from everyone who has things that probably happened today to cheer them, share with others, and enjoy in each other's good fortune. I don't have that and after eating my food and finishing my pint leave early for home.

Much to my surprise it is Danny who texts me to ask how today went; that is unusually thoughtful of him. I reply that it hasn't gone well again and ask how is life at his mum's but get no response. I can't be bothered to check the dating site or my emails to see if anyone has been in touch and take to my bed early with a book to try to distract me from everything.

DAY 59: MONDAY

I am at a bit of a loose end today. My original plan was to focus on Brian & Co.'s project for most of the day. With my decision to end my involvement I don't have too much to replace it with. Harry has some work that he needs doing this week, other than that I need to find some new clients. The best way is to put out feelers in my network and see if anyone hears of work that interests me.

I have a much-postponed call with Gill's company to follow up on more training later today. With work now scarcer this opportunity takes on more significance. I make sure I am well prepared to cover any question and to be as invaluable a prospect as possible so they will use me again. That is the best plan I can think of anyway and I cross my fingers and hope it works.

A quick call to my mum's new nursing home confirms that she is settling in nicely and seems happy and content with her new surroundings and people she lives with or cares for her. I ask them to pass on my love and say that I will visit her later this week.

Next up is another email from A Jewel who responded late

yesterday. I smile as I start to read it, as it is a lovely message.

'I admit that I tend to be a little reticent and do feel a bit uncomfortable if I am feeling rushed but I am enjoying conversing with you. You do sound as well as look like "a good guy" and I am definitely starting to feel less tense so yes it will be nice to meet and explore more. I also take it as a compliment that you like me so far and want to meet me.

Great that date suits you I also would prefer not to go anywhere too busy because I want to hear what you are saying! From midday is fine and going with the flow sounds good to me too. I hope that we get good weather but I always have the brolly ready so it'll be OK. T'

T! T? I don't have a name but I do have an initial so that is a step forward. It is becoming a more regular habit that I reply in the morning after A Jewel has written to me the previous evening. I think of my reply and settle on:

'One thing you will find with me is that I am also true to myself. I am truthful, trustworthy, and aim to be happy and help people in my life to be happy too. There is too much misery in the world now and I don't want to add to it but try to reduce some of it if I can.

I will start looking for suitable places and let you know my thoughts. I'm thinking of places where we can have private conversations in public places in central London and come up with as wide a range as I can think of. I love visiting London and worked there for a few years so I hope you like some of my suggestions.

Your comment about maybe needing a brolly reminded of one of the jokes at the Edinburgh Fringe. It was "I like to imagine the guy who invented the umbrella was going to call it the 'brella'. But he hesitated." It tickled me when I heard it.

With each email I like you more... Chris'

I send it to T (no longer just known as A Jewel) and sit back replaying our emails over in my mind as I bask in the pleasure it gives me. Not only is this a different way to dating, T seems different and in better ways compared with some other dates I have contacted.

Next up is my call with Gill's organisation. Part of the delay for this call was a handover to a new person, Emma Briggs, in their Training Department followed by a last-minute holiday. Finally we have the same date and time in our calendars to speak in real time but it doesn't go as I expect. After quick introductions by each of us on our roles and backgrounds Emma shows she is a straightforward, no-nonsense, person (a dream client as far as I am concerned) and wants to discuss her business requirements with me tomorrow in her office. Wow! Great I think and agree to see her. I can juggle this with seeing my mum after my meeting so that works for me too as she is now much closer to me.

I have lunch and with the sun coming out go for a long walk along the seafront and bump into Colin and Emma from the flat below me. We haven't spoken directly for a while but all I get is a muted "hello" and a nod as we walk past each other. Either they are both having a bad day or I am not flavour of the month after complaining to them and their landlord over the replacement key. Life is too short and as long as they don't disrupt my life I am happy to keep our contact to a minimum.

Feeling refreshed from my walk I start networking with close business friends to find out if they know of anything that could be of interest to me. These people don't work in the same area as me so it isn't such a strange thing to do. Sometimes we compete for work but more likely we collaborate as part of bigger project teams. They know I helped them in the past and we all want each other to succeed.

The afternoon is coming to a close when I get a call from the senior person in charge of Brian & Co. team's department. Leonard Stott or Len as he introduces himself wants to know what is happening and why the project is delayed. I explain what has happened and how we got to this position. Len asks what is needed to reboot the project and I give my increased fee to match the extra responsibilities. He gets that and doesn't have a problem with it.

Len's problem is not having the budget to meet it after it was cut recently. He asks if I will agree to do the work in a shorter period of time at the rate I want. Then he will find a project manager to complete the project when the budget runs out. That sounds a good way forward to me, the best way out of the impasse, and I accept providing it is confirmed in writing. Len says, "Leave it with me Chris. I'll be in touch tomorrow."

What a change from first thing today! An easy week with little work to do is now a busy week with extra work on top of my main client – peaks and troughs, feast or famine – no two days the same – typical life of a consultant.

Unexpectedly Gordon and James call within five minutes of each asking me the same questions. Have I seen the latest big signing? Am I going to the pre-season friendly this Saturday? The answers are "no" (but I quickly find out and approve of the new player my club signed) and "yes, probably" and my question to both of them "Who is buying the three tickets?". Predictably they both come back with the same answer "You!".

Knowing it is my turn at the traditional pre-season friendly where one of us buys all the tickets, I go online and buy three seats in the main stand and let them know they are buying all the drinks as I have the tickets, another tradition which I intend to make sure they fully comply with. It is hard to believe most of the summer has passed. August always feels too early for the football season to start to me. Nevertheless here we are almost at the start of nine months of highs and lows, dreams made or broken, excitement, stress, the lot as every football fan knows.

The rest of the afternoon and evening pass quietly and are uneventful until I am alerted to my dating site. Obi (my Brighton Lolly) has replied to my message that I sent after we met last week. She is very busy but hopes we can meet on Sunday at Brighton Marina; the weather forecast is promising and it can be a great place to continue our dating. It clashes with Letitia wanting to meet also on Sunday but I will wait until my next call with her before deciding what Sunday will be for me.

Before I take to my bed for an early night I see that A Jewel sent her daily (or so it now seems to be) email this evening. I resist reading it before I drift off to sleep not because I fear bad news; it should be something to start my day off that is positive.

DAY 60: TUESDAY

The day starts well as I read T's latest email with a cup of tea while lying in bed.

'Hi Chris,

How is your day?

I like that joke too, thanks for making me laugh! Always appreciated after a long day.

I love what you say - I totally agree that there really is too much misery - why make it worse by being a horrible person? A person who is true to themselves is so refreshing and meeting a truthful, trustworthy man called Chris who aims to be happy is exciting me so bring it on...

Which part of London did you work in? I am looking forward to your suggestions - it will be interesting to compare our similarities in taste or differences.

I'm glad that we are starting to build something through our conversations, I am feeling surprised about this and I'm liking you more too.

Have a good evening. Trish'

Trish! I have a name now. Slowly, very slowly progress is being made and a connection growing. Without any delay I reply to her.

'Hi Trish,

That is a lovely name!

My day is a mix of working with clients, calls, emails, etc., checking on how my mum is in her new nursing home and walking along the seafront. If you want to find out more about my business then let me know and I will share my website address with you.

I hate all forms of injustice, whatever they may be, and have supported various causes and charities over many years to try to contribute in my small way to change things. Trump, Brexit, North Korea, IS; all make this a very depressing world at the moment. But I still remain optimistic and positive that things will change for the better.

I believe the distant light at the end of the long tunnel is daylight and a better world, not a train coming towards me.

I worked near the City for a big blue chip organisation helping to train people then gradually combined that with communications before leaving to start my own business.

I will work on my suggestions over the next few days fitting it in with a busy week when I have any spare time.

What does your work entail?

I hope you also have a good day today and this joke makes you smile: "For me dying is a lot like going camping. I don't want to do it." Chris'

A high is followed quickly by a low in my roller coaster life. Debra calls me.

"Hi Chris, sorry to trouble you so early and with a wrinklet in your divorce. Due to a technicality your decree absolute can't happen immediately as Em's solicitors insist a formal document showing you have no other claim on her share of the assets is completed first. It's really irritating because I had already got them to sign one, called a Consent Order, weeks ago and did wonder why they hadn't done the same. Anyway they have but it's weeks later, probably an oversight on their part rather than Em raising it. The bottom line is your decree absolute won't happen this week or the money transferred. I hope that doesn't impact on your property purchase."

I pause to digest all this information. It is a setback to my plans but not disastrous and a delay rather than change what everyone finally agrees to settle the divorce. I try to think through how it affects the purchase of my new home.

"Chris… Chris, are you still there?"

"Yes Debra, sorry just trying to think through all the implications."

"Don't worry, this is all normal stuff that has to be done. They've just left it a little late and it will delay your decree absolute. Why not call Maureen and let her think it through and save stressing yourself?"

"Actually that's a great idea. Ok, thanks for letting me know. I'll call her now."

"Bye Chris, I'll keep you updated."

Maureen isn't available so I leave her a message briefly outlining the problem. I hope she will call back sooner rather than later. I don't have time to worry because I need to meet Emma Briggs hoping it will go as well as our call yesterday.

Arriving at the entrance I worry I might bump into Gill and my mood and preparation will be affected. Making my way quietly to Emma's office I don't see any sign of her, which I am grateful for. Emma is there, the meeting starts and finishes on time, nothing unexpected arose and I leave having experienced one of the more effective business meetings I have ever been to.

Emma requires 10 training days and whatever preparation time I need to train a group of managers to improve their communications and coaching skills. It is part of a new supportive management culture being rolled out across the company. We agree a rate for the project, timescales and success criteria – all in the one meeting. These have taken many painful calls, emails and meetings going on for weeks with a few clients I had the misfortune to encounter – some even led to nothing after all the time and effort. This meeting is the opposite of them.

Saying goodbye, I fly out of the room in a great mood, turn the corner and bump straight into Gill carrying a cup of coffee that she spills over herself and the carpet. She hasn't recognised me yet as she concentrates on where the coffee spilt before looking up angry until she sees it is me and shows her surprise.

"Oh! It's you. What are you doing here?"

Ignoring her question I say, "Sorry you've spilt your coffee. I didn't see you come round the corner so fast."

"I wasn't fast, you were! Anyway why are you here?"

"Sorry Gill, it's none of your business now."

"Cheek! I will find out. Why are you so nasty?"

"That's a bit rich from you after all you've done."

I walk past her before our conversation deteriorates to a slanging match about matters that should remain private.

"Bye!" is all I hear as I carry on to the exit.

Taking a few deep breaths after sitting in my car before I drive away I curse myself for breaking the golden rule of never mixing business with pleasure. The training will be for another part of Gill's organisation although in the same building. I don't think she wants to cause any problems for me, more it being I feeling awkward after what happened. There isn't anything I can do now and logically nothing should be needed.

My thoughts are interrupted by a call from Len who gives me the good news that my fee will be increased to the rate I asked for and backdated to last Monday. In return my contract will be shortened by around one month. That is the perfect outcome for me and I thank Len, promising to work on the project immediately. To have the money and end the work with a client who became troublesome is better than I hoped last week. Thank goodness Len can solve a problem that HR couldn't get their heads round!

The journey back home is smooth and full of promise after the call with Len. The rest of my day is spent responding to emails from last week, setting up meetings and calls with each of Brian & Co.'s project team. You can sense the palpable relief that they knew something was going on but now they can continue. My life for the next few days will be much busier and personal stuff will take a back seat for a while. One thing I will not do though is compromise on visiting my mum though and I vow to see her tomorrow.

By the end of the day I have that feeling of tiredness and satisfaction. It is good to have a solid day of progress to show for my work and know I am being paid for it. Maureen hasn't called back which is the only blemish on my day and I make a note to chase her up in the morning.

I turn to my dating site afterwards but can see that no one has shown interest in me. With all the activity and possibilities at play with women I contacted I don't have the appetite to introduce myself to anyone new. Of course I do search but no one stands out from the crowd and I hope something can happen with Brighton Lolly, Trish or Letitia. But the message I get next is not from them; it is from Gill of all people!

'Hi Chris, didn't expect to see you again so quickly!'

I hum and hah about replying but don't want anything to affect my work with her organisation. I haven't done anything wrong but I am uncomfortable after what happened between us.

'Hi Gill, yes, it was a surprise! Sorry about the coffee.'

'Coffee stains are the least of my worries now.'

Oh no, not again. What can I say that won't involve me more?

'Sorry to hear that.'

'Would you fancy a drink this week? For old times' sake.'

Oh no, it is the last thing I want to do.

'I'm a bit busy this week I'm afraid.'

'Oh go on Chris! I need to talk and you're a good guy, probably the only guy who understands me. Please!'

I groan inwardly as I realise I am becoming her 'agony aunt'. It is the last thing I want to do or be but I find myself saying.

'OK, how about Thursday?'

'I'm going round to Linda's then. Can you make tomorrow?'

I quickly realise Letitia is calling tomorrow and she is a higher priority than Gill.

'Sorry, no can do. Friday?'

'Yeah, that's good for me too.'

'OK, let's meet near the station.'

'Thanks. I'll text you where.'

'OK, take care.'

'I'll try. Bye.'

My mood changes with the prospect of an unpredictable Gill to meet. Why didn't I just firmly say "no" and not bother? Am I a good guy or a weak guy? The jury is out at the moment on what type of guy I am. Do I want to avoid difficult emotional moments as I think of when I left Em and recently in a certain café in London twice?

The exchange of texts with Gill drains me. What is an evening of conversation going to be like? I shudder at the thought. How do I let myself get into messy situations like this?

The mood spirals downwards further when I get a message from Melanie. We met once a few weeks ago and the evening was OK but I am not interested in picking it up again after so long. She wanted time to focus on her son for a while and that's what the first part of her message covers with what happened since we met. No problem with that so far with me but then it gets difficult, as she wants to meet me again. I really don't know how to answer that request and just sit and stare at the screen until the words blur.

It is late in the evening but I pour another glass of wine to help support my mood swing and try to find a way to respond but no matter how I try I can't. It is the implication that I just sat and waited for her to contact me that throws me most. How do I deal with that? Should I bother replying? The wine glass is empty without any conclusion so I take the dilemma to bed and fall into a restless sleep.

DAY 61: WEDNESDAY

Today was a complete non-event. My mood yesterday evening continued to spiral down and combined with a virus, chill or something nasty I was wiped out for the whole day.

Thankfully I had enough food to crawl along to the kitchen every now and again to try to eat something – cereal was my best effort – and drink water, plenty of water, in fact a whole reservoir wouldn't have been overstating it.

Aches and pains with my heavy head and lack of energy (my 'wine virus'?) meant I just slept, rested or did very, very, little in bed all day. Was this a warning sign that my body's wine allowance was overstretched? Was it just a virus that hits hard and goes quickly?

I say 'goes quickly' because by the end of the evening I had picked up somewhat and ate some supper before walking, not crawling, back to my bed.

Needless to say all my plans for the day, whatever they were I couldn't remember went out the window – hopefully the virus followed them. I didn't check my phone or laptop for any emails all day. I hadn't even pulled the curtains to see if the world still existed. Today won first prize for being the non-event day of the year and I didn't want any competition from other days!

DAY 62: THURSDAY

Unlike yesterday I wake with a clear head, refreshed from a very long and deep sleep and make myself a cup of tea and come back to bed, a second home for the past 36 hours or so. I don't feel 100% but I can go through most of the gears and start by reading the latest email from Trish. I am growing to rely on her communicating regularly and making me smile.

'Hi Chris,

It sounds like you have a lovely, close relationship with your mum and your children that's really good, it's good that you value family life - something else we have in common then.

You talk about hating injustice - again I'm the same, one of the things I always think I'd do if I won the lottery is to start a charity for children as I work with children. I have a degree in Law but decided not to follow that path.

I would very much like to hear about your job and see your website too - I'm intrigued - it sounds very interesting and exciting the work you do but keep me on tenterhooks and tell me more when we meet!

That joke I like, it echoes my feelings on camping and such a coincidence as I was just saying recently to someone how I'd do one night of camping - just for the experience after which I want four strong walls around me and the comfort of a proper bed, proper bath, proper food etc.!

Have a good night. Trish'

Sadly I didn't have a good night through no fault of Trish's of course. It begins to feel like we can be on the same wavelength. A meeting of minds maybe? Without any delay I reply, as I know my day will be jam-packed now as I catch up with work and visit my mum.

'Hi Trish,

Firstly, I'm sorry for the delay in replying. I caught one of those nasty 24-hour viruses that wiped out my day. Thankfully I'm feeling much better today. I am a very lucky man to have such a strong relationship with my mum and my daughter. My son is a bit different to his sister and while I also have a strong relationship with him, he doesn't want such frequent contact. But I am there for each of them whenever they need support. They are the most important people in my life.

I don't have a close family; just a sister who lives a long way away and we have little common. My father died a few years ago. It is lovely to hear you have family members that you are close to. I can see how much they mean by the way you talk about them. I hope we can talk about them when we meet.

I won't say much except my work is nothing compared with what you do. That is a very challenging and stressful at times and I will like to discuss it more. All I will say about my work before you Google my name is it is the people I help, not the technology or organisations, that I get a buzz from. Helping remove someone's stress by solving his or her problem is the best satisfaction.

I hope your day is good, you're healthy, happy, and you feel you have achieved something. Chris'

After I reply there is a fuzzy warm feeling in my mind. It is amazing that I seem so 'in tune' with someone I haven't met yet. And that is my worry! Is it much easier to converse digitally? Can you connect emotionally this way but not when you meet them? I am not prepared to hope after so many disappointments but just note that it is different and not so far in a bad way.

I spend the next couple of hours catching up on work emails ahead of calls this afternoon. I decide to visit my mum next, relieved that it is a shorter journey to her new home now. Going to see her is literally a breath of fresh air as I drive there; the sun is shining and the air is warm. I'm still feeling good and energised, grateful the virus has passed. What is there not to enjoy about this day?

My mum is in fine form and her memory seems better but that may have been wishful thinking on my part. We have a good chat; she is settling into her new place and comfortable with the layout and people. After leaving I send Danny and Liz a photo of my mum and me and ask them to visit her soon.

I still haven't heard back from Maureen and call again as it is getting urgent now. That's when I hear the bad news; Maureen has been in an accident and was taken to hospital Tuesday. This is shocking news and I ask her secretary, Debbie, how Maureen is. All the pressure from clients while concerned for Maureen at the same time frazzles Debbie; they have worked together for years.

Maureen is now recovering at home after being released from hospital with cuts and bruises suffered when her car collided with a 'hit and run' driver who appears unhurt and hasn't checked how she was after the collision. I ask Debbie to pass on my best wishes to Maureen. The downside for me of this is I don't know what is happening about my purchase and bury myself in work trying not to worry about it. I gripe a little about fate messing my life up when I don't want or need it to!

It is busy, busy, busy, with work for the rest of the day. I get a buzz when it is like this and a lot of satisfaction solving problems and making people's work easier. By the end of the working day I am knackered, pleased to sit down to a lovely spaghetti Bolognese I cook, one of my favourites, probably because it is easy for me to cook too. Relieved too that my virus hasn't reappeared.

As I eat loud music comes up from below thumping away with a bass beat. It breaks the mood as I eat the rest of my meal while the stress key in my back gradually turns round and round. Eventually after an hour of non-stop music without a pause I go downstairs to Colin and Emma's flat and knock on the door. There is no reply as I wait for the door to be open so I knock again a little louder. Still there is no response so I knock louder and longer while I go through my contacts on my phone for the landlord's number. The door suddenly opens and someone I haven't seen before and is not Colin or Emma stands and looks at me.

"Can you turn the music down please?"

"Why?"

"Why!"

"Yeah, why?"

"Because it is too loud."

"Col said I could do what I like while I stay here."

"I'm sure you can but not if it affects your neighbours."

"He said you wouldn't mind."

"Well he's wrong to say that and he's wrong because I do mind."

"I'm just letting off a bit of steam so cool it and go with the flow."

"If you don't turn the music down now I will complain to Colin and to his landlord!"

"Whatever..." and closes the door leaving me standing on my own outside.

As soon as I get back I try calling Colin but no reply or voicemail to leave a message so I call the landlord who also doesn't reply but at least has a voicemail so I leave a message. The uncertainty over my divorce and buying of my flat really eats away at me. The depressing thought of not being able to move for months to come doesn't even bear thinking about.

When Letitia calls I retreat to my bedroom where the noise is softened by the walls between downstairs and me. What then follows is a conversation that feels like I am peeling an onion layer by layer. We start off with the usual niceties, how we both are and what we have done since our last call. Letitia sounds like a lovely and interesting lady who I want to meet but then we peel away the layer exposing her plans.

"You like Portugal a lot?" I ask.

"Yes, I have taken quite a few holidays there."

"Are you planning to visit it again?"

"I hope so. I want to talk about it when we meet."

"Can you give me some information now? Like when you want to go there."

There is a long pause before Letitia replies. "Well... I am hoping to go at the end of the month."

"Oh, how many days will you be away?"

"I don't know yet. I'm not planning to come back any time soon."

"Oh!" then a very long pause from me. "So you're thinking of moving there permanently?"

"Probably. I'll see how it goes. Is that a problem?"

"Well... yes it is actually. I'm not sure how or if I fit with your plans. That's something I hoped we would discuss if we meet. I continue, "How fixed are your plans? Have you got somewhere to live? Do you know when you're flying out?"

"I have a place to rent from the start of next month and I have a flight booked at the end of this month."

I pause as I digest this news. There is no way I can see me developing such a strong relationship with Letitia before she flies. While I am not necessarily against long-distance relationships, the thought of having to fly there and back to see her isn't appealing or sustainable. It feels more like possibly the right person at the wrong time for both of us.

"I'm not sure how this can work. We haven't met yet you will leave in a few weeks. What are you expecting me to say?"

"Well, I hope we can discuss it and maybe you can join me for a while and see how things work out."

"Hmm, I suppose that is one option we can consider. My personal circumstances won't easily fit with that though. My mum is in a nursing home, I'm about to buy a flat and I want to see my children regularly which flying back and forth from Portugal won't make that easy. I really do like you and I do want to meet you but I can't see how this can work. Can you?"

Now there is a long pause from Letitia only broken by the sound of the music thumping even louder from downstairs.

"That's why I want to meet you, to see how we feel about each other, and then discuss our plans."

"Let me ask you one more question. Will you consider changing your plans and not moving to Portugal so you can continue seeing me here?"

An even longer pause followed this time with a long sigh.

"No."

With that response the end of any relationship is sealed. Maybe if we met at a different time in our lives it can have worked? The fact is now if we meet it is clear to me that it won't have a happy outcome.

"I'm sorry to hear that Letitia as I can't see me moving to Portugal with you at the moment. Another time in my life I may jump at the chance but not now."

"Yes, I understand Chris and I agree with you. I'm very sorry that it won't happen. Would you still like to meet, you know, just in case you might change your mind?"

Having two bad meetings in London recently, knowing what the outcome is going to be, it doesn't appeal at all.

"No, I think it will make the parting more painful than it is now."

"Maybe you're right but if you change your mind, please, please, let me know."

"I will but it is unlikely."

"I suppose this is goodbye then?"

"Yes, sadly it is. I wish you all the best for the future."

"Thank you and I wish the same for you."

"Bye."

"Bye Chris."

I am really upset after our call. I really like Letitia and how she behaves. But moving to Portugal isn't an option and so I look forward to meeting Obi and Trish. My life means I will be here for at least the next few weeks even if I wasn't going on these dates. Sometimes life just sucks and this is one of those occasions.

The music suddenly stops and the silence envelopes me, perpetuating my mood. Why does life have to be so frustrating and difficult? Two messages, one from Danny and the other from Liz, interrupt my reverie. Both say similar things asking how their nan is and hoping to see her soon. They also say things are more settled back home with their mum. I respond saying that is good news and that I hope they will see me soon.

Exhausted I make my way to bed and hope for another email from Trish to raise my mood tomorrow.

DAY 63: FRiDAY

My new normal routine takes place as I read Trish's latest email while sipping my cuppa:

'Hi Chris,

How are you today? Better I hope. I worked from home today, which I needed to, as I am actually quite sleepy - so happy not to be expending so much energy travelling in the rain!

Thanks for sharing about your family; it will be nice to talk more about our respective families when we meet up.

So I clicked the link and saw your website - so you are an Internet whizz kid - I am very impressed! I imagine you've always being a technology type, a good problem solver, maths and sciency type of person? You can teach me a thing or two then - those things are definitely not my strong suit. But you also write very well so you must be a multi talented soul.

I'm also looking forward to finding out why and how you started up your own business - I've always wanted to start my own so I can pick your brains. It must be so liberating working for yourself and getting the personal satisfaction knowing that it's all your creation. Well done; innovative people are so exciting!

My job is definitely not in the same league as you but I see we share the same sentiments about helping others - I love children and young people. I have a lot of empathy for them and love to help them to reach their potential but yes it's stressful emotionally and physically. I'm happy to share more with you later.

I'm glad that you had some good quality time with your friends and family and I have no complaints about how long you are taking to respond to me but I also look forward to hearing from you.

Speak to you soon - have a good evening. Trish'

Just the tonic I need after the turmoil of yesterday. Why am I seeing Gill? Why do I want to respond to Melanie? Why even see Brighton Lolly? One simple reason why is that I have no idea if we will meet or if we will want to see each other. I want to keep my options open until it is clear whom I want as my special friend and they feel the same. It seems so easy but proved so elusive so far.

I reply while still in bed to Trish's email:

'Hi Trish,

I'm feeling good, much better now. I hate to disillusion you over technology and me but I am not an IT expert. I understand how technology works but can be as puzzled as anyone why my smartphone, etc. won't do something. My background is in training and communications (thank you for saying I write well). I try to help organisations and people meet their business needs, basically making it easier for people to do their work better.

Better discussed in more detail when we meet if you want me to. I am amazed at what I have achieved on my own. To get away from poisonous office politics and be able to do what I'm best at has been liberating. I'm happy to help you to think about it. It's never too late. *Carpe diem*! Seize the day! Go for it!

Actually I see your job as above mine. I help organisations and it can have a big impact but you are helping some of the most vulnerable people in our society. I am not in the same league as you where that is concerned. I am very lucky my specialised skills are in demand and people are willing to pay to use them but that's all it is as I see it. Chris'

Nothing like starting the day with an uplifting exchange! While we still haven't met apart from our profile photos I am falling in love with Trish's personality already. Next Sunday seems a long, long, way away because I am keen to finally meet her. I realise I mustn't make assumptions and take each day and date as they come but I live in hope…

After reaching that high the rest of my day is spent continuing with work for Brian & Co. and keeping my other clients happy with progress updates. One thing I know is my accountant will be pleased with me when he audits my business accounts!

When work finishes and I have eaten dinner I turn to my dating life. My first port of call is Obi to confirm that I would love to meet her on Sunday at Brighton Marina. Where and when are my only questions?

Then I quickly get ready to meet Gill. I have been putting off whether to meet or not until it was too late or certainly too late for my conscience to cancel or postpone. I am not looking forward to it; question why on earth am I doing it and frankly can't wait to be back home again. Not the ideal mood for a happy evening I know.

I don't arrive on time as my train is late and as I enter the pub I see Gill in the corner glancing at her watch before looking up and smiling when she sees me. Quickly going over and giving her an air kiss on the cheek I ask what she is drinking and go to the bar and order a bottle of white wine for us to share. Taking it back with two glasses I sit opposite Gill and smile at her. We talk about our weeks and what we've done since bumping (literally!) into each other. I avoid any mention of dating; not because I want to make Gill jealous or fear she will pry into that part of my life. No, it is because Gill isn't relevant any more to that part of my life or probably any part of it now.

Gill seems to think otherwise though and tells me about her latest relationship breakup just over a week ago. The story has a familiar theme to the previous partners. As she tells her story it slowly dawns on me why she wants to meet me. She sees me as a stand-in for her until she finds a new boyfriend. She wants me to be her bit of fun, a "friend with benefits", and assumes I won't object! While the penny is dropping about the real purpose for our meeting I listen in wonder at her bafflement over why yet another boyfriend has left the scene.

Gill finishes her story with a look of expectancy at me; I believe she thinks I will embrace her or come and sit next to her, putting my arm around her. When I stay sitting opposite her a look of puzzlement comes across her face. She just doesn't get it as far as understanding people, especially potential and actual boyfriends. Slowly and politely I make it clear that I am not interested in being her boyfriend, pop-up lover or frankly any role in her life. Our time together wasn't great for me and I have moved on, long gone and far away now from my brief hookups with Gill.

By the time I finish Gill looks half the size she was and slunk into the corner of the bench she is sitting on.

"So you don't find me attractive then?"

"Not now Gill, not now."

"But you did so what's changed?"

"I've changed Gill. I've learnt from each woman I've met and use that to move on as I try to find the right woman."

"Don't you find me attractive any more?"

"It's not that Gill. I am different now and not interested in a relationship of any type with you now."

"There's no need to be that blunt!"

"But you can't see that I was never interested in just having sex with you on a no-strings basis."

"I never put it like that."

"You didn't have to but that is what you meant. We are very different people. The only thing we have in common is I'm working for the same organisation you work for. That's all."

Gill is like a balloon that is losing its air as she deflates further into the bench opposite. I do feel very sorry for her and responsible for how she feels now. But I know if I console her she will try to turn it into something sexual and meaningful.

"Look Gill, I want to leave here on good terms with you. I didn't have to come here and didn't know why you really wanted to meet me again. I'm flattered but the bottom line is I'm not that type of bloke, never was, never will be and that is your problem. You need to understand yourself better; what you are looking for and why? Please don't keep making the same mistake."

Gill bursts into tears as she sobs, "You're right, I know you are. I get so carried away, head over heels in love, and then bang, I'm dumped again. Linda tells me the same thing."

"Listen to how you can change and test it out. Try to resist your natural instinct and see what happens.'

"Thanks Chris. This can't be easy for you."

I shrug, "I just want to help if I can. I'm not sure if I have but at least I've tried to. I want you to be happy, in love and to be loved. It's not going to be with me though."

"Thanks, you're right. You will make a woman very happy as her special friend." She looks up and smiles brightly through the tears she is gently dabbing away from her cheeks and eyes. Looking at the empty bottle she says, "I haven't bought you a drink yet. Shall we have another bottle?"

"No, I think we've both had enough. It feels like the natural end to our evening. Let's go."

"You're right. I don't want to go home though."

"I can't help you there Gill. Sorry but I can't."

"I know but you can't blame me for trying one last time can you?

I smile back as we both get up. "No, you get top marks for trying."

We hug each other outside the pub as Gill gets into the taxi she called and I walk in the opposite direction to the station. It's been a long evening and a long day. The joy of reading Trish's email first thing this morning, feels like a lifetime ago.

DAY 64: SATURDAY

Today is going to follow an old tradition – seeing the final pre-season friendly that my football team play at home – and a new tradition – reading the latest email from Trish in bed while sipping my tea.

'Hi Chris,

It's nice to hear that you're feeling good and that you had a good day with work - if I left work on Monday I think there'd be about three people I'd keep in touch with.

I'm not disillusioned - just disgusted! Sorry just joking thanks for explaining - you should be proud and yes please explain more when we meet because I probably don't understand that well but I like learning new things so it'll be all good. I can imagine how happy you would have been when that offer came up - I will be exactly the same - I'm working from home on Monday and I already feel instantly lighter in mood... Office politics - don't get me started!

Tomorrow funnily enough I am planning to go to a local farm to pick fruit and veg and they said they have strawberries - so if you lived closer I would have picked you a few punnets. I am planning to go to the gym and may go to church as I do sometimes - are you a churchgoer at all? I'm not a stuffy churchgoer though - thoroughly modern.

Hope that you had a good day and are having a good evening too. Trish'

If only Trish knew what my evening had been like. I shudder at the memory of the awkward meeting and conversation with Gill. Maybe one day I can tell her and she will understand. I am amazed how well we connect with our sharing of jokes and views on work. We aren't going to be short of subjects to chat when we do meet and I am more confident it is when not if we do meet now.

My reply to Trish is:

'Hi Trish,

Now, if you can freeze some strawberries for me, you will have a friend for life! Whenever I go strawberry picking I seem to eat half of them while I'm picking! I'm tempted to see you this Sunday instead of next Sunday!

Thank you. I am proud of what I have achieved which means the people I have helped rather than the money I have saved organisations.

No, I am not religious but I accept and respect people who are. If you ask me to, I wouldn't have a problem going to church with you for instance. It is a pity that so many wars and conflicts have been fought in the name of different religions over the centuries. People should be free to do what they want and not feel victimised.

This afternoon I will follow a tradition over many years of watching the final pre-season friendly at home with my two football mates, James and Gordon. We've done this for years and go to the home matches together. If we win a game I won't need a train to get home, I will just float on a cloud home instead!

Tomorrow I'm going to... big drum roll please... send you my suggestions for you to laugh at and dismiss as hopelessly inadequate... well, hopefully not all of them. Relax and enjoy the weekend. You deserve it! Chris'

Next up is my reply to Melanie's text. I've been mulling this over for a while but decide I can't ignore, she deserves a reply even if it isn't what she will want to hear from me.

'Hi Melanie, I'm glad you enjoyed your time with your son and you have such a strong relationship. It's good to hear from you again but my life has moved on since we met a few weeks ago. I'm happy to stay in touch by texting but I'm not sure meeting up will be good for either of us. Sorry if that isn't what you hoped to hear from me. Take care, Chris.'

After breakfasting, showering and setting my football gear out on my bed to change into I make some coffee. The next message I receive nearly makes me fall off my chair as I drink my coffee while looking forward to meeting James and Gordon ahead of the game. It is from London Lady of all people. I haven't heard from her neither was I expecting to after the debacle of our one and only meeting. It is a simple enough text. 'How are you? Would you still like to meet up?' After all that happened and the period of time that has passed I am totally surprised by it.

Several thoughts go through my head: a) She really does fancy me! b) She doesn't mention my name c) Can she have sent this to other men? d) Why am I even bothering to think like this? I am not interested and that is that. Neither do I want to engage in messages that can go anywhere or nowhere.

ONLINE DATING FOR THE NERVOUS

A busy morning with online dating got that bit busier with a quick reply from Melanie.

'I'm sad to get your message Chris. I thought the whole point about online dating is you get to meet lots of people at the same time. Why can't we?'

I worry that further communication could spiral down into bitter debate. I also want to avoid saying that I don't like her enough to want to see her again and hurt her feelings. Sometimes I wish I don't have this compulsion to reply thinking I am doing the right thing. Is it just what I think is right? Of course it is but I aim to be objective and be OK with everyone I communicate with. I know I don't always get it right but that is my approach even if I do fail sometimes. This looks like being one of those occasions.

I focus now on the football; Melanie can wait for my response. It is time to change and meet Gordon and James. The anticipation of another football season just around the corner is starting to grip me. Dating has far too many permutations and potential outcomes but with football your team wins, loses or draws (unless it is postponed) which is much simpler and certain. There is something to be said for the enjoyment of football compared with the anxieties of online dating.

It is great to have a break from dating and just have some time with friends I have known through football for decades. I don't have to be careful about their feelings, remember their names or what they said in calls or messages before I meet them. They are Gordon and James and their focus is our local football team. After getting ready I catch the train to the station nearest to the ground where they are waiting for me.

We walk to the ground, catching up on chit-chat about each other and the latest gossip about who we are interested in buying, selling or just about our football club. Once inside I make my way to the bar for the first of many times to get three pints and we get on to more serious subjects. Both Gordon and James are interested, *very* interested, in my online dating. What have I done? Why that dating site? What are the women like? Lots and lots of questions, far more than I anticipated. After half an hour of this and still no let up in their curiosity a strange feeling comes over me. Maybe both Gordon and James's marriages are not as rock solid as I thought?

It is nearly an hour of grilling by the Gordon and James Inquisition before there is a pause so I can turn the conversation around by asking how they are then more importantly how are their wives. The candid questions they ask me about dating earlier become cautious and limited responses about their own situations. Slowly after buying more drinks it starts to come out that both their marriages are in trouble. Gordon's seems to be on life support and explain his vagueness when we chatted on the phone a while ago.

Wow! When we met at the end of the last football season there was sadness and sympathy for my divorce and plans to start online dating. Now at our next meeting there almost appears to be envy and jealousy for me being a single guy, free to choose whom I am with and what I do. It is devastating to see my two oldest friends possibly, no probably, going down the same slippery, painful, route that I went down over a year ago. Football for them is a sanctuary from the domestic stress they are experiencing. I know what that feels like and I am only too happy to buy the drinks and offer any insights.

By the time we go our separate ways after the match we have probably drunk too much and two out of the three of us will regret the journey home and the atmosphere they encounter from their loved one. For me there will be freedom and peace when I get home. We also cover the options they each face, practical options like should they go or stay and what they can do to save their marriages even at this late stage for Gordon and his wife. What an unexpected turnaround in our situations I think as I journey home on the train? The fact we thrashed the other team isn't the main focus for the first time in oh, I don't know, how many years, probably for the first time!

I sit down with some fish and chips and a cup of tea – I don't fancy wine after drinking so much beer at the football – and watch the TV but really churning over all that was said between us before and after the football. The journey I am on now has an upward feel about it after plummeting into depths of despair at the start of the last football season. I don't envy anyone but especially not my two football friends having to take the same route.

The loud music starts up again in the flat below. I toy with going down again and realise it will probably only make the situation worse and antagonise him further. Then there is a sharp knock on my door! Surely he hasn't come to talk to me? No, he hasn't because it is an angry and irate Meghan knocking on my door minus Blodwyn.

"Can you hear that awful racket in there Christoph… Chris?"

"Yes and I talked to him when it happened a few evenings ago and got nowhere."

"A few nights ago? I must have been out."

"Well apart from trying Colin and Emma or the landlord again I don't know what to do."

Her lips are very thin as Meghan says, "I know what to do. Leave it with me." So I do.

Five minutes or so later the music suddenly stops and everywhere is quiet again. In fact you could have heard the proverbial pin drop it is so quiet. Whatever Meghan said or did has been a complete success. It means I will be the one to thank her this time. I will miss Meghan a little when I leave!

Checking my dating site I see that Obi says she will meet me by the cinema around 3pm tomorrow. That is good with me and I confirm that with her. Next up is Melanie's message and I decide to just confirm I am no longer interested which is the truth and to wish her the best for the future. It is easier to say that after my afternoon with Gordon and James. My life is complex enough and I need to simplify it where possible. Saying goodbye to Melanie like Gill is the right thing to do now.

DAY 65: SUNDAY

Today I will meet Obi so it feels strange reading my daily email from Trish. The rules of online dating blur as far as contacting more than one person at the same time. It doesn't make sense to me to only be in contact with one woman at a time. It could take forever and a day to find my special friend. No, I can draw the line when I see someone regularly but until then I feel I have to see or at least be corresponding with more than one woman.

But even though logic tells me I am right emotionally I am uncomfortable with it. I am not 'two timing' anyone because I am not really 'one timing' anyone. In fact I only saw Obi once, same as Melanie and London Lady who contacted me yesterday and yet to meet Trish. How long before a relationship becomes 'exclusive' and you stop seeing anyone else or contacting or being contacted by other women? This brave new world of online dating is very difficult at times like this for me.

Trish's daily email begins:

'Hello Chris,

How are you doing today? Still elated from yesterday's win I imagine - well done.

I went fruit and vegetable picking this morning with my sister and got some beetroot, marrow, sweet corn, a few raspberries and strawberries - but the strawberries are not very impressive so I didn't bother getting much, so sorry none to freeze I'm afraid - next time and then maybe I can gain that friend for life.

It's good that you are open to the religious views of others, I believe in live and let live provided you are not hurting others ... Sometimes I get some peace and reassurance from attending church - perhaps we will attend a service together one day who knows?

I'm looking forward to meeting you.

Have a good night. Trish'

I relish the words she writes and the thought she puts in too. I start to reply with my suggestions of places to see and things to do when we meet next Sunday. It takes me a while during the morning with breaks for breakfast and getting ready for Obi before it I send it.

'Hi Trish,

Well here is my much anticipated list of places for my 'girly girl' to choose from! Trying to find somewhere where we can get to know each other better in a nice setting while taking account of the weather.

Meet at Covent Garden

While this will be very busy there are so many restaurants and cafes very close together. If you say "yes" then I will find a place that has a fish and vegetarian menu. We can walk on down to Trafalgar Square, etc. if we want to.

Meet at Embankment

ONLINE DATING FOR THE NERVOUS

There is a lovely walk over the bridge to the South Bank and a selection of places by the Thames that we can choose from. A walk along the riverbank afterwards if we want to.

Meet at Westminster

We can take the ferry down to Greenwich, have something to eat/drink there and enjoy the park or other places and take the ferry back.

Meet at Regent's Park

Obviously this is weather dependent but there are several cafes and restaurants to choose from and plenty of space to walk and chat.

Meet at Camden

Maybe too busy on Sunday to find a place we want to chat but there is plenty of choice and a lovely walk along the canal as well. Again, it's weather dependent.

If none of these appeal to you then I'm falling back on museums or parks or indoor places like Leadenhall.

I hope you like one of these suggestions.

Look forward to hearing your judgement and if I have managed to add another quality to my profile... or not. Chris'

I then follow up with a separate response to her email from yesterday.

'Well I'm absolutely gutted there are no strawberries for me. Sob, sob, sob... I will just somehow have to find the strength and willpower to get through today. Seriously, it was very thoughtful of you to consider them. I agree, their season is over, as I found recently when a punnet I bought went off in my fridge. Yes, more tears...

I don't think there are any sides to me. You can judge when we meet on Sunday. I am an open book with no secrets. What you see is what you get with me. I think you may be similar from what you have said so far. Chris'

I get a buzz from sending it and anticipating her response. It gives her insight into my thoughts and for me into her likes and dislikes. I do worry that it can miss the mark by a wide distance and cause a problem. Anything that is uncertain and can cause anxiety is not my cup of tea. I want life to be straightforward with a certain amount of stability. Don't we all? Well, most of us probably unless you are an adrenalin junkie seeking thrills!

After lunch I drive to Brighton Marina to meet with Obi. The sun is shining and it is hot – sunglasses yes but shorts? No it's too early to show my legs yet! I am really looking forward to finding out more about Obi and her life. It is good we want a second date, as I am not sure how attractive to me Obi is and vice versa. Maybe we are both still checking each other out? Maybe we can find that spark to ignite our relationship? Maybe, maybe, maybe… at least the weather puts me in a good mood.

I park my car and make my way to where we agreed to meet. It is packed with crowds of people milling around the boardwalk, enjoying the sunshine, bars and sailing boats moored in the marina. I wait and I wait over 30 minutes before I go to a nearby café and wait for her. I have no idea how long she will be or if she has changed her mind. I try to stay calm and not be too anxious as I sit back and soak up the sun while sipping a latte coffee. If we continue to meet then we need to exchange mobile numbers and Obi being more punctual are subjects I need to raise. It is a further half hour before Obi walks through the maze of tables, chairs and customers to join me at my table. I was about to give up and go and it was only the warm sun and interest in everyone and everything around me that prevented that.

"Hi Chris! How are you?" Fed up for being kept waiting so long is my honest answer but instead I say.

"I'm OK. How are you?"

"A bit frazzled to be honest but it's good to be here."

"Do you want to stay here or go somewhere else?"

"Let's stay. I don't see any spare tables as I walked here." Obi sits down and smiles at me.

This isn't going the way I want it to. She is late but no apology, no offer to buy me a drink to show any regret. It's not starting off on the right footing but there is time to retrieve things. Gritting my teeth I ask Obi what she wants to drink.

"Can I be cheeky and ask if we can get a bottle of wine? Push the boat out… nothing too strong, something light and refreshing?"

"I'll see what I can do." Getting up and moving through the tables to the bar I scan through the wine list. I start at the top and work down until I find a house white wine that is cheaper and isn't strong. That is about as generous as I want to be after my initial exchange with Obi. I walk back with the wine, four glasses and a jug of water on a tray but Obi isn't at the table. Feeling angry and anxious I look around quickly but can't see her until I see her waving her arm from a table in the corner.

"I think this is cosier for a chat than where we were; hope you don't mind."

I do mind actually but again keep it to myself. I smile and nod, putting the tray on the table and setting out its contents. After sitting down so Obi is to my right I realise it is a better place, certainly for private conversations. A switch has been flicked within Obi so the business-like woman has become a more engaging woman who shows interest in what I say and me.

Our conversation ranges over our careers, what is good, what can be better and what else we can do? It then focuses on Brighton and we realise how much we have in common, the same pubs, clubs and bars. We carry on chatting but there is something not right; the spark is just fizzing in the background and there is an invisible barrier that stops us getting any closer. Whatever the reasons why Obi is holding back it means we are unlikely to meet again. I resign myself to enjoying the company, location and sunshine; Obi is good company but doesn't feel like my special friend.

We both seem to come to the same conclusion around seven o'clock. It is either more drink with a meal and leaving our cars here or ending the meeting and going our separate ways, probably for good. The latter is both our choices and we part:

"Goodbye Obi and thanks for meeting me. I enjoyed our time together but don't think we will be meeting again. You're a lovely person but I think we are both looking for someone else."

"Oh!" is her reaction, which surprises me, "I think we are getting on well."

"Aren't you missing that all important spark?"

"Hmm, maybe but it might be you are a slow burner. My last boyfriend took a few months before the spark came to life."

"Really?"

"Yes, really. I think it's because we haven't confronted the elephant in the room."

Not sure what she means I just have a blank look of bafflement across my face.

"I'm talking about my size Chris. I'm rather on the large size aren't I?"

I admit she isn't the skinniest woman I have been with but it isn't a problem to me.

"Not really and I haven't a problem with your size. If I did I wouldn't have contacted you in the first place or want to meet you again, would I?"

"Hmm… I'll need to think about that."

"Well that's not why I'm saying goodbye I can assure you."

"I accept you're being sincere and like you feel there isn't a spark right now. Let's see how we feel over the next few days. OK?"

"OK."

"Bye Chris."

"Bye Obi."

That's how we part, no hug, no kiss, just a simple farewell. Any reflections about Obi are abruptly ended when I see my car has been damaged while parked. The bumper has two dents and some of the paintwork above scratched. Of course there is no note to apologise or admit liability and no eyewitnesses! That seriously lowers my mood as I drive home with an unwanted task to add to my list for Monday.

Another date full of hope and anticipation: another date ending with disappointment and depression. When will I find the right formula to meet that special friend I need? I still hope I will but I don't want to put any more pressure on myself. Getting back home the first thing I do is visit the dating site and review everyone who is new, check who has liked or viewed my profile and who I have already responded to and draw a complete blank.

I go to bed with a mood of despondency.

DAY 66: MONDAY

I sleep in late as it took me a long time to drop off to sleep as I chuntered away in my mind over Obi, my car and what next Sunday will be with no other dates on the horizon. Instead of my recent usual routine of reading and replying to Trish's emails I quickly shower and while I am breakfasting call my garage, then my insurance company and finally Maureen's secretary.

The car insurance excess mean it will probably be cheaper to pay for the repair than claim it and lose my no claims bonus. At least the insurance company accepts it is covered. The garage want to inspect it and if I pop round this afternoon they will assess the damage and cost of repairs.

Maureen's secretary can't give me any more information other than that she will let Maureen know I still need to speak with her. Her injuries include some to her face that make it difficult for her to speak but her hands are now free from the bandages so I may get an email sometime soon. I thank her but curse my bad luck that her accident happened at a critical stage in my flat purchase.

Over coffee I get round to reading Trish's email.

'Hi Chris,

You are a charmer and you have really excelled yourself. I do love some of those imaginative date choices! The ferry ride is my favourite so let's do it! Looking forward to meeting you in a week's time!

Apart from me spoiling it with news of "no strawberries" how was your weekend?

My Sunday wasn't great with my grandson being unwell but the good news is that he's improving. I do love babysitting - children are just so natural and fun - even when they're being a bit naughty, they can sometimes be so funny and you have to bite back the laughter so as not to encourage them.

I think that from the personality traits that I have picked up so far that you will enjoy having grandchildren - were you a "hands-on dad" - with the nappies, feeding, wiping up sick, etc.? How old are your son and daughter?

I'm having a study day today to get an assignment done - since you've told me what you have to do I'm feeling a hundred times better about it - so thank you.

Have a great day and all the best with your work. Trish'

My response to Trish is easy after reading her email.

'Hi Trish,

I'm glad you like my suggestions. I can't think of anything better than a cruise down the Thames to Greenwich with you next Sunday!

I hope your start to the week has been good. The sea is a short walk from me and I can hear the waves breaking on the beach. It's magnificent and helps sustain me while I knuckle down to lots of calls and implement Training and Comms plans for clients that I've developed. I've attached a photo I took while I was out walking of the waves.

I am very pleased that your grandson is improving and will be back at school soon. Yes, children that age are very entertaining and so funny. Yes, I was a "hands-on" dad and did my share of everything… except breastfeeding.

Umm, I will explain what I am doing when we meet. My website gives an overview but I don't expect you to read it again - once is enough!

One thing these daily emails have achieved is I don't feel I will be meeting a stranger on Sunday but someone who I already have got to know and like. Do you feel the same? There still are gaps but it isn't a blank canvas. I haven't asked you about your previous relationships, as you haven't about mine. I think these are best discussed in person.

To be honest though, most importantly to me is how you are now, I am now, and whether we can be happy together in the future whatever that relationship will be that we are both comfortable with. I always try to be positive and optimistic while being realistic. Chris (your humble consultant and strawberry taster)'

These daily communications do give me hope and partly restore my faith that I can meet the right woman for me. Maybe it will be Trish? Who knows? I am determined that I will not let my hopes get carried away; all can change in a day as I have experienced several times already.

Apart from a trip to my garage that say they can repair it later this week I just work through calls, emails and planning milestones and updates for each of my clients' projects. The damage to my car could have been worse which is some consolation for me. The repairs are expensive enough and I will have to claim the costs back. 'Touch up jobs' on paintwork and knocking out a dent or two are a thing of the past. Now it is replacing the whole part, sprayed beforehand, and brought in from outside by my garage. Oh for the good old days I think wistfully. At least I can still drive the car until it is repaired.

A quiet evening is disturbed by a call from my mum's nursing home. Can I come now, as they are concerned for her? They won't give me any more information over the phone just a sense of urgency to get there quickly. When I arrive they quickly escort me to my mum's room. As I enter she turns to me, bursts into tears and rushes to hug me.

"Bill, oh Bill! Why did you leave me? Where have you been?"

Bill was my dad's name. It looks like my mum mistakes me for my dad. We do look similar with the same colour hair but something is seriously wrong with my mum for her to assume I am my dad, her husband. I look over her shoulder at the nurses who share my look of concern. After a few minutes my mum relaxes her grip and slumps down on her bed where the nurses gently help her to lie down on top.

Later the sister tells me this is sadly normal but they hadn't expected my mum to deteriorate to this stage quite so quickly. It is difficult to forecast how fast her decline will be. I am determined to see her more often and to get my children to see her soon.

DAY 67: TUESDAY

Back to my normal routine and with cup in hand I sip my tea while reading Trish's latest email in bed.

'Hello Chris!

Thanks, that photo is absolutely amazing - I love it! How far from the sea do you live? Looks like you're standing right out there on the sea front.

How lovely to live by the sea - I remember you mentioning living near the seafront - I'll go back to your profile again and have another peek and as you say maybe see it for real one day.

My grandson is still a bit husky but getting there. It is very good that you are a "hands-on dad" not everybody is. The hardest bit of course was what I called the "night duty" - up every two hours for feeds. I certainly don't miss that bit but you're right it's all worth it. I'm happy to talk more about them when we meet as well as some of the other stuff.

I am on the same page as you regards our conversations, I am really enjoying talking to you and getting to know you better and feel that I'll be far more relaxed than if we'd met earlier. Your personality through the emails feels like someone that I can get on with well, yes there are gaps of course but I agree with you that talking about some things in person is better and I like what you said about the people we are now being what is most important...positive, optimistic and realistic are words that chime with me too.

Have a very good night humble strawberry tasting consultant. Trish'

My response to Trish for her uplifting email is:

'Hi my lovely word motivator!

You're right about the nightly feeds. I had it down to a fine art by singing songs I sang in the choir at junior school and knew exactly how many steps it was from the door to the window so I can close my eyes and try to rest while singing, walking, burping and helping settle Danny and Liz - multi-tasking (gosh, as a man I can do that!).

Have you heard of the song "Rock and Roll lullaby" by 10cc? Wonderfully talented and creative, best band in the 1970s in my humble opinion.

Your approach to get to know each other, enjoy the conversation and each other's personalities, for you to have key questions answered, has been absolutely right. I am really looking forward to meeting this funny, engaging, lady who is interested in me as much as I am in her.

For me today is a mix of interview calls and writing more action plans. Oh, and some food shopping...

Your very own humble strawberry consultant.'

Communicating with Trish raises my spirits and creates much

needed optimism with me. A call to my mum's nursing home gives me an update on how she slept and a request for me to visit again today which I am happy to fit in with my schedule of calls and meetings today.

It jogs my memory and I message both my children with the latest news about their Nan and implore them to go see her this week. I warn them in a series of texts that she is changing quickly from being the Nan they are used to seeing and talking to.

The rest of my morning is taken up with work – calls, emails, etc. – and it isn't until after lunch that I can visit my mum. Sadly, when I get there I can see instantly she is the same as last evening. Her question as soon as I come into the room :-

"Bill…?"

Follows with a confused look on her face is all I need to see and hear. The next hour or so I spend talking with her, reassuring her who I am, that she is safe and with people who care for her. I come away realising that visiting my mum is likely to become part of my daily routine from now on.

Feeling sad when I get back, I bump into Meghan going on another of her constitutionals with Blodwyn eagerly pulling on her lead.

"I don't what you did to stop the news but thank you all the same."

"I told him if he didn't stop I would call the police."

"But why would that stop him? They don't normally respond to a noisy party."

"They will do if said I heard a woman shouting 'Help!' loudly."

"Would you do that?" That is incredible!

"Yes and not for the first time."

"Wow! Well it did the trick, thanks," and I walk up to my flat in awe of Meghan. Outrageous and incorrect though it is, the threat had an immediate impact.

I call Maureen's secretary to complain that I still haven't heard by email or text what is happening. She again apologises and promises to let Maureen know. This is getting frustrating and I don't know what I can do which lowers my mood.

As I prepare dinner and look forward to a quiet evening at home my mobile rang. It is Rachel, very apologetic, asking if I am free if she pops over this evening. Surprised but pleased I say by all means and look forward to seeing her. It is rare for us to meet at each other's places; normally it is texts, calls or meetings at venues – the last time when we got drunk stuck in my mind.

Eating dinner and clearing everything away I ponder what can be so important or urgent? The buzzer sounds so I will soon find out! Rachel comes in breathless, full of excitement, says, "Hello!" and gives me a hug and then shouts out, "I'm pregnant!"

Wow! I know she is happy with her boyfriend but this is very sudden, she has only known him for a few weeks. "Congratulations! When is the baby due?" It sounds very clichéd but I am stunned and don't know what else to say.

"Not sure, I've only just found out! I haven't even told Roy yet."

"Why not? Why me? Why... ?"

"He's away working and his mobile is switched off and you're my best friend, always there for me with the big news. I *had* to tell someone or explode!"

"I would say let's celebrate, but I'm guessing you're not drinking now."

"Oh go on! Just a small glass won't do any harm will it?"

"If you say so." And go to the fridge to take a chilled bottle of white wine out.

"I haven't got champagne but this is the best I have to offer in wine."

"Mmm… that tastes good. Probably be the last I'll have for a long time." Sipping slowly Rachel relishes the flavour.

"I won't ask you how it happened but I'm surprised as you've only known Roy a relatively short time."

"A short time but beautiful so far. He's a wonderful man. We seem so right for each other."

"And ready to start a family so soon?"

"It isn't what we planned, but I'm sure Roy will be pleased."

Hmm, I wonder how he will react. I haven't met him yet so can only go on what Rachel says about him. My experience is unless it has been talked about beforehand it can be a shock and cause problems and split up rather than bond partners together more tightly.

"That's good. I'm sure he will be pleased."

"Anyway, what's the latest with you then Casanova?"

I recount the events of the past few weeks, some she was aware of, and she does giggle over my experiences in the café near London Bridge. Even I can smile a bit now as I tell her. I don't mention Gill for obvious reasons.

"I hope you do meet Trish. I wouldn't give up on Obi either. Are you sure about Melanie? Don't you want to meet her a second time… just to be sure?"

"I think I'll wait until after I've seen Trish on Sunday. Depending on how that goes, I will be clearer about Obi and Melanie."

"Yes, that makes sense. Ah well, it is good to see you and to share my brilliant news with. It's an early night for me, an expectant mum needs her sleep." She says, her eyes twinkling at me.

It is great to see Rachel so happy. I really, really hope that Roy will be pleased and is the right partner for her at last.

The rest of the evening passes quietly apart from texts from Danny and Liz saying they will go to see their nan on Friday. I hope so as I am uncertain how quickly she may decline.

DAY 68: WEDNESDAY

Normal service continues as I sit in bed reading my email that Trish sent late yesterday.

'Hi Charming Chris".

How lovely to be called "Charming" at the end of a very tiring day - I'm delighted.

"So, you can sing - that's great - do you still sing anywhere - apart from in the bath? I like singing but wait - I can't sing well and was just scored two and a half out of ten today by my son so I won't torture you with it so don't worry! I listened to 10cc - I don't know that song - I don't think I've heard them literally since getting ready for school in the 70s/80s on the radio - I like 'I'm not in love' and I remember 'Dreadlock holiday'. Gosh that takes me back!

I know that men can multitask - some just don't want to...your children were and are very lucky!"

I'm going to try and motivate myself now Mr. HSC - speak soon.

Enjoy your evening. Trish'

I did enjoy my evening and Rachel's good news. I respond:

'Hello my lovely Ms. Motivator,

I sing when I am happy and it can be anywhere in my place and at any time, normally to whatever is on my iTunes at the time. It takes me back to the 70s. As well as Bruce Forsyth and his Generation Game being part of my life my all-time comedy heroes are Morecambe and Wise.

10cc performed "Wall Street Shuffle", "I'm Mandy Fly Me" and "Art for Art's Sake" but I'm a little older than you so you may not remember them. Actually I got my old vinyl records out and played all my 10cc albums so it is a 10cc day today for me.

You will just have to get used to me complimenting you. It may get worse if I find you are as lovely on the outside as I can see you already are on the inside. I hope you don't mind. I don't say or write anything I don't mean.

Charming (I can't remember the last time someone paid me that compliment - thank you Trish, it means a lot to me). I feel very content with life and looking forward to Sunday and meeting you. I hope we have a wonderful time enjoying each other's company and conversation. Chris'

That exchange charges me up for a meeting with the project team at Brian & Co. that takes up the rest of the morning. After a sandwich for lunch I drive to my mum's nursing home. She is stable and not declined further neither has she improved. The Sister explains that it could be related to her move, a delayed reaction to the trauma of the change even if it will be for the better in the long term. I come away feeling guilty at moving her although her previous home pushed for her removal without any thought about the impact on her.

When I get home I finally receive an email from Maureen but it is no more than a holding reply. She is sorry for the delay caused by her car accident, is slowly getting back up to speed, can't talk but she is able to type a little. But there is nothing about the status of my purchase. Is it imminent? Has it hit a snag? Has it fallen through? I am very, very, frustrated. It raises more questions in my mind than give me answers. I am not a happy bunny.

The one consolation is Em's solicitors haven't transferred the money yet and so I couldn't exchange even if Maureen hadn't been injured and there were no delays. I email Debra asking for an update on the latest situation. Is the money ready to transfer? If not now, when?

A few emails and a couple of calls completes my work for today and I settle down to a relaxing evening and pizza. As I heat it up I open the wine and text Rachel asking how she is. Her response is rapid but not what I expect 'I'm OK but can't get hold of Roy. Left him a message with my BIG news but no response… yet. He is very busy when he works away'. Over dinner I consider what to say and settle for 'I'm sure he's just very busy and you'll hear from him soon'. 'Yeah, I hope so, I do miss him' is her response but it is not the most confident reply I ever saw.

While catching up on TV a message comes through from Obi. Now that is a big surprise, as I didn't expect to hear from her again. She wants to meet me on Saturday afternoon at a Jazz Club in Brighton. Well, that is different! I can't remember the last time I heard jazz live. It isn't my favourite type of music but I do like it when played live. The problem for me is that my football team play their first match of the season on Saturday at home. Unless we can meet afterwards I am going to decline and see what Obi wants to do.

I reply saying, 'Hi Obi, I am going to the football on Saturday afternoon. I can meet you afterwards if you still want to.' I wonder what brought this about. Maybe we will still meet and I will find out on Saturday?

Apart for an exchange of messages with Liz who asks if she can see me tomorrow the rest of my evening is uneventful.

DAY 69: THURSDAY

I wake up and my first thoughts are about the coming weekend, Brighton and Hove Albion, Obi and Trish although not necessarily in that order. Depending on what happens it can be a fun-packed weekend or a miserable one full of despair or probably something more in between these two extremes.

My mobile rings before I get out of bed. It is the nursing home checking that I will be visiting today as my mum had another bad night, confused and distressed at times. I confirm that I will come this morning and try to reassure my mum. Oh dear, this doesn't sound like good news.

Deciding to shower and breakfast first I look at my emails and find the one sent by Trish late yesterday.

'Hello Mr. Charming,

You are charming towards me and that's why you deserved that description. I may just be able to cope with one or two more compliments. I hope that today is a fruitful one for you and that you are making good headway - well done to you for getting more work -

indeed you must be doing a lot right - perhaps you are Mr. Right!

I remember well family viewing of programmes and game shows like the Generation Game, The Golden Shot, various comedies - you must remember them all like Dick Emery and Les Dawson etc. Oh my! In those days the family just sat down together on an evening and watched TV, fond memories for me.

It's nice to speak to someone who seems so content with life, I think sometimes people get into the habit of grumbling about one thing or the other and I know that often there are a lot of upsetting things happening but we also need sometimes to show gratitude for what we have and not take those things/people etc. for granted however little they may be. I'm glad that my emails have brought music to your ears and songs to your lips, I like hearing from you too.

We've made a good start so I hope it will continue when we meet (no pressure then), cheers to that if you're having another bottle of wine tonight.

Have a good night. Trish'

It certainly does feel like we have made a good start. However I know from past experience that it is when you meet someone that it can go horribly wrong. I reply.

'Hi Trish, my attractive achiever!

Of all the words I write it is those in my email to you each day that mean the most. I can't wait for your email each day to read and enjoy. I am a lucky man that you want to spend so much time and effort getting to know me.

While the scope of work has expanded my clients can be inconsistent and contradictory which takes away some of the satisfaction. I'm not sure how long each relationship lasts, it depends on how they behave. Deep sigh!

For me the 1970s was a golden age for family entertainment. Christmas evenings with everyone watching the Generation Game, Mike Yarwood, The Two Ronnies and Morecambe and Wise were amazing. I am getting misty eyed and nostalgic remembering.

I think we have similar tastes in music for the 70s and 80s with Soul, RnB and Blues just to start with. My range of music is eclectic. If you are very, very, nice I may give you a peak at my iTunes!

How is your grandson? Is he back at school now?

You are right (you have great insight!). I am content with my life, just need that special person to help share it with and make it even better. Maybe it will be you? I am looking forward to meeting you on Sunday.

Your charming consultant, Chris'

Only four days until we meet and it feels like things are moving along nicely. I feel a connection already with Trish that I struggled to find with anyone before. I haven't found it yet with Obi and don't think I will on Saturday but she wants to see me so who knows what might still happen.

Driving to my mum's I wonder what she will be like. Sadly again when I arrive I can see she hasn't improved; only confusion over whom anyone is including me. Talking with the nurses they assure me that episodes like this occur as my mum slowly declines. It doesn't mean it will continue and she can stabilise or even improve slightly. The main thing is to prepare and visit regularly if possible; I will aim to.

I spend the rest of my day meeting with my Brian & Co. team to review the project's progress then with Len who is tough but fair with his questions like he was over my fee dispute. By the time I'm back home there isn't long before Liz will arrive. I am looking forward to catching up with her, curious how life is at Em's house, and how Danny is doing.

After she arrives on time (that is a bonus) we start to chat as we prepare dinner together. As our conversation continues over dinner and we're washing up, several things become clear to me. Firstly that amazingly, Em now regrets what she caused – the hurt, the conflict, the turbulence – and wishes we had been able to work things out better. It's a case of too little, too late, for us to reconcile now though. I have moved on but the scars are still open and hurt badly at times.

Secondly, Liz wants to move on from living at her mum's place. She wants to stay for a few days with her, with me and then with other friends. It is clear after Liz completes her studies that she will not return to where she grew up. Where she does move to is up in the air but I am sure she will know long before she leaves university.

Lastly she and Danny are surprising themselves by how well they are now getting along. The splitting of their parents is helping them form a closer bond, be more tolerant of each other, share and help and stick up for each other. Some good has come out of the awful events of the past few months after all; every cloud has a silver lining. Not the best way to bring your offspring to maturity from adolescence nevertheless it is achieving a critical phase in their lives.

Liz completes this picture by saying Danny has messaged asking how she is doing and that he misses her company. Things really have changed for the better between them if he is now saying that! I can't stop myself smiling at her. Liz asks if she can stay the night and go with me to see her nan tomorrow morning. I say yes she can to both questions.

DAY 7o: FRiDAY

I wake up refreshed and jump out of bed to make my tea and read my email from Trish. To be honest I haven't checked, I just naturally assume there will be one such is my confidence in her. I am not disappointed either when I open my laptop or see my inbox.

'Ha ha - Hi Chris,

I am so glad that my emails cheer you - that's good and I really do hope that we will get on having made such a good start.

My grandson is feeling better I'm happy to say - he's prone to this and I've bought probiotics, olive leaf and other natural stuff to help his immunity. He is one today and we are having a party on Saturday.

I agree about the '70s - I loved those family times so much and treasure the memories too. It's only now however that we realise how un-PC a lot of the programmes were! I think I saw an old episode of Benny Hill and thought OMG I will never dream of letting younger children watch that nowadays and the portrayal of women is just really not on, we have moved forward but still not sufficiently. Do you remember a programme called Space 1999? I am telling my son how odd it was at the time that it feels so far away and we really believed that we would wear silver foil outfits once we got to 1999!

My favourite music is soul/R&B really -Marvin Gaye, Luther Vandross, Barry White, Aretha Franklin, Tina Turner, Whitney, Mariah, Michael Jackson - the list is endless - I think that the world is sooo lucky to have experienced this kind of music - there isn't anyone that can match them nowadays. It'll be interesting to see whether I get the peek at your iTunes. Trish'

Again, I relish reading and re-reading her latest email. I reply.

'Hi to the loveliest lady in London.

With much laughter and conversation I passed a relaxing evening with my daughter. We cooked all the leftovers in a dish that has no name (yet). Rice, vegetables and salmon with a few sauces and spices all washed down with a bottle of white wine.

Master (or mistress?) baker! I will love to sample some of your delicious bakes. What is your favourite bake? Are you a future Great British Bake Off contestant in *that* tent maybe?

I'm glad your grandson is better but understand your concerns for his health, a tough one. I would love to see the photos of his birthday.

All those artists apart from Mariah and Luther are on my iTunes. I like Motown (Diana Ross, Stevie Wonder) and the Sound of Philadelphia (Harold Melvin, etc.) created great songs. Disco and American rock (Eagles, Fleetwood Mac) I love too. Billy Joel and Eric Clapton are probably my top performers. An eclectic mix as I said before!

Love thy neighbour was another comedy to cringe at with its racism and yes, Benny Hill was very sexist. Comedy is better now but still has a very long way to go and reflects the problems generally in society. How people are treated unfairly because of their gender, ethnicity, faith and sexuality makes me angry, upset and frustrated that we don't improve quicker.

Yes, I'm looking forward to Sunday and building on a great start so far. I would like to share mobile no's in case there are any delays for me with the train (part of journey is a bus replacement service). Are you ok with that?

I'm aiming to be outside Westminster tube station in Bridge Street waiting for my favourite 'girly girl' to join me at noon. We can then walk and chat to the pier for the boat or have a coffee first somewhere. You choose, as long as I have your company nothing else will matter to me.

I hope you have a great day at work. Thank God It's Friday!

Your optimistic and hopeful, Chris.'

Liz notices my inner happiness and afterglow from reading and responding to Trish's email an hour later when I wake her up.

"And what's got you in such a good mood so early dad?"

"Just an email I received, that's all."

"Is this from the lady you're seeing at the weekend."

"That's right." Then I corrected, "One of them anyway."

Liz laughed. "One of them! Gosh you are spoilt for choice! Go dad!"

Our happy mood continues as we get ready and then drive to see my mum. Liz of course hasn't been there before so everything is new to her, sadly even her nan who in a short space of time is no longer able to quickly recognise her. By the time we leave the mood is more sombre.

"She's so different, nan looks and acts so different." It is all Liz can say for the first few minutes.

"Sadly she isn't going to get better. It's horrible watching her decline like this from the wonderful person we knew to the husk she is becoming. That's why you and Danny need to make the most of the time now with her before her memory goes completely."

"Yeah, I'll talk with Danny when I get back to mum's."

"Maybe you should both go together whenever you can? It might keep the conversation going and the mood more upbeat."

"Sure, I wouldn't want to go on my own."

It is strange for me to drive Liz to my old home but this time I don't feel so bad and park a few doors away without too much anxiety. I ask her if Danny wants to have a chat, I will wait for him to join me. I certainly am not going up to the door. Liz will let me know one way or the other. After about ten minutes Danny comes out looking like he's just woken up... which in fact he has!

"Hi dad how's things?" Danny's standard greeting now.

"Not so bad son. How about you?"

"It's ok at the moment. Liz and I are getting on fine. Mum is being easier on me since I've been back."

"That's good to hear. Keep on good terms with them. Liz can update you on nan. I hope you both go to see her soon."

"Sure dad, sorry I didn't go today but I will next time."

"OK, well I'd better get going. Look after yourself, love you." I gave him a big hug.

"Same back at you dad." Danny says with a grin on his face.

I start the car and drive off quickly. I don't want to see him open the door or Em be somewhere in the background. She may have looked from behind the curtains for all I know but the main thing for me is that I don't want to see her. Being outside her house (as it is now) is a huge step forward emotionally; that is enough for one day.

It is a good day at work; the work is prepared for Emily Briggs and the training can start next week. This time I know if I bump into Gill I will not feel awkward; she might but I will try not do anything to make that happen. Just seeing me may affect her but there isn't anything I can do about that. I am earning a living carrying out work for my client. The little project for Harry Stokes is also coming to a close with just a few loose ends to tie up. I can continue giving enough time and attention to Brian & Co.'s project and team as we enter a critical phase of the work for the next couple of weeks.

What happens after that with future work will sort itself out later. At least by the time I am paid for these projects there will be some breathing space. It is a common situation that I encounter many times and always something comes up; there is no reason to panic and think it won't this time too.

Work is interrupted by one piece of good news from Debra who confirms she has finally received the transfer of funds from Em's solicitors to her bank account. She will transfer the money to wherever I choose ready for my purchase. I thank her for managing this while wondering if it is in any way connected to me dropping Liz outside Em's house earlier. Probably pure coincidence but you never know…

It is earlier than I thought of finishing work but that news deserves a silent celebration and I take a short walk to the seafront. There are many parents with young children playing on the beach, the hot sun shining, the low tide revealing some sand after the pebbles for a short time. I absorb their fun and happiness and savour the moment as I walk to the end of the short pier and look out at the sea and horizon. Won't it be nice to feel like this always?

After coming back I make sure my best clothes and football stuff are ready for the weekend. I suddenly remember the match kicks off at lunchtime not the usual 3 o'clock, as it is live on TV. That means I can meet Obi at the original time. I kick myself for being stuck in an era when 3pm was always the time football matches started. I go to my dating site and see that Obi hasn't replied yet – she does seem to have a very busy life – and say I can still meet her at the original time as the football match finishes earlier than usual.

I cook dinner and open a special bottle of red wine to celebrate the amber light to buying my own place. Maybe the delay with Maureen will be a good thing after all? Not her accident of course! But I couldn't commit the funds with 100% confidence until the transfer from Em took place today. My future life becomes a little bit more straightforward today.

After dinner is eaten (did the news make it taste so good?) and everything washed up, I savour more of my wine and go back to my dating site. I want to avoid having all my eggs in one basket. What if Trish doesn't want to see me again? What if I don't? It will be a huge setback for me. I still don't think it can work with Obi. For one thing her life seems maxed out and there doesn't feel like there is much room for me as a priority. That isn't what I want or need from a new relationship.

Searching through all the women who joined since my last check I do find a few who could be of interest. I send my usual introduction message expressing my interest in them and asking for their view on my profile. My heart isn't fully in it and I don't want to mess them about but I need a Plan B. Next I review any woman who viewed or liked my profile that I haven't already contacted but only one woman meets that criteria. Lastly I check through the women I have liked but not heard back from and send a follow-up message to a few on the off-chance they may still be interested. I know it is unlikely but it is something I feel driven to do before my big weekend starts.

It puts my mind more at ease and I drop off to sleep quickly.

DAY 71: SATURDAY

My (hopefully) big weekend is about to start and the weather matches my mood as the sun shines brightly into my bedroom. Opening the window I take a deep breath of fresh air and hear the distant sound of the waves on the beach. Drinking my mug of tea I sit up in bed and read the latest email from Trish.

'Hi Chris,

You are very kind.

Thank you for asking about my grandson and I will be happy to show you the photos.

I like making and eating apple crumble with custard, and variations of it - it's the ultimate comfort dessert for me (yum). I bake chocolate, ginger, plain vanilla, fruit, banana cakes, cheesecake, etc., my repertoire is too small for GBBO - they get pretty adventurous on the show. One day I'll do a few novelty cakes and cake decorating courses.

Your evening with your daughter sounded lovely. I love many of your iTunes selections - very soulful - that's my bias but there are some jazz, pop, classical and country music that I like too, my daughter does too. Believe it or not my sons are into metal... but they like other stuff as well.

I think that you mentioned before your hatred of injustice and I am the same. It really upsets and frustrates me too - I can go on about it all day!

I will look forward to meeting you on Sunday Chris - today I'm not feeling so well but I hope that I will perk up considerably by Sunday, I've got your number so if anything changes I'll call you and you call me on this number. I admit I am not happy about the tube but as you say life has to go on. Since you have to take a bus replacement service, do you want to meet later - say 12.30 or 1pm?

Yes I second that - thank God it's Friday (that is a film I think) see you soon and have a good evening too. Trish'

Her news about not feeling well worries me and I hope she will perk up for tomorrow.

'Hi Trish,

I am sorry you are not well. I hope it isn't anything serious and you are better for Sunday.

Thanks for sharing your mobile no. with me. I am happy to meet you at 12:00 still. I know which train/bus/tube I need to get to Westminster by that time. If there are any last minute hitches then I will call you. If all goes to plan I hope we will have a lovely afternoon together.

We have so much to discuss on Sunday including an iTunes review and an extra round on my specialised subject. I can't wait!

Get well and I hope you enjoy Saturday. Chris'

My enjoyment of Saturday is pivotal on Trish's wellbeing. While I hope she will meet me on another day, I am desperate to avoid a delay. My wellbeing is linked to Trish's if only she knew it! There is still no response from Obi and I am beginning to wonder if she was serious with her invite this afternoon. Still there is the football that I need to get ready for and take a change of clothes in the hope I still see Obi after the match.

James and Gordon agree to meet me at the usual place, opposite the second bar on the concourse for the West Stand, with a pint waiting for me. It is early in the day to start drinking but the excuse for it is it being the first match of what we hope will be a successful season. Doesn't every football supporter have the same dreams about their team before the first game and reality then starts to set in?

The mood is buoyant after last week's result and their moods are lighter. Maybe our discussion over personal issues helped? Neither seems willing to open up in front of the other with everyone milling around talking loudly. We take our seats and enjoy an entertaining if inconclusive first half. Returning to the concourse and another drink courtesy of James buying this round I check my mobile for messages. Obi has finally responded and much to my relief is OK about the football and giving her mobile no. to me, asks me to call her after the game. Great! My Saturday is finally going as planned.

The second half is a repeat of the first half, good to watch but a draw with no goals. Disappointing but it could have been worse; early days; a foundation to build on, etc. I find most football supporters are eternal optimists and will only accept the reality of promotion or the dreaded relegation of their team when it is shown to be mathematically impossible to avoid. Declining another beer with Gordon and James who wish me luck with Obi and a few choice unrepeatable comments that I ignore; they are just jealous! I nip into the toilets and change in a cubicle from football outfit into something I hope is more suitable for meeting Obi at a jazz club.

While I wait in the long queue for the trains I call Obi but only get her voicemail. Damn. She is *really* difficult to get hold of! I leave a message saying I am queuing for a train and where and when should I meet her. It isn't until half an hour later as I finally get on a train to Brighton that Obi calls back.

"Hi Chris, sorry I missed your call. How about meeting me at the Clock Tower in 30 minutes? I'm just about to leave now."

"OK Obi, I'll be there in plenty of time." And I am but there is no sign of Obi and 30 minutes becomes 60 minutes before she shows up.

"Sorry I am a bit late. I got delayed by some friends I met on the way here."

Delayed by friends! On the way to me! Knowing I am just stood here waiting! It isn't the best of starts again with Obi and this isn't the first time either but I don't say anything.

"Good to see you again. What's the plan?"

"I've got some vouchers for a jazz club where we can hear live music and get a meal."

"OK, sounds good to me. I can't remember the last time I heard jazz live but I did like it."

"Let's go there now. It's somewhere near the seafront."

Obi sets a fast pace as we walk through the crowds towards the club, mainly me walking behind her in single file. With the noise of the traffic and people everywhere there is no chance for conversations. I trust her to find the place and she surprises me by abruptly stopping and I bump into her.

"Damn!"

"What's the problem?"

"The tickets!"

"What about the tickets?"

"I've left them back home."

"You what!"

"They're not with me."

"Are you sure?"

"Yeah, I was searching through my bag while we walked."

I don't know what to say. Part of me is stunned that she hasn't the tickets; partly because I didn't mind missing the live jazz and competing with it to talk; lastly I now hope we can go somewhere quieter.

Obi lets out a loud, deep sigh and looks up to the sky. "What shall we do?"

"How about a quieter place where we can talk?"

"Okay... where?"

"Are you hungry?"

"I'm not one to turn the right food down as you know."

"Okay, let's try the seafront. Weather's perfect for sitting outside."

This time I lead the way as we continue in single file down to the restaurants on the promenade. The problem is everyone else has the same idea and they are packed full with queues of people waiting to be seated. Unless we want to wait for ages this isn't going to work. We consult again...

"How about if we went inland where it should be less crowded

Chris?"

"Sounds like a plan. Have you anywhere in mind?"

"There's a nice Italian restaurant I know near the Royal Pavilion that usually has some space even when it is busy everywhere."

"OK, lets try there unless we see anywhere better on the way."

So we again walk in single file through holidaymakers, shoppers, locals, day-trippers, etc. with Obi leading this time. We stop outside a couple of cafes and a restaurant but don't see anything either of us really fancies and finally arrive at Obi's choice.

It is busy but we can see a couple of corner tables that could be ideal but they are reserved. We have to settle for a table in the middle of the main seating area, at least we have somewhere to relax and chat at last. The effects of the alcohol, sun and exercise make me want to stay still for a few moments to collect my wits about me before ordering.

Obi wants to order wine while we decide what to order. That is fine with me as long as they bring some water too and I leave her to choose which bottle. I can see Obi knows her way around a wine list and she makes a good choice or rather I like it too!

After ordering food we finally take stock of each other, raise a glass and drink slowly; neither of us seems to want to start the conversation. I feel that any relationship with Obi can only be as a friend; there is still no spark. I am unhappy with the casual way she makes arrangements with me and I know that it will drive me mad.

Slowly we engage as we discuss our time since we last saw each other. Then Obi moves on to her work and career and what she could do. It is a repeat of the same subject we covered twice already and I am relieved when our first course arrives to stop my frustration.

The food is tasty and the wine helps it to slide down into my empty tummy very nicely.

However once we finish, Obi returns to the same subject. Talk about a record stuck in the groove! After we go round the same circle and are starting on it again I interrupt her. I make it clear this isn't what I want to discuss again. Obi needs to act, not talk about her career and decide for herself what she is going to do. It won't help going over and over the same thing without moving on by trying something.

Clearly this is a mistake as far as Obi is concerned and not something she is used to hearing but I won't back down or apologise for giving direct and clear advice. Our main course arrives which helps distract us and focus on food until she makes some reference to her size again so that causes more silence.

Although they are dangerous areas for both of us we venture to talk about our past relationships; something we have brushed over on our first two meetings. After I talk about my marriage and why it failed I ask Obi about her previous partners, which she is reticent to talk about. When I probe a bit deeper it is too much as far as Obi is concerned and she stops me by spreading her hand out and putting her palm firmly in my face.

"No!" she says sharply.

"Sorry Obi, I am curious and didn't mean to pry."

"You have gone too far."

"I hope I haven't burnt my bridges over this."

"Oh you don't know how many bridges you have burnt today, no idea."

Genuinely puzzled by this I ask, "What do you mean by that?"

"It seems my daughter took a real shine to you when you met her on our first meet up. When I told her we wouldn't see each other again she thought I was wrong and should reconsider. So here we are but it's not working out for me still."

"I only saw our meeting up today as friends. There's still no spark for me either. I was curious why you wanted to see me again but now I know why."

"Let's get the bill and go."

"OK."

And that was the end of our time together. As we leave the restaurant there is an awkward hug and kiss on the cheek from both of us. I go to the train station, Obi in the opposite direction to the bus stop. As my train makes its way to Worborne I don't feel disappointed just settled that events ran their course with Obi. I wonder if she will ever give the right person enough time and priority in her life to make a relationship last. For me it means that tomorrow's meeting with Trish is more significant.

Just before I am home Danny texts me to say that he and Liz saw nan in the afternoon. Like Liz he is shocked by her decline. He promises to not leave it so long before seeing her next time. My mum recognised both of them after a little prompting so that is slightly better news.

There is nothing to do when I get back but I can't resist checking if Trish emailed me today. She has!

'Thanks Chris for your kind wishes - I am feeling much better after resting today and am also very much looking forward to meeting you in person tomorrow to continue the conversations that we have started + hear more that I haven't yet heard!

Enjoy your Saturday too.

Speak soon. Trish'

I can't wait until tomorrow before replying and send a quick response.

'Hi Trish,

That's great news you're feeling better now.

So, tomorrow we finally meet! I'm looking forward also to continuing our conversations and extending into new areas we both want to explore. I don't have to leave by a certain time so I'm happy to see how things go until a natural ending is reached that we're both happy with...just so you know.

Shall I text you when I catch the train to London and when it arrives at Victoria? We can call each other if there are any travel problems as we have already agreed. Chris'

The effects of the alcohol, football and Obi mean an early night for me with the thought that tomorrow I will finally meet Trish.

DAY 72: SUNDAY

Today is 'T Day', the day when I will finally meet Trish! It is either going to be an amazing or despairing day! I try to play down my expectations but it is difficult. I am so pleased I reached out to Trish and she was brave enough to respond. What feels different from my other first dates is the wealth of information we have already shared with each other. The rapport we are establishing, even laughing at each other's jokes and funny comments. I am so looking forward to carrying on that conversation in person today!

I make a cup of tea and go back to bed. Out of habit I check my emails not expecting anything but to my surprise Trish replied quite late yesterday evening. I love her dedication.

'Hi Chris,

I'm happy to see how the day goes - the only thing is the coach turns to a pumpkin, my footman to mice and my clothes to rags if I don't get home by midnight.

Yes do let me know when you get to Victoria and we'll let each other know of any delays - although you must remember that it is a woman's prerogative to be late.

See you soon and good night Chris. Trish'

What a wonderful woman! My 'Wonder Woman'! I smile as I realise I am falling in love with her personality. Her sense of humour, interest in me, shared views; make for what could be a memorable day. A little voice in my brain keeps saying 'don't get carried away' but it is easy to ignore with the lovely warm words that Trish wrote in each email to me.

'It is a woman's prerogative to be late.' Is that a subtle hint for me not to expect Trish to be on time? So far I have 'no shows', 'late shows' or even 'different shows' thinking of how different Melanie looks so much older than her profile photo. I am prepared for any eventuality even an 'early show'; now that will be a first for me meeting my dates.

That stimulates me to go through the gears and get myself ready to meet Trish and it is at a record pace that I make myself presentable and able to catch an earlier train than I planned. I am happy just to wait until she arrives, whenever that is, with plenty of messages to send and respond to from friends and children. I message Trish when I arrive at Victoria as we agreed. The weather is sunny and warm as I emerge from the exit at Westminster tube station, prepared for a long wait for her to arrive if necessary after her cryptic clue on time keeping.

Taking my phone out I start to send and to respond to messages while keeping a close eye on the exit. There are many passersby as tourists stare at Big Ben and the Houses of Parliament as they walk by but thankfully very few stay where I am waiting for Trish so I have a clear line of sight on anyone coming out the exit.

So, it is a big surprise when someone resembling Trish appears at that exit ten minutes early! I almost drop my smartphone as I realise this is Trish! Early! Smiling at me! A few fireworks explode inside my head as all this registers. I try to recover and step towards her to give her a hug and check it is Trish. Two tourists get in our way and I go to my left as does Trish and we miss each other until we have completed a circle and can hold each other as we burst into laughter and the ridiculousness of what is happening.

And what a lovely sound her laugh has, the smile on her face is wonderful. Her hair is black, short and styled to show her face off. Even her eyes are smiling, maybe twinkling, and are a very deep brown. Trish is even more stunning than her profile pictures. A light blue coat sets off her complexion perfectly and a bright orange dress compliments the coat. Trish has style and looks that match the personality I am in love with already. I just hope and pray she feels similarly about me.

We say "hello" to each other and I suggest we walk towards where the pier to board the boat is. However we have to rush across the road to avoid the traffic and I get a gentle scolding for risking our lives in my impatience to get going. She smiles as she does this so I know she isn't too serious, just making a point that I accept. I want this date to last and last and definitely not risk anyone's life by my actions.

Trish then says, "I need to take a sea sickness tablet before we go on the boat down the Thames to Greenwich."

I am speechless for a second before blurting out, "Why did you choose this option?"

"Because I will like being in Greenwich with you. It's just a precaution."

"Ah, OK, what shall we do?"

"Maybe buy a bottle of water now and wander over the bridge, and have a coffee or something while it kicks in before we board?"

It isn't how I thought our date would start but I am intoxicated by her presence and will go anywhere as long as she is with me. We buy water and she takes her tablet and stroll over the bridge, happy in each other's company, to find a café on the other side of the Thames where we sit at the only table free with two chairs. I can't stop smiling; I am so happy and thankfully Trish is smiling too.

The conversation is completely different from any previous first meeting with a date because I know so much about Trish. Likewise I shared a lot with Trish. We are far more comfortable with each other's company because of this. My usual awkwardness and anxiety don't exist because I feel I know enough about Trish to be confident to pick areas to talk about we are both okay about. She is assertive and happy to take the lead over which areas she wants to talk about too.

We are content sitting there enjoying each other's company so much that it is a shame we have to move after finishing our coffees, seasickness tablets kicking in if needed, and make our way to the ferry and on to Greenwich. As we pass the landmarks on our journey we realise that we have similar likes and dislikes. To be honest with you I am already enraptured with Trish, the journey and scenery are secondary to her – her looks, voice, personality, dress sense, actions, everything!

When we arrive at Greenwich it is packed full of people as we amble around happy to be side by side as we look for a suitable restaurant where we can eat but most importantly get to know each other better. The more I find out about Trish, the more I like her and I want to find out more and more. Eventually after looking in many windows at menus we choose an Italian restaurant with space and no background music so we can talk easily. The menu has a wide range of dishes so there is plenty of choice to cater for our appetites. After ordering we sit and gaze at each other and smile. There has been a lot of smiling so far!

"I am so pleased we have finally met Trish," I start, "but the strange thing is I feel as if I know you already."

"Yes, I feel the same," says Trish. "Those daily emails help me to feel comfortable about meeting you now."

"It feels a bit like an old-fashioned romance with daily letters being written expressing affection and what has happened."

"I am naturally a cautious person so I'm glad you had the patience even if you did want to meet much quicker. Such impatience Chris!" Her rich brown eyes are twinkling again as she says the last part.

I grin back. "I do find I get on best with people when I meet them face to face but I do enjoy your emails every morning. It helps start my day so well."

"That's good to hear. I enjoyed reading your emails each evening and replying to you. You are a very interesting man."

"Thank you and you are a very interesting lady. You don't look old enough," and I say the next part very quietly "to be a grandma."

"Ssshh!" Trish says while smiling. "Thank you. And you don't look your age either."

We then discuss each of our families in more detail, Trish about her children, siblings and grandchild, I talk about Danny and Liz and the situation with my mum and a little about my sister. Trish is understanding and genuinely concerned about how I feel and it makes me feel very warm and cared for inside.

Our first course arrives and we tuck into our dishes. I am ravenous, my appetite stimulated being with Trish at last and I quickly eat my starter, so quickly Trish jokes that I attacked rather than ate my food. I blush and apologise which makes her laugh.

"It's good to see you have a hearty appetite Chris. It will help you stay a strong and fit man."

Wow, a compliment! This is going well so far. I don't want to spoil it or for it to end. "Thank you. I will try my best." This causes Trish to burst into giggles and when she sees my puzzled look can only say,

"Your voice is so cute when you say that." I am bemused but take it as another compliment. Like London buses, there are none for ages then several all at once!

Our main courses arrive at that moment and I am able to demonstrate my healthy appetite as I eat my pizza while Trish enjoys her risotto. A few comments are exchanged about our dishes and if we are enjoying them. We are also comfortable with silences while we eat; neither of us feels we have to say things to fill this natural gap. Just being in each other's company is enough, which I find wonderful.

After we finish our main course - two cleared plates by the way – we sit back and gaze at each other. I take note of the lovely orange dress Trish wears, very stylish, with a blue cardigan that is unbuttoned to show more of the dress. It sets off her Caribbean complexion perfectly; I think she looks stunning but I am afraid to say in case it frightens her away because she thinks I am being too forward.

Our conversation turns to what next week looks like being for both of us – both have a busy week of work ahead – then to mutual areas of interest. It doesn't matter where the talking leads us; there aren't any awkward pauses or sudden shifts away from sensitive subjects. The benefit of our daily emails shows through strongly as it instinctively guides us along the right paths.

After a decent period to let our tummies settle we choose desserts; I can only manage ice cream after eating my enormous pizza; Trish picks sticky toffee pudding saying she is having a treat as it is a special occasion. Again I feel very pleased at the compliment.

After eating our pudding and ice cream we agree that a walk towards and around Greenwich Park will be good to enjoy the weather and beautiful scenery. As we walk together I feel I have known Trish for much longer than a few hours because of the emails exchanged leading up to today. It is tempting to take her arm to escort her or hold her hand but I resist the temptation without a signal from Trish first.

The park is perfect, quiet, more space and less crowded. We admire the view of the Royal Observatory up the hill and the magnificent buildings that make up the Old Royal Naval College. I suggest we walk to the Observatory but Trish wants to sit down on a nearby bench.

As we sit on the bench enjoying the sun and views she admits to me that she badly twisted her ankle while on her way to meet me. It is only because she was determined to meet me that she didn't turn back to rest it. It is now very painful to walk on and she has to rest before being able to put her weight on it again. I don't know what to say or do first. Can I rub her ankle? Can I get her painkillers? Trish smiles and said it is great that I show such concern but it is going to need rest over the next few days as the same thing happened recently and needed at least one week's rest.

Over those few moments the success of our date is confirmed for me; I wasn't sure until then how Trish felt until then. We sit happily side by side watching people who walk part us, looking at each other and smiling, generally letting time pass so Trish can rest her ankle. We talk more about our past relationships – good and bad times – and what we would like from a relationship (this is code to me for if we continue to see each other). There is nothing contentious, in fact there is hardly any difference between what we each want, another good sign for us I hope.

After half an hour Trish gingerly puts her foot on the ground and then slowly rises up to put some weight on it. Her face winces in pain and she cries out. Without thinking I immediately stand up and put her arm over my shoulder so she can take the weight off it and stand on one leg.

"Thanks Chris. You are a true gentleman." Yet another compliment but I don't register it immediately as I think about how we can get back to the ferry.

"My pleasure, anything for a lady like you Trish." I pivot around while supporting her arm to pick up her handbag from the seat. "Let's slowly move towards the ferry and rest whenever you need to."

"OK, thanks." We must look a comical sight to some with Trish limping slowly while leaning against me holding a leather handbag on my other arm.

Slowly, very slowly at times, we make our way to the park's exit then take the shortest walk to get to the ferry. Glancing down I can see Trish's ankle ballooning out from the sprain. It doesn't look good but I keep my thoughts to myself; Trish doesn't need me to remind her and will know better than me how bad it is.

After what seems like hours we board the ferry and make our way back to Westminster Pier. Her mobile is pinging with text messages and when she checks they are from her children checking how she is. I think it is great they are concerned for her. I hope she says good things about her time with me.

Finally we arrive at Westminster and disembark. The rest on the ferry has helped a little but I still support her as we make our way to the tube station. This is going to be the hardest part – saying goodbye but I hope it will just be for a short time – as the French say, *au revoir*, a temporary farewell not *adieu* like a final goodbye.

We stand inside the tube entrance and look at each other, gazing into each other's eyes, I'm sure mine are moist because the day has been brilliant, exceeding even my high expectations. But all good things must come to an end as they say, my problem is I don't know for certain if my feelings are reciprocated and we can repeat this. I am almost too frightened to ask for fear of hearing the wrong answer.

I sense that Trish is waiting for me to speak first and that she doesn't want to wait forever while standing on her sprained ankle so I speak first.

"Trish, today has been amazing, you are amazing, and I have loved every second of our time together. I want to see you again. Do you?"

"I've enjoyed our time together Chris. It's been a lovely day. Yes, I would like to see more of you." Silently fireworks are erupting inside my brain on hearing this.

"I'm so pleased. Can I call rather than email you? It will be good to call you tomorrow if you want me to."

"Yes, that's a good way forward. I will like hearing your voice rather than reading your thoughts." More fireworks erupt inside.

"I have seen other women through online dating but I feel like this about them," pointing to the ground. "But my feelings for you are like this," pointing above Trish's head. "May I kiss you before you go?"

"That's a lovely thing to say. Yes you can kiss me."

The best moment since I separated from Em, maybe the best moment of my whole life then happens as we kiss. Touching her lips with mine feels like a bolt of lightning going through my whole body it is so wonderful. It is probably only for a few seconds but feels like it is a lifetime so strong are my feelings.

We separate, smile, and wave goodbye and go our separate ways on the underground to our homes. To be honest I don't remember much of the journey except I must have made my way to the right station and train because I arrive home later that evening. It feels as if I floated home on a cloud of loveliness. All I can think about is Trish; her personality, looks, conversation, stylish clothes, humour and her interest in me. I have not felt like this about anyone I met - nowhere near – and can't imagine meeting anyone else now. It is Trish or no one as far as I am concerned.

I send texts to Danny, Liz and Rachel updating them on my day, how it went and how I feel - not that I can find words to express fully my true feelings for Trish. I am exhausted but tempted to send a text to Trish about how I feel but resist being too gushing and risking her feeling pressured by me in any way.

Wanting this to work and Trish to be my special friend are my only thoughts and then my dreams as I fall into a deep, restful, sleep.

DAY 73: MONDAY

As I wake up it doesn't feel like the morning after the night or rather the day before. Nope, absolutely not, none of those feelings; I am still flying on the memories of Trish yesterday. I sit up in bed and indulge myself by going over again in my mind all the wonderful moments I experienced while with her. From our first meeting through to the café, then first ferry, the meal, walk in the park and journey back with Trish limping until we parted.

Is it me or does the sky look bluer this morning? Isn't that sun shining through my window just a little bit brighter? I breathe very deeply and just wallow in bed for a few minutes indulging, wrapped up in the warmth of my feelings for Trish. Eventually the need for the loo and a cup of tea drive me from my reverie.

After a few minutes settling back in bed with my tea gazing out the window I automatically open my laptop to check my emails. This time there isn't one from Trish and I am not disappointed. For me this signals our relationship moving to another level, which pleases me. Talking over the phone will be even better than reading her words; to hear her voice again will be enough for me.

Yes, life is good and worth all the effort, setbacks, false hopes when you meet the right person. I believe Trish could be my special friend, lover, and life partner, best friend… hopefully all of these. Finding my special friend has been very elusive for me, some people never succeed despite many years of trying sometimes with many failures. I am very fortunate to have found it with Trish. I have only found one other woman who I felt that same spark for or rather a huge bolt of electricity for. That was many years ago and it faded and blew out a while ago; we are now divorced.

Online dating gave me an insight into women that I haven't gained while with Em and wouldn't have gained otherwise. It helps my understanding and to appreciate people even more. At times I felt like a male agony aunt as women I dated sobbed at times and told me of how they had been damaged by bad relationships. At times I felt ashamed being a man after hearing the mental and physical harm women suffered.

There are questions that Trish wouldn't answer yesterday about her previous relationship; neither did she explain why she asked me those questions when we started communicating by email. They are not important now. Answers and explanations will come when it is the natural time and place for them; I am in no hurry to push for them. I want to take our relationship a day at a time, savouring every minute of it. While I hope it will ideally be for the rest of my life, I am not going to worry about the future or plan. I want to focus on the here and now.

There are still some ongoing matters that need my time and attention and slowly integrate into my new relationship with Trish. Buying my new place, caring for my mum as well as business clients.

All these things matter but it is the change in my status that I feel counts most.

For the past few weeks I wanted to change my status from a divorcing, unattached, man to being divorced and then attached to a new partner who I love and loves me. While it is still at an early stage, Trish is this new partner, of that I have no doubt judging by her behaviour yesterday and in the lead up to our meeting. It feels natural already to think of life in terms of "we" and "us" rather than "me" and "I". I am amazed how quickly my brain has shifted towards that!

Taking this journey has been difficult, stressful, upsetting and on a few occasions despairing but... but... it has been worthwhile, every second and step of that journey if you find that (love) needle in the haystack or pot of (emotional) gold at end of the rainbow. Words can't express that wonderful special feeling being with someone you truly love and who loves you equally. It is true that love does conquer all; love is the most important thing in life; love makes everything else seem less important yet at the same time more worthwhile.

For Trish I want it to be onwards and upwards together! Forever!

ABOUT THE AUTHOR

I live near Brighton, UK, where I was born. After a long career working in communications and information management I turned my hand to writing my first book based loosely on my own and other friends' experiences. I spend time enjoying the little things in life like walking by the seashore, gazing at the sea and sky from my place, and appreciating everything and everyone each day..

Printed in Great Britain
by Amazon

51870189R00254